*These milli...*
*but w...*

# The Mistresses

Powerful tales of passion and seduction
from Katherine Garbera

# The Mistresses

### KATHERINE GARBERA

MILLS & BOON

First published in Great Britain 2012
by Mills & Boon, an imprint of Harlequin (UK) Limited,
Eton House, 18-24 Paradise Road, Richmond, Surrey TW9 1SR

THE MISTRESSES © by Harlequin Enterprises II B.V./S.à.r.l 2012

*Make-Believe Mistress*, *Six-Month Mistress* and *High-Society Mistress* were first published in Great Britain by Harlequin (UK) Limited in separate, single volumes.

*Make-Believe Mistress* © Katherine Garbera 2007
*Six-Month Mistress* © Katherine Garbera 2007
*High-Society Mistress* © Katherine Garbera 2007

ISBN: 978 0 263 89689 3
ebook ISBN: 978 1 408 97052 2

05-0512

Printed and bound in Spain
by Blackprint CPI, Barcelona

# MAKE-BELIEVE MISTRESS

BY
KATHERINE GARBERA

**Katherine Garbera** is the *USA TODAY* bestselling author of more than forty books. She's always believed in happy endings and lives in Southern California with her husband, children and their pampered pet, Godiva. Visit Katherine on the web at www.katherinegarbera. com, or catch up with her on Facebook and Twitter.

Since I'm now officially an Evelette, I'd like to say thanks to Janet, Roz, Denise and Leonora for welcoming me to the gang. And special thanks to the leader of the Evelette pack…Eve Gaddy!!

# One

Adam walked into her office like he owned the place, closing the door behind him and locking it. He brushed his hand along the side of her cheek and tunneled his fingers into her hair, tipping her head back. She shook from the brief contact and bit her lip to keep from asking for more.

Excerpt from "Adam's Mistress" by Stephanie Grace

Grace Stephens found it hard to think when Adam Bowen turned that intense blue-green stare on her. Her pulse beat loudly in the back of her head. Even though she'd rehearsed what she'd say at this meeting a hundred times, in the presence of her secret crush, she couldn't talk.

"Ms. Stephens, I asked you what action you think this board should take," he said.

His voice was deep and slightly gravelly. But it fit him. He was a big man, almost six-foot-two, muscular and totally ripped. She'd never seen him without a healthy tan. However, usually he just glanced over her and moved on. She hadn't anticipated what effect being the center of his attention would have on her.

"Mr. Bowen," she said, sorting through her notes on the table. As soon as she looked away from Adam her concentration returned. She was the headmistress of Tremmel-Bowen Preparatory, a very prestigious school in Plano, Texas, she reminded herself. It was an institution that had long been the breeding ground of powerful world politicians and future captains of industry.

Though lately they'd been in the news more for their scandals.

*Get it together, girl.*

She cleared her throat and pushed to her feet, wishing her five-foot-two frame was just a little bit taller. She walked to the front of the boardroom where her assistant, Bruce, had set up her laptop and a projector. The vice principal, Jose Martinez, rubbed the back of his neck as she fumbled with her presentation. It wasn't just her job on the line, but the jobs of all her staff. Bruce, Jose and seventy-five teachers and support staff.

"I'm sorry for the delay. I was gathering my thoughts to talk to you and the rest of the board of regents."

She was incredibly nervous about this meeting. The thought of disgrace and unemployment were enough to make her sweat. She refused to go back to the life she'd struggled so hard to escape. The idea was enough to draw her attention back to the matter at hand.

"Tremmel-Bowen has long been the place where diplomats and world leaders send their children for polishing and training to become future world leaders."

"In recent years, that reputation has suffered," Sue-Ellen Hanshaw said. The head of the PTA was a former beauty pageant queen and always made Grace feel like a country mouse. Sue-Ellen's makeup was flawless, her hair salon perfect and her body, of course, in the best shape money could buy.

"I'm aware of that. We've made a lot of changes this year to get the school back on track. But of course, we've had this one minor setback."

"I wouldn't call it minor," Malcolm O'Shea said. As the most active regent on the board, Malcolm had the power to influence the others, to keep the school open.

Of course he wouldn't. It had been his wife—Dawn—whose photo, in a torrid embrace with another teacher, had been splashed across the Internet. Scuttlebutt said that Malcolm and Dawn were currently in mediation preparing for their divorce.

But Adam was still staring at her and his eyes held more than their usual hint of boredom. They held anger, too. She couldn't blame him. After all, she was ultimately responsible for two of her teachers getting caught having sex by her students. She might have been able to manage the students if a picture of the incident hadn't been made public on the school's Web site. Stupid cell-phone cameras.

She felt flames of embarrassment sweep up her neck. Dawn had tried to explain that she'd gotten caught up in the moment and forgotten where she was, but Grace hadn't bought it. She'd kissed her share of guys—okay, maybe fewer than her share—and not once had she forgotten where she was.

Adam cleared his throat and Grace swallowed hard. His eyes held determination; she knew he and the other regents were here to deliver bad news.

The prep school that bore his name, which at one time enjoyed a reputation for being one of the most prestigious in the world, was now mired in scandal and debt. Not at all what his great-grandfather and Angus Tremmel had envisioned when the school was founded more than one hundred years ago. And as headmistress she was ultimately the one to blame. But she had a plan—a plan that had absolutely nothing to do with staring into Adam's deep-blue eyes.

She took a breath and moved to the front of the room. "I want to thank you all for agreeing to this meeting today. I understand your position on closing the school. However, I think once you see the plan that we have ready to implement, you'll give us a second chance."

She skimmed her gaze over the regents, parents and student council, who were also in attendance, keeping a determined and confident smile fixed to her face.

Most of them didn't exactly looked inspired by her speech. And Malcolm didn't look close to even listening to any kind of save-the-school plan.

"We've terminated the contracts of Dawn O'Shea and Vernon Balder. The fraternization policy at the school is very clear. They both understood the reasons for their dismissal. I've made it clear to the staff that there are no exceptions to any of our rules."

"That's a good course of action, but it's not enough to change the board's decision, Ms. Stephens," Malcolm said.

Grace was disappointed by his comment but had expected nothing less. Malcolm had to have been humiliated when the pictures of Dawn were published first on the Internet and then in the local paper. He was out for blood.

"What Malcolm means is that we're also concerned with the school's financial state. As you know, the incident caused many families to withdraw their students and we had to refund tuition, which affected the operating budget for the remainder of the school year," Adam said.

Grace took a deep breath. It was January and the start of the second semester—enrollment had dropped by half. Parents didn't want their future leaders touched by any kind of scandal. She was painfully aware that the school was barely going to cover operating expenses until the school year ended in May.

This was the first conversation she'd had with Adam that had involved more than one- or two-word answers.

"I know that. I've been working with our school accountant and I think we have a plan that will keep us under budget until the end of the year."

"Even if we keep the school open until the end of the semester, we'll be back here discussing the same situation in the fall."

Grace felt her heart drop. Though the board had agreed to this meeting, they'd already made up their minds and there seemed to be nothing she could say to change them. But giving up without a fight wasn't her style.

"I don't agree with that point of view, Mr. Bowen," she said. "Our remaining student body wants to return next year and, together with the student council, we've started an aggressive recruiting campaign."

She'd spent her entire life in pursuit of this one goal—living a proper life and working at this school. She wanted the conservative reputation she now had. She'd wanted to be anything other than the sinful daughter of the Preacher Reverend Stephens.

She forced that to the back of her mind. She definitely wasn't going to dwell on the terribly clichéd fact that her mother had run off with a traveling salesman. Jenny Stephens had left long before Grace had been old enough to ask to go with her, and the reverend had made sure Jenny had little time with Grace thereafter. Although he'd taken her to her mother's funeral after Jenny's death from an aneurysm.

She rubbed the back of her neck and tried to concentrate, but the smell of Adam's cologne distracted her. It was earthy, woodsy, a scent that titillated her senses.

"I'd like the chance to show you our entire presentation before the board votes," she said.

"That's why we're here, Ms. Stephens."

Adam's BlackBerry twittered and he pulled the unit closer to him. His hands were large, his fingers long and his nails nicer looking than hers, which were chewed to the quick.

"Excuse me," Adam said. "I need to see Ms. Stephens outside for a minute."

"Of course, that will give Bruce and me time to set up the presentation for our fiscal reconstruction plan. Will fifteen minutes be enough?" Jose asked.

"Perfect," Adam said.

He gestured for her to lead the way. She was conscious of him walking close behind her until they were outside the boardroom and in the relative privacy of the hallway in the administrative building. He had his hand on the small of her back. She felt the heat of his touch through the layers of her clothing.

She hoped that none of what she'd thought earlier showed on her face. She tried to keep her breathing even and told herself that she was at work, not a place for desire.

"What can I do for you, Mr. Bowen?" she asked, trying to keep her mind on business and not the way his suit jacket fit his broad shoulders.

"I've asked you to call me Adam when we're not in the presence of the other regents," he said.

"It wouldn't be proper," she said, trying not to notice

that the dark-blue shirt he wore made his eyes even brighter and more penetrating than usual.

"And are you always proper, Grace?"

Yes, sadly she was. She nodded. Too bad other members of her staff weren't as vigilant. "I think maybe that's a good thing, considering the problems our school is facing."

He gave her a wry grin. "I need to use your office computer to print an e-mail that I just received and fax back a response."

She led him down the hall to her office. She logged on to her computer and then left him to his work. "I'll be right outside if you need anything."

Adam accessed the Internet and read the e-mail Lana, his assistant, had sent him. Every business had its headaches, but lately running AXIOM was no longer just a fun adventure, especially where Viper was concerned.

Viper had been one of the first bands he'd signed to his label and he felt a sense of loyalty to them. And the last year and a half had been hard on both the band and the label. Lead singer Stevie Taylor's mother had been sick and dying of cancer. Stevie had reacted to his grief by partying harder, and when Stevie drank he got violent. The latest episode involved three staff members at a Paris hotel and the authorities.

Adam rubbed his brow as the list of people he had to talk to lengthened. He needed a conference call with Mitch Hollaran, Stevie's attorney, and Nico DeTrio, AXIOM's attorney.

He picked up the phone and called Lana, giving her specific instructions for dealing with Stevie, who was more trouble than he was worth as far as the bottom line was concerned. But since Viper had made Adam his first million independent of his inheritance, he would put up with more crap from them than any other band he had. He hit the print icon and waited for his document.

As he turned back from the printer, he bumped into Grace's desk. Her office was a decent size, but not really big enough for the large oak desk. Two file folders fell to the floor and papers spilled out of both of them.

He dropped to one knee to pick them up, glancing at the papers for a second. The words *breast* and *mouth* caught his eye, and he pulled that page farther from the folder, reading it. He was surprised to see a very racy story that opened with the boss and secretary engaged in a steamy embrace on an office conference table. It was titled "Adam's Mistress," by Stephanie Grace. Not much of a stretch to conclude that this was Grace's pen name.

But even more intriguing was the fact that "Adam" bore a startling resemblance, both physically and financially, to *him*. And the heroine's name was Grace.

He finished reading that first scene, feeling more than a little aroused by the sexy images he assumed Grace had created. There were almost five pages of first-person fantasy there.

There was a knock on the door. Adam stuffed the

scene back into the folder and covered it with his own papers. "Come in."

Grace stood in the doorway, looking the same as she always had. But for the first time, he really noticed her. Not as a school administrator but as a woman. He couldn't help but see that the silky shirt she wore matched the one her heroine had on. Grace's real blouse was covered with a boxy jacket.

"I'm sorry to interrupt, but Mr. O'Shea is anxious to continue the meeting. Will you need just a few more minutes, or should we reconvene after lunch?"

He was in no hurry to return to the meeting until he had a chance to think about the contents of the folder, but he knew the situation with the school needed to be resolved. Adam followed Grace back down the hall, trying not to dwell on what he'd read. He still saw the professional front she presented to him and the board, but his image of her was shifting. He saw more.

There was a hint of vulnerability in her eyes as she stood at the front of the room, knotting her fingers together as she waited for everyone's attention to return to her. When she spoke her voice was soft but firm. Not loud, not booming. There were layers to this woman he'd never realized were there.

She glanced at the student-council president and her entire demeanor changed. A fire lit in her eyes.

"We're not willing to let one mistake close our school. I've spent the entire weekend meeting with our teachers and staff and then with the student council, and we are all committed to keeping Tremmel-Bowen open. The plan that we've devised is multipronged."

"That's admirable, Ms. Stephens, but—"

"Let her finish, Malcolm," Adam said. "Then we can analyze her plan."

"It's not really my plan, we've all had a say in it."

"Even the PTA?" Malcolm asked.

"We've negotiated a few things with the PTA to get them to buy into this plan, Malcolm."

"Let Sue-Ellen answer for the PTA."

"Yes, we are willing to work with the teachers on this new plan," Sue-Ellen said a bit reluctantly.

Adam leaned back in his chair, listening as Grace talked about fiscal responsibility, community service and new teacher standards and guidelines. She sparkled when she talked about the school, her passion coming to the fore.

"Thank you, Grace," Adam said as she finished her presentation.

"Yes, thank you. I do feel, though, that this is too little too late," Malcolm said.

"Malcolm, why don't we table this discussion until the next meeting?" Adam suggested.

"Sounds like a great idea," Grace said.

Adam called for a vote and Malcolm was the only one to vote against taking a break. Slowly the conference room emptied. Adam held back, waiting until only he and Grace were left in the room.

"I'll see you later," she said, brushing past him and heading back to her office.

Adam knew he should just let her go. That reading the rest of the story he'd found in her office was a bad idea. Pursuing her was an even worse one, but she'd caught his attention. And not just with her passion for getting the school back on track.

She turned to walk out of the room, and for the first time he really watched her. Saw the feminine body beneath the dull clothes that were really too big for her body. Observed the curve of her calf and the sway of her hips. It was pure temptation. Her stride was slow and measured; she moved teasingly with each step she took. She favored skirts that ended at her knee and two-inch heels.

He followed her into her office and found her chatting with her assistant, Bruce.

"Grace, can I have a minute?"

She bit her lower lip and then nodded, closing the door as her assistant left.

"What's the matter?"

She took a seat in one of the guest chairs. As she crossed her legs, the hem of her skirt rose over her knee. He realized for the first time that her legs were bare. Her skin looked satiny smooth.

Adam wasn't sure how to bring up the sexy story he'd read earlier. The fantasy revealed a vulnerability in the woman sitting across from him. One he didn't want anyone else to see.

Her fantasy story was racy, but also very sweet, revealing more of the woman than he'd bet she'd be comfortable knowing she exposed in her writing.

He realized he couldn't confront her with the story he'd slipped into his briefcase. He leaned back in the other guest chair, just watching her. She fidgeted and then a blush stole over her face as she twisted her fingers together. She took a deep breath and glanced away from him.

He'd wanted the meeting to finish so they could officially close the school. His last tie to the lie that was his legacy. But now…now he wanted to linger in town and in her office. Find out how deep those still waters ran in Ms. Grace Stephens.

"I think if we work together we might be able to convince Malcolm and the rest of the board of regents to give you and the school a second chance."

Her eyes widened. "What? I thought you were…"

He smiled at her. "Some new information has come to light and I think that with a little attention both you and the school will benefit."

"It's not like you to be so mysterious, Mr. Bowen."

"No, it's not. We can discuss it over lunch, *Grace*."

She bit her lower lip, tipping her head to one side to study him. "Let's be honest here. Why are you really interested in helping me out?"

Her cheeks were flushed and a tendril of hair that had escaped the clip at the back of her neck curled temptingly against her cheek.

Damned if he wasn't interested in getting to know this woman better. Now that he'd seen those tantalizing glimpses of the woman beneath the very prim headmistress persona.

"Adam? Are you paying attention to anything I've said?"

"Of course," he said. "We can discuss everything over lunch." He repeated the invitation, knowing it sounded more like an order.

He knew there were risks involved—Malcolm was hot on keeping everyone in their very proper place—but Adam wasn't an employee of the school. Just on the advisory board.

He wanted to know more about Grace. And he'd always gotten what he wanted. Sometimes he'd paid a high price for achieving it, but in the end that price had always been worth it. This time, he could oversee getting the school back on track financially—making money was something he was good at. And he could get to know the real Grace Stephens. The one she hid from the world.

"Why are you staring at me?" she asked, crossing her arms under her breasts.

He was momentarily distracted by the view. "I just realized how pretty you are."

She tucked the strand of hair back behind her ear, tilting her head to the side to study him. He wanted her to find whatever it was she was looking for in his face. Some kind of realness or sincerity. The kind of thing that he was never sure that he had.

"Mr. Bowen, are you feeling okay?"

"More than okay. I'll have my chauffeur meet us at the gates of the school. We can discuss your plans for Tremmel-Bowen and other things."

"What other things?" she asked, a trace of panic in her voice. "Do you want me to resign? I don't think that would be in the best interests of the school. I'm a good administrator, Adam."

"No, Grace. I don't want you to resign." He liked the way she said his name. But she only did when she was passionate about something. About the school. When she forgot herself, forgot to be nervous around him.

What would happen if she forgot herself more often?

"What do you want?"

"You."

# Two

He swept the papers off her desk and lifted her up
onto the polished walnut surface. Slowly, exquisitely he unbuttoned her blouse. Ran his finger
down the center of her body, over her sternum and
between her ribs. Lingered on her belly button
and then stopped at the waistband of her shirt.
He slowly retraced the path over her torso. This
time his fingers feathered under the demi-cups of
her ice-blue bra. A shaft of desire pierced Grace.

*Excerpt from "Adam's Mistress" by Stephanie Grace*

Grace swallowed hard and reminded herself that he'd
just been planning on firing her, so he certainly hadn't
meant anything by saying he wanted her. He was

probably being clever. What would a sophisticated woman do?

She had no clue. At heart she was a small-town girl who lost herself in her books and imagination. And the attention of a man, the kind of attention that she thought she glimpsed in his eyes—awareness and attraction—that she had absolutely no idea how to handle.

"Grace?"

"Yes?"

"Did I scare you?"

Heck, yes, he'd scared her. But she was the headmistress of this school, a job she intended to keep. So she wasn't going to allow him to see that slight bit of insecurity. "Of course not. You mentioned lunch…"

"That's right, I did, but I don't want you to be afraid of me."

"I'm not afraid of you, Adam." She really wasn't. She was afraid of that inner temptress that her father the preacher had always warned her about. The woman hidden beneath the baggy clothes with the hour glass figure and features that just naturally drew masculine attention. From the time she was thirteen she'd had to repent for this body and now that she had Adam's attention, she wasn't exactly sure what to do with it.

She preferred him to continue to be her secret crush.

"Grace…"

"What?" she asked, not even aware of how long she'd been standing there staring at him.

"Stop it."

"I have no idea what you're talking about," she said,

nibbling on her bottom lip and hoping he wouldn't call her on her lie.

"You're thinking about this too hard. It's just a meal."

There was a tone in his voice that made her feel really ridiculous but she knew she hadn't imagined what he'd said to her. "Then why are you looking at me like I'm on the menu?"

He laughed, a deep masculine sound. "Am I?" he asked, with his charming grin. The one she'd seen him bestow on other women but never on her.

She felt giddy for a second at having captured his attention just by being herself. Not because of her made-for-sin figure, but because of who she was.

Oh, my, she was in over her head. She needed to get this conversation back on to the topic of the school. She shook her head.

"Malcolm wants this place closed down for good, doesn't he?" she asked, desperate to focus on the school and not Adam.

"Can you blame him?" Adam asked. He rose and moved closer to her, leaning one hip against her desk and crossing his legs at the ankles.

It was a totally masculine pose and should have put her at ease, but didn't. There was something measured, calculated in the way he stood there, waiting for her reaction.

She sighed, wondering if he somehow blamed her for the downward spiral of the Vernon-Dawn-Malcolm mess. God knew that she blamed herself for not paying better attention to Dawn and Vernon, but to be honest they'd been two of her best teachers.

"No, I don't. That kind of betrayal would cut so deep. I wish I'd been more observant and realized what was going on."

"What would you have done?" he asked.

"I don't know. Something. Anything to prevent the situation from getting out of hand."

"You can't control the actions of others," he said. There was an emotion in his words that she struggled to define.

"I know. Just think how nice it would be if I could. We wouldn't have to go to lunch to discuss the school, you'd just agree to keep it open."

"Let's go."

She followed him out of her office, trying not to wonder what it would feel like to have his lips on her skin.

He put his hand on the small of her back again. She liked the feeling of his big hand on her. She stumbled a little and he steadied her with his other hand.

"Are you okay?"

"Yes," she said, but inside she wasn't okay. She'd been so careful for her entire life. Made sure to keep her private fantasies carefully tucked away from the reality of the life she carved out for herself.

For the first time she understood that the lines between them were blurry. That they could be crossed. And she wasn't prepared to deal with that.

When would she be? She'd spent the twenty years

since she'd turned thirteen running from her body and the way men reacted to it. When was she going to stop running?

The bell rang while they were in the hallway and she drew Adam to a stop. She wanted him to see the camaraderie between the students. She wanted him to have a glimpse of what he'd be taking from the kids if he didn't vote to let her try to save the school. She wanted him to see that there was something worth saving here.

And nothing could serve as a stronger reminder of what she stood to lose if she let herself contemplate stepping out of the shadows she'd carefully built around herself.

Adam looked down at her as if he wasn't sure what to do with her, and she understood that. She didn't know what to do with herself. She only knew that the life she'd been living wasn't acceptable anymore. It was going to change, because of the situation at the school and because of this man. And if he was interested in her, the way he seemed to be, then she wasn't going to retreat and let this moment pass her by.

Adam had his driver take them to a local chain restaurant and soon was seated across from Grace in a booth.

Something had changed in her demeanor since they'd left her office, but he couldn't put his finger on it. She was starting to relax around him. She still had a barrier in place around her, a formality that she didn't drop, but he could tell she was trying to be friendlier.

"What should I do differently to win over the board members?" she asked after taking a delicate sip of her water.

"Nothing. Most of them are tired of the problems that the school has," he said bluntly.

"Well that was honest." She entwined her long fingers together on the table. He wanted to reach out and touch her, rub his thumb over her knuckles. But he didn't.

"I'm not going to get a chance if Malcolm has anything to say about it."

"You're right about that. But I can override the board's decision or possibly table the formal vote until the end of the school year.

"Your plan has a lot of merit on its own. The board of regents will only be swayed by action and results. I'll be happy to help you implement the changes personally. I think that will be enough to convince the board to give you some extra time."

She flushed as she stared at him. He wanted to know more about what made her tick. Why hadn't he paid attention to Grace before now? "You'd do that?"

She made him feel like a better man than he really was. Maybe it was the knowledge that he was only sitting across from her because she'd aroused his interest with her fictional story about being his mistress. There was something in her eyes that made him feel…well, not empty the way he usually did.

"I don't say things I don't mean."

"I'd heard that about you," she said. "That you don't tolerate lies."

"That's right. I don't," he said, not willing to talk about why. "What else have you heard?"

Not all of the stories that circulated about him were nice. In business, he was ruthless.

"That's all," she said, smiling at him.

He caught his breath as her entire visage changed. Grace Stephens was a stunning beauty when she smiled. A goodness shone through in that smile.

"What have you heard about me?" she asked, her voice suddenly shy.

Not much really. Commendations from parents and students prior to the incident but nothing personal about her. "I've heard very little about the woman behind the headmistress role, but I'd say that you are a woman of hidden depths and passions and that one day some lucky man is going to unlock those secrets."

She tipped her head to the side. "I'm getting a glimpse of that charm of yours."

He was a bit offended that she thought so little of his compliment. "I'm not flirting with you, Grace. Don't belittle the both of us by asking for honesty and then reacting as if it were a lie."

She flushed. "I'm sorry. Anything too close to the truth unsettles me."

"Why?"

She shrugged and looked away from him.

"Look at me, Grace."

She lifted her head, her gaze meeting his squarely. A tendril of her hair had escaped the barrette she'd used to clip it at the back of her neck.

"Why?" he asked again.

"Because I'm afraid of that kind of truth, Adam. I'm not sure how to act around you. You've never looked at me this way before."

"I'm looking now," he said.

"Yes, you are, and I'm not sure why."

He knew that he should come clean and tell her he'd found her erotic story, but his gut said she'd shut him out and he'd never see this Grace Stephens again. Instead he captured her hand, tracing his finger over her fragile wrist and the veins running under her pale skin.

"Does there have to be a reason?"

"I guess not. But I'm sure there is one."

"You're passionate about your students and your school, Grace. There's something different about you when you're defending them, fighting for them."

She licked her lips and he tracked the movement, realizing she didn't wear lipstick. Her mouth was lush, her top lip bow-shaped and the lower one fuller. He wanted to draw her across the table and taste her. To see how she'd react to a kiss. How long would it take to shatter her composure?

"I just know how hard it can be to lose your school at that age. To have to move to a new place."

"Personal experience?"

"Yes."

"I had the feeling that you were practically rooted to Texas."

"I am. I've always wanted to find a place where I fit in and put down roots and I found that at Tremmel-Bowen."

"You didn't grow up in Plano?" he asked, realizing how little he knew about her. It made him feel a little ashamed that they'd known each other for more than three years and he'd never paid any attention to her before this moment.

"No. I didn't."

There was a quiet note in her voice that made him realize there was more to her past than she'd probably want to tell him. "Where'd you grow up?"

"West Texas."

"What city?"

"Why does this matter? I'd rather discuss the school—"

"I give you my word that I'll step in and delay the vote. There's nothing left to discuss about the prep school. I'd rather talk about you," he said.

"Is that the only reason you're willing to help me convince the board to keep the school open? A personal interest in me?"

He was a smart man and knew there wasn't a good answer to this question. But he realized he'd pushed too hard and too personally for her. "No, of course not."

Grace didn't want to talk about herself. Men rarely wanted to know about her. She had no idea what she'd say. She stunk at making small talk and if they weren't going to talk about the school then she was going to have to be sparkling or interesting and, frankly, she didn't think she had that in her.

Luckily their food arrived and she gave it more attention than it deserved. She closed her eyes and offered a brief prayer of thanks for the food. Some of the preacher's teachings she'd never been able to shed.

Okay, none of his teachings, but she didn't like to dwell on the fact that her father was still controlling her behavior years after she'd left him behind.

She tried not to be nervous as their lunch progressed and Adam coaxed the conversation through a lot of different topics. She was surprised by how much he revealed about himself. He didn't seem to have the barriers she always kept in place between herself and everyone else.

She felt a twinge of embarrassment at how professionally he was now behaving toward her. Had she completely misread his interest earlier?

She tucked a strand of hair back toward her clip while the waitress cleared their plates and Adam reached over to capture her hand in his.

"Isn't this cozy?" Sue-Ellen Hanshaw asked as she approached their table.

Grace jerked her hand from Adam's and tried to remind herself that they weren't doing anything untoward. "Adam was giving me some input into the presentation I made earlier."

"I'm sure he was."

"Can we help you with something?" Adam asked.

"I hope you can help get our school back on track," she said. "My son has a year and half left at Tremmel-Bowen and I'd hate to have to pull him out before he can graduate."

"We all want to avoid that situation," Grace said. "I'd love to talk to you and get your input."

"Adam, will you be helping Grace?"

"Not that Grace needs my help, but yes, I'm going to be an active part of the school community until the end of the year."

"I'll be happy to serve on a committee with both of you."

Grace had absolutely no idea how this had happened. She didn't work well in groups. There was no way she wanted both Adam and Sue-Ellen in her office on a regular basis.

"We can work out the details of our committee after the board meets this afternoon," Adam replied.

"I'll look forward to it," Sue-Ellen said and walked away.

Grace glared after her, hating the fact that Sue-Ellen had bullied her way onto a committee that Grace wasn't even sure she wanted to be a part of. If she was on a committee with Sue-Ellen, she'd have a hard time holding her tongue and being the nice little headmistress she was supposed to be. Of all the parents she dealt with, Sue-Ellen was the one who pushed her buttons.

Sue-Ellen glanced back over her shoulder with a smug half-smile. Grace had the feeling Sue-Ellen knew exactly what she did to her.

"Will you do something for me?" Adam asked.

"In return for your help at the school?" She didn't want to say no since he was doing her a huge favor but she'd learned a long time ago not to agree to something without hearing all the details first.

"No. I'm going to help you without you being in my debt."

He seemed a little offended that she'd thought she'd have to pay him for being nice to her. But he was a savvy businessman, and she knew he didn't just donate his time to help anyone out. Even the school that was his family's legacy.

"Then why?"

"Curiosity," he said.

"What do you want me to do?" she asked after a few seconds.

"Have dinner with me," he said.

Dinner with Adam Bowen…oh, my God. She wanted to say yes. She wanted to run and hide at the same time. Her resolution to change herself and not wait for her life to change around her was still so new that she had a moment's thought that she'd just forget about it and sink back into her old life. After all, it was Monday night and she didn't have TiVo. She'd miss her favorite television show.

This was it, she thought, glancing up at him.

"You're staring at me," he said.

She blinked and realized she had been. Just looking at that perfectly formed mouth. Wondering for the millionth time what it would feel like pressed to hers. "Am I?"

He quirked one eyebrow at her. She fought to keep her expression serene. To somehow keep him from guessing that he had any effect on her. But she knew

that he was used to being around much more sophisticated women and a small-town girl from west Texas
was going to be no match for him.

"Yes, you are," he said.

"You're a very attractive man."

"I can't believe you're just noticing," he said.

Startled she had to laugh. "You aren't going to deny
it?"

"Women seem to find the arrangement of my
features pleasing."

She shook her head. An innate charm imbued everything he did and said. She wondered if it stemmed from
his childhood. She knew he was the pampered son of
older parents. And her own childhood had been very
different. Was that the key to adult success?

"I wish I had your confidence," she said before she
could stop the words. She'd gone to school this morning
knowing she was going to have to fight to keep her
career going, never imagining that she'd find herself in
a different relationship with a man she'd fantasized
about for a long time.

"Have dinner with me and I'll teach you how to get
it."

She nodded, unable to say more. This was a fantasy
come true. So why did she feel as if she were about to
start something more potentially scandalous than the
mess she was already in?

# Three

Grace needed more of Adam. She wanted more. Her heart beat so swiftly and loudly she was sure he could hear it. She scraped her fingernails lightly down his upper body. He groaned, the sound rumbling up from his chest. He leaned back, bracing himself on his elbows.

And let her explore. This was different than the hurried couplings she'd had with boyfriends in the past. Encounters that had happened in the dark and were over almost before they'd begun.

"Last chance to stop before we go too far, Grace."

*Excerpt from "Adam's Mistress" by Stephanie Grace*

Adam paid the check and escorted Grace out of the restaurant. He wasn't sure what had happened in there.

Seduction for him was a well-thought-out game and caressing her in the middle of a restaurant had not been
his intent.

He put his hand on the small of her back seemingly
for the courtesy the gesture afforded, but he acknowledged to himself that he wanted to touch her. He wanted
to pull her into his arms and feel her curves nestled
against him.

He wanted to kiss her, He wanted to take all the time
he wanted to explore her. To figure out the mysterious
depths that he sensed were hidden inside her.

He didn't want to go back to the school and drop her
off. He didn't want to spend the afternoon in meetings
with Malcolm, who was out for revenge and wanted to
close the school and then sell it. He didn't want…to leave
her.

He liked the quietness she brought to him. The way
she really listened when he talked. And the shyness
that he had been able to coax her into forgetting while
they'd been eating. He also liked her honesty. She
wasn't pretending to be someone else or hiding from
the mess the school was in.

Lies were something he simply couldn't tolerate,
even well-meaning ones, and with Grace he got the impression that she was as honest as the day was long.
Though she didn't see herself the same way he did.

He loved her hair and wanted to see it falling around
her shoulders instead of clasped at the back of her neck.
He seated her in his car, a black Ferrari 599 GTB
Fiorano, and walked around to the driver's side.

She fussed with her hair as he started the car.

"What are you doing?"

She glanced over at him, her head tipped to one side. But her hands stayed at the back of her neck. "My hair is a little wild and not very professional."

He could think of no woman who embodied professionalism more than Grace. He captured her wrist and pulled her hands free of her hair. The thick brown length of it spilled around her shoulders. She watched him with wide eyes, clearly waiting to see what he'd do next.

"It's not the hair that makes you professional." She had no idea how upstanding she seemed. He'd never even glanced past the surface of who she was until he'd seen her secret fantasies written on the page. To be honest, a big part of the reason was that she gave the impression of being a no-nonsense, by-the-book administrator.

"Easily said by a man. You have no idea what it's like to be in a room full of perfectly coiffed, straight-haired women and be the only one with this hair," she said, gesturing to her head.

"Does putting it up make you more confident?" he asked. There was a sparkle in her eyes that he thought might be temper. But he knew she wouldn't lose it with him. He was coming to know Grace better than he suspected she wanted him to. The fact of the matter was, Grace needed him to help save her school so she wouldn't tell him off no matter how much he ticked him off.

She shrugged, and he knew that he'd stumbled onto something more than a hairstyle choice. She glanced out the window as he turned on the car. He didn't put the car in gear, only turned on the air conditioning so they didn't roast while they continued the conversation.

Which, it seemed, had stalled. She wasn't going to say anything else and probably expected him to behave in a polite, gentlemanly fashion and let the subject drop. But this woman had written about him in a way that no other woman ever had. On page, she'd made him seem to be a hero. And Adam Bowen had never been anyone's hero.

"Grace…" he said, softly, reaching over to stroke her face. Her skin was the softest he'd ever touched.

She flinched away from him. "Don't, Adam. We can't."

She was right. With the intense public scrutiny of the school, the last thing he should be thinking about was Grace and himself alone. But his mind was consumed with images of the two of them.

He was careful to keep a barrier between himself and other people because he knew he'd always move on. Moving on was the way he survived, something he'd learned the hard way after the death of his parents. He remembered standing in the foyer of that big empty house that had always been filled with their presence and realizing he was all alone. Their deaths when his father's twin-engine Cessna crashed had rocked his world.

But even then he hadn't realized how truly alone he was.

She touched his hand, rubbing her finger over the back of his knuckles and making him realize how soft and small she was compared to him.

"It's not like we even know each other," she said.

"I want to change that. After all, you oversee one of my investment properties."

"Investment property? I thought the school was your family's legacy."

"It's a Bowen legacy, but I view it more from a financial angle," he said in a way that didn't invite more questions.

"And if I don't pull it out of trouble, you're going to lose money—that's your main concern?"

He took her chin in his hand, moving her head up so that their eyes met. He waited a full minute before saying anything to her. Making sure she realized that he was not just using practiced lines to charm her.

"No, Grace. Because you are the kind of woman who makes a man realize there's more to life than investments."

"I am not. Why would you think that?"

"The passion you have for Tremmel-Bowen."

"I've always had it, and you've never noticed me before today."

She had a point, but he wasn't going to mention the story he'd read…"Adam's Mistress." He wanted her to reveal it to him. "It's the way you defended the school and the students."

She took his wrist in both of her hands and tried to move his hand from her face. He let her push him away, his fingers caressing her skin as he dropped his hand to his lap.

When he reached for her again, to tuck a strand of

hair behind her ear, she shifted in the seat and gave him a hard stare.

"I'm warning you."

"Warning me?"

"Yes. This kind of behavior and comments like you just made—that's what I was talking about. Do you think I've never glanced in a mirror and seen myself? I know exactly the type of woman you usually have on your arm."

"I don't have a type," he said. He really didn't. He liked all women no matter what their shape or style. He liked that their bodies were different than his. The feminine grace they used when they moved. The way they really got to the heart of the matter. Just as Grace was doing now, though it was making him uncomfortable. Hell, he thought, he even liked that with Grace. Liked the way she didn't pretend that this was something casual.

"Yeah, right," she said. "I think it's time we returned to the school."

He wondered if she'd sound so sure if she knew the thoughts that prim, school-headmistress tone gave him. He wanted to argue with her, get her to admit he didn't have a type. But there would be time for that later. Tonight.

The problems she'd left behind when she'd gone to lunch with Adam waited for her when she returned. Sue-Ellen had set up an appointment for the next morning. She was gathering the PTA troops and would be bringing other parents who wanted to take an active part in reshaping the school.

Grace had the beginnings of a headache, no doubt brought on by the pressure of trying to convince the board not to close the school. But she thought the intensity that Adam had shown her was also a part of it. She'd wanted him for a long time and now it seemed he was finally noticing her as a woman.

Why?

She sighed and searched around for the budget file that Jose had made notes on.

"Bruce, have you seen my budget file?" she called out the door.

"I put it on the corner of your desk before we left for the meeting," her assistant replied.

Grace went back to her desk and picked up a pile of folders, suddenly remembering that she'd put a story she'd meant to enter in a romance writing contest in a similar folder.

Oh, my God.

Frantic, she started searching through all the folders, not finding the budget report or her story "Adam's Mistress."

Oh, this was so not good. She had absolutely no excuse to have printed the document out here at work, but her printer at home was almost eight years old and it was difficult to find printer ink for it. Currently, she was out.

There was a knock on the door and she glanced up. Jose stood there with a folder in his hand. A folder that was identical to…well, every other folder in her office, since they purchased folders in bulk.

Calm down, Grace.

"Got a minute?"

"Sure," she said, amazed that her voice sounded so calm and serene when inside she was ready to scream.

"I grabbed the budget report to double-check over lunch. I think we need to reevaluate the funds we have."

She was partially relieved that Jose was holding the budget and not her story. "Please tell me we have more money than we thought."

"I wish I could."

She sank down in her chair and gestured for Jose to come farther into the room. "I think we're going to need fifty thousand to make it until the end of the school year."

"That's a lot of car washes," she said. The school had never held many fundraisers. They had a golf tournament every year in the fall to raise funds. But parents and alumni had already contributed to that.

"The kids are willing to participate to some extent, but the one thing we haven't slipped on is our academic excellence."

She understood what Jose was saying. If they asked the students to start participating in a variety of fund-raising activities, it would distract them from their studies.

"I have a meeting tomorrow morning with Sue-Ellen. I think the parents will be a great resource for this. Jose, will you please call our alumni president and see if he's available tomorrow at ten?"

"Yes."

"Thanks," she said. As Jose got up and left her office, she sank back into the chair. The next few months were going to be difficult. And she had to find that story she'd printed out.

She didn't need the additional worry that a student would find it. Or worse, Sue-Ellen or Malcolm.

Oh, no. What if Adam had found it?

Was that why he'd taken her to lunch and said he'd help her with the school? Was he setting her up for a private meeting where he'd tell Malcolm about the story and fire her?

She had no time to dwell on that possibility as she spent the afternoon meeting with individual board members. Meetings that Adam had set up for her. The support she garnered was worth the time she spent with them.

The afternoon went by quickly. She had a small break and searched every inch of her office but couldn't find her story. Jose e-mailed her his ideas for their fund shortage, and they were all really good.

"Grace, Dawn O'Shea called while you were in a meeting. She wants to talk to you about possibly getting her job back." Bruce hovered in her doorway uncertainly.

"I can't talk to her today," Grace said. She felt sorry for Dawn, losing her job and her husband. But Dawn's actions had greatly hurt the school, and saving Tremmel-Bowen was Grace's priority.

"I told her you'd call next week."

"Thanks."

Bruce left at six. Grace researched fundraising ideas on the Internet and sent a few links to Jose and Sue-Ellen. She glanced up from her computer at seven-thirty when she heard voices in the outer office. Her head ached at the thought of how much work she still had to do.

The missing story scared her. It had the potential to put all the work she'd done today to save the school to waste. At least she hadn't put her real name on it as the author. But the characters' names—Adam and Grace— were pretty damning. She'd have to change those before she submitted it anywhere. *If* she submitted it.

She knew her assistant would rush back to help her if she called him. But she didn't exactly want Bruce searching her office for that file folder.

"Grace? Got a minute?"

Adam stood in her doorway with Malcolm just behind him. The smile of welcome froze on her face as she noted the file folder held loosely in his hands.

The sinking feeling in her stomach grew as she waited for Malcolm or Adam to speak. She was a nervous wreck and she hated that. This was her domain. The one place in the world that she'd found where she really fit.

*"Good evening, gentlemen."*

"Ms. Stephens, do you have time to discuss your financial plan with me now?" Malcolm asked.

She wanted to say no. But she wasn't going to turn away from the olive branch that Malcolm offered. All day long she'd heard from other board members that the decision to keep the school open had to be unanimous, so if Malcolm wasn't on board by the end of the school year, Tremmel-Bowen would be closed.

"Sure. I was just about to order some dinner, can I get something for you both?"

"We won't be that long. We can go down to the conference room so we'll have more room."

Grace followed Malcolm down the hall. She empathized with him. She would want to shut down the school as well if she were in Malcolm's shoes. *Betrayal.* It was one thing she understood better than most.

Adam dropped behind to speak to the night-maintenance supervisor and Grace found herself alone with Malcolm. She explained the shortage error they'd just found and then spent forty-five minutes arguing over the tiniest details in the budget. Grace was careful to keep her temper, but she was beginning to believe it was going to be impossible to convince Malcolm to give the school a reprieve.

In the back of her mind was the fear that all the work that she and Adam had done today would be undone by her story surfacing somewhere. She thought of all the people who'd been in and out of her office throughout the day. She'd had the student council representatives in there and, to be honest, she would be even more horrified if one of them had found the folder than if Adam had.

"Ms. Stephens, if you aren't going to pay attention you're just wasting our time."

"I am paying attention. I don't see this as a waste of time."

"I do," he said. She felt the noose tighten and realized that Malcolm might have given in until the end of semester but beyond that he wasn't vested in seeing the school survive.

She reached across the table and touched the back of his hand. He glanced up at her. "Yes?"

"What can I say to you?"

He didn't pretend not to understand her. "*Nothing.* I'm sorry, Grace. I have a lot of respect for you personally but I can't get around the fact that this school needs to be closed."

"You know that knot you have in the pit of your stomach?" she asked, waiting only for his nod.

"That's what you are going to give to the kids. Some of them don't make friends easily. Some of them have their whole life planned with this school, with this education. And no matter that we're in the red financially or that we've had an unfortunate scandal— educationally, we're still top-rated."

"And your point is?"

"That we'll be betraying the trust those students put in this institution. And I know that someone who understands betrayal wouldn't want to do that to anyone, especially not teenagers who are already struggling just to grow up."

Malcolm leaned back in his chair, studying her with an impenetrable gaze. He gathered his papers and put them into his briefcase. "You make a good point, Grace. And I'll consider what you've said until the end of the semester when the board meets again."

She said nothing as the older man left her alone in the boardroom. But she knew she'd scored a victory. A temporary one, a small battle, but still she'd convinced him to give her until the end of the school year to make some significant changes.

And if she didn't find her file folder, it could all be for nothing.

She frowned, thinking of what she had to accomplish. The short time frame she had to accomplish it made her want to scream.

Someone brushed her fingers aside and she glanced over her shoulder to see Adam standing there.

He massaged her shoulders and the tension of the day started to recede. Not totally of course. "Malcolm mentioned he was giving you until the end of the semester to prove the school should be left open."

"Yes, he agreed to that. Thank you, Adam. For arranging all those meetings and for standing behind me. I don't think the board would have given me a chance without that."

She tried to keep her mind on the school. It was the most important thing in her life. But a part of her stared up at Adam and wondered if he'd somehow found the seeds to shut down her school anyway. If he was toying with her because…why? From what she'd seen of him, he wasn't a cruel man.

"No problem. Everyone agrees that if anyone can turn the school around it's you," he said.

"Why do they believe that?" she asked, hating the weakness that question revealed. But tonight, she was a little overwhelmed. Maybe she'd bitten off more than she could chew. Maybe she should have taken the out the board had given her. She could have walked away from the school with a nice recommendation and gotten another job.

"Because you have this inner strength that makes everyone around you realize that you won't settle for anything other than excellence."

She wished she felt that what he'd said was true. But inside she feared she was a fraud. That the fear of having to look for another job, the fear of having to go to some new place and try to fit in had in large part motivated her to save Tremmel-Bowen.

"I'm not that woman," she said.

"Yes, you are," Adam said, using his hands on her shoulders to turn her around and draw her to her feet.

"I don't feel like it."

"You will tomorrow."

"What's going to change between now and then?"

"I'm going to make you dinner and convince you of the faith I have in you."

"We can't. I thought about it this afternoon, you know we can't have dinner together."

"We both have to eat," he said.

She shook her head. If she wanted to save the school, she needed to stay focused on the school and not let Adam distract her. "Our being seen together is too risky. I don't want to chance it."

"Dinner isn't a torrid affair."

"I know that."

"How about if I cook for you?"

"You can cook?"

He quirked one eyebrow at her and gave her a half smile that she felt all the way to her toes. "Yes, ma'am."

She gave her unspoken consent by following him out the door. Already she felt lighter, not as tired, just at the thought of spending more time with him. Adam really was a one-of-a-kind guy. The kind of man worthy of a woman who wasn't always pretending to be someone she wasn't.

Her secrets felt like a heavy burden. And Adam might actually be privy to one that she wanted to keep very private. Going to dinner at his house would give her an opportunity to fish around and see if he'd found "Adam's Mistress" on her desk.

# Four

She knew she should tell him to leave, that her job was at stake, but she couldn't give up the chance to be with him. To know him intimately. She caressed his chest, lingering over the well-developed pectorals.

His muscle jumped under her touch. She scraped her nail down the center line of his body. Following the fine dusting of hair that narrowed and disappeared into the waistband of his pants.

*"Don't go,"* she said softly.

*Excerpt from "Adam's Mistress" by Stephanie Grace*

Adam enjoyed cooking because so many people expected him not to know how to do it. Like he was nothing more than a stereotype instead of a real person. He'd been on his own for the better part of the last fifteen years and survival demanded that he at least make an effort to learn how to feed himself.

He'd employed his parents' staff for the first five years after his parents' death, but when he learned the truth of his family's secret he felt like a fraud and couldn't in good faith continue to pretend to be someone he wasn't. One of the hardest things he'd had to do was let go of the staff. But if Molly and Hubert Johnson were working for him he wasn't going to learn to stand on his own, so he'd asked them both what they wanted to do. Molly had always longed to open a small craft store in her hometown and Adam had helped her do that. Hubert had been happy to move back home with his wife and work in the shop.

Slowly Adam had started learning what he needed to do to carve a life for himself. A life that he was in control of.

Grace wasn't one of those women who made false assumptions about him. She'd taken one look at the state of the art kitchen and understood that he would know his way around a good pot roast.

"I guess you really can cook," she said, a wry grin lighting her face.

"Yes."

"Most guys consider dinner throwing something on the grill or heating up rice in the microwave."

He wanted to groan. "A man offered to cook for you and then made microwave rice?"

She laughed but the tension didn't really ease from

her face. She was still nervous and tense. Still unsure of something.

Him, he suspected. The situation that he was engineering to hopefully get her comfortable enough that she'd share the secrets hidden behind those shadowed eyes.

"No. My dad used to make rice for us for dinner whenever there was nothing else to eat."

"Where was your mom?"

She fidgeted with the stem of her wineglass and he realized he'd probed past the bounds of what was polite conversation and gone straight into that forbidden territory marked personal. A place that it was obvious she wasn't ready to go.

"This is a really nice house. I can't believe how big all the houses are in this area."

Actually, the house was rather modest for the neighborhood, only 4,000 square feet. Certainly small compared to other properties he had around the world. But he'd liked the soaring windows and the large deck outside was a terrific place to work on the laptop on nice days. Well, it would be if he were ever here long enough to enjoy it.

Since the Johnsons had gone, he had a cleaning service come in periodically to check on things and dust. He'd had them stock the kitchen before he'd arrived. He might have to have them in more often if he truly was going to stay in Plano for the next six months.

"Where do you live?" he asked, because every detail

about her life was becoming important to him. He'd certainly be happier discussing her and her life. Maybe get her to confess she'd always been attracted to him and had written a sexy little story about the two of them.

"Not so far from the school. My subdivision is a few years old. It's a good thing I moved there when it was first built. I don't think I could afford to buy there now."

"What do you like about where you live?"

She took a sip of her wine. He finished putting the tomatoes and onions on the salmon and wrapped them in foil before putting them in the oven. He checked the boiling water and dumped in the couscous and then turned back to her. She was staring at him.

"What?"

"I thought you were faking it. That you were going to pretend to know how to cook, but then when I turned my back you'd be pulling ready-made meals from the freezer."

"No matter what else you believe about me, Grace, know that I never lie."

"*Never?* What if I asked you if this suit looked nice on me?"

"I would say that the color is good with your skin tone but that the cut isn't flattering."

She arched one eyebrow at him. "What if you get pulled over for a speeding ticket?"

"Not even then. I just don't see the point in making up a story."

"Even when you're starting a relationship? When you want to make a good impression?"

He shook his head. "That would set a tone for the relationship that I think I can fool the other person and I don't like it."

"Did someone lie to you?"

Deep inside the icy part of his soul where he hid the truth of what he was, he cringed. Lies were the very foundation his life had been built on and he hadn't even realized that until he was twenty-five. At that age when most people were coming to terms with their past, he'd learned his was a sham. "That's in the same closet that you closed the door on."

"What closet? When did I close that door?"

"The one marked personal. You closed it when you changed the subject from your mother."

"Oh. If I tell you about her…"

"I'm not trying to make a deal with you. Just saying some areas aren't meant to be trod this early in a relationship."

There were some places he didn't ever want to go. Digging into her secrets and finding out more about Grace was his only goal. He didn't want her to see him in a different light.

"Are we going to have a relationship?"

"I didn't invite the rest of the board back to my house for dinner."

"No, you didn't." She set her wineglass on the counter and walked around the island so that she stood right next to him. "Why is that? Why are you suddenly noticing me as a woman and not just as a coworker?"

He realized that he'd boxed himself into a corner. "I saw a different side of you today. I was—I am—intrigued." That was the truth.

"Desperate and willing to do anything to save the school—no wonder you're interested in me."

He laughed because he could tell she wanted to lighten the moment, but inside he knew that he shouldn't seduce her until she revealed the truth. Until she acknowledged that she'd been attracted to him for a long time.

"I don't see you as desperate."

"Well, I was. And you are turning out to be a very nice person to have in my corner."

Thinking of why he'd invited her over, he knew he wasn't nice. "No one would ever call me nice."

"I would, Adam. I know you don't see it that way, but taking a chance on me and the school…it was a very kind thing you did. And I really appreciate it."

"I don't want your appreciation."

"No?"

He shook his head, closing the distance between them and drawing her into his arms. He lowered his head, brushing his lips over hers. He told himself that he was just telling her the truth with his body because he still couldn't reveal it with his words, but he knew that something else was going on here. For the first time since he was twenty-five, he wanted to pull a woman into his arms and keep her there forever.

For a man who liked living a solitary life, that was a scary thought.

* * *

Grace rose on her tiptoes to meet Adam's mouth. She snaked her arms around his waist and held on to him, afraid to wake from the dream that he'd enveloped her in. For some reason, Adam Bowen was suddenly paying attention to her and she didn't want to let him go.

The worries she'd carried for the last ten days faded to the back of her mind. He opened his mouth and she knew he'd said something but for the life of her she couldn't hear him over the roaring in her ears. She kept her eyes open as he moved closer to her.

"Grace?"

"Hmm?"

"Last chance…"

She realized he was telling her to pull back but she couldn't. He was her fantasy and after the long stressful day she'd had, she wanted—no, needed—to put her needs first. She'd wanted to kiss Adam since the first moment they'd met.

His lips brushed over hers. *Adam Bowen was kissing her.* He tasted way better than she'd imagined he would. He kept his touch light, his tongue tracing the seam between her lips. She let her eyes drift closed and knew that she'd made a choice that was going to change the nice safe world she'd created for herself.

The timer on the oven beeped and he pulled back. Reluctantly. He directed her toward the dining room and she went in by herself, knowing she needed to collect her thoughts and find her center.

What if he was toying with her? One other time, she'd believed in a man and he'd disappointed her badly. She didn't want to be a fool again, but Adam had always seemed different to her.

The dining room was ultra-formal, decorated in dark wood and antiques. This was the kind of showplace house her father would have eyed with a fanatical gleam, sure the owner had plenty of spare cash to donate to the church. The kind of place she'd never have been invited into as a child.

She heard Adam's footsteps behind her and turned as he entered the room. He set the plates on the table and held out a chair for her. Once seated she muttered a quick prayer of thanks under her breath.

Then glanced up in time to see him take his seat. The meal was delicious and she wanted to keep the conversation light. To remind herself that no matter what Adam intimated, this wasn't the beginning of a personal relationship.

But she wanted to know more about him. She wanted to find out why he had a thing about lying. Most people paid lip service to believing in that, but in real life often rattled off falsehoods without a second thought.

She should just ask him straight out if he'd seen the story in her office and maybe picked it up. But she'd be so embarrassed if she had to explain about it. What if it wasn't Adam? Jose, Bruce and other staffers went in and out of her office all the time. Even students and other teachers had access.

For just one night, she wanted to see the real man so *that when she got home* after this strange day was over, she could write down her impressions of him. The way his hand had felt on hers. The way his lips had moved over hers. The way he'd cocked his head to the side and really listened while she talked about subjects on which no one else wanted her opinion.

Even if she never saw him again, she knew he'd given her a gift. But she *would* see him again. And she didn't want to slip back into invisible mode with him. The weight of her hair against her shoulders reminded her that he already saw her in a different light.

"What were your parents like?" she asked, when they'd finished their main course and were having coffee on his deck. It overlooked the well-landscaped backyard. In the center of the yard was a large pool with a waterfall on the far end.

"Ward and June Cleaver. Are you old enough to know who they are?" he asked.

"I think everyone has seen *Leave It to Beaver* on Nick@Nite."

"Very funny. My mom and dad were the perfect parents, doting, supportive, strict when they needed to be."

"So why haven't you settled down?" she asked. It was the one thing she'd always wondered about him. He seemed so perfect—what was stopping him from committing to one of the perfect women he dated?

"Why haven't you?" he asked.

She swallowed hard. This was why she didn't do

close relationships. Sooner or later you had to talk about your past. Small talk only lasted so long. "I didn't grow up with the perfect parents."

"What kind of childhood did you have?" he asked.

It was an innocent question. She wanted to counter with a change of topic—something to turn the spotlight back on him—but she wasn't going to, because she did want to get to know Adam better. And that thing he'd said earlier about trust had struck a nerve. Here was a man she thought she could trust.

"I don't know. One like most kids. I think you're the exception, Adam." In her small town, he would have been the exception. They'd had rich kids like everywhere else, but no one who'd grown up the way Adam had. Traveling every season, going to trendy ski resorts and all-inclusive Caribbean getaways instead of riding in the backseat of a cramped car to some dreary relative's house several hours away.

"How?" he asked, his interest genuine.

"Just that a lot of parents weren't that supportive of kids in my neighborhood."

"You're from a small town, right?"

"Yes. A poor one. Most families really scrambled to make a living."

"Yours?"

"Yes."

"What did your folks do?"

She should never have started this conversation. How could she talk about being deprived when her father had been a preacher and had provided a nice house for her? How could she explain, without sounding like a whiner, exactly the way she'd been deprived? How could she explain what she herself never wanted to understand?

"My dad's a preacher."

"So you're the rebellious preacher's daughter?"

"No. Not a rebel. I prefer to just blend into the walls."

"I've noticed."

"Well I must be doing something wrong, because you weren't supposed to notice."

"I didn't until today."

She smiled at the way he said it. Like it was an important thing. That having noticed her had made a difference to him.

Was it because of the story?

"I've noticed you before."

"Really? Tell me what you observed."

She took her time trying to figure out how to tell him what she'd seen in him without revealing how deeply she'd studied him. Now that she was here with him, she felt a little silly that she'd given him a starring role in her fantasies without really knowing the man behind the good looks.

Adam knew he was pushing. But the more he learned about Grace, the more he realized that his knowing about her fantasies was going to wound her. She gave off the image of being so superefficient and competent that only tonight had he glimpsed the vulnerabilities she had underneath.

He didn't want her to think he'd exploited those weaknesses. And guilt ate at him. Omissions were lies, he thought. Hell, he knew that omissions were the biggest kind of lies.

But he wanted to hear from her lips that she found him attractive. That he hadn't imagined the story that he'd reread during the day about five times. He knew exactly what she liked. How she wanted a man who was forceful in the bedroom but sensitive and understanding outside.

To be honest, that wasn't how he normally operated with a woman, but everything about Grace was different. She made him want to be more. He didn't know why. He couldn't explain it to himself. But tonight, with a cool breeze in the air and the fragrance of the blooming vegetation around his pool filling the air, he didn't care.

He didn't want to think of anything other than this woman and how he could convince her she'd be safe in his arms. And he wanted her in his arms. He wanted her mouth under his with no dinner buzzer about to go off. No crowded restaurant of people too close to them. Just the two of them and the night and nothing between them.

"Come on, Grace, what did you think about me the first time we met?" he asked, having the feeling that she was going to just keep quiet and let the conversation die an awkward death.

"It's complicated," she said, leaving the deck and

walking toward the pool. She stopped by a potted hibiscus and bent to smell the bloom.

She ran whenever he pushed too far into her barriers. The ones she used to keep everyone at arm's length. She was subtle and only someone who spent a significant amount of time with her as he had today would notice it.

"I understand complicated. Is it such a bad impression that you're worried about hurting my feelings?"

"Give me a break. You must know that no one has a bad first impression of you."

"I don't know that, Gracie. You won't tell me what you thought."

She took a deep breath and faced him, her eyes alive with an emotion he couldn't name. "I thought, this man is someone who knows how to really live his life."

He was taken aback by her comment. To be honest, he'd been fishing for a compliment. Having read her story, he knew she liked his shoulders and his backside. He was chagrined to realize that he'd expected her impressions to just be physical. If they had been, he would have felt comfortable using the physical attraction between the two of them to seduce her.

"Not what you were expecting?" she asked.

"No," he said. What she'd observed in him revealed what she herself was afraid she was missing. It took him a moment to identify fragility and fear as the emotions in her eyes. Grace didn't lie, either. The knowledge made him feel protective of her.

"Well, there it is. You also have very nice eyes."

She took a step closer to him. There were still a few

inches of space between them, but she'd made a move toward him—the first she'd made since they met. He was a little thrown by her compliment. Nice eyes? "No one has ever mentioned that before."

She wiggled her eyebrows at him. "Probably because they were busy ogling your physique."

"Ah, that's more what I was expecting."

She laughed at him. But there was something in her eyes that told him she'd said it to distract him. And he let her because he already knew more of her secrets than he intended. More than she'd probably intended him to know.

"Anything specific about my physique?" he asked, letting her turn this moment a little lighter. He had to touch her again. She'd left her hair down. The silky length of it fell around her shoulders, curling gently.

He caught one of the curls and let it wrap around his hand and wrist, drawing her closer to him. She was short, shorter than he'd realized until he held her in his arms. She came only to his shoulders.

He lowered his head, brushing his lips against hers. He felt her fingers move restlessly on him and wished he didn't have his shirt on so he could feel her touch on his skin.

Her fingers were small and her touch light. So light and tentative, as if she wasn't sure what to do next. He groaned deep in his chest, thinking of this fragile, beautiful woman and wondering if he had a right to touch her like this. Because he was a rambler. A rolling stone that had learned that life was less painful when he kept moving. He didn't notice the emptiness when he moved from place to place.

And if ever a woman was rooted to one place, it was Grace.

She opened her lips under his and he stopped thinking. He just felt. The soft brush of her tongue over the seam of his lips made his blood flow heavy. He felt a tingle of arousal spread down his spine. He pulled her closer with his hand in her hair at the back of her neck.

His other hand skimmed down her curves to rest on her hip, drawing her into his body before he took control of the kiss, thrusting his tongue deep into her mouth and tasting her deeply. The flavor of the wine they'd had with dinner was on her tongue, but also something he was beginning to identify with only Grace. That was what he hungered for. More Grace.

He lifted her to his body, canted his hips and wrapped his arm strongly around her hips to enable him to kiss her deeper. To thrust his tongue into her mouth again and again, trying to assuage a hunger that he'd never had before. A hunger that made all the emptiness in his life pale in comparison. A hunger that came from this small, complicated woman.

# Five

He traced her lips, his finger following the path
his mouth had taken a few moments earlier. He
caressed the pulse point where he'd suckled her
neck and then moved lower.

His stomach was rock hard and rippled when he
moved. He reached around her back and
unhooked her bra and then pushed the cups out
of his way. He pulled her closer until the tips of
her breasts brushed his chest.

"Grace." He said her name like a promise.

*Excerpt from "Adam's Mistress" by Stephanie Grace*

He overwhelmed her. Adam had literally swept Grace
off her feet and she didn't care. For once it felt good to

just forget about everything and feel. She wrapped her arms around his shoulders and gave herself up to his embrace.

She shifted restlessly in his arms, trying to get closer to him. She felt the world spinning around her and found and felt the padded cushion of a lounge chair under her back. Adam pulled back for a second, shifting her to her side and sliding down on the chair next to her. He pulled her back into his arms.

Actually being in his embrace, feeling the length of his body pressed against hers was so much better than she'd imagined. He was dominant and a little aggressive but she felt cherished in his arms. She knew he'd never hurt her. She was startled by that thought. It had been years since she'd thought of a man's strength being used against her.

He traced his hand over her face as if he were memorizing her features. There was so much heat in his eyes, she was surprised she could still breathe. She wanted to feed that fire and make him forget the outer trappings of the plain woman she'd worked so hard to project. But she wanted to be equal to him in this moment. She wanted to be alive instead of just blending into the background.

She tunneled her fingers through his hair, holding his head still. He waited for her to make her next move. She shifted in his arms so that her head was above his, her elbows resting on his chest, and she lowered her mouth to his. Rubbed her lips over his. Because she wanted to make this moment last forever.

She wanted to remember every millisecond of this

kiss and how he tasted and felt. His lips were firm and strong and she just breathed into his mouth for a second before sliding her tongue beyond his teeth deep into his mouth.

He groaned and tightened his hand on the back of her head, rolling her to her side again so that she was cradled in the crook of his arm as he took complete control of the kiss. His other hand rubbed her back, then slowly slipped around to the front of her body. He rested his hand on her abdomen and she tensed, knowing she wasn't model slim or perfect, but he soothed her with long, drugging kisses that proved he was attracted to her.

Really attracted. She couldn't think as he unbuttoned her blouse. He pulled back from her mouth, trailing kisses down her jaw to her neck. He buried his face against her and inhaled deeply and she held him to her. As he nibbled on her skin, his tongue found the pulse beating strongly at the base of her neck and suckled it.

Shivers coursed down her arms and torso. Her breasts felt full and achy and she arched in his arms, trying to rub them against his chest. But there was just enough distance between their bodies that she couldn't.

He put his hand between her breasts. His palm, hot against her skin where the edges of her blouse parted, made her nipples tighten and she tried to rotate her shoulders to bring them in contact with his hand. But he held her still underneath him.

He pushed the sleeves of her blouse down her arms.

She sat up to let him remove it. She reached for the buttons on his shirt, wanting to keep things equal between them because she knew she was already out of control.

He urged her back again, with his hand between her breasts, and leaned up over her, his hand moving over her torso. Her breasts were covered by the lacy cups of her bra and her stomach was only partially visible, her suit skirt covering her belly button. She was wearing control-top panty hose, she thought, but then he brought a finger to her face.

Tracing a path down her nose to her mouth, he outlined her lips and then moved lower, his finger following the path his mouth had taken a few minutes earlier. He caressed the pulse point where he'd suckled her neck and then feathered over the fabric of her bra, tracing the edges until she was shifting underneath him, trying to get him to touch her without having to ask.

He slid his finger under the fabric of her bra and caressed the globe of her breast briefly before withdrawing and tracing the line between her breasts down to the waistband of her skirt.

He did this over and over again until she was out of her mind with needing him.

She grabbed his hand and placed it over her breast. Held his palm over her lace-covered nipple and rubbed herself against him. She closed her eyes and shifted under him. Needing more.

He tugged his hand out from under hers and lowered his head. His warm breath brushed over her distended nipple first, then his lips rubbed back and forth over her before she felt the delicate bite of his teeth.

She moaned, wanting so much more. There was an ache deep inside her that she thought would never be alleviated. He started suckling her breast. Her legs moved restlessly and she tried to draw him over her. She wanted his weight on her. She wanted something solid to hold on to while his mouth drove her further down the path of arousal.

She felt his hand on her thigh, moving up a pantyhose-clad leg and under her skirt. He continued to suckle her as his fingers teased her inner thighs, moving closer and closer to the warm center of her body. To the place where she wanted to feel his fingers so badly. But he held her in his embrace, building her passion to the breaking point but not letting her go over.

He moved to her other breast and the cool evening air on her wet, tight nipple made her groan again. She moved her hands restlessly up and down his back and finally she felt his hand slip under the waistband of her panty hose.

He rested his hand on her lower stomach, lifted his head and glanced down at her. Waiting for permission to touch her so intimately. She knew she'd die if he didn't but she had no words to say what she wanted.

"Please, Adam."

He smiled at her, lowering his head to take her mouth again in a passionate kiss while his fingers moved through the damp curls between her legs.

* * *

Adam hadn't meant the evening to go as far as it had, but there was something so addictive about the feel and taste of Grace that he couldn't stop. He didn't want to stop until he was buried hilt deep in her silky body.

She responded so beautifully to him. He wanted to surround himself completely in her. She was damp and ready for him. He pushed his forefinger through her damp curls, touching her intimately. She clutched at his shoulders, holding him tightly as if to keep him from leaving her. As if he'd leave at this moment. He needed her response. It made him feel alive in a way he didn't want to examine too closely.

He bent to her breast again, drawing her turgid nipple into his mouth. Sucking on her strongly, trying to draw some essence of Grace into his own body. She lifted herself up into his embrace, her legs falling open to give his hand more room to move between them.

He lifted his head from her breast, pushing her skirt to her waist and drawing her panty hose and underwear down her body and off. Her legs were firm and soft and her body much slimmer than the boxy clothing she wore revealed. She had lush hips that he sank his fingers into. Once he had bared her to his gaze, he pushed her legs apart. She shifted on the lounge chair, moving restlessly.

He parted her with his fingers, lowering his head, needing to know if she tasted as good here as her mouth and breasts had. He tongued her gently and parted her with his thumbs. She cried out, her hips rising to meet his mouth. Her hands moved restlessly from his head to his shoulders, her thighs clenching around him and then falling apart.

He sensed it wouldn't take much to drive her over the edge. Licking delicately at her, he lifted her hips in his hands, his fingers sinking into her buttocks and cradling her so that he held her completely open to him.

"Adam…"

"Hmm?"

"I'm not going to last much longer."

"Good," he said. He draped her thighs over his shoulders and gave himself up to making Grace lose control, to seeing the flush of her skin deepen and listen to the breathy moans that were the sweetest music he'd heard in a long time.

He used his fingers to tease her until she was arching into his touch, and then he bit carefully on her most delicate flesh, sucking her into his mouth while he pushed one finger deep inside her.

Her body clenched around his fingers, heels digging into his back as she moved frantically.

His name was a long sigh on her lips as her climax rushed through her body. He kept his mouth and fingers on her until the internal clenching of her body stopped and then he moved up her body, keeping his hand between her legs as he found her breasts once again, suckling on them, hoping to find some satisfaction from just touching her.

She reached between their bodies, found him painfully engorged. She scraped her fingernail down the side of his zipper. He tightened even more.

Slowly she pulled the tab of his zipper, reaching into his pants and through the opening in his boxers to touch his hot flesh.

She circled him with her hand, stroking up and down and he lifted his head from her breast, brought his mouth down on hers, letting her taste herself.

She pulled her mouth from his. "Open your legs, Adam."

He shifted them apart and felt her hand move lower, cupping him and rolling her fingers over him. He tightened.

"Grace, you need to stop."

"Why?"

He explained why in blunt detail.

"Yes," she said.

"Yes?"

"I want that," she said.

He growled her name and bent to take her mouth again. Her hand worked up and down his length until he knew he wouldn't be able to hold back any longer.

He shifted his hips, wanting to move away from her, but she tightened her grip, driving him over the edge. She tangled her other hand in the hair at the back of his neck and drew his mouth down to hers.

He lowered his head to her breast, resting there. Feeling the emptiness that was always inside him ebb for the first time in a long time.

She wrapped her arms around his shoulders and one

of her legs over his hips. And held him, and he let her. Not wanting to acknowledge that he had found a weakness in himself that only this woman had brought out.

Adam lifted her into his arms and carried her into the dark house. She wrapped her arms around his shoulders, not really wanting to talk. She was afraid that if she did this moment would drift away and she'd wake up. Realize this was a beautiful fantasy instead of reality.

She caught a glimpse of his bedroom—king-size bed dominating one side of the room, floor-to-ceiling windows with crisp sheers pulled across them—as he walked into the master bath and set her on her feet. He turned on the lighting over the garden tub and the largest shower she'd ever seen. It was a glass enclosed structure with two showerheads on opposite ends.

She was aware of her state of disarray. A twinge of embarrassment went through her. But then she glanced at Adam, who was equally disheveled.

He caught her glance and drew her closer to him, kissing her once again. She wanted more. She wanted to feel him hot and hard between her legs. She wanted him to lose control again only this time inside her so that she'd carry his mark on her and in her.

He drew back. "I'll put some clean clothes on the counter."

She watched him walk away and felt a little colder. She didn't do sex well. She always associated it with some kind of deeper feelings, and maybe Adam didn't.

Of course he didn't. He'd said at dinner that he'd never noticed her until today. She wrapped her arms around her waist, feeling small and oh, she didn't like this feeling.

She removed her clothing quickly and turned on the shower, wanting—no, needing—to get clean and get out of here. What the hell had she been thinking? She had to *work* with Adam. He was staying in town to help her and she was going to have to sit across from him in meetings and remember the way his mouth had felt on her breasts. The way he had felt in her hand.

She stepped into the shower and lifted her head toward the water, hoping it would wash away the feelings that were overwhelming her. She braced one arm on the wall and tried to find her center.

But her center had always come from that core deep inside her that no one had ever realized was there. And tonight she'd let Adam see it. She knew it was going to be impossible to pretend this hadn't happened.

The shower door opened and Adam stepped into the cubicle. She glanced up at him, praying that what she felt wasn't on her face.

He didn't say anything, just drew her into his arms, holding her naked body against his. She closed her eyes and rested her head on his chest. His scent surrounded her and diminished the panic that had been growing steadily since he'd brought her into the bathroom.

"What's wrong?" he asked.

His deep voice brushed over her, sounding like

something straight out of her dreams. Tears burned the back of her eyes, because she had dreamed so many times of him holding her like this.

"I'm not…oh, heck, Adam. I'm not used to getting so intimate so fast."

He rubbed his hand up and down her back. "Don't think about that. Whatever's between us is different."

For her, she knew that. But she was positive that Adam was used to women falling all over him and she wanted to be distinctive, not part of the pack.

He tipped her head back. "What are you thinking?"

"That I'm an idiot."

"Gracie…"

"No one's ever called me a nickname before," she said, the words slipping out without her permission.

She'd had two serious relationships since she'd left home and neither of them had lasted more than a year. She was afraid suddenly that Adam would be gone as quickly. Not because she needed a man to cling to, but because he was the first person to make her feel like who she was was enough. That she didn't have to pretend to be someone else. And that really scared her, because she'd never been comfortable in her own skin.

"Can I ask you a personal question?" he asked.

"I'm standing naked in your shower. I think we've gone past the point where personal questions are out of bounds."

"Why do you wear baggy clothes?"

"I… They're just more comfortable."

"I thought we agreed there'd be no lies between us."

"Did we agree to that?"

"Stop stalling."

She reached for the loofah sponge and put some shower gel on it. "Turn around and I'll wash your back."

He arched one eyebrow at her but did as she asked. She scrubbed his back and noticed the scar that ran along the base of his spine. She touched it, wondering where it came from. "I wear the baggy clothes because my body distracts men. Makes them think of sin instead of business."

"Grace."

She stepped away from him, retreating to the far corner of the shower, sponging herself. Actually, now that she'd said the words out loud, she knew that she'd revealed too much. She felt more naked than she had on the lounge chair with his mouth between her legs.

"I don't know who said that to you, but that is not what your body makes me think of."

She tipped her head to the side, studying him. Trying to gauge the truth in his words. "What do I make you think of, Adam?"

He dropped his gaze from her for a second and then lifted his eyes to hers again. "You make me think of home, Gracie."

She didn't know how to respond to that, and it seemed neither did Adam. They each washed their own hair and got out of the shower without saying another word. It scared her to realize that Adam knew some of her deepest secrets, but she knew she also knew one of his. The man who had everything his heart desired was searching for something the same way she was.

# <u>Six</u>

The sound of raised voices filtered through her
locked office door. Panicked at the thought of
getting caught half naked in his arms, she started
to push away from him.
But he held her close, wrapping his strong arms
around her. "I've got you."
Grace hugged him to her and closed her eyes, reminding herself that this was just loneliness and
she hadn't found the man she'd been secretly
dreaming of.

*Excerpt from "Adam's Mistress" by Stephanie Grace*

Two weeks later, Grace had managed to keep Adam at
arm's length. Not an easy decision on her part, but she

knew that dating him publicly was the absolute worst thing she could do as an administrator. Plus, she was scared.

She would admit it only to herself, but she'd let Adam get much closer in one night that she'd ever intended to. Seeing him every day at the school was a bittersweet thing. After hearing from two concerned parents about the amount of time she was spending with Adam on campus, she was almost afraid to be alone with him.

Afraid that if anyone thought there was something inappropriate going on between her and Adam, it might fuel Malcolm's campaign to close the school. Sue-Ellen and the PTA had really run with the fundraising and money was starting to come in from the alumni group. But Grace knew any small mistake could set Malcolm off.

More disconcerting, her file folder with the story had shown back up on her desk. Where had it been? Had it been there the entire time?

She glanced at the pages and knew she should probably shred the thing before someone definitely saw it. The office shredder was in Bruce's cubicle and she'd tried a couple of times to use it but someone always walked by.

There was a brief knock on her door before it opened and Adam filled the doorway.

She shoved the folder under the blotter on her desk. She flushed a little and hated that. She wanted to come off as more sophisticated than she was, but no matter how hard she tried she was always going to be a small-town girl.

"Good afternoon, Grace. Do you have a minute?" Adam asked.

Quickly she closed the Internet window on her computer where she'd been reading an article about Adam that had been in *Entrepreneur* magazine last fall.

"Sure," she said.

He closed the door behind him. He wore a pair of dark dress pants and a blue shirt that really brought out his eyes.

"Please leave the door open."

"What?"

"Sue-Ellen thinks I'm spending too much time with you behind closed doors. You know she goes straight to Malcolm with her concerns, so I really don't want to give her any more fodder."

He crossed his arms over his chest and made no move to open the door. She didn't want to force the issue. Worrying about a closed door seemed kind of silly to her, but she was willing to do whatever was needed to keep the school open.

"Is that why you've been too busy to have dinner with me the last two weeks?" he asked.

"No. I have a life. I wasn't just sitting alone in my house waiting for you to start asking me out." She hoped he'd never know how many nights she'd spent sitting alone in her house thinking of him. Fantasizing about what it would be like to be in his arms. Her dreams had now become fevered remembrances of his mouth on her body. Her hands on him. She squirmed a little in her chair just at the thought of the intimacies they'd shared.

"Too bad for me," he said with a self-deprecating grin that made her smile back at him.

"What did you want to discuss?" she asked, knowing if she didn't change the subject she was going to do something she'd regret, like tell him to lock the door then seduce him on her desk.

"The gym needs a new floor. And that's not in your budget," he said, leaning back against the still-closed door.

"What do you suggest we do?" she asked. The school needed a lot of repairs. The tuitions that they'd had to refund after the scandal broke had left them in a sticky place.

"Coach Jarrett and the boys' team suggested a charity basketball game to raise money. We'd use the outdoor courts for play."

That was a great idea, but she wondered how many games they'd have to play to earn enough money to re-surface the floor. "Okay. But I don't think we're going to raise enough with just our team. Attendance at the games hasn't been that high."

"I'm going to contact a few of the musicians on my label and get them to come and play."

"I approve that idea. When were you thinking of having the event?"

"The weekend prior to spring break. I think that will give us some high-profile press coverage and we can maximize it to bring our enrollment numbers up."

"Sounds good. I have some local media contacts we can use. And Barbara Langdon would be a great parent to coordinate this. She's super-organized. Do you want me to set that up?"

"Yes. I've given Bruce all the information on the artists I think will participate."

She made a few notes on her computer calendar. Adam came farther into her office, leaning one hip on the side of her desk right next to her.

"Now that we've got school business out of the way…."

She pushed her chair away from the desk to put more space between them. "Yes?"

"I've got tickets to the Stars. Want to join me?" he asked.

She wanted to say yes. She'd never been to a professional sports game. Ever. And the Dallas Stars were a really good hockey team. She knew they were going for the Stanley Cup.

But more than any interest in sports, she wanted to spend time with Adam. To feed the obsession that had grown in the weeks when they'd been dealing with each other only for the school's business. "I'm not sure that's a good idea. What will the board think?"

"I don't care."

"That's easy for you to say. If the school closes down, you still have a job."

"Do you think I'm that callous?"

"No," she said. "But I do think you're used to everyone doing what you want them to."

"What are you afraid of?"

"Why do I have to be afraid? Malcolm is just looking for an excuse to get the board to fire me."

"Going to a hockey game with me isn't going to affect your job."

He had a point. She knew it. But she was starting to care for him and she was afraid if they got any closer that she was never going to recover when he moved on. And he would move on, because there wasn't anything to hold him here in Plano. She wasn't the kind of woman that made a man stop roaming around. Much as she wanted to be.

"Okay," she said, realizing that she was running from herself again. She had to stop running away if she really wanted to find herself.

Adam was surprised by how challenging he found the work at Tremmel-Bowen. The school was one of those connections to his parents that he'd distanced himself from. They'd been very involved in the running of the school and, at twenty-five, when he'd learned the truth about himself, he'd been angry. Carrying on his family's traditions hadn't seemed important.

But without intending to, Grace was giving him a chance to see the pride that his father must have felt in the school. Talking to the students and seeing the campus, he felt a connection to the Bowens that he'd lost when he'd heard a few sentences uttered from a distant relative. A relative who had made the loving family he'd always taken for granted a big lie.

It was why he was a stickler about the truth.

Tonight he promised himself that he would bring up the subject of Grace's erotic story. He'd find a way to make her tell him about it and then admit he'd read it.

He knew they'd both retreated after the intimacy they'd shared on his pool deck. And he'd come to some strange conclusions about himself and Grace. No matter why he'd first become attracted to her, the need to know her and bind her to him had grown.

He rang the doorbell at her house a few minutes early. Grace lived in a neatly kept townhome community. A small, wrought-iron bench sat to the left on her small porch and a Welcome wreath hung on the door. The scene felt welcoming in a way he associated only with Grace.

He heard her footsteps on some kind of hardwood or tile floor before the door opened. She had her hair pulled back in a ponytail and wore a pair of baggy jeans and a cute pink T-shirt. He smiled to himself at the way she carefully concealed her curvy body.

He didn't like that she hid that part of herself. She had the kind of body that he'd always dreamed of holding. And she was embarrassed by it. Her words—that she was made for sin—still lingered in the back of his mind.

Even if he left Grace with nothing other than the school, he'd first make her see herself through his eyes. To see that she was so much more than that long-ago image she had of herself.

"I just need to put on my shoes and change my purse. Do you want to come in for a drink?"

"That would be nice," he said, catching a glimpse of

her decor over her shoulder. The floor was a dark hardwood, probably oak. A coat tree stood to one side, hung with Grace's coats, and a brightly colored scarf lay draped over a small table.

She led the way through her house. It was elegantly decorated with some homey touches—photos on the mantel, antiques in the hallways. As he glanced around her private sanctuary he realized he was seeing another layer of that private woman. The house suited her.

"I've got iced tea, beer and some white wine," she said, opening the refrigerator and glancing inside it.

"Tea would be great."

"It's not sweet."

"Perfect." He realized she was nervous about having him here. And he liked that. She was always so confident of herself, moving through life as though nothing really bothered her, that he liked shaking her up.

She got a glass with ice and poured the tea. She set it on the breakfast bar and moved to the other side of the kitchen, leaning against the counter next to the refrigerator and watching him as if she wasn't sure what to do with him.

"I'm not going to pounce on you now that we're finally alone again." Though he wanted to. His arms were empty without her in them. He wanted to kiss and caress her, to keep their relationship on a level that he easily understood, and fit the mold of what he expected from the women in his life, instead of dealing with all the other things that she brought to the surface. The longings for home and permanency that he'd thought he'd shed a long time ago.

"I didn't think you would," she said with a tart note in her voice.

"Then what's up?" he asked, after taking a sip of his iced tea.

She shrugged. "My house is so much smaller than yours."

He was coming to realize that one of Grace's major hang-ups was the fact that she was conscious of what other people had and measured herself against them. Why would she think he'd be judging her by the size of her house?

If she knew the truth about him—the fact that he was a fake Bowen—she might not care that his house was bigger than hers. But he knew it was *his* money, the money he'd earned on his own, that provided the basis for his wealth. He'd taken his parents' entire fortune and donated it to charities that he knew his mother would have supported.

"I like your house, Gracie. It's a lot like you."

"How?" she asked, wrapping her arms around her waist. He had the feeling that if he said the wrong thing she was going to retreat even further into herself and disappear completely.

"Well, this kitchen is bright and welcoming. Your house if filled with photos and antiques, stuff that has a lasting feeling to it."

She nodded and her arms dropped to her sides. "I always wanted roots. When I was growing up, my father served in a lot of different communities in Texas. We were constantly moving."

"And you've put them down." He knew she had. The way she spoke about moving made it very clear exactly what she thought of it. He realized that, if there was going to be any real lasting relationship between the two of them, he'd have to change his ways. And he wondered if she would be worth staying for.

She nodded. "The antiques aren't heirlooms. I bought them at auctions and estate sales."

"That doesn't change what they represent about you."

She bit her lower lip. "I'll be quick getting ready."

"Take your time. Do you mind if I explore your house?"

She released a long breath. "Okay."

Grace enjoyed having Adam in her house. He was the missing piece of the puzzle that she'd created of a picture-perfect life. He'd been the fantasy in her head for a long time, the man who'd make this little empty house feel more like home—and now he was here.

Her fear was that she only liked him because he did fill the hole in her life. That she wasn't infatuated with a real man. It was complicated and she wanted it to be simple. For a relationship with Adam to be easier than it was.

She'd wasted some time when she'd gotten home, writing down her latest fantasy about him. In her dream relationship, he was completely enthralled with her and her body.

She finished getting ready and then went to find Adam. To her dismay, he was in her home office, sitting at her desk. She knew that her handwritten notes on "Adam's Mistress" were there. The printed copy of her story was still at work, but she'd been editing a handwritten version of it earlier that day, adding in details from the night at his home.

She noticed he was studying something on her desk. For a second, she couldn't breathe. She'd die if he'd found that story. In fact, tomorrow she was going to shred the thing at work and destroy this copy.

"You like Viper?" he asked.

For a minute it was as if he were speaking a different language. Then she realized her mouse pad featured the heavy metal alternative band.

"Yes. I do. Their music is different."

"You know they're one of my artists. Actually, the first band I signed."

"I did know that," she said. She'd checked them out originally because she knew that Adam liked them.

"I can get you an autograph," he said, with one of those silly grins of his.

"Really. Then maybe I'll like you."

He laughed, a full-bodied one that made her feel good. "All the girls say that, but as soon as they get their autograph…"

"I'm not like other girls, Adam."

He pushed to his feet and came around the front of her desk. It was a cheap one that she'd gotten at a scratch-and-dent sale. He leaned against the front of it, legs crossed at the ankles, arms resting on either side of his hips.

"I know that."

"Why are you here? I mean really. I'm not your usual type of date."

She'd tried not to think about him. Had focused on the school and keeping it going. But in the back of her mind she'd been looking for excuses to keep him at arm's length. Not because she didn't want him closer but because she feared what would happen if she did and it turned out he wasn't as interested in her.

"I think we've discussed this before."

She envied him his ease and self-confidence in this situation. She'd handled herself with aplomb when she'd had to confront two teachers having sex in a classroom but this was simply beyond the scope of her experience. Adam was beyond that scope, and she hoped he'd never realize by how much.

"I think you're right, but I still don't get it. It seems like this is some sort of dream and that I'm going to wake up and you'll still be treating me like a stranger."

"Am I your dream man?" he asked.

She slid her gaze down his body. Dressed in an oxford shirt with the collar open and a pair of faded, tight jeans, he looked like every woman's dream man. But it was way more than just his sexy, muscular body that made him her fantasy.

She shrugged, afraid of saying something and revealing too much to him. Afraid of increasing the very real chance that he might see her as a pathetic woman who'd somehow gotten hold of him and wouldn't let go. Afraid that he'd realize she wasn't the kind of woman who could hold his attention.

"Am I, Grace?" he asked, pushing away from the desk and walking toward her.

"Yes."

"For how long?" he asked.

"Why? Why does that matter?"

"Because I want to know every one of your secrets," he said, stopping with just an inch of space between them.

He was in her personal space but she didn't care. She wanted him closer. It had been two long weeks since she'd felt his arms around her, and it had been too easy to convince herself that she'd simply dreamed the way he'd felt in her arms.

"My secrets?" He could never know her secrets. She didn't like the fact that he'd even guessed that there was more to her than what she presented to the people she worked with.

But at the same time, that was what drew her even closer to him. She liked that he was the only man who saw beyond her facade. And if there was some safe way to let him in and still protect her tender heart, she'd do it.

"Yes, Gracie, your secrets," he said. He cupped her jaw and tipped her head back, his fingers supporting the back of her neck as he kissed her.

"Do you have secrets, Adam?" she whispered.

"We all do."

She clenched her hands together and stood still in his

embrace. She didn't know if she trusted him enough. If she'd ever trust him enough—because even after spending time in his arms, she still didn't think he was real. He was still just a fantasy, and if they were ever going to get to a point of trust she was going to have to let him be real.

And the real man was complicated. He had problems and issues just like she did. He moved on. He always moved on. What kind of secrets did he have that he was always searching for something but never finding it?

She realized in that instant with his mouth on hers and his hand on her neck that she wanted to be the keeper of his secrets. That she wanted to find a way to understand the complex man who had been her fantasy for too long and that she now wanted to be her reality.

But he couldn't be as long as their relationship remained hidden. She knew what happened to secrets like this. Forbidden desires were forbidden for a reason. A relationship that started in lies would never survive.

She had the uneasy feeling that she was going to be forced to choose between the safe place she'd made for herself at Tremmel-Bowen and Adam. The tightening in her gut told her the day was closer than she wanted it to be.

# Seven

"I don't know why we have to hide from the world," he said.

He wouldn't understand. But she wasn't one of the glamorous women he was always seen with. Everyone would take one look at them and know she wasn't meant to be on his arm.

"Please, Adam. I don't want to share what we have found together. They'll think I'm your mistress." And she was, wasn't she?

"Okay, Grace. For you."

The voices moved on down the hallway and he stared down at her. She knew that something had changed between them in those few moments.

*Excerpt from "Adam's Mistress" by Stephanie Grace*

Adam had never enjoyed a hockey game more. Though Grace knew little about the sport, she learned quickly. Normally he would have been annoyed but wasn't surprised to find that with Grace he wasn't.

They were sitting alone in the luxury box that Adam shared. The box had a wet bar staffed by an arena worker plus two TV monitors so they wouldn't miss any of the action they might not catch from the bird's-eye view through the huge bay window that overlooked the arena. Adam had asked that one TV be tuned to CNN so he could keep track of Viper lead singer Stevie Taylor, who was Larry King's guest for the evening.

"I've never really gotten into professional sports," Grace said as the game reached the end of the second quarter.

"My dad was a huge hockey fan. We went to every Stars game, even the away ones."

"What was he like? I know he was big on community involvement, and the community-service program he established at Tremmel-Bowen is one of the things that really makes us stand out from other schools."

Adam noticed that Grace never forgot about the school or her commitment to it. He wished there was a way for Malcolm to see this side of Grace. So he'd understand that just because Dawn had made him look like a chump, the school didn't need to be closed down.

"He was a good man like you said, big on community involvement, but he also made sure that he had time for me. My folks were in their forties and well established before I came along."

"I didn't realize that. Were you a very spoiled only child?"

"To some extent. Not in material things." It had been a long time since he'd really thought about his parents and his childhood. He'd pushed those memories away at twenty-five and had been afraid to look back and see if he'd fooled himself into believing that the love they'd showered on him had been a lie.

"I never had a lot of material things, either," she said quietly.

"Are you an only child? I thought there were some pictures on your mantel of some other people your age. I assumed they were siblings."

She flushed and looked away, reaching over to pick up her soda cup she took a long swallow. What was she hiding about her family?

He already had the impression that she hadn't had a very nice upbringing. He sensed that the key to figuring this woman out lay in her past. After all, the things *he* was hiding all stemmed from that one incident. That one comment that had shaped his life from twenty-five forward and made him question everything that had gone on before.

"Tell me," he said, wanting her to trust him. He didn't question why gaining her trust was so important. He only knew that with Grace it was one of the things he wouldn't compromise on.

"Tell you what?"

"Whatever it is about those pictures that made you turn several interesting shades of red."

"I'm going to sound like a loser," she said.

He cupped the back of her neck and drew her toward him, leaning down to kiss her. To tell her with his embrace that he believed in her. "Never."

"I don't know what to do with you," she said. The words sounded like a confession and he knew to some extent they were.

Because he'd read the words she'd written. He'd returned her story to her office and noticed it had disappeared from her desk. He'd sat in her chair in her home office and imagined her writing there, having sexy dreams about him.

He lifted his head and rubbed his thumb over her lower lip. Touching her was an addiction. A craving that never really left him.

"Tell me," he said again.

She wrapped her small hand around his wrist, turned her face into his hand, breathing deeply and keeping her eyes closed.

"They are pictures of… Well, I don't spend a lot of holidays with my father and those are photos taken with other people's families."

He felt a punch in his gut. She had more hidden depths than he'd realized and he had no idea if he knew how to sort them out. Why did he even want to?

The answer was simple and easy. He wanted to be her hero. He wanted to be worthy of the fantasies she'd weaved about him. He wanted to be the kind of man she'd still look up to when she knew him well.

Instead, he was stuck with being the man he'd always been. Someone who took one look around him when the going got rough and then packed his bags and looked for a different challenge. One that wasn't personal. One that didn't really affect him.

But it was too late where Grace was concerned. He liked the personal connection they had.

She watched him with her wide, sad eyes, waiting for him to say something.

"*No one's life is picture perfect,*" he said, *trying to* share with her what he'd learned in the last fifteen years. How he'd struggled to come to terms with having his entire life turn out to be a lie. Not a malicious one, but a lie nonetheless.

"I don't want perfection," she said. She shifted away from him, wrapping her arms around her own waist.

He didn't want her to soothe herself when he was right there and more than willing to offer her comfort. He wrapped his arm around her shoulder and pulled her into his body.

"I've got to go to the restroom," she said.

He guessed she was just using it as an excuse but got to his feet. "I'll show you where they are."

Adam was easy to follow as they moved through the arena hallway toward the restrooms. Since this was a Platinum Club floor there wasn't a lot of foot traffic. She knew asking to go to the bathroom was lame and had avoidance written all over it, but Adam had been pushing too hard and she was about to just give in and tell him another one of her secrets. Peel away another layer of her carefully crafted facade and bare her soul.

She didn't want to get into a heavy conversation. She'd been having fun. Having a normal date and, somehow, she'd blundered and ruined it.

"You don't have to wait for me. I can find my way back to the box."

"I don't mind."

She ducked into the ladies' room. When she came back out she glanced around for him. The hallway was a little more crowded now. For a second she couldn't find him and wondered if he'd gone back without her. She started that way when she felt his heavy hand on her shoulder. He drew her to a stop.

"I'm not going to stop asking you questions about those pictures."

"I'm making it into too big a deal. Really it's nothing. A group of teachers and I have a wine and supper club. There are twelve of us and we take turns hosting the monthly dinner. The last time they were at my place someone commented on the fact that I had no family snapshots anywhere."

"So you started displaying photos taken with other people's families?"

"Yes. Until then, I never noticed that I didn't have any photos and other people had them. I'm not one for looking back."

"Yet you crave roots."

"That's different. I just want to have a place I belong. I don't need decades of ancestry for that."

A couple brushed past them, oblivious to the world. They had their arms around each other. She realized it would be easy to look at them and assume life was simple for them—and maybe it was.

She always wanted relationships to fall into nice, straightforward categories. The work relationships she had with Bruce and the teachers on her staff. The mentoring role she had with her students. But she couldn't put an easy label on Adam. She wanted him more than she'd ever wanted any man.

It was a weakness to want him. Because he didn't fit into the safe boxes that others did and she had the feeling he never would. He was never going to be someone she felt completely comfortable with.

"Let's go back to our box," he said, cupping his hand under her elbow and leading her back to the stairs. She couldn't read his expression but had the distinct impression that he was angry.

"Adam?"

They stopped walking and turned. Grace wanted to groan out loud when she saw Sue-Ellen Hanshaw. Of course she always looked well put-together and made Grace feel every bit the small-town poor kid she'd always been.

She suspected the other woman didn't do it intentionally. Sue-Ellen definitely put her kids and family first, which Grace could admire.

"Hi, Sue-Ellen, enjoying the game?"

"I am. I thought I saw you earlier with Grace."

Wasn't she clever?

"Adam was just giving me a quick lesson in hockey."

"Where are you two sitting?" Sue-Ellen asked.

"Up in one of the private boxes." Adam's tone didn't broker an invitation to join them.

"Do you have other guests?"

Sue-Ellen sounded suspicious. With each question Grace felt her skin get tighter. She wanted to disappear—heck, if she hadn't been running away from Adam's questions, they'd never have seen Sue-Ellen.

"No. It's just the two of us," Adam said.

"Is that wise?"

"We've been discussing the school," Grace said quickly. "Did you hear Adam has arranged for a few celebrities to come play in the charity basketball tournament to raise money for the school's gym?"

Sue-Ellen smiled and the expression almost reached her eyes. "Thank you, Adam, for doing that."

"It was no problem. To be honest, it was Christian's idea."

Sue-Ellen's son was one of the many students who were working hard to keep the school going.

"I think he had an ulterior motive. He's a huge Bottle Rocket fan," Sue-Ellen said, naming one of the bands on Adam's record label. She was being friendly, but Grace sensed disapproval under the surface.

Grace knew practically his entire artist base thanks to some time spent on the Internet. She wasn't surprised to hear that Sue-Ellen's son, a junior, had come up with the idea. She wondered if Sue-Ellen realized how badly her son wanted the school to stay open. If she knew how much the changes in their personal lives over the last two years had affected her son.

"It was a great suggestion," Grace said.

Sue-Ellen flushed at the compliment to her son. "I'm so impressed at the way he's gotten involved with saving the school."

"You should be proud of him," Adam said.

"I am. I'll see you both at the meeting on Thursday, right?"

"Yes," Grace said. "I'm looking forward to hearing all the parents' ideas."

Sue-Ellen moved on. Adam made no move to go back to the box to watch the rest of the game.

"Are you embarrassed to be seen with me?" he asked, pulling her out of the walkway and into the shadows.

"No. Why would you think that?" she asked. Her back was against the wall. He leaned closer to her, putting one arm on either side of her head, caging her with his body. She put her hand on his chest to keep him from coming any closer. Because she wanted more than anything to say to hell with Sue-Ellen and Malcolm and the morality patrol and just give in to the temptation that was Adam.

"Your comments to Sue-Ellen made it seem like we weren't on a date," he said, canting his hips forward so that he was nestled against the center of her body. Flashes of light flickered in from the arena. Or was that her, reacting to him?

"Good. The last thing we need is for anyone to know

that you and I are dating. That's the kind of publicity the school doesn't need," she said. Even to her own ears, her voice sounded breathless.

"Why good? This feels like a date to me, Gracie."

She was mesmerized by the latent passion in his eyes and leaned up toward him. Brushed her lips over his once and then again. She had never had a man so completely take over every part of her life before. She suspected that Adam didn't even know that he was doing it.

He kept his lips out of reach. "Explain to me about Sue-Ellen."

"She's reporting everything I do to Malcolm."

"I didn't realize it was that bad. You don't have to pretend we aren't dating."

"Are we dating?"

"I think I just said we were."

"We've only had dinner once. And now, the game. It's not like we've really had a chance to get to know one another."

"We know each other intimately," Adam said, wrapping his arms around her and pulling her fully into his body. He lowered his head and brushed his lips over hers. "Don't we, Grace?"

She knew he was asking her something important, but she couldn't think or answer. She just wanted to lose herself in this moment and in this man. *This* was what she'd been wanting when she put those photos on her mantel, snapshots of a life that wasn't really her own. She'd always craved this. This, what she felt right now with Adam.

And she knew exactly what *this* was. A feeling of belonging and acceptance that had been missing all of her life.

Adam lifted his head after a long moment had passed. He drew her out of the shadows, leading her down the hallway and toward the exit. "Let's get out of here."

Adam parked his car at the curb in front of Grace's house. A quiet had fallen between them as they'd left American Airlines Center. He didn't know what to say to her, unusual for him. He usually had no problem filling awkward silences with small talk. But he and Grace had somehow moved beyond small talk and now he had nothing to say. No way to communicate with words. The charm that he usually employed with women wasn't going to be enough.

She watched him with her wide, wounded eyes and he knew that he couldn't leave her. Not tonight, he told himself, but a part of him recognized that as a lie.

"Thanks for taking me to the game," she said in that quiet, polite way of hers.

"It was my pleasure. I'd like to take you out again tomorrow night," he said, stretching his arm along the back of her seat. She tipped her head to the side.

"I could make us dinner at my place."

"I'd like that. I'll bring the wine."

She smiled at him and for a moment he felt something that he hadn't realized had been missing in his life. A sense of total normalcy. Like they *were* just two people dating. Like there were no secrets between them. No lies that were quietly waiting to jump out.

On one level it angered him because he knew that the lies were his own and having been on the other side, having been the person who'd been lied to, he knew how much that was going to hurt. Unless he could figure out a way to make Grace tell him about the erotic story. Her fantasy of being his mistress.

"What's your dream date?" he asked.

She quirked one of her eyebrows at him and licked her lower lip. "Something like tonight, I guess."

"You guess?" he asked, flirting with her. Finding his rhythm in the new, easy way she held herself. This was something he knew how to do.

"Yeah, I guess."

"Are you going to invite me in for a nightcap?"

She gathered her purse from the floor and opened it pulling out her keys. "I wasn't planning on it."

"Come on, Gracie. I want to hear what you'd change about tonight." He turned off the car and leaned back in the seat to watch her, his hand stretched over the back of her headrest. Her flowery perfume filled the air, and when she moved her head strands of her hair rubbed over his wrist. He wanted to wrap his hand in her hair to not have to play the waiting game that dating couples did. Instead he wanted to claim her, to throw her over his shoulder and take her to bed.

In her fantasies he already had. Even in his own, he'd claimed her. He wanted her with a bone-deep fascination that made everything else pale. He needed to be inside her silky curvy body, marking her as his own. Finding a way to bind her to him. He didn't understand the need, didn't want to question it too closely. He only knew that he wanted Grace.

"Why?" she asked.

He didn't want to have to explain himself. Didn't want to have to come up with more reasons to drag this conversation out until she felt comfortable enough to invite him into her home. "So I can better plan next time."

"What if you're the thing I'd change?" she asked, a saucy grin on her face.

She knew what she was doing. She was playing him to see how much he would take. He had the suspicion that this was new to her—flirting with a man, finding her feet with him—so he tugged on a strand of her hair and brought her face closer to his.

"Then you're out of luck. I'm not going anywhere."

The words resonated inside him and he realized that he wanted to stay with her. To stay as long as he could.

She watched him with those wide, serious eyes and then said, "Not even in the house for a drink?" She opened her door and stepped out of the car.

He watched her for a moment. Something had changed from earlier. There was more confidence in the way she moved. As if she knew he was going to follow her. And he was. He was going to follow her and give her a night straight out of her dreams.

Grace was sure and competent and very in charge in real life, but in her fantasy she wanted a man to dominate her. To take control of her passion. He followed her up her walk, pressing his remote to lock the doors on his car and set the alarm.

He followed her as if she'd promised him the answers to questions he'd always posed. And he knew she didn't have them. Knew that, like women or projects in the past, he wouldn't really find what he'd been chasing. He'd thought he'd found the answers before only to be disappointed.

But tonight none of that mattered. All that he cared about was that she'd invited him in. She'd made a move in real life, not just in her written fantasies, and that was good enough for him.

She had something he wanted and because he was a guy it was partially tied up in lust for her curvy body. But he knew there was more to it than lust.

She led him into her house and got them both a glass of wine, a California merlot that was full-bodied and fruity. She sat on one edge of her couch, leaving plenty of space between the two of them.

"I thought we were beyond this," he said, quietly. She blew hot and cold with him, one minute flirty and sexy as hell, the next retreating behind her walls. Watching him with those enigmatic eyes of hers that made him realize he might never know any of her secrets.

"Beyond what?"

"This space between us," he said.

She took a sip of her wine. "Whenever I think about you here with me, I can't help thinking—what is this man doing with *me?*"

"I'm here because you make the world come alive for me."

"That sounds hokey."

"I know. But I can't think of any other way to describe it."

"Your life is pretty exciting without me in it."

"No, Grace, it isn't. My life is full of events and people, but it's all routine. I learned a long time ago that routine is important to survival."

"Routine is getting up at six every morning, eating cereal and driving to work. Routine is not spending your day surrounded by rock stars and celebrities."

"I guess it just depends on your perspective," he said quietly. Thinking about how one little detail could change a life. The lies his parents had told had changed his life. The story of Grace's he'd read had changed their lives. And though he knew he needed to say something, to somehow reveal the secret he was keeping, he still wasn't able to find the right words.

# Eight

"Where were we?" he asked, his voice a sexy whisper in her ear.

He nudged her center and she shifted against him, trying to get even closer. It was impossible with the layers of cloth between them. Her skirt was hiked up, but not enough.

"I think we were here," she said, looking down at her bare breasts.

"Show me where I left off," he said.

She drew his head down to her lips. He kissed his way down her neck and bit lightly at her nape. She shuddered, clutching at his shoulders, pressing her body harder against him. He bent his head and his tongue stroked her nipple.

*Excerpt from "Adam's Mistress" by Stephanie Grace*

Adam looked like he belonged in her house as he sat next to her on the couch. A part of her was afraid she was building too much around him and their relationship the same way she did with those photos of her with other people's families on the mantel. Creating the illusion that there was more to her life than there really was.

He spread his arms along the back of the sofa, his body open and relaxed. She thought about the story she'd written. The story that, for her, was bold and erotic. A fictional account that she used to fill the empty part of her life. The part that she'd always really been afraid to admit that she wanted.

But she and Adam had already made love once. She'd already had an orgasm in his arms and watched him have one next to her. They'd been intimate in a way—

"What are you thinking so hard about?"

She shrugged. What could she say to him that wouldn't make her sound…like herself? Like the scared and insecure woman she was deep inside?

"Nothing," she said, wanting to believe that it was strategy and not fear of rejection that held her still on her side of the couch.

"If it doesn't feel right don't do it," he said, a wry grin on his face. But the expression seemed forced.

She guessed he was experiencing something similar to what she felt. She skimmed her gaze down his body, stopping when she noticed his erection. She hadn't even touched him, how could he be aroused by her?

"I guess you can tell how much I like you," he said, gesturing to his body.

"Why?"

He turned to her then, putting one hand on her face, his fingers gentle as he traced the line of her cheek-bones. But when he started to speak she put her fingers over his lips. She didn't want to hear what he had to say. Whatever expectations he had of her, she didn't want to know them. Didn't want her fears of living up to what he wanted to stop her.

"Forget I asked. I like you, too."

"Show me," he said.

Grace pushed all her doubts from her mind about why Adam was here. He *was* here, and that was enough for her. She wasn't going to waste the opportunity to be with him. Not like the last time at his house in the shower, when she'd wanted to reach for him again but had stopped herself. Her fantasies, which had fed her secret life, paled in comparison to the real thing.

How could the imagined feel of his hand on the back of her neck match the actual warmth and weight of the real thing?

He watched her steadily, awareness of him growing in her until she had to lean forward and capture his lips with hers. His mouth was firm and hard. He didn't open his lips, just waited to see how far she'd take it. She brushed her mouth back and forth over his.

She licked at his lips before using her teeth to draw his lower lip into her mouth, scraping her teeth over the plump flesh. She rested her hands on his shoulders for balance as she leaned over him. The angle forced his head back so that she was in complete control.

He moaned and pulled her down on his lap, shifting the balance of power in that one move. He took control, his hands sliding up to hold her head still as he plundered the depths of her mouth.

She shifted her legs so that she straddled his hips. She lifted her head and stared down at him. His eyes were narrowed and intense as he looked up at her.

"Take off your T-shirt."

"Only if you take off your shirt."

He nodded. She sank back on his thighs, reaching for the waistband of her shirt. She pulled it up over her head and then held it awkwardly in front of her for a minute. She knew what her body looked like with just jeans on. Her white belly was visible. Some of her skin swelled over the waistband.

He unbuttoned his shirt and pushed it off his shoulders. He was lean and ripped with rock-hard, defined muscles that a businessman shouldn't have. "You work out."

"Yeah, I get restless and no matter where I am there's always a gym."

"There are also bars and women."

"That's not who I really am, Gracie. Why are you holding on to that shirt?"

She shrugged. No way was she going to say something derogatory about her body when she had him half-naked and wanting her. She pushed her concerns from her head and focused instead on Adam.

She dropped her shirt and his hands were on her immediately. His fingers traced the lines of her torso before sliding around her back and up her spine. He found the back clasp of her bra and she felt him undo it. He left the fabric on her, continuing his path up her back to her neck.

He drew her forward, his mouth meeting hers again. Making her forget the lingering doubts she had. There was no room in her mind for anything but Adam when he touched her.

His hands kept moving while his mouth held hers captive. He swept her bra aside and then pressed between her shoulders until her breasts were against his naked chest.

Her breath caught in her throat and she closed her eyes, wanting to capture this moment forever. Wanting to never forget the way he felt against her.

He lifted his head, skimming his mouth down her jaw to her neck. He nibbled on her skin, making her feel like a meal being offered up to him. His hands and his mouth made her come alive in his arms.

Her nipples tightened as his fingers drew near them but he only skimmed the fleshy part of her breasts and then moved downward to the swell of skin above the waistband of her jeans. He traced the seam where fabric and skin met all the way around to her back where the jeans gaped away from her body.

He dipped his finger down, touching the silky fabric of her panties and then slipping underneath to caress the sensitive skin at the base of her spine. She shifted in his arms as his mouth moved down her neck.

He sucked on the pulse beating at the base of her neck. She felt an answering pull from the center of her body. She shifted on his lap, rubbing her center over his erection.

He groaned deep in his throat, his finger on her back caressing the cleft in her buttocks. She canted her hips away from that unfamiliar touch as his mouth moved lower, finding her nipple and kissing it.

"You have very pretty breasts, Gracie."

She didn't know what to say to that. She could barely think coherently while her body was in this state of need—aching need—and chaos.

He kept his one hand in the back of her jeans and drew the other one down her body, tracing her face and then her neck, lingering on the spot where he'd sucked on her skin, then going right between her breasts. He didn't stop there, kept tracing a line down the center of her body. He flicked open the snap of her jeans and lowered the zipper so he could keep touching her.

She had braced her hands on his shoulders and sank back on his thighs so that she didn't have to use her hands for balance. She scraped her nails down his chest. She loved the muscled steel of him.

The light dusting of hair on his chest tickled her fingers. She lowered her head to taste his skin, licking delicately at him before nipping him with her teeth. His hands tightened on her, his fingers finding one nipple and pinching her lightly.

He tangled his fingers in her hair and drew her head up to his. Both of his hands slipped down to her breasts as he rotated his palms over her. She lost herself in a wave of feeling as he drew her forward, urging her up on her knees.

"Offer your breasts to me," he said in a gravelly voice.

Nerves assailed her for a minute and she was stuck in that place where she came up against what she'd never done and what she wanted to do. This was almost exactly what she'd fantasized when she'd written her story. The fire in Adam's eyes and the heat between her legs convinced her not to back down.

She cupped herself and leaned forward. The line between reality and fantasy blurred. She felt the Grace Stephens she'd always been drop away and the Grace Stephens she'd always wanted to be take center stage.

Her eyes met Adam's and he watched her with that level, steady gaze of his filled with passion and heat. A shiver of awareness slid down her spine. She aroused him. She made him want her. It was a heady feeling and she savored it.

She tipped her head to the side, enjoying the feel of her hair sliding over her shoulders. "Taste me."

"With pleasure," he said.

He kept one hand at the small of her back, urging her forward. Dropping kisses along the tops of her breasts, tracing the lines of her fingers with his tongue before suckling her nipple deep into his mouth. She let go of *her breasts and grabbed his shoulders for support as the* entire world tipped on its axis.

Everything narrowed down to the two of them. To his mouth on her breast, his hand on her back sliding lower and pushing her down against his erection. She wished she'd taken off her jeans.

Reaching between their bodies, she caressed his hard length though the fabric of his pants. Everything he did turned her on.

He suckled her breast and urged her to rock her hips against him. She felt the weight of her hair against her back and, as she leaned forward into his body, she felt him surround her. She felt cherished, safe, wanted in a way that awakened the hidden woman inside her.

She arched into his touch, felt him everywhere. His hands touching and caressing her, driving her to the edge. His mouth and teeth nibbling at her breasts until they felt too full, too heavy. She needed more. Needed something from him that she couldn't find.

She rocked against him, her nails digging into his shoulders as everything inside her tightened. Every nerve ending she had was so sensitized to the slightest brush of him against her that she felt herself close to the edge.

"Are you close?"

"Yes…."

"Come for me," he said, touching her intimately. The pressure pushed her over the edge. Everything in her body clenched down and she rocked against him.

She held his head to her body as waves washed over, leaving her shivering in his arms. He pushed to his feet, holding her high in his arms and walked down the hallway to her bedroom.

Adam tried not to analyze what he felt as he walked into Grace's bedroom with her in his arms. She was so wonderfully responsive to his every touch that she made him feel like the king of the world. The king of her world, really. The only man who existed for her.

He felt almost as if, for the first time, he knew who he really was. That Adam Bowen wasn't a fraud.

Tonight, when they were at the hockey game, he'd realized that her attention never wandered from him. That she didn't want to be with anyone else.

And when she let him make love to her, he had her trust whether she wanted to admit it or not.

He set her down in the center of her bed. The head of the bed was covered in pillows. Only the light from the hallway spilled into the room. Not enough. He wanted to see more of Grace.

He reached over to turn on the lamp on her nightstand.

"What are you doing?" she asked.

"Making sure every detail is right."

"Here in my room?"

"Yes."

"Why?"

"We're only going to have one first time together. I want it to be everything you've ever imagined it would be."

"I can't imagine anything better than you in my arms, Adam."

His heart ached a little. There it was again. That sweet honesty that made him remember he knew more about her fantasies than she would want him to. Knowing that made it easier for him to keep his control though he was rock hard. Knowing he was going to fulfill them made his spine tingle.

He unsnapped his jeans and pushed them down his legs. He'd forgotten his shoes and had an awkward moment where he had to bend over to remove them.

He felt the butterfly-light touch of her hand on the back of his thigh. Her fingers explored him while he was doubled over. He got his shoes and socks off and pushed his jeans to the floor.

Standing there in just his jockey shorts he let her explore him. Her fingers traced the line of a scar he'd always had, which wrapped from the front of his hip around to his back.

"How'd you get this?"

Adam shrugged. His mother had told him it had happened when he was only six months old. She'd never said anything more and he'd never asked about it. But when he'd learned that she was really his adoptive mother he'd wondered again how he'd gotten the scar.

"I've always had it," he said. She traced it again with her fingers then hooked her other arm around his waist and drew him back to the edge of the bed. He felt her lips along his flank. Kissing and nibbling, tasting him. He tightened painfully and he knew that the slow and easy round of lovemaking he'd wanted for their first time wasn't going to happen.

He wanted her. He needed her soft touches. He needed her combination of shy looks and bold caresses. He needed…her. He sank down on the bed, moving over her.

She smiled up at him, her hands still exploring him everywhere. Touching his chest, tangling in the hair there and tugging on it.

He pushed her jeans down her legs, removing her shoes and socks, too. He sank back on his haunches and just stared at her. She was bare except for the brief fabric of her bright blue bikini panties. They were made of silk and lace and he remembered the feel of her warmth against his fingers, the fabric under his hand as he'd touched her on the couch.

He wanted more than memory. He wanted to feel her again. To feel her now. "Are you on the pill?"

"No. I don't have any condoms, either."

"I brought my own."

"Always prepared?" she asked. There was something in her tone that made him realize the answer to this next question was very important.

"I'm prepared for you. I don't carry condoms around as a rule but you are pure temptation, Gracie, and I knew I wouldn't be able to resist."

"Come to me," she said, leaning back against the pile of pillows. She pushed her panties down her hips and kicked them to the floor. She opened her arms and bent her knees.

He shed his underwear in record time and grabbed the condom from his pocket. He'd put it there earlier in the hopes that the evening would end this way.

He took her feet in each of his hands and drew her down until she lay flat on the bed. He pushed her legs wide open and held himself over her, braced on his forearms leaving only an inch of space between their bodies.

He lowered his hips and felt her moist center. His control slipped. She shifted, reaching down to encircle him with her hand.

"Where's your condom?"

"Right here." He dropped it next to her. He kissed her, starting at her neck and moving down her body, unable to resist the temptation to taste her. He leaned down to lick each nipple until it tightened. Then he blew gently on the tips. She raked her nails down his back.

He held her still with a hand on her stomach as he suckled on each of her breasts until her nipples were hard and red. He glanced up at her and saw her swallow. Her hands shifted on the bed next to her hips.

He traced a path down her center until he got to her belly button. He loved the small mound of her belly. He kissed her flesh there then moved lower, dipping his fingers into the warm moisture in her center.

"Adam, please."

She took his hard length in her hand and followed with her tongue, teasing him with quick licks and light touches.

He arched on the bed, thrusting up before he realized what he was doing. He pulled her away from his body, wanting to be inside her.

He pulled her up to his body until she straddled his hips. He fumbled for the condom, finding it a few feet from them, then ripping the packet open with one hand.

He sheathed himself and then, using his grip on her hips, he pulled her down and slipped into her body. With one quick movement, he rolled them over to take command.

She arched her back, reaching up to entwine her arms around his shoulders. He thrust harder, slid deeper still into her, and felt every nerve in his body tense. Reaching between their bodies he touched her between her legs until he felt her body start to tighten around him.

He let himself go in a rush, continuing to thrust into her until his body was drained. He then collapsed on top of her, laying his head between her breasts.

A feeling of contentment started to wash over him. But Grace's soft sigh and the emotions coursing through him made him tense. There was a wealth of caring in that sigh and in the arms that wrapped trustingly around him. How would she feel when she realized the man she'd honored with her body and let past her guard, the man who claimed to hold the truth in highest regard, had been lying to her?

# Nine

"I need you, Grace."
She took his jaw in her hands and pulled his face
up to hers. His pupils were dilated, and between
her legs she felt him, hot and hard.
"I need you, too."

*Excerpt from "Adam's Mistress" by Stephanie Grace*

Grace rolled over, glancing at the clock. Three a.m.
Too early for the alarm, but something had woken her.
She shifted in the bed and encountered Adam. He was
warm and solid. *Real.*

Her thighs ached and her breasts were tender from
making love with him, but she didn't mind. She liked
the feeling being possessed by him left in her. She

realized she'd forgotten about the scents and smells of sex when she'd written her story about Adam.

Adam moved in his sleep, rolling from his side to his back. She shifted up on her elbow and tried to see him in the darkened room. Tried to make out the features of this man who'd made her realize that she'd been half asleep until he'd come into her life a few weeks ago.

But she couldn't. He didn't snore and other than that movement he was a pretty solid sleeper. She rested one hand on his chest, lightly, just over his heart. She felt it beating under her palm. She wanted to lay her head on his chest, but didn't want to wake him.

Didn't want to have to endure him holding her until he thought she was asleep before he slipped away. Just the way Dean had the few nights they'd spent together. She'd only slept with him a few times, unable to bear having been so close physically to someone who didn't want her to touch him unless they were having sex.

"Gracie?"

"Hmm?"

"What are you doing way over there?" he asked.

"Trying not to disturb you."

He moved his arm, wrapping it around her waist and drew her next to him on the bed. Her breasts pressed to the side of his chest and her head came to rest on his shoulder. He tangled his hand in her hair, something she realized he did a lot. Wrapping his fingers in her curls, he tipped her head back.

"I like having you next to me."

Sleepily he found her mouth with his and then gently

guided her head down to his chest. His hand on her back swept up and down her spine as he anchored her to him.

Sex, she thought. It was okay, really it was.

"You smell and feel so good, Gracie. I'm almost afraid to wake up and find I dreamed you." He tucked her even closer to his side.

No man had ever held her as closely as Adam held her now. She tried to tell herself not to read too much into the embrace but when he held her like this he felt solid, real. Like the very thing she'd been searching for.

When she'd written the story "Adam's Mistress," she'd focused on the physical details of what making love with him would be like. How it would feel to have his masculine attention turned on her.

She hadn't let herself hope that some kind of caring or affection would be there on his side. She just wasn't the kind of woman who inspired that in men. Her father had been the first one to teach her that lesson and Dean had followed it up. But Adam made her feel like she wasn't the kind of woman that men left.

This spot on his chest, right over his heart, seemed to be made for her head. It was the perfect place for her to rest. His hand in her hair, caressing her, made her feel wanted in a way that nothing else had in a long time. No, she thought, she'd never felt wanted like this before.

She was afraid to believe that this thing with Adam could be more than just a short-term relationship. The complications she'd made for herself by lying here in his arms were too many to count.

But she didn't care anymore. She'd gladly take on the challenge for more nights like this one.

She should sleep but couldn't. Nighttime was always when she was plagued with doubts and fears of the future. Nighttime was when she remembered vividly the words her father had said to her in his quiet, preaching voice as she'd packed her bags and left his house at age sixteen.

Nighttime was the one time when she was truly alone with all the ghosts of her mistakes. And she'd never liked it.

Nighttime had also always been her time for dreaming—and for the past three years, those dreams had been of Adam Bowen.

Now he was here and she should be sleeping blissfully. But she couldn't. What was it about her that could never just be happy? Never just be content with what she had? Why did she always want more?

And she did want more from Adam. As nice as this was, she wanted him to wake up and tell her…oh, man, this was pathetic. She'd only really known the man for a few weeks but she wanted him to be in love with her.

She wanted him to somehow realize what they could have together and be the embodiment of her fantasy Adam. The one she'd never been able to make commit to her on the pages she wrote. And the one she'd wanted to.

She turned away from Adam. Unable to lie there in the dark with her mind so full of those thoughts and her heart so full of longing that it felt like it might really break. And not because of anything that Adam did, but because of what she'd always wanted.

Adam followed her, his arms staying around her. She felt his mouth against her neck as he pulled her back against his body.

"What is it?" he asked.

She couldn't think for a minute of what to say or do. She could only feel a bittersweet mixture of hope and realism as he held her. He was naturally affectionate and it was going to be so hard to keep herself from falling in love with him.

No sooner had the words formed in her mind than she realized it was already too late. That she did love Adam. She'd been half in love with him from the moment they'd met and getting to know the man behind the fantasy had left her vulnerable to herself.

"Gracie?"

She smiled at the way he said her name. She'd always been too serious to be a Gracie but somehow Adam saw her differently.

"Nothing's wrong. Just a bad dream."

Adam woke a little after six, surprised he'd slept so soundly. But then Grace seemed to calm the chaotic, restless part of his soul. That knowledge took him aback and made him want to analyze it. But he wasn't good at looking for answers to emotional questions. That was why he'd spent so much time avoiding Plano and the school his family had started.

He remembered her waking in the middle of the

night and knew that she probably wasn't used to a man sleeping with her. He wasn't really used to sleeping with a woman in his bed. But he always stayed the night even though he usually found it difficult to get a good night's sleep. He was sensitive enough to know that no woman wanted a man she'd just had sex with to sneak out while she was sleeping, however much he wanted to go.

He didn't want to with his Grace.

The morning sunlight spilled through the small cracks in the plantation blinds. The ones on the top of the window had been left open and the light was moving across the floor toward the bed.

He glanced down at Grace, aware that he wanted to make promises. Promises that the past had proven he couldn't keep. Vowing to always be there to hold her in the darkest part of the night and keep her bad dreams at bay. Pledging that she'd never want for anything again. Assuring her and himself that the lonely restlessness that had always plagued him and, he suspected, her would never haunt either of them again.

But those were words he couldn't form. No matter that it felt right to have Grace in his arms. To sleep in her embrace through the long night. He was afraid to let go of the past long enough to believe that this woman in his arms could be the future.

Because he knew that security was the ultimate illusion. His parents' death had been the first time he realized that there was no such thing as a safety net. Learning the truth of his birth had confirmed it. And every relationship he'd had since then had simply reinforced those beliefs.

He hated that about himself. Knew that it stemmed from the darkest part of his own fears—fears that he usually only examined when he was out getting drunk with Stevie Taylor of Viper. The two of them questioned why money couldn't buy happiness.

He looked down at Grace's fragile features, her face soft and relaxed in slumber. All the money in his bank accounts didn't mean a thing to her. He'd read her secret fantasies, he knew that as far as she was concerned it was the man who made the difference. Not his finances.

A part of him was soothed by that. The twenty-five-year-old guy who'd learned that the legacy he thought he'd been entitled to was a sham liked the fact that this woman wanted him, not the Bowen name.

Damn, he was getting maudlin. He closed his eyes, burying his face against the back of her neck, in those soft curls of hers that he couldn't get enough of touching. She shifted in his arms, her backside brushing his morning erection, and he groaned deep inside. Wanting her again. After last night he should be well sated for at least 24 hours, but he knew with Grace nothing was the way it usually was.

He'd never get enough of caressing her soft curves. Of making love to her. He canted his hips forward, nestling himself in the curves of her buttocks. She shifted in his arms, rubbing her back against his chest, moving until they were pressed together from shoulder to thighs.

One of his hands was nestled between her breasts

and he shifted it to cup her right one. He held her in his palm, forefinger caressing the soft weight of her. He liked the textures of her body.

He pushed the covers off them so he could see her. Her skin was smooth and creamy, her breasts topped with pretty dark pink nipples. His hand looked big and dark against her pale skin. He used his thumb and finger to caress her nipple until it hardened under his touch.

Her legs moved restlessly against him. He wedged his thigh between hers and felt her heat on his leg. He used his other hand to hold her to him low at her stomach, one finger snaking lower to caress the small bud at the center of her body.

"Adam…"

Her voice was sleepy and husky and he knew what she wanted. Knew that he'd brought her from sleep into a world of aching need. That suited him, because he ached for her. He needed her in ways that he hoped she'd never realize.

"Hmm…"

She rocked her hips against him until his erection was poised at the damp opening of her body. He wanted to thrust into her just like this. Forget about the future or the consequences of taking her totally naked.

But he knew better. He didn't want Grace to have to confront an unwanted pregnancy. He shifted around on the bed, leaving her for a minute to get another condom out of the pocket of his pants.

He sheathed himself and came back to her. Pulled her back against him. She shifted around until she was where she'd been before, her right leg draped over his hip, her breast nestled in his hand.

"Look at me," he said.

She tipped her head back against his shoulder, her eyes slumberous. He leaned down and took her mouth, thrust his tongue deep inside her. He guided himself to her opening, then plunged into her with one steady thrust. She gently nipped his tongue and thrust her own back into his mouth. He held her tightly to him as he slid hilt deep into her body before pulling all the way out. He dropped kisses down the side of her neck, biting lightly at the pulse that beat steadily at its base as he thrust back into her.

She rocked against him, tightening herself as he pulled out one more time. She drew his hand from her hip down to the center of her body. He pushed his finger into the curls at her mound, finding the sensitive bundle of her nerves between her legs.

He rubbed her as he plunged back into her body again and again. He sucked hard on her neck, she moaned deeply and he felt her tighten. Knew what that sound signaled. He shifted her over onto her back, lifted her hips and thrust harder into her until the world coalesced around the woman in his arms and they climaxed together.

And he knew that the vows and promises he wanted to make had already been made as he held her like this, because he couldn't imagine leaving her.

Grace had never made breakfast for any man other than her father. She'd pretty much avoided the meal since she didn't like to eat it. But Adam was a big guy and he obviously needed to eat, so here she was in the kitchen staring into her refrigerator. Trying to pretend this morning was like any other when she was still trying to calm down from the last time they'd made love.

Her body still tingled. She couldn't believe the way he'd held her. She forgot about trying not to fall for him. Forgot about not making this night—this relationship—into more than it was. Forgot that heartbreak was inevitable.

"What are you looking for?" Adam asked, coming up behind her. He wore only his slacks from last night. His hair was unruly.

"Something to make you for breakfast," she said over her shoulder.

"Why?" he asked, wrapping one arm around her waist and pulling her back against him.

"Because…" She tipped her head back to look up at him. He leaned down and kissed her. Sipped at her mouth like she was all he'd need to find sustenance. She opened her mouth for him, knowing that she couldn't possibly make love to him again but that her body was readying for him.

He arched one eyebrow at her. "You were saying?"

She had no idea what they'd been talking about…oh, yeah, breakfast. "You seem like the kind of man who'd want a hearty breakfast."

He smiled down at her. "I have worked up an appetite this morning and I do like breakfast."

She blushed at the thought of what he'd done to work

up an appetite. She knew it was silly and she wished she didn't react that way but this was all too new to her.

He kissed her again and this time it was tender and almost sweet. When he lifted his head, she stared at his moist lips.

"I knew it," she said, trying desperately to marshal her thoughts back in order.

"I'm not picky. What do you usually eat?"

"A cereal bar," she said, nibbling on her lower lip. There was nothing in the refrigerator except a six-pack of fat-free yogurt that might have expired. She searched past the take-out containers for something that might feed Adam.

He made a face. "That's not breakfast."

"I know. That's why I'm searching my fridge."

He pulled her away from the appliance and shut the door. He lifted her up on the countertop and stood between her legs. She wrapped her arms around his waist, holding him to her. Resting her head on his shoulder, she closed her eyes, happy for this moment just to savor being with him.

He held her for a long time, his hands moving on her back, his head resting on the top of hers. Then his stomach growled and she pulled back.

"We've got to find you something to eat," she said.

He looked chagrined by his growling stomach. "Do you like omelets?"

"Yes, but I don't even have a carton of Egg Beaters," she said, deciding that she'd have to go grocery shopping and keep some real food in her fridge before he came back again.

"Egg Beaters? Woman, they aren't even real eggs. I'll run out and get everything we need and make you breakfast."

She frowned at him. "I wanted to do it."

"Gracie, it's clear you're not a cook." There was a teasing note in his voice that she'd never heard before. She suspected Adam felt like she did. That this moment was a respite from their realities. A chance to drop their guards and be themselves. She knew it couldn't last. That sooner or later reality would intrude and they'd be forced back into the roles they both knew so well.

"That obvious?" she asked, tipping her head to the side.

"Well, your fridge is full of take-out containers and expired food. I'll make us breakfast."

She didn't like it and knew why. *She* wanted to take care of *him*. To give him something here, in her home, that he wouldn't find anywhere else. It was part of her fantasy to cook for him, but he was right—she wasn't a cook.

"I want to do this. I like taking care of you."

Those words had a profound impact on her deep inside. She knew that he meant *cooking* for her, but it felt somehow like more.

"I could go to the store with you," she suggested. She enjoyed being with him and she didn't want to be apart. Actually that made her feel a little weak but it wasn't because she couldn't function without him. It was because she wanted to spend as much time together as they could before he left.

"Okay."

Her phone rang. Adam reached over to grab the cordless unit and handed it to her. She glanced down at the caller ID and saw that it was Sue-Ellen Hanshaw. Reality, intruding big-time.

She answered the call. "Good morning, Sue-Ellen."

"Not really a good one, Grace."

Her stomach sank. "What's up?"

"Our school is in the paper again and it's not good. The headline calls us a hotbed of sexy encounters."

"Who is it this time?"

"You. You and Adam."

# Ten

He growled deep in his throat and lowered his head to hers again. This time there was no gentle seduction but a full out taking of her mouth. He didn't mask what he wanted—he took. And she let him.

One of his hands left her waist and cupped her butt, pulling her closer until her mound rested against his hardness.

Grace threw her head back and moaned. His other hand slid up her leg, not stopping until she reached the center of her. She moaned again as his fingers skimmed the pulsating center of her desire.

*Excerpt from "Adam's Mistress" by Stephanie Grace*

Adam wrapped his arm around Grace's shoulder and pulled her close to his side. All of the color had left her face and he knew Sue-Ellen had delivered bad news.

"What's going on?" he asked her.

"Hold on, Sue-Ellen," she said, putting her hand over the mouthpiece. "There's a story about us in *The Dallas Morning News.*"

Crap. The last thing he needed was press, but he should have anticipated it. The society column gossips loved to talk about him. He could guess what the article said about the two of them, but he didn't want to. He needed to see the article. Find out exactly what they were up against.

"Do you get the paper delivered?"

"Yes."

"Tell Sue-Ellen we'll call her back once we know what the article said."

He left the kitchen and walked outside, finding the paper under the tree in her front yard. There were cheery yellow and blue daffodils planted around the base of the tree.

It underscored what he knew about Grace. That she'd put down roots here. That the closing of the school wasn't just about losing a job. It was about changing the life she'd worked hard to carve out for herself here.

He went back into her house, vowing to himself that he'd do whatever he had to keep her safe. To make this latest hiccup go away.

He went back inside, hesitating in the doorway of the kitchen when he saw her leaning against the counter staring out the back window. Her arms were wrapped around her waist and she seemed so alone. It was an almost palpable feeling.

Dammit, how could a morning that had been going so perfectly have turned into this? He cleared his throat so he didn't startle her, but she didn't even turn toward him.

Hell, this wasn't good. She was breaking his heart. Because he could tell from the way she was focused so deep inside that she'd experienced this kind of wrenching, world-wrecking situation before. Whereas he always rolled on down the road when it happened, she hunkered down and shored up her defenses.

He wondered how many times she'd faced this kind of situation. He hoped that this time he could be there for her. But he'd never stayed. Could he this time?

"Gracie."

She lifted her head, her eyes filled with fatigue and weariness and something else he couldn't define.

"Did you get the paper?"

He held it up, shaking it out of the plastic bag. He set the bag on the counter and walked toward her. He drew her onto the bench seat in her breakfast nook.

"Whatever is in here, we'll face it together."

She gave him a sad smile that made him angry. She expected him to leave her. To let her face whatever was in the paper by herself. He couldn't battle the ghosts of her past any more than she could take on his. But together they had to face what was happening now.

"Don't do this," he said, getting a little angry that she was giving up on him before she'd even let him fail. The hard part was, he expected to disappoint her. He'd been doing that steadily to people since his parents had died.

"Don't do what?" she asked, in that school-administrator voice of hers, making him feel like a senior who'd been caught pulling a prank.

But he was a grown man and he knew how to handle these kinds of situations. He dealt with temperamental artists and negative media all the time. "Act like I'm just saying words that I don't mean. I don't know who let you down in the past, but it wasn't me. Let me fail on my own before you look at me with disappointment."

She bit her lower lip and then touched his face with those long cold fingers of hers. "I'm sorry. I didn't mean to make you feel like I was disappointed in you. I'm not."

He wanted to crush her to him and give her the promises she needed. The ones that would clear the clouds from her eyes and make her stop trembling.

"Then why do you look like you're about to cry?" he asked.

She shook her head. Pushing against his chest she moved away from him. Put a few inches of space between them but the gap felt bigger. And he knew that crossing it was going to be a trial. Suddenly he wondered if it was worth it. Was she worth it?

He was fighting to save a school he didn't care about so that he could get to know this woman better. And what he'd found was incredible, a woman who had touched him in ways no one else ever had.

"It'll sound really stupid if I have to say it out loud," she said.

And he had his answer. Of course Grace was worth the effort.

"Then whisper it to me," he said, putting his arm around and tucking her up against his side. He liked the feeling of her there. He didn't question it, only knew that he wanted her by his side.

"I'm so tired of struggling for everything. I wanted our relationship and the school's future to just go smoothly, but we've been sneaking around and I should have expected this to happen."

He cupped her jaw and tipped her head back. He sipped at her lips, kissing her languidly like there wasn't an urgent matter waiting for them. Like time had stood still and their morning was still ideal. Like he could give her what she wished for.

"You're right. Sneaking around was a mistake."

The worst part was, he knew that her fantasy man would be able to do those things for her. But this was real life and it ticked him off that he wasn't going to measure up to what she needed from a man. Even though her other man was a romanticized version of himself.

Grace didn't want to read the article. The headline said it all: How Far Will She Go to Save the School? Once she saw the picture of her and Adam in the hallway outside the Platinum Club at the American Airlines Center, the photograph seemed cheap and tawdry.

The photographer had captured them after Sue-Ellen had left, when Adam had caged her between his big body and the wall. She was staring up at him with her heart in her eyes. She'd had no idea her emotions were so transparent when she looked at him.

It was impossible to see Adam's expression from the angle of the photograph. But his body language was easy to read. His hips were canted toward her. His head was lowered, their mouths a breath apart.

It was worse than she'd anticipated. Everyone was going to know immediately that they were involved in a relationship. Analytically she knew that the photo wasn't anywhere near as bad as the one that had been taken of Dawn O'Shea and her lover. But it wasn't good, and the article accompanying it was downright salacious. Malcolm was going to be all over this.

"It's not as bad as I feared."

"It's bad enough," she said.

"Don't be like that. I'll call Malcolm and then the newspaper."

"What are you going to tell the newspaper?"

"That we're dating and have been for a while. I have a great spin doctor who will come up with an angle to help promote the school."

She didn't like this side of Adam, but knew she should be thankful he was going to step in and take care of the problem this photo had generated. The thing was—she didn't want him to. As adverse as it seemed, she didn't want him to take on the problems of the school and solve them the way he described.

"What about truth?"

"I'm not going to lie, Grace. We've known each other for three years."

She didn't know why it bothered her, but it did. A big part of her was saying to just shut up but she couldn't. "You barely knew I was there for three years."

"And your point is?"

"Nothing. I don't have a point, except that you said the truth was important to you and what you're proposing is a gross exaggeration of the truth."

He put the paper down. "What's really going on here?"

She shook her head. How could she explain to him what she didn't understand herself? She knew it wasn't fair, but she'd expected Adam to live up to the pedestal she'd put him on. And seeing that he had feet of clay, that he was human and made mistakes just like her…. Well, it was a little too much like real life.

She didn't like that about herself. That she'd expected him to act the way her fantasy man would.

"Sorry. I'm not sure how to handle this. I was starting to believe that we were going to save the school."

He took her hand in his. She looked up at him, knowing now that she had little chance of keeping him from seeing the hope and anticipation in her eyes.

"Don't give up yet. This isn't anything other than a minor setback. And we've done nothing wrong or immoral."

"I don't think Malcolm will see it that way."

"I'll handle Malcolm."

"Thanks, but I'm the one who's responsible for the school's reputation."

He sat back in his seat. "You don't want me to fight your battles for you."

"No, I don't." He was too attuned to her. She'd let down her guard last night and now she regretted it. In the middle of the night it had been comforting to realize that he was with her, but this morning… This morning she saw the danger in having a man such as Adam around. He would take over every corner of her life. Until he moved on.

"Why not?" he asked. She could tell he wanted the conversation done so he could take action. Call Sue-Ellen, call Malcolm, bend them both to his will with charm or threats or however he operated. She didn't know what he'd use for the two of them because she was realizing that he changed his way depending on the person he dealt with. He had a gift for seeing into a person's soul.

She shook her head at him. There was no way she was going to tell him why she didn't want him fighting her battles. If she started talking about that she'd probably end up confessing that she was afraid that she'd become too dependent on him. Which was bound to freak him out.

She had to stop thinking like a woman who'd been caught with her lover, a man in a position to make decisions about her own job. She had to be the administrator. The professional woman who knew how to handle a crisis.

"Let's not go into that. I better call Sue-Ellen back

and then call Malcolm." She scooted around the bench to get out.

Adam shackled her wrist in his big hand, holding her still. She glanced back at him, trying to figure out what he was doing.

"You're not calling anyone until you answer me."

"I don't answer to you, Adam." She tugged on her wrist but she couldn't budge it. "Let me go."

"Not yet."

*Not yet.* She knew he meant right this instant, but a part of her felt like those words summed up their relationship.

And she knew why she was so upset. Because when they'd been dating quietly, only the two of them had witnessed it. Now the world knew. Her world knew that she'd gone out with superstud Adam Bowen and if their relationship ended badly she'd have to spend the rest of her life dealing with pitying glances.

And she didn't want that. She'd left that behind in West Texas when she'd left the preacher and his sanctimonious ways.

She started struggling in a totally undignified way, needing to get away from him. Wanting to escape before she did something really stupid and begged him to not spin this situation. To just ignore it, even if it meant closing the school—anything that would leave her pride intact. But she didn't like what that said about her.

"Please, Adam. I need a minute to myself."

He held her for another second and then dropped her hand. "I'll be here, waiting for you."

* * *

Adam let her go because he knew he had no choice and he wasn't sure how to make her stay. He heard the shower come on and went into her bedroom, finding his BlackBerry on the floor near her bed.

Malcolm had called him twice. No matter that Grace wanted to handle the newspaper article, which was salacious and full of innuendo, he knew that he was responsible for this. The article added complications that he and Grace didn't need. But he wasn't really surprised by it. He should have anticipated that sooner or later a gossip columnist would find out he'd been spending time with Grace. And he planned to spend a lot more time with her.

He could get them to print a retraction and hope that would be enough to make things better for Grace. Only Adam knew that it wouldn't. He wanted to fill her life with all she'd missed. To somehow be her benefactor because it would insulate him from what he felt right now. From the pain of disappointing her.

He called Malcolm and got his voicemail. "It's Adam. We need to talk. Call me back."

He sat down on the bed to wait for her. Picked up the book she had lying on her nightstand and flipped through it. It was a romance novel. A business one in which the hero had come into the heroine's life for revenge but fell in love with her instead.

This was what Grace thought romance should be. He wanted to give it to her. He wanted to be her white knight, her hero. And a man who let his woman fight her own battles wasn't a hero.

She came out dressed in a large terrycloth robe, her hair wrapped in a towel. Her eyes were damp and he knew she'd been crying. He swallowed a curse.

He didn't know how to handle this. Should he keep the topic all business? Hell, he should just pull her into his arms and make love to her. Then the distance put between them by one phone call and one photo would disappear.

"I left a message for Malcolm. I'll take care of him. You can handle the parents since I don't have much contact with them."

She walked over to her dresser and opened a drawer, pulling out matching panties and bra in a light blue color. She held them in her hand. And he totally forgot what they were talking about.

All he could think of was how she'd look wearing only those small scraps of fabric. How the light blue would look against her creamy skin.

"That sounds like a good plan. The more I think about this, the more I think a clean break between the two of us will be the right solution," she said. Her words drew his mind away from his erotic daydream.

"I'm not ready for a break, Grace. I'm still getting to know you." He was still trying to unravel the many mysteries that were Grace. He hoped that she hadn't figured him out in such a short time. But he knew he wasn't that complicated. That he had no hidden depths for her to plumb. Just one secret that he kept to himself because he didn't know how to verbalize it.

"After you get to know me, will you be ready?" she asked, and he heard the hurt in her voice.

He shrugged his shoulders, unwilling to give her the words that would reassure her. He wasn't about to tell her that with the way she made him feel, he doubted he'd ever be ready to break up with her.

He wanted her in his life, but realistically didn't know how to make that happen. Articles like the one that had her so upset were a part of his life.

She made his fuller, gave him a different perspective…made him feel. And that had been missing since his parents died.

"We're so different, Adam. I thought that wouldn't matter, but I think it does."

"It doesn't matter," he said, pushing to his feet and going to her. There was no way he was letting her brush him off and push him out of her life. This was a minor problem. "I'm not going anywhere, Gracie."

The words crystallized everything for him. He didn't have the answers, but for once packing up and moving wasn't the most appealing route. He wanted to do whatever would make this work for him and Grace.

"Why not? It would be simpler for both of us if we just stopped seeing each other."

He thought about last night. And the last few weeks when they'd been working together. How his life had changed when he'd stumbled across an erotic story penned by her and knew that he couldn't go back to being the man he was before.

"I don't know what to say to you, Grace. But I do know that I can't let perception rule my life."

"Perception?"

"What other people think." He couldn't say more than that. Sometime he'd be able to tell her that he wasn't really who she thought he was, but not right now. Right now, he needed Grace.

He slowly unwrapped the towel from her head, dropping it to the floor. He held her face in both of his hands, lowered his head to hers and kissed her with all the emotions that he was afraid to identify.

She kept her hands between them. The satin fabric of the undergarments she still clutched felt cool and silky against his stomach. He wanted to crush her to him. To take her into his body so she couldn't get away. So that he could keep her safe from being hurt like she had been this morning.

He wanted to keep kissing her until time stood still and once again there were only the two them. He'd always been a practical person, but with Grace he wanted to be that fairy-tale hero.

He lifted her in his arms and carried her back to her bed, knowing that making love to her wasn't going to solve anything. Wasn't going to resolve any of the questions she had that he couldn't answer. Wasn't going to make the problems outside of her cozy little house go away.

But he needed her in the most basic and elemental way. He needed to feel her arms and legs wrapped around him. To feel her nails scratching down his back and her body melting around him.

Welcoming him into her embrace in a way that felt like forever. Because forever had just gotten a hell of a lot shorter than he'd expected it to be.

# Eleven

He pulled his hips back, teased her with the promise of more. She shifted herself against his touch and finally felt him at the entrance of her body. He thrust deep inside her and she clutched at his shoulders.

His thumb rubbed at the center of her pleasure and the fire stormed through her, throwing her closer and closer to the pinnacle. Her breathing increased, she could scarcely catch her breath. His hand on her bottom held her hips steady as he rocked against her.

*Excerpt from "Adam's Mistress" by Stephanie Grace*

Grace walked into her office on Monday feeling a lot less confident than she had back in January when she thought the scandal of two teachers was going to close her school.

"Good morning, Bruce."

"Morning, Grace. Um, you've got a guest in your office."

"Who?"

"Dawn O'Shea."

Grace groaned. She'd been putting the fired teacher off but should have guessed that Dawn wouldn't let her do it indefinitely.

"This is really a bad time for her to be here."

"I know. That's why I put her in your office. Figured it was better if she was out of sight."

"Good thinking. I hate to ask this, but will you interrupt in five minutes?"

"No problem."

She entered her office. Dawn was standing behind Grace's desk staring out at the campus green. "I'm sorry I kept you waiting."

Dawn jerked around at the sound of Grace's voice. "We didn't have an appointment."

"Well, we have been trying to meet. I'm glad you stopped by, but today is going to be a little crazy."

"I saw the picture of you in the paper."

"Everyone did. What can I help you with?"

"I want my job back."

"It's too soon, Dawn. We're going to need at least another term before I can bring your name up to the board."

Dawn nodded. "I was afraid you'd say that."

"I wish there was something else I could do."

"Me, too," Dawn said, picking up her large brown leather purse and leaving.

This was really not what she needed. She made a mental note to contact the other administrators she knew in schools outside of Texas. Maybe one of them would have an opening for Dawn.

She was tired. Adam had left Saturday afternoon and she hadn't seen him since. He'd called a couple of times, but she'd refused to pick up the calls. The full board was meeting that afternoon and she needed to appear before them feeling fresh and strong. On her own.

But she'd missed him. She'd slept horribly the last two nights, which really ticked her off because she'd only spent one night in his arms. She shouldn't be missing him already.

She went to the sideboard and fixed herself a cup of coffee. She heard someone behind her and knew it was Adam without turning around. The spicy scent of his aftershave surrounded her and she closed her eyes, breathing deeply.

Her concentration coalesced. He reached around her for a coffee mug, his body brushing against her back, and she shifted slightly, letting her shoulder rub his chest.

"Good morning, Adam."

"Grace. Did you have a good weekend?"

She looked at him and realized that she had hurt him by ignoring him. Instead of giving her a sense of power, it made her feel small and petty. She put her cup down and took his hand, pulling him from the almost empty room. She took him down the hall into her office and shut the door.

Letting go of his wrist she stepped away from him. Even though she was in her office, the place where she always felt competent, she didn't. If this was what falling in love with a man did to her, she didn't want to be in love.

"I'm sorry," she said.

"You couldn't say that in the boardroom?" he asked, leaning back against the walnut paneled wall and watching her with that enigmatic gaze of his.

Over his shoulder was the portrait of her predecessor, the stern, matronly Marilyn Tremmel. The last Tremmel to be in charge. Grace wondered if Marilyn had ever had to deal with the problems she was facing.

"No, I couldn't. I don't want there to be any witnesses to this."

"Still trying to avoid bad publicity?" he asked.

She couldn't read his emotions in his tone or in his expression. Had she killed whatever he felt for her with her silence and distance? She still could feel him moving over her on her bed before he'd left to talk to Malcolm. She wanted him in her arms again.

"That's not it. What I feel for you is personal and no one else's business."

"What do you feel for me, Grace?" he asked. His tone begged honesty but she knew that his definition of honesty and hers were different.

He had no problem stretching the truth. There had been an article in Sunday's gossip column stating that he and she were old friends who'd been dating for a while. Not a lie exactly, but not the truth, either.

"I missed you this weekend," she said at last.

"You didn't have to."

"I know. That's what I'm trying to say. I'm not good at relationships."

"Neither am I," he said.

But she thought he was good at them. He had that knowledge of what they were supposed to be like from his *Ozzie & Harriet* upbringing. He didn't have her screwed-up relationship ruler that came from the preacher telling her that her mother left because Grace wasn't someone worth staying for.

"You had the perfect family growing up," she said.

"I thought I did, but it turned out to be a lie."

"What was a lie?"

Silence stretched. Adam blew out a deep breath.

"I'm not really a Bowen. I was adopted. All that *Father Knows Best* image that we had wasn't real."

She ached for Adam. For what he was saying. "Just because you were adopted doesn't mean that your parents didn't love you. They chose you, Adam."

"I don't know that. They never discussed my birth with me. They pretended I was theirs."

She couldn't stand not touching him so she grabbed his hand but kept at arm's length. "Maybe because they really thought you were their son."

"I've never been able to figure that out."

She wanted to wrap her arms around him and hold

him forever. But she heard voices in the outer office and knew the real world was about to intrude.

She didn't want him to realize what a mess she was inside but she needed them to be okay before the meeting. She needed to know that this thing between them was solid.

"I really am sorry. I thought it would be better to put some distance between us."

"Was it?" he asked, leaving his spot and walking toward her. More like stalking her, she thought, backing up until the desk stopped her retreat.

He kept on coming until his chest brushed her breasts and his hands came to rest on the desk on either side of her hips.

"No."

"Good."

"I don't like this, Adam, but I need you."

"That's what it's supposed to be like."

"Easy for you to say."

He tipped her face up toward his. "It's not easy for me to say, Grace. I don't like this any more than you do, but I know that until we figure out what kind of relationship we have, we can't both keep running."

"I'm not a runner." She said the words out loud but knew they were a lie. Hiding was another form of running. She'd created a life for herself based on who she'd always wanted to be. That was where her problems stemmed from with Adam.

She'd always thought he could belong to her only in her dreams. And having him in her life made her nervous.

Made her doubt the things she'd always taken for granted. The parts of herself that she'd been most sure of.

She realized that the closing of the school and loss of her job paled in comparison to living her life without Adam. And that was why her weekend had been so long and so hard. Because she wanted him by her side and she was very afraid that once the school situation was straightened out he'd be on the road again and she'd be in her hiding place all alone, with only her fantasies to keep her company.

Adam had his bags packed in his car and was ready to head to the airport when this meeting was over. He knew when to cut his losses and move on, but now he had a few doubts. He knew he was running away. He'd learned long ago that when things got too messy emotionally, he did better moving on. His assistant was already working on the final details of the basketball tournament.

Grace had given him the impression that she was serious about not wanting him in her life anymore. But today she was different. As always, she was running hot and cold. He understood that part of her because he was the same way. He left usually because it was easier than staying and dealing with people. But Grace wasn't just people and he wanted her.

He'd gone out of his way to make amends for ruining her reputation. He knew that most people wouldn't care if they had their picture in the paper, but Grace was different. She was intensely private and her reputation had always been above reproach. *He knew she savored that.*

But that still wasn't enough for her. She was skittish and scared. Watching him with those big wounded eyes of hers as if she were waiting for the next bad thing to happen. And his life, which, romantically, had always been fluid and carefree—safe—had been threatened by the deep need he had for her.

"I don't know what to do with you," he said, tugging her off balance and into his arms. The only time he felt like he knew what he was doing was when she was in his arms.

"Me, neither, Adam," she said, leaning forward, wrapping her arms around his waist and resting against him. He pulled her closer. He'd thought he'd never have the chance to hold her again but now he did.

He didn't want to let her go. For the first time since his parents' deaths he felt vulnerable.

After this weekend, he'd begun to understand why Viper bad-boy Stevie Taylor drank to escape. Understand how confusion and alcohol could lead to violence. Adam had wanted to put his foot through the wall or his fist through the door this weekend when he kept trying to call Grace and got no answer.

He wrapped his hand in her hair and pulled her head back. He found her mouth with his and plundered it ruthlessly, punished her with his teeth and lips and tongue for making him feel vulnerable…for leaving him.

She didn't try to pull away and after a moment the rightness of having her in his arms soothed that troubled part of him. He gentled his embrace, sucking gently at her mouth. Skimming his lips over her jaw and rocking her in his arms.

When he lifted his head her lips were wet and swollen from his kiss. Her eyes were half-closed and she was clinging to him. It made him feel complete in a way he hadn't realized he was missing until that moment.

Until he'd lived through a weekend without her. How the hell had Grace wound herself so deeply into his soul?

"Um…what was that about?" she asked.

Her hands were tracing a pattern on the small of his back under his suit jacket. He liked the feeling a lot. Okay, too much, he thought as he felt his body harden.

"Just showing you how much I missed you," he said. *He could do a better job* of it if she'd let him set her on her desk and push her skirt to her waist, like her story character. But he sensed that Grace wouldn't want to walk into an important meeting with damp panties and the knowledge that she'd just had an earth-shattering orgasm with one of the participants.

"I don't know that I won't retreat like that again," she said. "I mean, if something else happens like the photo. I am trying though. Can you have patience with me?"

"Yes," he said. Walking away from her wasn't going to be easy. He knew that he was going to unpack his bags and figure out a way to run his company from here in Texas. Not because it was his home, but because it was where Grace was.

"Thank you, Adam," she said, tipping her head back.

She leaned the slightest bit toward him. Watching the implicit trust she'd just given him by turning to him affected him. He refused to acknowledge it. He should have walked away.

He leaned down and brushed his lips over hers, meaning the embrace to be an apology for the rough kiss he'd just given her. She slid her hands down his chest and held on to his waist. He didn't rush her or try to intimidate her with his kiss. Instead he teased her lips with his own.

Finally she opened her mouth and tilted her head to the side, inviting him to deepen the embrace.

A knock sounded on the door and he pulled back from her. He dropped nibbling kisses under her ear and then spoke into it.

"Gracie, I think someone wants you."

"You?"

"Other than me," he said.

Awareness pulsed through him. He wanted to lead her to that leather couch in the corner of her office. But if he did, she'd never forgive him. There was a boardroom full of people waiting for them.

"Fix your lipstick. I'll meet you in the boardroom." He walked away while he could. Knowing that they'd turned a corner and not sure how to navigate the future.

He opened the door to find Malcolm there, regarding them gravely. Without a word, he led the other man away to give Grace time to compose herself. It was the least he could do.

Grace needed more than a minute to fix her lipstick. She sat down at her desk, realizing her desk blotter was crooked. She'd forgotten about the file folder with "Adam's Mistress" in it. Dammit. This time she was shredding it, Bruce or no Bruce, on the way to the meeting.

She lifted the blotter and realized the story was gone. Nothing remained, not the folder nor the pages that were in it.

She started opening drawers searching for it but she couldn't find it. Oh, God, she really didn't need to have that on the loose right now. *Why* hadn't she destroyed it already?

"Grace, the board of regents is seated and they are waiting for you." Bruce stood in her doorway, looking uncertain.

"I'm on my way," she said to Bruce.

"What are you looking for?"

"A file folder I'd tucked under my blotter. Have you seen it?"

"No, but I can ask the cleaning service. They were in last night for the bi-weekly cleaning."

"Please do," she said, forcing herself to stay calm and not panic. The file would show up and then she'd feel silly having worried about it being missing. Again.

The meeting went quickly. Malcolm and the other regents as well as the parents' representative were all surprisingly supportive of her and Adam dating. But they made it very clear that there could be no more public photos or stories about them.

Having her private life discussed was her worst kind of nightmare, but Adam was seated next to her, and he reached over and squeezed her thigh just when she thought she'd try disappearing under the table.

"We don't have a problem with you and Adam dating, we just don't want to see it in the papers again," Malcolm said for the third time.

"I've already apologized," Adam said. "I think the article in yesterday's *Dallas Morning News* more than compensated for the salaciousness of the photo and its caption."

"I agree," Sue-Ellen said. "But I see Malcolm's point. The school is at a critical stage."

"I'm aware of that. It won't happen again," Grace said. "Adam, would you please bring everyone up to speed on the plans for the celebrity basketball fundraiser?"

As everyone's attention shifted to Adam, she breathed a sigh of relief and enjoyed listening to the low rumble of his voice. Finally she understood what Dawn had meant when she'd said she'd been carried away with passion. Adam was the only man who'd made Grace forget everything but him.

The meeting adjourned and she hurried down the hall to her office while Adam lingered with the board. She searched her office, every single inch of it, and couldn't find the file folder with that story in it. She'd double-check at home but knew that it wasn't there.

The story was definitely missing again. She wondered if the same person had taken it. What did they plan to do with it?

She needed to let Adam know. How embarrassing, she thought. Just when they were moving on to having a real relationship, she was going to have to tell him she'd written an erotic story about the two of them.

There was a knock on her door and she opened it. Adam stood there. She could see Bruce behind him at his desk, checking his e-mail.

"Got a minute?" Adam asked.

Bruce didn't even glance up. She opened the door wider and let Adam in.

"That went better than I expected," she said.

"I told you to leave everything to me."

"You're taking credit for that?"

"Yes. I was your hero, Gracie. Admit it."

Her heart melted at his words. "You are definitely my hero."

"Damn straight," he said, pulling her into his arms. He kissed her while lifting her into his arms and carrying her to the desk. He set her on the edge of it.

"Now that the meeting is out of the way…"

"Yes?"

"I need you, Grace." He brought his face down to hers. His pupils were dilated and between her legs she felt him, hot and hard. "But this isn't the time or place."

The offer to stop touched her as little in life had in a long time. But she'd never experienced a tenth of this passion with other men.

"The world is waiting for us outside that door."

"I'd forgotten," she said.

"I'm glad."

She was glad, too. In ways she didn't want to comment on. But she knew in her heart, as he held her in his arms, that she'd found the home she'd always been searching for. And that it would be taken from her if she didn't find that fantasy she'd written.

# Twelve

All of her nerves tightened. Everything inside her clenched and then there was the release she'd been driving toward. She shivered in the aftermath. Adam groaned her name as his own release washed over him.

She collapsed against his chest. He held her close. "I'm falling for you, Grace. I want you to be more than my mistress."

She wanted to believe him, but a part of her wasn't sure that she could ever be anything more than Adam's mistress. But with his arms around her, his body completely surrounding her, she felt the truth in his words.

*Excerpt from "Adam's Mistress" by Stephanie Grace*

$F$riday evening Adam picked up a pizza at Campisi's and drove to Grace's house. The Dallas-area pizzeria had rumored mob ties but Adam didn't care. They also had the best thin-crust pizza he'd ever eaten.

He had a bottle of prosecco in the soft-sided cooler in the back seat chilling. After the long week they'd had he thought a celebration was in order. It had also been a week since they'd made love and he wanted to commemorate that. He'd stopped by his jeweler after leaving the school this afternoon and picked up the custom bangle bracelet he'd ordered for Grace.

In two weeks, at the start of spring break, Tremmel-Bowen would host its first basketball tournament fundraiser. Registration for the coming school year was up and the financial picture wasn't as bleak as it had once seemed.

All in all Adam felt very good about the way things were going in Plano. The only wrinkle was Grace. She still hadn't said anything about the story she'd written about the two of them. He'd looked for it in her office to try to see if there were any new additions to it that he could use to make this night even more special for her, but she must have removed it.

Probably a good idea, he thought. He parked on the street in front of her house, grabbed their dinner and went up the walk to her front door.

*She opened the door before he got there and smiled* up at him. Her dark hair was down, curling around her shoulders. She wore a simple sleeveless sundress that fit her curves. She was the embodiment of every womanly fantasy he'd ever had and he couldn't think when he saw her.

She led him through her home and he followed her, unable to keep his eyes off her curvy body. He knew he wasn't going to make it through a meal before he had her. He put the pizza in the oven on the way by and left the prosecco in its cooler bag as she stepped out on to the patio.

Her doorbell rang and Adam groaned. "I'm never going to have you all to myself."

Grace smiled at the way he said that. He made her feel so wanted. It was a new feeling and one she planned to get used to. Though she knew it would take some time before she could really accept that he wanted her. "I'm sure it's nothing major."

She walked through the house feeling well-loved with the mild rhythm of Miles Davis' music still echoing in her mind. She was vaguely aware of Adam following her to the door.

She glanced back at him. "Are you planning to answer my door?"

"I have a gift for you out in my car. I forgot it."

"Geez, I wonder why?" she teased him. But her mind was dwelling on the fact that he had a gift for her. What was it?

"Because you clouded my mind with sex appeal." He dragged her to a stop and dropped a quick kiss on her lips.

She laughed. No one would have ever suspected her of distracting any man with sex. But that was the old

Grace. Prim and proper Grace, who'd never been confident enough to be herself with any man. The new Grace could seduce Adam into forgetting a gift. She was very proud of the changes in herself.

She was shocked to see Malcolm standing on her doorstep. He wore a suit, as if he'd come from work, but the tie was gone and his hair was disheveled as if he'd been running his hands through it.

"Good you're both here," he said, looking over her shoulder at Adam. But then he glanced out toward her street.

"Why are you here?" she asked.

"We've got a big problem."

"Another one?" She was beginning to think that Tremmel-Bowen was never going to get out of trouble. Every time they took one step forward something dragged them two steps backward.

"Yes," Malcolm said. "Can I come in?"

She stepped back, holding the door open for him. The evening air was dry and cool but she saw a sheen of sweat on Malcolm's brow. What the heck was going on?

She led the way to the living room, but none of them sat down.

Adam put his arm around her waist and tucked her up against his side. It made her feel so much better to have him there. Holding her, supporting her. It reminded her that she was no longer all alone.

"We've been careful. We haven't been out in public one time since that photo last week."

Malcolm scrutinized her before glancing up at Adam. "She hasn't been careful."

Grace's stomach fell and she dreaded what Malcolm would say next. She tried to pull away from Adam. To put some distance between them before Malcolm dropped whatever bombshell he had.

But Adam's grip was firm. The message in his embrace was clear—they were in this together. He wasn't going to run and she wasn't going to hide. But damn, it was hard to stand her ground.

"What do you mean?" she asked, her voice a thready whisper.

"A story called 'Adam's Mistress' has surfaced. The heroine's name is Grace and the couple resembles the two of you. The local media is all over it. I'm surprised they aren't camping on your door."

"Oh, my God. I don't know what to say." She wanted to run into her bedroom and close the door. Never open it up. She couldn't face Adam. Not right now.

"Grace?" Adam's voice was deep and concerned. She pulled away from him. She was going to feel like a big idiot when she told him what was going on.

"Are you okay?" Malcolm asked.

She realized she was swaying on her feet and she could see spots dancing before her eyes, but she refused to pass out. "Give me a minute."

She wanted to throw herself on her bed and start crying but that wouldn't solve anything. Who had her story? And why would they release it to the media?

"I wrote the story," she said.

"I figured," Malcolm said.

"How did it get released?" she asked, not looking at Adam. Later she'd deal with him. And telling him about her secret fantasy.

Malcolm rubbed a hand over the top of his head and then cleared his throat. "My sources said it was Dawn. But I can't figure out how she got a copy of it."

Her heart sank. She'd tried to set up some interviews for the other woman out of state. But Dawn hadn't returned any of her calls over the past week. "I printed it out at work because my home printer was out of ink. Dawn was in my office alone for a minute—she must have taken it."

"This isn't going to be easy to manage," Malcolm said.

"Let me get my people on it," Adam said. "I'll call you later and let you know what we're doing."

Malcolm agreed and left a few minutes later. Grace sank further into herself, trying to figure out how to explain the story to Adam. She risked a glance up at him.

"I bet you have a lot of questions."

"I do."

"It's going to be hard to explain."

"I'm sure it won't be that complicated. Want to go out on the patio?"

"Yes," she said, wondering why he was being so calm. If she'd heard he'd written a story about her, she'd demand answers.

"Um…I don't know where to start, except to say that

I wrote an erotic story about you and me. I was going to enter it in a writing contest but then changed my mind. I mean, I'm the headmistress at a prep school, I can't exactly publish an erotic story, even under a pseudonym."

He didn't say anything. Finally she looked at him to find him watching her with a very steady and serious gaze. "I knew about the story you wrote."

She was totally shocked and couldn't think at first. Then she thought too much and she realized when he must have seen it.

"Did you read it before you decided to help me save the school?"

"Yes."

Adam knew he'd made a mistake. From their first lunch he'd known that he'd crossed a barrier she'd find unforgivable. But the action had been taken and it was too late to go back and undo it.

"I thought you said that truth was important to you," she said, pacing away from him. But she didn't stop and face him, she kept walking around the patio.

"It is." He knew that he wasn't going to convince her with just words. He was scrambling to think of something to say or do to make this right. To fix the hurt she felt and get her to move past it. But he had no easy answers.

"What do you call reading my story…oh, my God, that's not all you did," she said. She stopped pacing to stand in front of him. Her hands were on her hips and her eyes blazed at him.

He saw her eyes widen as she recalled the first time they'd made out on his couch. She'd described something very similar in her story and he'd borrowed from it. Used her own fantasies to seduce her.

He saw a shimmer of tears in her eyes and felt like a bastard. He never should have let it go on this long.

"I can explain," he said, knowing that he really couldn't. He hadn't planned on being around long enough for the truth to come to light. He might have thought it but he'd known from the beginning that he'd be moving on.

"I don't care." She was trembling and he took a step toward her, wanting to comfort her. "Please leave."

"Grace…you're hiding again. Let's talk this out." He took another step toward her but she held her hand out to ward him off. He stopped where he was, though every instinct he had shouted for him to take her into his arms where he could soothe the hurt he'd inflicted on her.

"I'm not hiding. I'm furious. And if you don't leave I'm going to do something I might regret."

"You have a right to be angry with me."

"Stop being so calm and rational, Adam. I'm not in the mood for it."

"I'm not leaving. I made a promise to myself that I wouldn't run this time. That with you I'd stay and fight."

"Is a promise anything like the truth?"

He cursed savagely under his breath.

"I'll take that as a yes. I think we both know that you

view the truth as something that can be bent to fit your needs. I'm asking you to leave my house."

He didn't want to hurt her any more than he already had. Any other woman and he'd suspect she was being melodramatic, but with Grace he knew how hard it was for her to let anyone see the real woman. And her story had been one-hundred-percent real wants and needs.

"If I leave I'm not coming back."

"What does that mean?"

"Just that you're not the only one who feels betrayed." He didn't add that he'd betrayed himself. He didn't want to focus too clearly on himself. He'd known that staying in one place wasn't a great idea and now he had the proof. The reason he'd been waiting for to move on.

"How did I betray you?"

She stood before him almost sanctimonious in her anger and he realized that he really did feel cheated. Cheated out of all the time when he'd never noticed her. "All those years of lusting after me. All those years of pretending to be someone you weren't."

"Look what happened when I stopped pretending. This isn't exactly happily ever after," she said, starting to cry.

He closed the gap between them. He really couldn't stand to see her crying. He wrapped her in his arms, held her as close to him as he could. "It could be. You just have to forgive me for reading your fantasies."

"That's not why I'm angry," she said, her voice muffled against his chest. Her arms were held limply by her sides but she wasn't pushing him away.

"Then why are you?"

"Because I was falling for you. Because I believed you when you said that the truth really mattered. And I just found out that was a lie. How can I trust anything you've said to me?"

He had no answer for her. No way to make this right with his words or actions. "I honestly didn't know how to tell you I'd read your story."

"How did you even find it?"

"It fell off your desk. The papers spilled out and I skimmed them to make sure it wasn't my file. When I saw the word breast…well, I'm a guy, I had to read more."

She pushed out of his arms and walked away from him again. This time it felt permanent.

"That's what I was afraid of."

He didn't say anything, wanting her to continue and afraid he'd screw up even further if he tried to say something now.

"You made me believe that you noticed me as a woman because of the way I acted in the boardroom, but all the time you were interested because you thought I was some kind of repressed spinster."

"I never thought that."

She was shaking now. "It was the truth. I hadn't been on a date in more than five years, Adam. Until I walked into Tremmel-Bowen and saw you. Then I became obsessed with you."

He was kind of flattered, but knew that she'd never seen the real man when she'd been dreaming of him. "I can't be your fantasy man."

"I never asked you to be."

"You just did. I'm sorry I disappointed you, but everyone has to deal with crap like this."

"Not everyone. Just those of us who don't live charmed lives."

"Everyone," he said, getting close to her. "Just because my life looks perfect on the outside doesn't mean that it is."

She looked taken aback. She retreated again, this time turning to the edge of the patio. He wanted to make love to her again and again until she forgot to be sad and angry that her private story was now in the public domain.

"I'm sorry, you're right. I was making you into a television-perfect version of a modern Prince Charming."

He came up behind her and put his hand on her shoulder. "Don't be sorry for that. I wanted to be that guy for you. But I'm only human and I screw up and make mistakes. And unlike a television sitcom, I can't fix them in less than thirty minutes."

She wiped her tears away and wrapped her arms around her waist. "I'm not sure I'd want that anyway."

"What do you want?"

"I don't know. I need some time to think."

He could understand that. He didn't like it but he could give her the distance she needed. He gathered his stuff together.

He walked away, knowing it was a mistake but not knowing what else to do.

# Thirteen

Adam knew he had this one chance to make things right for Grace. But he was scared to say what was in his heart. Scared he wouldn't have the right words to convince her that she was the only woman in the world who made him complete.

"Was there something you wanted, Adam?" she asked, sitting there behind that wide walnut desk where he'd had her.

"Yes, Gracie, there is. Marry me."

*Excerpt from "Adam's Mistress" by Stephanie Grace*

Grace sent in an official resignation from her job at Tremmel-Bowen in the mail on Monday. She'd spent the weekend dodging calls from reporters and local television media, both of whom had shown up about ten minutes after Adam had left.

He'd called a few times and she'd let the machine take his calls. She didn't know what to say to him. She was so embarrassed by what she'd written and by how she'd acted when she'd realized he'd known how she felt the entire time.

She wanted to cry when she thought of how he'd taken her erotic dreams and made them come true. He hadn't deserved her anger but she'd been unable to stop herself from acting out.

She'd never had a short fuse until Adam. And she knew that was only because she'd wanted to be wanted by him. Really *wanted,* not wanted because she'd aroused him.

She'd had two calls from different magazine publishers offering to publish her story. Adam was big-time news and any sensational story featuring him interested the national media.

She knew she couldn't hide in her house forever. For one thing, she was going to run out of food before too much longer. And her house was closing in around her. The place that she'd created to be her sanctuary had turned out to be a bed of thorns since Adam had left.

*She saw him everywhere. Every place they'd made* love. Every inch of her house seemed to be imbued with him and she felt lonelier than she'd ever felt before.

Her doorbell rang and she peaked out the small

window on the side to see who was there. Adam stood on her doorstep. He wore a pair of faded jeans and a long oxford shirt with the tails hanging out. He had on dark sunglasses and held something in his left hand.

"I can see you," he said.

She unlocked the door and opened it. He stepped inside just as the Fox 4 van pulled up at the curb. He closed her door for her, locking it.

"Thanks for letting me in."

"I couldn't let you face the media by yourself."

She still felt raw and had no idea what to say to Adam. No idea how to move past what had happened.

"I know you don't want to talk to me."

"I didn't say that."

"Yes, you did, when you let every call of mine go to voicemail. I'm not just here to talk about our relationship."

"You're not?"

"No. I'm here as an official representative of Tremmel-Bowen. We aren't going to accept your resignation. You are a viable part of the school, and this particular scandal isn't going to break the school."

"Oh, are you sure?"

"Yes. Have you been watching the news or reading the papers?"

"No. I've just been hiding out."

"Well, Dawn felt bad about what she did. She's gone to the media and told them that she wrote the story to get back at you and I for firing her."

"That's not true."

"Well, she did do it for revenge but she regretted it almost immediately."

"I wonder why?"

"She said something about owning up to the mistakes she'd made and not blaming you for her problems."

Grace was glad to hear it, but still wasn't entirely sure that she could go back to her job.

"I think you should know that Sue-Ellen and Malcolm are giving me an hour to convince you to come back."

"Really?"

"Yes. The past month has really brought us all together as a school community and everyone agreed you are part of the school. An important part."

"I don't know what to say to you. I'm still embarrassed."

He rubbed the back of his neck. "You didn't do anything to be ashamed of."

"I'm the only one who can decide that."

"Gracie, your passion and your desires were so sexy and sweet. Please don't ever think that there was anything wrong with that. Your story changed my life."

"Sexy scenarios changed your life?"

"Your sexy scenario led me to you."

She blushed at his words and stepped farther into her house. "Want to come in and sit down?"

"Not yet. I wrote something for you."

"What?"

"A short story, like the one you wrote. I figured turn-about was fair play."

He handed her a file folder. A plain manila one like she'd used. She peaked inside and saw the title of the story.

"Grace's Husband."

She was almost afraid to read the pages. But Adam was standing in her foyer and she knew she wasn't going to have another chance with him.

She took the folder into her living room and sat on her couch and read it. It was a sweet story…their story, with a happy ending. Adam was brutally honest when it came to his own faults, but glossed over her own like they didn't exist.

She realized as she got to the part where they moved into his big house and started having children that Adam wanted to stay here with her. That he saw his home and his future in her. Tears stung the back of her eyes and she looked down. How had she gotten so lucky? To find a man like Adam, a man who loved her for who she was. A man who wanted a future with her.

She looked up to see him standing over her. "I think you might be a better writer."

"I don't know about that. Did you mean this?"

"Yes," he said. He scooped her up and then sat down on the couch, cradling her in his arms. She slipped her arm around his shoulder, resting her head on his shoulder and closing her eyes.

She felt safe again. For the first time in three days she felt the knot in her stomach ease. He tangled one hand in her hair, tipping her head back for a long slow kiss.

When he lifted his head, she caught his face in her hands. "I want that story, Adam."

"Me, too, Gracie. I've been playing at living, pretending I had a full life but deep inside I knew I was running from the emptiness of the life I once believed was mine."

"What were you running from?"

"I told you about being adopted, but I hated that people saw me as something I wasn't. A real Bowen, you know."

"Oh, well, you are a real Bowen. You proved that when you worked so hard to save the school that your family established.

"Are you ready to stop running?" she asked.

"Only if you stay with me. I've found what I was looking for here, with you. I've talked to Malcolm and the board, we want you to stay on as headmistress. Together I want us to run the school and raise a new generation of Bowens."

"Are you sure, Adam?" she asked, because she couldn't believe that she'd finally have everything she'd dreamed of.

"I love you, Gracie. I've never said those words to anyone except my parents. But I know that I can't live without you."

She hugged him tight, burying her face against his shoulder. "I love you, too."

He carried her down the hall to her bedroom and

made love to her all afternoon. They made plans for the future and talked about their fantasies and dreams.

Adam promised to always make all of hers come true. And he did.

\* \* \* \* \*

# SIX-MONTH MISTRESS

BY
KATHERINE GARBERA

This book is dedicated to my sisters…
Donna and Linda, sisters by birth. Nancy,
Mary Louise, Eve and Beverly, sisters by chance.

# One

"Jeremy Harper is here to see you."

"Send him in," Isabella McNamara said, even though he wasn't on her calendar. She hung up the phone and settled back in her leather executive chair, blowing out a long breath. This was just another meeting. She faced heads of Fortune 500 companies all the time—facing Jeremy would be no different.

*Yeah, right.*

She wiped her sweaty palms on the fabric of her silk skirt and immediately regretted it. She wanted to look her best, to pull off some of Angelina Jolie's charm and confidence. Taking a deep breath, she repeated a few words in her head—calm, cool, clever.

Everything was always different with Jeremy. She'd seen him exactly twelve times in the last three years. And each of those meetings had left her shaken, hungry and wanting more of the man. Of course, since she'd pretty much signed away her body to him, every time they'd met all she could think about was what it would be like to feel his naked skin rubbing against hers.

Oh, God, he'd turned her into a sex fiend. She knew that being a man's mistress wasn't about sex; it was about money. But Bella had never been able to think of anything to do with Jeremy as only business.

She didn't have to guess why he was here. Three short years ago, she'd made a deal with Jeremy and now it was time to pay up. She didn't kid herself that he was here for any reason other than to collect on that debt.

The door to her office opened and she stood to greet him. He wore a Dolce & Gabbana suit with the same ease that teenagers wore jeans and T-shirts. He sauntered into the room as if he owned it.

She caught her breath, wishing for a minute she didn't find him so attractive. But she always had. And that was probably why she was in the position she was: Owing this man a debt she had no idea if she would survive paying.

The door closed firmly behind him, but she

barely noticed. Instead she tried to ignore the spicy scent of his aftershave and the way his bluer-than-blue eyes watched her.

He was her devil. The man she'd sold her soul to—and he was here to collect. She twisted her fingers together, trying desperately to believe that she wasn't scared of a six-foot-two man. But she was.

"Hello, Bella."

His voice was deep and low-pitched. She'd spoken to him on the phone countless times, yet his voice always sent little shivers of awareness pulsing through her veins.

"Jeremy," she said, then remembered a very important lesson that her mother had taught her. *Never let them see you sweat.* Of course, her mom had been referring to the Palm Beach jet set they'd once been a part of, but Bella figured the same rule applied to sexy billionaires. "Please have a seat."

He moved farther into the room, seating himself in one of her guest chairs. She sank down into her leather chair, opening her center desk drawer and touching the jewel-encrusted Montblanc fountain pen that had once been her mother's and was now Bella's lucky charm. She rubbed her fingers over it before taking it out of the drawer and placing it on the desk.

"What can I do for you?" she asked carefully. He might be here for another reason. Maybe he wanted her to cater an event for his company or his family's annual Fourth of July bash.

"I think you know."

She sighed. Not an event after all. "Time's up."

He laughed, a rich sound that filled the room, and for a moment she forgot to be afraid. Forgot that he held all the cards in this situation by her own design.

"I was hoping time would have helped alleviate your fears."

"I'm not afraid of you," she said, very aware that her words were a lie.

She didn't care if Jeremy knew it, either. She'd spent most of her life dealing with people she was afraid of, ever since her father had died when she was fourteen and they'd gotten the news that his entire fortune was gone. She'd learned to deal with the fear of being mocked by the same people she'd once called friends.

She'd faced fear again when her mother died four years later and the sole responsibility for raising her fourteen-year-old brother, Dare, had fallen to her. She'd known real fear—survival fear—and she'd never once admitted to it out loud.

Jeremy arched one eyebrow at her—an arrogant gesture that fit him to a tee.

She forced a smile. "Dare is still in college."

"He's graduating at the end of summer. And he has a job lined up with Fidelity starting in the fall."

"How do you know that?" she asked. Dare had only just called this afternoon with the job news. She'd known then that she needed to call Jeremy.

To let him know that she was now ready to fulfill her part of the bargain.

"I told you I'd make sure your brother's future was taken care of."

"I thought you meant the scholarship." But she'd suspected he'd done more. Dare had mentioned a few times that Jeremy had visited him at school.

He shook his head. "I'm not here to discuss your brother."

No, of course he wasn't. He was here to discuss her and the contract she'd signed three years ago. A contract in which she'd agreed to be his mistress for six months in return for the help he'd given both her and her brother.

"So, it starts tonight?" she asked at last. For three years he'd been waiting for her to be free of her obligation to her brother. For three years she'd seen him every three months to affirm that the deal was still on. For three years she'd dreamed of his passionate embraces…and the hope that, once they started their affair, she'd be able to convince him that she was meant to be more than his mistress. Because she wanted to be Jeremy's wife.

"I believe you're free," he said.

She was available tonight. The new manager she'd hired had proven himself capable of handling all the events, so she was taking a rare night off. How did he know? "Did Dare tell you?"

"He didn't have to. I asked your assistant."

"You're a very thorough man." She was going to have a talk with Shelley about giving out personal information. Her hands were shaking and she clenched them together so he wouldn't notice. He was just a man. But for some reason he'd always been more to her.

"When I see something I want…" he said.

"And you want me?"

"After the kisses we've shared, I know you don't doubt that."

She didn't. But by the same token, she'd always sort of wished she'd just imagined the intensity in Jeremy's eyes when he looked at her.

She had no real idea how to respond to that. "Um…I…"

He stood up and walked around her desk to stand next to her chair. She tipped her head back to look up at him. "Changed your mind?"

She couldn't read the emotion in his eyes—there wasn't any. For all the reaction she saw, he might not care either way. And that was why she was afraid. She'd been desperate when she'd agreed to the contract, wanting to stop feeling so alone in the world. People she knew left but, if she had the chance, she knew she could convince Jeremy to stay.

Jeremy had gone beyond what he'd said he would do, introducing her to business partners of his and recommending her party-planning services before she had any real references. He'd helped tremendously to get her business off the ground, and to ensure its success.

And she wanted him, she did. She was just afraid that the secret crush she'd always had on him would make it too easy for her to believe there was something more between them than a contract.

She was attracted to Jeremy. She'd been in lust with him since she'd first met him when she was sixteen. She'd been working at the Palm Beach Yacht Club as a waitress and he'd been dining with a bunch of his college friends. He'd been tan and fit and incredibly handsome. And polite—the nicest to her by far.

When he'd finally approached her a few years later, she'd been thrilled at first. Until she realized that what he was offering was a business arrangement. An arrangement that she'd never regretted not turning down.

"I haven't changed my mind. I gave you my word." She didn't feel guilty about the contract she'd signed. A lot of women married for money and then divorced and married again. In essence she was doing the same thing.

"And your word is your bond?"

"It has to be. I didn't have anything else when you made your offer." She didn't like to remember those days, the despair and the sense of failure that she'd been mired in.

"You had your pride," he said softly, running one finger down the side of her face. He cupped her jaw in his hand and she held her breath.

His gaze fell to her mouth and stayed there. She licked her dry lips and his gaze narrowed. Silly as it sounded, she could feel his eyes on her lips.

"I still do."

"Good."

She leaned away from him. "It would make me feel more comfortable if everything you said didn't sound so arrogant."

"I can't help that."

"You can, you just choose not to."

"I've had thirty-four years to get this way."

"And no one has ever complained?"

"Not to my face."

"I don't think I'm going to be able to keep my comments to myself."

"I wouldn't want you to. I'm not asking you to pretend to be someone you aren't."

But he was. The woman she was today was different from the one she'd been three years ago. And at twenty-six she wasn't sure she could pretend they were dating when she knew the truth. That she was his mistress. That the relationship was stamped with an expiration date. And that he was planning to walk away from her without looking back or leaving any of his emotions behind.

* * *

Jeremy stared down into Bella's big brown eyes and felt like he'd taken a punch to the gut. He'd waited lifetimes for this night. True, he knew it had been only three years, but they seemed long—too long. His skin felt too tight and if she didn't lose the nervous look, he wasn't sure what he was going to do.

She was his. For the last three years that knowledge had been in the back of his mind. His life had gone the same as always. But in the back of his mind he knew that Bella McNamara belonged to him. Finally he could claim her.

He had a contract with her signature on it. A legal document that proclaimed she'd be his mistress for six months. But even he wasn't that big of a bastard—he wouldn't force Bella into his arms and his bed if she didn't want to be there.

Still, he'd have absolutely no qualms about seducing her into his bed. About using the passion that had always been between them to gain her acceptance and get her where he wanted her.

"Um…how is this going to work? Will we go to your place right now?" she asked. A strand of her hair had escaped the clip at the back and curled against her cheek. She tucked it behind her ear absently.

She bit her lower lip. Her mouth was full and enticing. It was the second thing he'd noticed about her. He had tasted her lips before, when he'd held her in his arms. But the way he felt about her was…hell, he couldn't define what he felt for her. He wanted to groan out loud.

"No, not now. We're attending the Tristan-Andrew Cancer Institute charity benefit tonight. Our arrangement will stay private. In public, it will seem like we're dating."

"Thank you," she said.

"For?"

"For keeping our arrangement private. I don't really want the world to know," she said, her words breathy. A soft little confession.

Jeremy didn't pretend he understood women but he did know that socially a girlfriend and a mistress *weren't in the same league. He'd seen that firsthand* with his own father's women. Bella had enough marks against her socially. But this was the only arrangement she would accept from him. And mistresses he understood.

He'd hoped for a different sort of evening—an intimate dinner for two on his yacht, followed by dancing under the stars. But at least at the charity benefit there would be music and he could hold her in his arms.

The last three years had been the longest of his life. He hadn't been celibate, but every woman he'd slept with had become Bella in his head. He wanted *her.* When he woke in the morning he imagined her soft brown eyes opening to meet his. She'd become an obsession—and a successful businessman couldn't afford to be obsessed with anything other than business.

She licked her lips again and his body clenched. He wanted to know the taste of her mouth. It had been too long since he'd last kissed her. This time he did groan out loud.

"What?"

He shrugged. The safe bet would be to play it off as not wanting to go to the charity event. He liked social events, normally. Tonight he was being generous in letting her have this time to adjust to being in a relationship with him.

The event had been organized by his mother. His family was a major benefactor to the local cancer institute. They were hosting the charity fashion event this evening at Neiman Marcus. His mother had called to remind him that plenty of single ladies would be in attendance, all of them suitable to become Mrs. Jeremy Harper III.

Which made this the perfect night to be seen with Bella.

He rubbed the back of his neck to keep from reaching out and capturing that strand of hair that was once again curled against her cheek. "Are you familiar with the event?"

"We lost the bid to cater it." She said it almost absently. She straightened some papers on her desk and only then did he notice the fine trembling of her hand.

"Forget about your business for one night," he said, trying to process her reaction. His own hands shook at the thought of being alone with her. The feelings she evoked in him were that intense.

"I don't think that's a good idea."

"Why not?" he asked.

"Business is all we have between us," she said, staring up at him. He knew he was missing something in the words and her expression, but he couldn't figure out what it was. If it *was* just business between them, then he couldn't have her. He never wanted to be more involved than his partner in an intimate relationship.

"Our business is very personal," he said at last, capturing that curl and wrapping it around his finger. It was what he wanted to do with her. Wrap himself in her curvy body and silky limbs.

"Yes, it is. And, oh God, I'm not sure—"

He covered her mouth with his fingers. Her lips were plump and moist from her breath. "You can change your mind."

She shook her head. "I don't want to."

He smiled then, hoping his relief didn't show. It was unnerving to be so attracted to a woman. He'd jumped through hoops for Bella that he wouldn't have for any other woman. After all, he'd waited three years for her.

"Then let's go to the party and see where the night leads."

"What about the contract?" she asked, clearly still uneasy with him.

He struggled for a way to put her at ease. He knew he could be charming, but with Bella he wasn't his usual self. From the moment he'd suggested that she become his mistress, he'd been out of control.

At the time she'd seemed so young—only twenty-three—and so fragile.

"We can discuss it over dinner after the party," he said. He wasn't ready to let her out of the contract. He knew a better man would have torn the document up a long time ago, but frankly it was the only leverage he had with Bella. Leverage he didn't want to let go of.

"Okay. I can have my secretary make us a reservation," she said, trying to take control of the situation.

He held back a smile. He admired her bid for power but there was no way he was letting her take charge. "I'll take care of that. Just get your purse or briefcase and we can leave."

"Leave?" she asked. Her face flushed and she looked like she wanted to tell him off. Finally he felt like they were getting somewhere. He saw the real Bella in that instant. The woman he'd first been attracted to. The woman of passion and pride and determination. Not someone who was biddable and afraid of him, something he didn't want.

"Yes. My driver is waiting out front."

She smiled sweetly at him. "Thanks for the offer of a ride, but I have to go home and get changed."

"I have a dress for you."

"That's nice, but I'd prefer to wear my own clothes."

"And I'd prefer you to wear the dress I selected."

"I think we're at a stalemate."

"No, we're not."

"We're not?"

"No."

She shook her head. "I know you think you're going to get your way, but—"

"I don't think it, Bella, I know it."

"Why?"

"Because as my mistress you'll put my preferences first."

# Two

Bella laced her fingers together under the desk to keep from doing something she was sure she'd regret. She wished she had a mentor when it came to filling the role of a mistress, but she didn't. She sensed it would be easier to just let her pride go. *Once you agree to be a man's mistress, your pride means nothing.*

*If only.* Suddenly it wasn't the sex that concerned her, but the attitude that she'd have to pretend to have. She tried to smile, but couldn't force herself. If only she owed him money, then she could go to the bank and take out a loan, but he'd given her a lot more than money. He'd given her contacts, business advice and provided a male role model for Dare. Those were things that couldn't be paid back in dollars.

"This isn't going to work. I'm sorry that I didn't realize it before, but I'm not the kind of woman who can—"

He put his fingers over her lips again. Her tongue brushed his skin for a second before she closed her mouth, staring up at him.

She felt her resolve melting and it had absolutely nothing to do with not wanting to be in breach of the contract she'd signed. It had to do with his eyes.

His touch was featherlight and almost tentative. Like he wasn't sure he had the right to touch her, but couldn't help himself. That reassured her. No matter what he'd said before, there was more to this than a contract.

He must know he was pushing her. Did he want her to renege? Had that been his plan all along? She wanted to take his arrogance down a peg or two.

She had no idea how to handle herself with him. He had something she wanted. Something he *knew* she wanted. That elusive stamp of approval from the crowd that had tossed her out without a backward glance—and the only sure way to get that back was to marry into the crowd. And she was willing to do anything to make that happen.

If she had to swallow her pride and her temper, then she would. Being a mistress should be easy enough. She had to do nothing but live for pleasure and smile at her man. Make him feel like he was the sexiest, smartest, wealthiest man in the room.

God, she didn't think she could do it. Even for the chance to walk into a room with him, that most elusive of men, the ultimate bachelor. A man whom every single woman in that elite social jet set wanted to claim. And she thought—no, knew—she could win him over for a lifetime.

It was small and petty, but that thought made her tip her head to the side and smile up at him. "Of course, I'll wear the dress you selected."

"Let's go then."

"I'll need a few minutes to get ready. I'll meet you in the waiting room."

He nodded and walked out of the room. She collapsed into her chair as soon as he was gone.

There was a brief knock on the door and then it opened again.

"Bella?"

"Yes, Shelley?"

"He asked me to give you this."

Shelley handed her a small, gold-foil-wrapped box. "I had no idea the two of you were dating."

And so it starts. "We've known each other for years."

"I know that. Are you going to open it?"

She didn't want to know what was inside. A gift for a mistress might be different than a gift for a girlfriend. She thought maybe she should open it by herself, but Shelley didn't look like she was leaving. Her assistant was also the closest thing that Bella had to a friend.

"Yes, I'll open it."

She didn't let herself dwell on the fact that it had been almost ten years since she'd received a wrapped present. Dare gave her gifts, but generally left them in the bag from the store they'd come from. She slipped the ribbon off the box and set it aside.

"Oh, man, I can't wait to see what it is. How can you go so slowly?"

"I don't get that many gifts."

"Me neither. Not like this. Not from men."

Bella slipped her fingernail under the seam in the paper and ripped it away. The box was long and narrow, and when the paper fell away she saw it was that distinctive Tiffany blue. *Jewelry.* He'd gotten her jewelry.

Shelley perched her hip on the desk and leaned forward as Bella lifted the lid. It was a platinum, diamond-encrusted choker.

Shelley gasped a little and reached out to touch it. "It's gorgeous."

"Yes, it is," Bella said. She realized that he'd done her a favor, insisting she wear a dress he'd purchased. She would have worn one of her mother's old haute couture dresses and costume jewelry and all the time she'd have felt like a fraud.

Did he realize that? Or had buying her a dress and, she assumed, a wardrobe simply been part of preparing her to be his?

She closed the jewelry box and slipped it into her leather Coach bag. She'd skimped and saved until she could afford the large, classy bag that she wanted and needed for work.

Her stomach was still a knot of nerves, but she refused to think about it. Instead she fell back on her business. "Remind Randall to call me when the event tonight is over. I want to know how it went."

"Are you sure about that?"

"Of course I'm sure."

"If I was going out with someone like Jeremy Harper I wouldn't want my phone ringing."

"Shelley…"

"None of my business, I know. Have fun tonight, boss lady."

Bella knew she'd have a lot *of things tonight* and wasn't sure fun was one of them. But she was excited and nervous and a million other things that she'd never expected. It wasn't just Jeremy. It was her return to Palm Beach society and the ten long years it had taken to get there.

Jeremy escaped from his partner's spouse, who desperately wanted to find him a wife. Despite the fact that he'd arrived tonight with Bella on his arm, Lucinda wasn't deterred. She had a friend she wanted him hooked up with and nothing would stop her.

Ever since Daniel and Lucinda had married, Lucinda Cannon-Posner had been trying to pair him up with her oh-so-proper society friends. The moment Bella had stepped away to powder her nose, Lucinda and her friend Marianne had pounced.

Jeremy eased deeper into the shadows, waiting for Bella to reappear. He was surprised by how much he was enjoying the evening. Normally these events were a total bore. But tonight, with Bella at his side, he'd been enjoying himself—until Lucinda and her friend had made their move.

"Hiding from Marianne?"

Jeremy glanced over at Kell Ottenberg. He and his cousin had been best friends forever. Their mothers were sisters and the two men had been raised together. Kell handed him a martini glass.

"Waiting for Bella."

"Ah, the mystery lady. Rumor has it she's been hired for the evening."

Jeremy knew Kell was trying to get a rise out of him. The fact that he'd hit so close to the mark was something Jeremy chose to ignore. "You're the one who has to pay for companionship."

"I don't have to pay, but it does make life easier. None of those messy entanglements that come from getting involved."

Jeremy shrugged. Kell had a bad attitude toward

women and it was understandable. He'd been raked over the coals by a first-class, gold-plated bitch.

"So who is she?"

"Isabella McNamara," Jeremy said. Kell leaned back against the wall. The fashion show was going on next door and this room was relatively quiet.

"Where did you find her?" Kell asked.

"Hiding." She'd been living in a small duplex in Fort Pierce. Not that many miles from Palm Beach, but a world away.

"Ah, so that's what you two have in common."

Jeremy punched Kell on the arm. "I'm not hiding, I'm waiting."

Kell glanced around the area. "In the corner?"

Jeremy shrugged.

"Why don't you tell Daniel to have a talk with Lucinda?"

"I have. He doesn't want to upset her."

"After seven years of marriage he shouldn't be so concerned about that."

Jeremy knew from observing Daniel with his wife that he loved Lucinda and he'd do anything to keep her happy. Frankly, Jeremy didn't understand Daniel and Lucinda's relationship. His own parents had been happiest apart. His father had always kept a mistress on the side and everyone had seemed pleased with that arrangement.

"She is beautiful," Kell said.

"Marianne? I'll tell Lucinda you *think* so."

"No, thanks. I meant your lady," Kell said, gesturing to Bella, who was walking slowly toward them. She glanced up, caught him watching her and smiled.

"Later."

"Later? Don't I get to meet her?"

"I'm taking her to the dance floor. I think three would be a crowd."

"I'll just cut in."

Jeremy glanced at his friend. "Why?"

"I want to meet her."

He knew from Kell's tone that he wanted to question her. "She's not like—"

"I'm sure she's not. I'll be good, I promise."

"Somehow I doubt that," Jeremy said under his breath.

He went to meet her, aware that Kell was only a few steps behind him. Jeremy cupped his hand under her elbow and drew her away from the fashion show into a third room where the DJ and dance floor were set up, ready for the party to spill over once the fashion show ended.

"I'm sorry if I kept you waiting," she said.

"No problem." He heard Kell chuckle behind him and suspected it was because he sounded like an idiot. What the hell was it about this woman that made his brain short circuit?

He'd dated beautiful women before, so it wasn't that. There was something else about her. The dress he'd selected was perfect for her. It was a summer cocktail dress with a slim-fitting skirt and a scoop neck.

"Hello, Isabella," Kell said, reaching past him and offering her his hand. "I'm Kell."

She took his hand. Kell lifted it to his lips, kissing the back of it and smirking at Jeremy while he did so.

Bella smiled at Kell and Jeremy felt his gut tighten. He knew she was his, and she knew it, too. But he still felt a twinge of jealousy.

"Let's dance," Jeremy said, drawing her away from Kell and tucking her up against his side.

Kell's laughter followed them as they walked away. Jeremy ignored it. He wanted to believe his reaction had absolutely nothing to do with jealousy. She was his mistress for six months, nothing more. He told himself that he only wanted to keep Bella from being hurt by Kell, who could be charming but would never be sincere.

"What was that about?" she asked, a different note in her voice. He glanced down at her and saw the smile lingering at her mouth. She was still nervous, but the exchange with Kell had relaxed her. She was teasing him.

"Kell's a goofball. Don't pay any attention to him," he said.

"You have a friend who's a goofball?"

"Unfortunately, I'm related to him."

"How?"

"Cousins. Our moms are sisters."

"Ah, so the crazy gene…"

He pulled her into his arms as the DJ played a slow song. "Skipped my branch of the family."

"Whatever you say."

He didn't say anything else, just pulled her closer in his arms. She relaxed against him, following his lead. They fit together perfectly.

He kept stroking his hand down her back, completely obliterating her thought process. She liked the strength in his arms. The way they felt wrapped around her.

For a minute Bella bought into the illusion of security that his arms offered. She closed her eyes and let the spicy scent of his aftershave fill each breath she took. The music was slow with a funky beat. With her eyes closed, she could let her worries and fears and the past years drop away.

She could just be Bella and pretend this was her teenage fantasy come to life. She thought she'd known all about Jeremy from her crush those many summers ago, but she was coming to realize there was so much more to the man.

She remembered seeing Kell back then. He and Jeremy were photo negatives of each other, both tall, one blond and outgoing, the other dark and dangerous.

More than once she'd wondered why Jeremy

had made his offer to her. What had he seen in her that had made him offer to help her?

Was it only sex, a desire for her to be his mistress?

She looked up and met his gaze. She was surprised that he was watching her. If he was pretending, then he was a better actor than she was. He held her and looked at her like she was his. His for more than six months and because of more than a contract. She knew it was an illusion, but she hoped to make it a reality.

"What?" he asked with a hint of tenderness in his voice.

"Uh…" She couldn't remember what she'd been about to say. She wrapped her arms around his shoulders, let her fingers caress the back of his neck. Held him. This was what she'd dreamed of for the last three years.

Bella realized that giving herself up to Jeremy freed her to just be herself.

He continued to stare down at her, making her wish she could remember what she'd been about to say. She started to worry that something was wrong with the way she looked. She resisted the urge to pat her hair. Oh, man, she hoped she didn't have a bit of spinach in her teeth or something like that. Something that marked her clearly as an outsider. This was the kind of event her mother had missed the most when they'd had to move out of the mansion and into that shabby apartment.

It was odd to Bella that she was actually attending this event and not working it as a caterer—or standing on the sidewalk with her mother, pretending they were window-shopping. A shiver of embarrassment crawled down her spine as she remembered arriving tonight and seeing Lucinda Cannon and friends spot her outside.

"Why me?" she asked, finally remembering what she'd wanted to say.

He brushed his finger down her cheek before he cupped her jaw. His hand enveloped the side of her face, his fingers caressing her neck. His gaze was compelling. She couldn't decipher what she saw in his eyes. He lowered his head until there was barely an inch of space between them.

"You're not like any other woman I know," he said.

That wasn't what she had wanted to hear. She didn't want to be so different that everyone could see it in a glance. She wanted to blend into the moneyed set that she'd partly grown up in. She wanted to forget that she'd ever been cast out and use Jeremy to find her place again. But that wasn't what she was doing tonight.

Instead she was enjoying his arms around her and wishing they were alone. Wishing for a minute that this entire night was real. Wishing he'd asked her because he cared for her, and not because she was going to be his mistress.

This was the very thing that woke her in the middle of the night. How was she going to make Jeremy fall for her? She knew she had to keep him from seeing that she wanted so much more than to be his mistress. Somehow, she had to seduce him into seeing her as more.

"I'm sure of that," she said at last. She *was* different from the other women in the room. She'd had to scrape and struggle to get back to this glitzy world. She doubted even Jeremy understood the toll those years had taken on her.

"I meant it as a compliment," he said, brushing his lips over hers. His lips were full and firm.

All night he'd been touching her. Accustoming her to his touch and taste. The feel of his body brushing against her.

He didn't push his tongue into her mouth, just pressed his lips lightly against hers. Someone cleared his throat, but Jeremy didn't pull away. He lifted his head slowly, caressing her face before he turned to face a man she didn't know.

"I see now why you're avoiding Marianne."

"Who's Marianne?" she asked, trying to calm her racing blood. She didn't like the fact he'd rattled her with that one brief touch of his lips on hers.

Jeremy kept his arm around her waist, but turned them toward the man who'd interrupted them. The music changed again to a more lively number and Jeremy led her off the dance floor.

"One of my wife's friends. I'm Daniel Posner," the man said, following close behind them.

"Isabella McNamara," she said.

"What do you want, Daniel?" Jeremy asked.

"To invite you and your date to join us at our table," he said, gesturing to a round of eight set near the dance floor.

Bella smiled over at the table until she recognized Lucinda Cannon. Her heart started racing and the blood drained from her face. She'd hoped to see Lucinda again, hoped to have the chance to meet her onetime friend as an equal once more. But she wasn't ready yet. It was too soon.

Daniel wrapped his arm around Lucinda as she approached. "This is my wife, Lucinda. Honey, this is Isabella McNamara."

"We know each other," Lucinda said.

Bella could only nod at Lucinda, not sure what to say or how to fill the awkward gap of silence that grew between all four of them.

She pulled away from Jeremy and then realized how cowardly that was. She wasn't at this event as part of the staff. Jeremy glanced down at her. She shook her head, afraid to open her mouth. Afraid she'd blurt out something she didn't want to say.

Jeremy took charge. "We'd love to join you, but we have a dinner reservation and have to leave now. Another time?"

"Certainly. Enjoy your dinner."

The look Lucinda gave Bella before she and Daniel walked away was haughty and telling. And the good feelings Bella had had about being back in this high-society world suddenly dissipated.

# Three

No one would ever call him a sensitive man, but even he could tell something was wrong when his date lost all color from her face. While they waited for the valet to bring his convertible Jaguar up, he watched Bella slowly sink deeper and deeper into herself. She wrapped her arms around her waist and kept her eyes down.

The June evening was hot and humid. He pulled Bella to his side and stepped away from the crowd waiting for their cars. She pulled away from him as soon as they were out of the crowd.

"Are you okay?"

"Yes," she said, but he knew she wasn't.

"You're pale as a ghost."

"Can't you just ignore it? I'll be back to normal in a minute."

"No, I can't ignore it. I didn't realize you knew Lucinda."

"Well, I do, and it's been years since I saw her…I thought I'd feel differently."

"How did you feel?"

"What are you, my shrink?"

"I'd like to think I'm your friend." Friend, he thought. Was that really what he wanted?

"I just expected it to be different."

"It?"

His car was brought up, but he signaled the valet that they'd be a minute more. The feeling of protectiveness was disturbing. He wanted to keep her in the safe box labeled *mistress*. He didn't want her upsets to affect him. Yet they did.

"Being back in that room was different," she said, her voice very soft.

He had the feeling she was talking more to herself than to him. For the first time he realized that he wanted more than Bella's body. He wanted her secrets, too.

"Different meaning better?" he asked.

"Not necessarily. I think I may have been feeling a bit vindictive when I imagined it."

He laughed at the way she said that. He already knew she wasn't all sweetness and light. He'd seen her temper and her sheer force of will, both of which she'd used to support herself and her brother.

He cupped her elbow and led her to his car. As he held the door for her and she slid into the seat, the skirt of her dress rose slightly on her thighs. He stared at her leg until she put her hand on the exposed skin and tugged the fabric down.

He closed the door and walked around the car, using the few seconds to regain his control. The entire mistress contract was supposed to enable him to control his feelings around her. Instead he had the feeling that it had backfired on him.

He saw Kell come outside just as he closed the car door. The expression on Kell's face wasn't a good one and he wondered what had happened after they'd left.

He lifted one eyebrow, a silent question to Kell: *Should he stay?* Kell shook his head and motioned that he'd call later.

Bella fixed her lipstick in the visor mirror and then turned toward him, putting her hand on his thigh.

He glanced at her. It was the first time she'd initiated contact. She scraped her fingernail over the fabric of his pants and he felt that touch echo all the way to his core.

"Thank you," she said.

He had no idea what she was thanking him for, but if she moved her hand a little bit higher she'd see how much he appreciated her touch. He shook his head, trying to clear it.

"For?"

She rubbed his leg one more time and then pulled her hand back. "For pretending you care."

He didn't like the way that sounded.

"I'm not pretending, Bella," he said, capturing her hand and putting it back on his leg. After tonight he hoped she'd have no doubts about how he felt toward her. "I've always cared for you."

She gave him a sideways look and stroked her finger up the inside of his thigh. "Most people don't consider lust caring."

She made him want to laugh at the wry way she said it. It was one of a hundred things about Bella that made him want to be around her. He knew she was scared of any intimacy between them, yet she played that down and treated the attraction with a frankness that was refreshingly honest.

"It's always been more than lust where you're concerned," he said, putting the car in gear and leaving Neiman Marcus behind. And that one crucial point disturbed him more than he thought it would. It was why he'd decided to ask her to be his mistress. His father said that the women who affected a man most deeply were the ones a man had to be careful of.

She said nothing as the miles passed. Then she turned off the radio and reached for his arm.

"Yes?"

"I'm sorry about that. When I'm not sure of myself I can be mean."

"You weren't mean."

"Yes I was. And you were really trying to be nice to me."

"So why did you have a self-confidence attack?"

"Lucinda Cannon," she said, and pulled her hand back to her own side of the car.

Bella knew she was ruining her image, but could only deal with so much at a time. She was losing control of the evening. Losing the perfect bubble that she'd managed to wrap herself in at the charity event.

Pretending she was someone else—a mysterious stranger who belonged—had helped. But one glimpse of Lucinda Cannon had brought her back to herself. Back to the girl who'd been sent home from the exclusive Swedish boarding school for failure to pay her tuition. Back to the girl whose mother had turned to her society friends for help and had volunteered her to clean the homes of people she'd once considered friends.

She could hear Lucinda's pitying words from long ago still echoing in her head. And she knew that this night wasn't about the past. This night was about establishing herself as Jeremy's mistress and securing her future so that she'd never have to endure pitying looks or charity again.

That was one of the reasons she'd signed the mistress contract. She couldn't stand the thought of taking charity from another person. She shook her head to clear it as Jeremy turned off the road and into the parking lot at the public beach.

"What are we doing here?" she asked, trying not to feel relieved that they weren't at a restaurant. She wasn't ready to face anyone, not even strangers. Her reaction to seeing Lucinda had left her raw and exposed and she had no idea how to pull her shell back around her.

Jeremy didn't say a word. He put down the windows and then the top of his car. The moon was only a sliver and stars were visible in the evening sky. It was still light enough to see.

The sound of the rolling waves hitting the shore filled the car as did the warm, ocean-scented breeze. She leaned her head back against the seat and closed her eyes, breathing in nature.

She focused internally as he fiddled with the radio. The mellow sound of the Dave Matthews Band flowed from the speakers. She loved the group and somehow wasn't surprised that Jeremy would know that. He was a thorough man. The kind who noticed details and remembered them.

"I think you need to mellow out," he said, shrugging out of his jacket and tossing it in the backseat. He loosened his tie and unbuttoned the top button of his shirt.

"Mellow out?" she asked. The words were incongruous with Jeremy. He personified hard work and drive. She'd heard his Blackberry beep a couple of times while they'd been driving, and at Neiman Marcus he'd excused himself twice to take calls from his office.

He slanted her a look as he slid his arm along the back of her seat, his hand came to rest on her shoulder. "It means relax."

She struggled to concentrate on what he was saying as his finger drew lazy circles on her upper arm. He turned toward her, his intense attention focused on her.

"I know what it means. I just didn't think you did," she said, knowing she was grasping at this conversation and trying to make something out of nothing. Anything to keep him from bringing up Lucinda again.

"Oh, honey, I know how to relax."

He was being sweet and she knew he'd deny it if she called him on it. Seeing this side of him made her believe that he could want her for more than six months. *This* was the man she could fall for, not the arrogant man who'd walked into her office this afternoon and told her that his mistresses wore what he provided.

She fingered the diamond choker at her neck. She was something he'd bought and paid for, like his fancy car with more gadgets than anything she owned. She was an accoutrement and she struggled to remember that he thought of her that way.

"Again with the lust thing."

The circles he was drawing on her arm got wider until the tip of his forefinger slipped under the strap of her dress, moving with slow sensual sweeps over her collarbone. "You're obsessed with making every conversation we have sexual."

No, she wasn't. She had just learned from dealing with men that they were easily led off topic when sex was introduced into the conversation. And hey, she was honest enough to admit that it was easier to resist him in the moonlight when she thought he was only after one thing.

"Isn't that what being a mistress is about?" she asked.

"I don't know. I suppose each woman has a different reason."

Somehow that made her feel a little better. "What about you? Why do you want a mistress?"

"My father was always happier with his mistresses than he was with my mother. I guess I just want to be happy. Does that make sense?"

"Yes," she said. More sense than she wanted it to.

Making Jeremy want more than six months with her was going to be harder than she'd first thought.

He left off caressing her arm and shoulder and traced the line of the choker. Her pulse sped up and the slow, steady rhythm of the music mirrored the beat of her heart.

She forgot about vindication and contracts. She forgot about wanting something that had been taken away from her too soon. She forgot about everything except the man sitting next to her.

The man filling her head with thoughts that she'd never had before. Thoughts of nighttime walks on the beach; thoughts of forever. The future had always been nebulous for her. As a young girl, the princess of her family, she'd awaited her future, sure that it would hold only more pampering and treasures. She'd never guessed that it could be such a harsh and cold place.

Despite what she might feel in this moment for Jeremy, she had to remember that the future wasn't a rosy, cheery place. The future, even one with him, would be filled with moments like the one she'd had tonight when she'd seen Lucinda. A moment that could make her stomach feel filled with lead.

"Don't think so much, honey."

"I can't help it."

"Yes, you can," he said, wrapping his arm around her and bending to kiss her. A sweet, gentle kiss….

Maybe the future wouldn't be so cold and harsh after all.

Jeremy's good intentions of relaxing Bella faded quickly when she melted in his arms. He held her loosely, trying to remember why he'd thought stopping at this very public spot would be a good idea.

He'd wanted to slow things down, to slow himself down and not rush his seduction. But at this moment, with her lips so tender under his, he couldn't recall why.

His cell phone rang again. Reluctantly he pulled away from Bella to glance at the caller ID. Kell. *Again.*

"I've got to take this."

She nodded and opened her door. "I'll give you some privacy."

He stopped her with his hand on her wrist. "Stay."

She sank back into the seat as he accepted the call.

"Kell, man, you know I'm on a date."

"I wanted to make sure you had all the information you needed."

"About?" he asked.

"Isabella."

He glanced over at the woman in question. She had her head tipped back against the headrest and her eyes closed. She tapped her fingers to the rhythm of the music playing. He had a sinking feeling in his gut that Kell wasn't calling to recommend Bella's event-planning company.

"And?"

Kell took a deep breath and Jeremy worried what his friend might have heard. "She's a gold digger, man. Lucinda remembers her. Don't be fooled by her designer gown or jewelry—she's penniless. And there's more you should know about her father."

Jeremy felt a twinge of guilt at the thought of his friends gossiping about them when they'd left. Talking about her gown and the jewelry that he'd insisted she wear. He had an inkling of understanding as to why Bella had blanched when she saw Lucinda. What had happened between those two?

"Thanks, I'll keep that in mind." Since they had a contractual arrangement, he wasn't too worried about any designs that Bella had on his money.

"You're still going to—"

"Do whatever I damn well please."

"It's your funeral."

"Thanks for the encouragement."

"Jeremy, I, uh, I just don't want to see you make the same mistake I did."

He knew that Kell didn't interfere unless he had a good reason. And Jeremy did appreciate his cousin looking out for him. Maybe he should set Kell straight on Bella. As soon as she wasn't sitting next to him. "Thanks, Kell. I won't. Are we still on for golf tomorrow?"

"Yeah," Kell said, and disconnected the call.

He tossed his phone into the center console and turned toward Bella. She opened her eyes and looked at him.

"Everything okay?" she asked, with a note of

caring in her voice that made him wonder yet again why she'd settle for a business relationship with him instead of a more personal one.

"Yes, fine."

"So what's next? Sorry about wigging out earlier. I'm not usually like that. You knocked me off balance by showing up out of the blue like you did."

He raised an eyebrow at her. "Glad to know that my plan worked."

She smiled. "You have a very devious mind."

"I'm a planner."

"Really? I'm more a reactor."

He had seen that firsthand. She seldom made plans for the long term. When he'd run into her three years ago, she'd been focused on getting Dare through college and hadn't thought beyond that. Even when making her business strategy, she seldom wanted to look more than six months ahead.

"I don't like to have to react. When you have a plan, you're in control."

She shook her head.

"You don't agree."

"Ah, sorry, but no. When you have a plan all you have is the illusion of control. You can't expect the unexpected."

"Like me coming to your office tonight."

"Exactly. I knew it was time to pay up, but thought I'd manage it from my end."

He'd meant to catch her off guard. When Bella

was prepared she was hard to read. She gave the scripted reactions to everything instead of letting him see a glimpse of the real woman. He'd only caught her by surprise twice, counting tonight. The first time, he'd kissed her—and offered to make her his mistress.

But then, her responses to him each time never failed to stagger him. He always built variables into his strategic plans for business and for his personal life, but she never responded the way he expected her to.

"We have two choices," he said.

"And they are?"

"We can still make our dinner reservation, or we can take a walk on the beach and then I'll take you home and cook for you."

"I'm not ready to be with other people right now," she said.

"Want to talk about it?"

"No. I'll deal with it."

"The way you always have," he said under his breath.

"What does that mean?"

"That you're too used to being on your own. I'm in your life now."

"For six months, Jeremy. When you're gone I'll be back where I started."

"I'm not gone yet."

"But you will be and I don't want to forget that."

"Until then I think we can have one hell of a ride, Bella."

She said nothing, and he wondered if this would be it. The moment when she decided that she'd had enough of him and his contract and walked away.

She sighed and put her hand on his thigh again. "I think I'd like for you to cook me dinner."

# Four

Jeremy's house was plush and sophisticated. The trappings of his family's legacy of wealth were everywhere. It reminded her at once of her childhood home and she felt a pang in her heart as they walked by the pool in the back of the house.

The smell of hibiscus was thick in the air. The meal he'd prepared had been simple and delicious and she savored the novelty of having a man cook for her. He'd offered her an after-dinner drink but she declined. This wasn't the time to do too much drinking and the wine she'd had with dinner was giving her a sweet buzz.

She was a little sleepy, but wasn't ready for this

night to end. It had been a tumultuous ride, but she was getting used to that. It seemed everything with Jeremy was unexpected.

"What are you thinking of?" he asked, quietly coming up behind her.

She bit her lower lip. Honesty had been her policy since she'd realized that lying hurt her more than the truth.

"You."

"Hmm, that sounds good."

"Maybe."

"Maybe? That's all I get?"

"Yes. You're too arrogant for your own good," she said, but her words lacked heat. Tonight she'd seen a different side to him. A side that wasn't entirely unexpected. She'd been telling him the truth in the car—she was a reactor. But this situation was difficult for her. She wasn't sure how to react.

Inside she battled with her physical responses to him as a woman and what her mind was telling her. She needed to find a way to balance honesty with self-preservation. Because if she responded to him in the way she truly felt, she was so afraid she'd lose part of herself—her heart.

It would be so easy to melt into this role. To stop worrying about the future and just let the next six months bump along according to his design. But at the end of that six months what would she have left? The same things she had now…unless she planted the seeds of the future with Jeremy.

"You're thinking again."

She smiled at him and hoped her expression didn't reveal the sadness that was tingeing this moment.

"Sorry." She didn't say more than that, afraid that she'd blurt out more than she wanted him to know.

"Don't be. I do have some papers for you to go over. I've leased a luxury townhome for you to live in and I set up some accounts for you."

"I don't need any of that," she said. He'd already mentioned that he would provide housing and accounts, but the last thing she wanted was to take anything else from Jeremy. And she needed her real life. Her small home and her friends. They were what kept her grounded.

"I have certain standards."

"Just because I'm not in your financial tax bracket doesn't mean I live in a dump." To be fair, there was a time when it would have meant exactly that. But the last three years had been good to her and her business. She didn't live in the most prestigious neighborhood, like he did. But she lived in a nice area. A comfortable, middle-class neighborhood where people genuinely cared for each other, and not because of their social status or connections.

"I wasn't implying you lived in a dump."

Had she overreacted? She had no idea. Suddenly she wanted this night to end. She wanted to be back in her nice, safe little home, tucked under the quilt that used to grace her parents' bed, hidden away from the world so she could regroup.

"I can't put my life on hold for six months," she said, rubbing the back of her neck. This was the part she'd never been able to imagine when she'd thought of their contract. The part that made this temporary business arrangement all too real.

"I'm not asking you to." He brushed her hand aside and massaged the back of her neck and shoulders. His touch was just right, strong and firm.

Chills spread down her neck and arms. Her breasts felt fuller. Even though his touch wasn't sexual, she wanted it to be. She wanted more of the passion-filled kisses that had punctuated the last three years of her life.

"Relax, Bella. This is going to work out the way we both envision it," he said.

He slid his hands down her arms and drew her back against his body. His breath stirred the hair at the nape of her neck. She was completely surrounded by him and sank back against his tall, lean frame.

Why did he sound so reasonable? He was making her feel like she was being difficult, and that had never been her intention. She needed to be up front about what limitations she wanted on the relationship.

But she couldn't do it while she was in his arms.

Taking a deep breath, she stepped away from him, turning to face him. "I need to stay in my home. I'll be available for you on evenings and weekends. There will be some nights when I have to work, but I can come over here or even to that townhome if you want all of our sexual encounters to take place there."

"Sexual encounters."

"Aren't those the words you used in the contract we both signed?"

He closed the distance she'd put between them in one long stride. She couldn't help taking a step backward. Gone was the soft, tender lover. She couldn't really tell what he felt at this moment, but she suspected it was close to anger. She thought her blunt summation of their relationship might have been too baldly stated.

He'd let things get out of control in an effort to relax her and perhaps to make up for the encounter with Lucinda. But letting her boil down what was between them to nothing more than sexual encounters left a bad taste in his mouth, no matter that it was the truth.

From the very beginning the attraction between them had been electric. He couldn't explain it any other way. He knew that real sexual chemistry was rare. He had experienced it to lesser degrees with other women he'd dated, but from the first instant he'd seen her, his entire body had gone on high alert.

She'd been too thin and too tired to be interested in any advances he made, but she'd still responded. Responded and turned him down with regret because she had a teenage brother at home for whom she was responsible.

That had been part of the attraction, he admitted. Her total selflessness where her brother was concerned. He didn't have one acquaintance who would have done the same, except Kell. Kell would sacrifice himself for Jeremy, and Jeremy would do the same for his cousin.

But never for the women he'd been involved with. He'd thought perhaps that novel situation had been the driving factor in the attraction. He could have walked away from her—hell, who was he kidding? Walking away was never something he'd considered.

When he saw something he wanted, he went after it until he made it his own. And he was going to make her his. Completely his, no matter what she thought or how she tried to manage him and their time together. *Sexual encounters* was too tame a term to describe what he intended between them.

She bit her lower lip and he groaned out loud. Her mouth was full and lush and beckoned him like nothing else ever had.

He caught her hips in his hands and pulled her

toward him. Her eyes widened and she inhaled sharply but she didn't resist him.

"We're going to have more than sexual encounters, Bella."

"We are?"

"Yes," he said, lowering his head to hers. He dropped nibbling kisses along her brow and then slowly found her lips with his. All night long he'd kept a tight rein on his desire to devour her mouth. He knew how it tasted, always thought it couldn't be as lush and welcoming as he remembered. Yet it always was.

Her hands found his shoulders and she clung to him as he traced the seam of her lips with his tongue.

There had been something of a challenge in those words she'd uttered. And he didn't know if he *would be able* to prove her right or wrong. Part of him—the hard, hungry part of him—wanted sex. Craved the feel of her silky limbs against his.

There was a spark of wildness in her eyes that called to him. Her hands clasped his shoulders, making him feel like the strongest man in the world. He tilted his head to the side and plundered her mouth.

If she wanted this, then he'd be happy to oblige. He'd seduce her into his bed and use her until the passion between them ran its course and then send her on her way. She'd fulfill her promise to him and he'd have…he'd have Bella for a short time.

She tasted of some essence of woman that he was coming to associate only with her. She moaned deep in her throat as he thrust his tongue into her mouth. Her tongue stroked tentatively against his.

Sliding his hands down her back, he cupped her hips and pulled her more firmly against his body. He'd meant to keep the embrace light, but Bella made it too easy to forget his intentions.

He rubbed his growing erection against her and she made another soft sound in the back of her throat. Her nails dug into his shoulders through the layer of his shirt. She undulated against him.

He lifted his head. Her eyes were closed and her face was flushed with desire. He knew that it would take very little for him to persuade her to have sex with him, but with a few words she'd made him want her to admit there was more than sex between them.

He traced a path down the side of her neck to the choker he'd given her. He wanted to see her wearing just that and the moonlight. The image almost brought him to his knees.

He didn't know if she'd meant to remind him or herself with those words. Part of him wanted to just take what he needed. Show her how it would be if he really did just use her for sex.

But then her eyes opened and she looked at him and did something no woman had ever done before. Bella cupped his face and stood on tiptoe, touching her lips to his and whispering his name.

His heart beat too quickly in his chest and the lust that had taken control of his body abated as fear slowly crept through him. He wanted her more than he should.

He let his hands fall away from her body and turned on his heel, heading back up to the house. Once inside, he went to the wet bar and mixed himself a drink.

How had the evening gotten so out of control? Bella stayed on the patio for a few extra minutes, trying to gather her senses and make some kind of plan to get safely out the door without throwing herself into Jeremy's arms.

His arms around her always felt so right. She shook her head, refusing to dwell on that. They needed to come to a compromise about their living arrangements for the next six months. She'd angered him with her summation of their relationship and she couldn't blame him.

Half the time she said things just to get a rise out of him. As she belatedly followed him into the house, she smiled to herself. She'd gotten more than one kind of rise out of him just now.

"What's so funny?"

"Oh, it was kind of an inside joke."

He waited, highball glass in one hand, hip cocked. He looked so virile and masculine standing there in the dim light provided by the wall sconces.

He took her breath away with the way he moved. And his contradictions. Why couldn't he have stuck to ordering her around?

She could resist Jeremy all day long when he was arrogant, but as soon as she felt his arms around her she was lost. Or was she found? She'd been lost for so long that she'd almost accepted it as the norm. But then he reminded her that there were still things she wanted in the world that had nothing to do with money, status or business success.

"You might not think it's funny."

"Try me," he said, knocking back his drink.

"Um…I was just thinking that I said what I did to get a rise out of you…"

He gave her a wry grin, but didn't move from the doorway.

"I'm sorry about what I said earlier. I should try to remember what Shelley advised."

"Your assistant?"

"She's more than just an employee, she's a friend."

"What did she say?"

"To enjoy you," she said.

"Tell me more."

She shook her head. "I don't want to talk about my friends," she said quietly, reluctant to reveal more than she had.

"Me either."

She took a few steps closer to him. They had to

come to some kind of compromise. "I kind of want to have things my way on everything."

"Yeah, I can understand that. I've been dealing with people for a long time. And I've learned that having everything in a contract is the only way to keep all sides from getting upset."

It sounded so cold, hearing him talk about sleeping with her the same way he'd approach a deal he brokered. Guard your heart, Bella, she thought. This man could hurt you.

"I've never been a mistress before. And I haven't experienced relationships the way you have. Most of the people I deal with are good on their word."

"What if they aren't?"

"Then I'm disappointed in them."

"With a contract there's no room for disappointment."

"Do you realize how cold that sounds?" she said before she could help herself. Her doubts were circling back to her.

He shrugged a shoulder and turned to the bar, pouring himself another mixed drink. "Can I get you something?"

She shook her head. She knew how Alice must have felt when she'd stumbled down the rabbit hole. Bella only wished there'd been a talking white rabbit to alert her that she was now in an alternate universe.

"Where are the papers you had for me to look at?"

"On the table," he said, gesturing with his glass toward the dining room.

The dining room was bigger than the master bedroom in her current house and recalled images of the one from her childhood. She remembered playing on hardwood floors just like this, sock-skating around the table while her mother sang in her beautiful contralto voice.

Oh, man. What was she doing here? No matter how many times she asked the question, she still hadn't found the answer she was looking for.

There was a manila file folder with her name written across it. She drew out a chair and sat down, opening the folder. Inside was an addendum to the contract she'd already signed. It listed the start and end dates for their relationship.

He had been thorough and very generous. The accounts he'd set up would last only as long as their relationship did, but the annuity he was providing for her for the six months would continue. He wouldn't be adding money into it, but by the terms and stipulations she read, he'd given her a cushion that would ensure she'd never again have to leave her house in the middle of the night one step ahead of the creditors.

She struck out the clause about the townhome, but left the accounts with the stipulation that they be paid from the annuity. She didn't want to take any more than was absolutely necessary. She changed the start and end dates by one day because she couldn't start tonight.

And hoped he'd understand. She added one addendum of her own and then initialed her changes and signed her name.

She glanced up to where he waited in the doorway and pushed the papers across the table toward him. "I made a few changes."

He walked into the room, glanced at the changes and initialed all of them, including the clause she'd added, without any questions. "I'll have my driver see you home. And I'll pick you up tomorrow night around eight."

"I'll be at an event. I'll send the address to your secretary in the morning."

He nodded. The emotionless set of his face and his dispassionate eyes made her feel cold. She stood, rubbing her hands up and down her arms.

He cursed under his breath, closing the distance between them in two long strides. He pulled her into his arms and kissed her. Not a tentative meeting of the mouths, but the kind of kiss that went beyond the barriers of two people attracted to each other and straight to the souls of two lonely people.

In his kiss she felt a desperation that echoed what was inside her. She wrapped her arms around his waist and held on to him like she'd never let go. Only she knew, deep inside, that she never wanted to.

# Five

Jeremy checked his watch for the second time, realizing that Bella was late. He got out of his car, leaving the keys with the valet, and entered the Norton Museum of Art in West Palm Beach.

"Sorry," Bella said, hurrying over to him. She wore a blue crepe dress that ended just above her knees and she had her hair pulled back in a professional-looking twist. She smiled at him but he could tell she was harried.

"Is something wrong?"

"Just horribly short-staffed. I'm going to be at least forty-five more minutes. If you want to go ahead to the restaurant I can meet you at the bar there."

Drinking alone had never appealed to him. Especially when Bella waited somewhere else. Thoughts of her had crept into his mind throughout the day until Daniel had text-messaged him to get his head in the game. It was the first time he could recall a woman interfering with his business and he didn't like it.

"No."

She put her hand on his wrist. Her slim, cool fingers rested right above the Swiss Army watch that his dad had given him. The watch was a constant reminder of his old man.

"I really can't leave right now, Jeremy."

He twisted his hand around to capture hers, rubbing his thumb over the back of her knuckles. "I'll come with you. Putting out fires is my specialty."

She didn't pull her hand free as she led the way back down the hallway to the theater room in the museum.

"It is? You don't look like a firefighter."

"Well, there's more than one kind of fire."

"I know that," she said under her breath.

"Are you feeling a few flames?"

"Don't even start. Twice today I—"

He pulled them to a stop in the doorway leading toward the service corridor when she didn't go on. "What?"

She shook her head. "I really need to go back to the ballroom."

"Then tell me what you were going to say."

She nibbled on her lower lip, a gesture that never failed to make him want to kiss her.

"Just that twice today I called one of our staffers by your name."

"Does he look like me?"

"Not at all. I was just—" She pulled away from him. "Don't let this go to your head, but you were on my mind."

How could he not? He tugged her back toward the main hallway. "Let's get your problems solved so we can go somewhere private. Then you can tell me all the details."

"I don't need you to solve my problems."

"I know that. It's just that I'm rather effective at it."

"Really? What's the most effective way?" she asked, tipping her head to the side in a flirtatious gesture. "I've never had a billionaire businessman give me advice on managing my workforce before."

"Keep being sassy and you still won't."

"Sassy?"

"Sassy."

"Hmm…no one's ever called me that before. Is that the key to keeping the staff in line?"

"Intimidation is. You scare the bejeezus out of your staff and then they work more efficiently."

She laughed, just like he hoped she would. "I'm not very intimidating."

"Have you ever tried to be?" he asked. He

doubted she had. There was an innate goodness that surrounded Bella. He suspected that was part of what had originally drawn him to her. Despite the fact that she'd been down on her luck, she'd still been looking out for those around her instead of just focusing on herself.

"Well, no. That's not my style, really. Even when Dare was rebelling and I knew I should be tough on him, I couldn't." In her voice he heard the echoes of what he'd heard that night three years ago when they'd struck their deal. Her doubts in herself and her abilities to pull her brother back from the edge.

He let go of her hand, sliding his arm around her waist and drawing her into his side. She held her body stiff until he stroked his free hand down her spine. Then she relaxed against him.

"He respects you," she said quietly.

"He admires you," Jeremy said. He didn't know how he'd become a father-confessor to Dare McNamara, but somehow he had. The young man e-mailed him a couple times a week and called every few days to check in.

Jeremy knew part of it was that Dare expected him to keep an eye on Isabella. Her brother wanted to make sure she was looked after. And as Dare said, he wasn't man enough to do it yet.

Since taking care of Bella played into his plans, that was an easy enough promise to give Dare. Sometimes he had a few qualms about how Dare would feel if he knew the nature of the relationship between him and Bella, but that was no one else's business.

"I really don't have time to be talking about my brother or leaning on you."

"What do we need to do?"

"The florist dumped the arrangements in the kitchen and I need someone to place one on each round table."

"Um…"

"Come on, Jeremy. It'll be good for you. It'll build character and earn you my gratitude."

"That's all well and good but I want more than gratitude."

"Help me out and I'll give you whatever you ask for."

"Deal," he said, holding open the door to the convention space and entering Bella's world. He watched her direct her staff and realized he respected the way she worked. She didn't micromanage anyone—just expected them to do the job they'd been assigned. And he noticed that everyone worked harder when she was around them. Not because they were afraid of her, he suspected, but to bask in the glow of her smile and the praise that accompanied it.

He told himself he wasn't the same as these workers. That he was here to collect the woman who was contractually bound to him. But when she glanced at the finished tables and smiled at him, he felt something stir inside him.

Something that had nothing to do with lust. Something that wasn't bound by a contract. Something he hoped like hell was going to go away when his time with Bella was up.

"I'm so glad you're here," she said.

He walked away without saying a word because he wasn't too sure that *he* was happy. He'd wanted Bella and gone after her with the single-minded determination he went after anything he wanted, and was only now realizing that getting her might not be his smartest business decision.

She'd expected Jeremy to whisk her out of the museum and to a private place where they'd be intimate. But when the bar association members started to arrive, some acquaintances of his were in the group. He signaled her to join him but she shook her head and motioned that she'd be a few minutes.

Every time she was in his presence he knocked her a little further off-kilter. She pulled her cell phone from her pocket to check the time and pretend she was busy instead of going to his side. She wasn't ready to be at his side. Not now. She needed a reality check. The kind that focusing on the details of her job could deliver.

"There you are," Shelley said, coming up behind her. She had a clipboard in one hand and a radio in the other. She looked like a staffer, unlike Bella, who was dressed for her date with Jeremy. She realized that she was right where she'd never wanted to be. Right on the cusp of two worlds. Her two worlds.

Her two lives. The one she'd once had and dreamed of getting back. And this one, the one she'd built from the wreckage.

"Please don't give me bad news," she said when Shelley reached her side.

The blonde had her hair pulled back in a ponytail and her button-down, oxford shirt open at the collar. She looked young but competent. "Geez. Is that my rep now?"

"Well you did keep coming to find me with another challenge to report."

"Challenge…I like that. I'm going to use it the next time my boyfriend says I'm too much work."

Shelley was a dear, sweet person who didn't have a mean bone in her body. And her boyfriend took advantage of that. "Did you need something?"

"Yes. I'm playing delivery girl again." She reached into her pocket and pulled out a small envelope. One that the florist had inadvertently put in the arrangements. That had been one of the first challenges of the day—removing all those picks with the blank cards in them.

Her name was written across the back of the cream-colored envelope. "Thanks, Shelley."

"No problem. He's very romantic."

Bella had no idea how to respond to that. "We need to double-check the jackets on the waitstaff. I don't want anyone going out there with stains."

"I'll double-check. You need to leave."

"Are you sure?" she asked. Her duty manager had been involved in a car accident, so there was no senior person at the event. Bella had toyed with canceling on Jeremy, but Shelley had made a bid to be in charge, wanting to use this event to prove herself.

Shelley rolled her eyes. "Yes."

"You've got my cell number, right?"

Shelley shook her head, reached over and took the museum radio from her hand. "You're being challenging."

Bella laughed. "You're right. Sorry about that. I'll see you in the morning."

"Have fun tonight," Shelley said as she walked away.

Bella left the theater and went in the back to collect her purse. She'd left her car at the office since Jeremy had said he'd pick her up.

She lifted the back flap and stared down at the card inside. She pulled it out. It was a cheap generic one, the kind that florists used for bulk arrangements.

On it was simply a phone number. This was what Shelley had thought was romantic?

What had she expected? Some kind of love note?

She was his mistress, not a woman he was seducing. She was a sure thing. And she was beginning to realize she had absolutely no idea how to convince him she should be more than a mistress.

She dialed it, a little disappointed. And mad at herself for being upset. She had no claims to Jeremy other than those he'd laid out in writing. Why had she forgotten that?

"Harper."

"It's Bella," she said, moving away from the convention food and beverage staff, who were making a lot of noise as they readied all the dishes to go out to the tables at one time.

"Are you free now?" he asked.

"Yes. I'm all yours."

"Mine? Not quite."

"What do you mean?"

"Why didn't you join me earlier?"

"I had some stuff to finish up."

"Stuff? That sounds like an excuse. You're my mistress, Bella. That means that when we are together—"

"I'm working tonight, Jeremy. That's my first priority."

"Why?"

"Why what?" she asked, stalling. She really had to figure out how to filter every thought that came into her head so that they didn't all end up coming out of her mouth.

"Are we going to play this kind of game?"

"You started it," she said.

She hated that he'd called her on avoiding him. She was nervous again, and that was beginning to bother her. Why hadn't she figured him out yet? Normally it took her maybe two meetings with a person to decide how to deal with them. But with him...

She sighed. "I'm sorry. I was being sarcastic and it was uncalled for."

"Bella, what am I going to do with you?"

"Anything your contract gives you the right to."

He said nothing for a long moment and she heard the head of the Palm Beach Bar Association get up and start talking.

"I'll meet you in the Tsai atrium and we can start our night."

"Okay."

She hung up before he had a chance to say anything else. No more nerves. She'd promised herself that this morning. She wanted more from Jeremy than six months and she wasn't going to get that by hiding.

Seeing her tonight with her staff and the way she'd treated him when they were with other people showed him that she was still nervous about any intimacy between them. And he knew the quickest way to push past it was through seduction.

He had been to many events at the Norton during his lifetime and knew the museum like the back of his hand. He'd attended most of the events with one of his parents. Never the two of them together. They were happier apart, something his father had explained to Jeremy when he'd turned nine.

That talk about marriage and relationships had been diverted by a few innocent questions about sex. Because nine-year-old Jeremy hadn't been too sure that Kell had known what he was talking about when he said that a boy's penis had to get hard before he could have sex.

The sex part…well, his dad had firm opinions about it. He'd said that women saw sex as more than just a physical release. That a gentleman didn't marry for sex, he had mistresses for sex. And that when a man found the right woman, sex was an incredible thing.

Bella stood in the center of the now empty atrium on the cracked ice terrazzo floor. Remembering his father's advice about women and sex made him realize that he wanted Bella to be different. To somehow be the kind of woman that Lucinda must be for Daniel to still be so into her.

But he was afraid to take the risk of caring for her. He would likely only confirm that he was essentially his father's son. After all, he was definitely his father's progeny in the business world. Making money and turning a profit was something that came easily to him. As did the women…and there had never been anyone he wanted to marry.

And now, there Bella stood, her dress so close to the same deep blue as the tiles that she looked like part of the decor. An ethereal woman that he could only glimpse. He hated that. For most of his life he'd struggled with trying to hold on to people in his life. He didn't have a lot of lasting relationships.

The heels of his Italian loafers made a soft sound as he approached and she pivoted to face him. He hesitated there, unable to move toward her. Feeling once again that punch in the gut. She was more beautiful than any woman he'd ever seen.

He walked up to her and had to fight the urge to put his arms around her. She was a mistress. His mistress. *His.*

That word resonated inside him. He knew it wasn't politically correct but it suited him to claim her even if only in his own mind. There was something soothing about knowing exactly what to expect from another person.

She turned to look at him. "I love this place. It's so soothing and quiet at night."

"Then you're going to love the surprise I have planned for you."

"Love it?"

There was skepticism in her voice, but he wasn't daunted. Now that he had a plan, he was back on his game. Seduction was the key to wooing her and having her.

"Wait and see."

He took her hand in his and led her to a small, wedge-shaped room off the atrium. The J. Ira and Nick Harris Family Pavilion. There was a small table set in the middle of the room in front of the glass doors that led to the Italian gardens outside.

But it was the ceiling that made the room. The Chihuly glass was spectacular and Jeremy knew he'd made the right decision when he heard her breath catch.

Her hand fell away from his and she walked farther into the room. The lighting behind the Chihuly ceiling painted the room in hues of aquatic blues and greens.

"Jeremy…this is lovely. Are we having dinner here?"

"Yes," he said, crossing to the freestanding ice-bucket to pour them both a glass of champagne.

"This is…okay, I do love it."

"What did I tell you?"

"You're doing the arrogance thing again."

"In this case I think I've earned the right."

"Okay, I'll give you that."

He handed her the champagne flute and then tipped his glass to hers. "To the next six months."

She nodded and took a delicate sip of her drink, keeping eye contact with him the entire time. But he saw her hand tremble as she lifted the glass to her lips.

She put her glass on the table and walked slowly around the room, observing the ceiling from every angle. When she came back to the table, he signaled to the waitstaff to begin serving their meal.

He held her chair, seating her. When he pulled his own chair out he saw the small gift box he'd asked to be put there.

He picked it up and placed it on the table.

She glanced at the gift box and then back up at him. He couldn't read the expression in her usually expressive eyes.

"You don't have to seduce me," she said carefully.

"That's my privilege."

"Oh."

"Yes, oh." He handed her the package and watched as she held it carefully between her fingers.

"I'd rather you make a donation to charity than keep giving me gifts."

He shook his head. "Mistresses should take as many gifts from their lovers as possible."

He'd hurt her. He could see it in the way she subtly flinched and sank back in her chair. She let the small present fall to the table.

He felt like an ass. He'd been on his game just a few moments earlier. Why had he said that? It shouldn't matter to him if she didn't want his gifts—and yet it did. She was already blurring the lines between mistress and…girlfriend.

"Just open the present, Bella."

She removed the ribbon and the wrapping and then opened the box. Inside was a small placard that showed a Chihuly sculpture he'd ordered for her. It would be delivered in three weeks time.

"Thank you, Jeremy."

He shrugged like it meant nothing to him, but it was too late to pretend with himself. His gut-deep confirmation earlier that she was his made that impossible. He could only fall back on the contract they had between them. Hope that six months of holding her would be enough.

After they ate, he took her on a moonlit stroll through the Renaissance-inspired gardens and then led the way back to his car.

She'd relaxed during the walk but his tension had increased. He wanted her. And that seemed more dangerous now then it had at the beginning of the evening when he'd felt safe and protected by his contract. He could have everything he wanted from her. But now he knew that their arrangement wasn't going to protect him from the emotions that she brought swirling to the surface.

# Six

Bella had no idea where they were going as they flew down the highway. The top was down on Jeremy's convertible and the breeze made it impossible to talk, which was something of a relief.

Tonight had made her feel every inch the pampered woman of a wealthy man. There was something very attractive to her about being Jeremy's mistress. The problem was that the glimpses she'd seen of the possessive man Jeremy was made her want him for more than a temporary affair.

She hoped they weren't headed for the town house he'd leased. Suddenly, she thought of it as a test for him. If he took her to the townhome, then she'd know she hadn't made any progress in getting him to see her as more than a mistress. But it wouldn't make it any easier for her to remember that this was an arrangement and not a real love affair.

But damn it all, it was starting to feel that way. He should have just taken her to dinner instead of going out of his way to have a meal catered for them. And she knew the Norton's convention policy—they had minimums like everyone else. He must have spent a fortune on dinner.

Money wasn't an issue for Jeremy. She should have remembered that. Maybe the evening was nothing more than a convenience. Maybe what she'd interpreted as a romantic gesture was just the way he operated.

She didn't think so. The Chihuly glass sculpture was breathtaking, even in a picture. She wanted to take the card out of her purse and look at it again. But she didn't.

As they neared town, she glanced over at him. His attention stayed focused on the road and she noticed that he handled the car with ease. Not surprising. He did everything with ease.

He slowed even further and pulled into the parking lot of the Palm Beach hotel. The hotel was old and refined, a grande dame in the area. It was known for luxury and quality.

*Please don't let this be where he is taking me,* she

thought. She didn't want the first time they made love to be in a hotel. She wanted it to be in a place that meant something to one of them.

As he neared the valet parking station, she reached over and put her hand on his thigh. "What are we doing here?"

"Meeting some business associates for a drink."

More time spent waiting. The tension that had been riding her for the last two days—heck, to be honest, the last three years—tightened painfully inside her. She knew that Daniel Posner was his business partner. And Lucinda Cannon was Daniel's wife. She wasn't ready for another meeting with either of them.

She didn't want to add another nerve-inducing element to the evening, and talking to his business associates wasn't going to relax her. But she'd never say that to him. She owed him. He'd spent an insane amount of money on her already and she hadn't done anything other than kiss him.

"Is that okay?" he asked, looking pointedly down at his leg.

She was digging her nails into his thigh. "Of course."

She hastily removed her hand, putting it back in her lap. Oh, my God, this was getting out of control. Why had she ever thought she could do this? Because she'd been desperate. And desperation was the creator of opportunity.

It didn't feel like opportunity right now, as she looked at the beautiful hotel entrance. A place where she'd once attended cotillion dances and afternoon teas with her mother's circle of friends. She'd taken tennis lessons from a Wimbledon champion at this hotel. And played golf with her father a lifetime ago.

"Who are we meeting?"

"My partner and his wife, plus a very important client, and his wife."

"Daniel?"

"Yes. Is that a problem?" he asked.

She shrugged, determined to play it cool this evening. She refused to give Lucinda the power of unnerving her, though her sweaty palms said the other woman already had done so.

"Not at all. Who's the client?" she asked. This might be the perfect opportunity for her to show him that she'd make a better wife than mistress. The kind of woman he'd want by his side in business and pleasure.

"Frederick Merriweather. We've been trying to convince him to merge with our company."

"And tonight is another attempt?"

Jeremy pulled the car to the side of the driveway and stopped. "Yes, it is. I'm glad to see that you're so interested in this meeting."

"Why?"

He shrugged.

She waited. But he didn't say anything else. She started to feel small and insignificant. And very much, she realized, like a mistress.

She turned her head away from him. She didn't want to play games. Games were their own form of lying. And she had played enough of them when her mom was alive.

*Let's pretend we don't see the Cannons or the Fell-Murrays or anyone else we used to know.*

"Just tell me why, Jeremy."

He reached across the space in the car, fingers on her cheek. "Because it's the first interest you've shown in something for me."

Didn't he realize she paid attention to every detail that was his life? It was probably a good thing that he didn't, at least not yet. But she took as a good sign that he wanted her attention. "Then tell me what you need me to do. I'm pretty good at putting people at ease."

"Just be yourself," he said.

He cupped his fingers around the back of her head and drew her steadily toward him. In his eyes she saw the light of something more than desire.

It made her want to trust him, she thought. But then his head bent toward hers and everything in her body tensed in awareness and need. Her blood flowed heavier in her veins. Her breasts felt fuller and her lips tingled. She started to close her eyes but then kept them open.

She wanted to know how he felt when he kissed her. Did he reveal anything? She noticed the tiny gold flecks in his light green-gray eyes. She noticed the way his pupils had dilated and his nostrils flared right before she felt his mouth on hers.

She closed her eyes then. It was impossible to think of anything other than Jeremy when his mouth touched hers. The details of their deal dropped away as she created new memories of this man.

Of the way his hands moved over her skin like he was trying to learn her by feel. The way his tongue conquered her mouth with languid thrusts as if he had all night to learn the taste of it. The way he rubbed his thumb over her moist lips and then held her hand as he drove to the entrance of the hotel.

When he put his hand low on her back and escorted her into the hotel, she no longer felt like an outsider.

The bar was crowded, but Jeremy found Daniel and Frederick with no trouble. He wanted this meeting to go smoothly and quickly so he could hustle Bella home. And then take her to bed. He'd set up the meeting to put Bella more at ease in his world, part of his deal with her.

But his body was tight and his mind was only on the woman at his side, not the upcoming meeting. He'd been a little rattled when she'd asked him what he needed of her. He didn't want to analyze it, yet the words kept circling around in his head. He needed her there because the other men would have their wives and it would keep the party even.

There was a sense of rightness in having her by his side. But he knew that it was a mistake to feel possessive about her. He wasn't a man who kept things. He prided himself on looking to the future. On moving through life unencumbered.

Bella was just one more pleasure to be enjoyed as he moved forward. Once he had her silky body under his and he claimed her, had her, he could move on.

That elusive thing about her would be realized and she'd become like every other woman he'd had a relationship with. Just another mistress.

Frederick was an older man in his late forties with a leonine mane of blond hair that made him look like an aging hippie. He wore a Brooks Brothers suit and a pinky ring. Frederick was a self-made man who didn't care what anyone thought about the way he and his wife dressed.

"Evening, Frederick. Where's Mary?"

"She saw something in the window of the boutique that she had to have. Who is this?"

"Bella McNamara. Bella, this is Frederick Merriweather."

"It's nice to meet you, Frederick," Bella said.

Jeremy nodded toward Daniel. "And I'm sure you remember my partner, Daniel Posner."

"Yes. Good to see you again, Daniel."

They shook hands and then Jeremy seated Bella at the table.

"You'll have to go to the bar if you want a drink," Daniel said.

"What would you like?" he asked Bella.

"Drambuie, please," she said.

He made his way to the bar to get their drinks.

"She doesn't look the way she used to."

Jeremy glanced over to see Lucinda standing next to him. Lucinda was one of the most beautiful women he'd ever met. She had classically good looks and she'd been raised in a moneyed world that showed in every graceful movement she made.

His family had socialized with hers, but he'd never noticed her as a child or teenager. In fact, until Daniel had started dating her, he'd never paid much attention to her.

"What did she look like?"

"At fourteen?"

He nodded. God, he hadn't realized how young she'd been when her world had fallen apart.

"More like me. Manicured, pedicured and hair chemically perfect."

He smiled at the faint mocking tone in Lucinda's voice. "Circumstances change."

"Yes, they do," Lucinda said.

"What are you trying to tell me?"

"I'm not sure. Her family and mine were once very close…"

Jeremy had done some Internet research on Bella and had read the AP newswire accounts of her father's fall and consequent suicide. And then just a tiny article when her mother died a few short years later. But there were details of her life that he couldn't fill in. How did a girl who was a princess turn into the single-mother type she'd been when he met her? True, it was her brother she'd been raising, but...

"When did you lose touch?" he asked, prying the way he would if this were a business deal. He'd never expected to glean information from Lucinda, whom he thought of usually as someone to be avoided since she was always trying to foist her single friends on him.

She shrugged and bit her lower lip. "When she stopped moving in our circle. She's not like us anymore, Jeremy."

He wasn't sure where she was going with this conversation, but had an inkling of why Bella had been so upset when she'd seen Lucinda the other night.

"Just spit it out. I'm not good at guessing games."

"No, you're not. That's why you need Daniel."

"In business I do need him and the subtle way he has of smoothing over my rough edges, but that still doesn't tell me about Bella and you."

"When she lost everything, she became a different person. She wasn't the girl she used to be, and to be honest I'm not sure that she isn't dating you for some kind of revenge."

"I don't understand."

"She means I wasn't suitable to speak to any longer."

He hadn't heard Bella come up to them. Lucinda shrugged delicately and stepped away from them. She stopped a few steps away to look back at Bella, and there was tension between the women that went beyond not talking to one another.

"Well, you and I both know that we don't socialize with the staff."

Bella froze. He wrapped his arm around her shoulder and pulled her solidly against him. She put her hand on his lapel and he felt the fine tremors in her body.

"Bella's not the staff any longer, Lucinda."

"Of course she isn't. She's your…what exactly is she, Jeremy?"

Bella cleared her throat and he saw a flash of her temper. That same temper that she always tried to hide. "None of your business, Lucinda. We're not friends any longer."

"And whose fault is that?"

"Assigning blame is a juvenile thing to do," Bella said in a small voice.

He had the feeling that there was much more between the two women than a change in Bella's financial circumstances. And though he was curious, he knew it was past time to put an end to this.

"We need to get back to the table. We're here for a business meeting."

"Of course," Lucinda said and made her way to Daniel's side.

He handed Bella her Drambuie. "Want to talk about it?"

She shook her head.

He couldn't stand the hurt in her eyes and wanted to do whatever he could to soothe it—to soothe her. "Bella—"

"Leave it, Jeremy. I'm not your girlfriend. I'm your mistress."

Her words struck him like a barb. And this was why he didn't want to allow her any closer than he had to.

"That's right. You are."

They didn't talk much on the car ride back to his place and Bella was glad of it. She had no idea how to make amends for her stupid comments. Once again she'd allowed Lucinda to get the better of her and to threaten a relationship that was coming to mean a lot to her.

She needed to apologize to Jeremy. Wanted to get the tension between them out of the way before they were intimate. And she knew without a shadow of a doubt that Jeremy was going to take her to his bed tonight. If for no other reason than to prove to them both that she was nothing more than his mistress.

She swallowed hard, searching for some words. Any words. *I'm sorry* wouldn't do, because then she'd have to admit that she realized she'd hurt his feelings earlier.

But once they entered his house, she was nervous about more than the apology, which was so silly because she wanted Jeremy. Her lips still tingled from his kiss in the car earlier.

Maybe that had played a part in her remarks to him. She had a history of shooting herself in the foot socially when she was…

"Jeremy?"

"Yes." He tossed his keys on the table in the hallway leading from the garage to the house. Standing on the threshold of the media room, he didn't turn to look at her.

"I…" She just couldn't say it. Didn't want to have to talk about Lucinda and the bad blood between them. Lucinda hadn't been particularly nice to her, but Bella knew she hadn't been all that good to Lucinda, either.

"You?" He pivoted on his heel.

She took a deep breath. "You know I've said that you're arrogant."

He nodded.

"Well, I'm not. When I'm unsure of myself—

and it happens more than I like to admit—I lash out. It's my way of protecting myself."

He leaned against the wall, crossing his arms over his chest.

"When did you start doing that?" he asked.

She took a deep breath. "Probably the summer I was fifteen and my mother started working for the Cannons as their upstairs maid. I helped her sometimes. It was awkward. I…I've never been able to just be quiet and pretend nothing bothers me."

"So you attack?"

"Yes."

He nodded. "Was there anything else?"

She shook her head.

"Then let's go have another drink before we head upstairs."

"Jeremy."

"What?"

"I don't like this tension between us. Despite everything, we've always been friendly. Let me do something to make it up to you."

He rubbed the back of his neck, and she realized that tonight might really be a sexual encounter. And she'd have to renege on her word.

She didn't give herself easily and had slept with only one other man. An event which was singularly unmemorable. She wanted earth-shattering passion with Jeremy, but a big part of her believed that was just the stuff of romantic stories—that in real life, sex was just sweaty and somewhat enjoyable.

"Come inside and we can discuss this," he said.

She followed him into the media room. He shrugged out of his jacket, tossing it over the back of the couch.

"I really enjoyed meeting Frederick and Mary," she said. As soon as they'd returned to the group, she'd realized her faux pas with Jeremy and had tried to make up for it by charming his would-be business associate.

She didn't know why she was talking about the business meeting he'd had. She certainly didn't want to open up the conversation to Lucinda. God knows she didn't want to think about the way she'd felt when she saw the two of them talking at the bar. A part of her knew that there was nothing Lucinda could say that Jeremy didn't already know. He'd seen her at rock-bottom.

"They liked you, too. I'm having a party on my yacht for them on Saturday."

She was grateful for the subject change.

"Do you want to use my caterer?" she asked, trying to ignore the fact that he'd removed his tie and loosened the top two buttons of his shirt.

"No. I want you by my side and not thinking about business."

"Oh," she said, feeling a little hurt. "I'm really the best event planner in the area."

"I don't doubt that."

"Then why don't you want me to take care of the details? It's short notice but I can—"

"Bella."

"Yes?"

"I have a personal chef who'll attend to the details, and if it's really so important to you, you can make the menu choices."

"Okay. I can hire servers for you, too."

"Forget about business. You have only one thing to think about right now."

"And that is?"

"Being my mistress," he said, and took her in his arms.

He tipped her head back and she met his gaze. He was serious now. And she realized she was seeing the real man. The trappings of society were stripped away as he watched her.

He wanted her.

She shivered. No man had ever wanted her this much. She was acutely aware of her femininity and the primitive power that she carried with it.

She caressed his back, felt the power in his shoulders. His arms shifted around her. One around her waist, the other low on her hips.

He didn't speak, didn't have to. At this moment words would be superfluous and neither of them needed to talk about anything.

His hair was cool and silky under her fingers.

She cupped his head in both of her hands, standing on her tiptoes as she drew his head down to hers.

She pressed her lips to his and traced the seam between them with her tongue. He tasted faintly of the scotch he'd consumed at the hotel and something else that she associated only with Jeremy.

He groaned deep in his throat, shifting her in his arms, lifting her off her feet. His mouth never left hers as he carried her up the stairs to his bedroom.

# Seven

He set her on her feet next to his bed. The bedroom had one wall that was all windows. Framed in glass Bella saw the stars and the subtle lighting around the pool.

At this moment she was so very afraid that Jeremy would think she was only here because of the contract. And yet, at the same time, it would make things so much easier if that's what he believed.

*Liar.*

She grimaced. No matter how many times she said the words, they weren't true. She was here with Jeremy because she wanted the man and he'd…he'd gone to a lot of trouble for her. She was touched in a way that she didn't want to be.

He looked at her through half-lidded eyes, making her hyperaware of him and at the same time of her own body. She felt his gaze moving over her. She shifted her legs and let her arms drop to her sides.

She didn't need to protect herself from the past tonight. She was here with Jeremy. The man she'd been thinking about too much of the time. And damned if she wasn't going to enjoy him.

"Still want to talk about my party on Saturday?"

She bit her lip to keep from laughing. He was too confident, too sure of himself and with plenty of cause. He reached for her and pulled her into his arms. He lowered his head and she held her breath.

Brushing his lips over her cheek, he held her close but with a tenderness no man had shown her before. His long fingers caressed her neck, slow sweeps up and down until she shivered in his arms. She needed more from him. She grabbed his shoulders, tipped her head and opened her mouth under his.

He sighed her name as she thrust her tongue into his mouth. Sliding his arms down her back, he edged her toward the bed. It hit the backs of her legs and she sat down. He followed her, never breaking their kiss.

His tongue moved on hers with ease, tempting her further, tasting her deeper and making her long for him. Her skin felt too tight. Her breasts were heavy, craving his touch. Between her legs she was moistening for him, ready for him.

Squirming, she shifted around until she was on his lap, her legs straddling him. She lifted her head to look down at him. His skin was flushed, his lips wet from her kisses. She flexed her fingers against his shoulders.

God, he really was solid muscle.

"Take your shirt off," she said. She'd been longing to touch his chest since that long-ago summer day when she'd served him at the yacht club.

He reached between them, the backs of his fingers brushing her breasts as he unbuttoned his shirt. She shook from the brief contact and bit her lip to keep from asking for more.

He unbuttoned the small pearl buttons that held the bodice of her dress. Ran his finger down the center of her body, over her sternum and between her ribs. Lingered on her belly button and then stopped at the waistband of her high-cut thong panties.

He slowly traced the same path upward again. This time his fingers feathered under the demi-cups of her ice-blue bra, barely touching her nipples. Both beaded, and a shaft of desire pierced Bella, shaking her.

She needed more. She wanted more. Her heart beat so swiftly and loudly she was sure he could hear it. She scraped her fingernails lightly down his chest. He groaned, the sound rumbling up from his chest. He leaned back, bracing himself on his elbows.

And let her explore. This was so different from the hurried couplings she'd had with that one boyfriend in the past. Encounters that had happened in the dark and were over almost before they'd begun.

His muscles jumped under her touch. She circled his nipple but didn't touch it. Scraped her nail down the center line of his body, following the fine dusting of hair that narrowed and disappeared into the waistband of his pants.

His stomach was rock-hard and rippled when he sat up. He reached around her back and unhooked her bra and then pushed the cups up out of his way. He pulled her closer until the tips of her breasts brushed his chest.

"Bella." He said her name like a prayer.

His hard-on nudged her center and she shifted on him, trying to find a better touch, but it was impossible with the layers of cloth between them. Her dress was hiked up but it wasn't enough.

He kissed his way down her neck and bit lightly at her nape. She shuddered, clutching at his shoulders, grinding her body harder against him.

He pulled the fabric of her dress up to her waist, slipping his hands under the cloth. Those big hands burned hot on her skin as he cupped her butt and urged her to ride him faster, guiding her motions against him. He bent his head and his tongue stroked her nipple.

Everything in her body clenched. She clutched at Jeremy's shoulders as her climax washed over her. She collapsed against his chest, and he held her close. Bella hugged him to her and closed her eyes, reminding herself that to Jeremy this was just an agreement. But it didn't change the fact that she felt like she'd just found the man she'd been secretly dreaming of.

Jeremy had never seen anything more beautiful than the woman in his arms. She was so responsive to his touch and he wanted more. It fed his obsession in a way he hadn't expected. If he didn't take her soon he was going to self-combust.

The word *mine* swirled around in his head.

She pushed his shirt off his shoulders and he tugged it off, tossing it away. She shrugged out of her dress and bra. She was exquisitely built, soft, feminine. Her breasts were full and her skin flushed from her recent orgasm.

He ran his hands slowly over her torso, almost afraid to believe that after all these years, after all his negotiating, she was really here. Finally, in his bed, where he'd been fantasizing about her for so long.

Her nipples were tight little buds beckoning his mouth. He'd barely explored her before and he needed to now. He needed to find out how she reacted to his every touch.

He fingered her nipples carefully and she shifted her shoulders, trying to increase the pressure of his touch. "Tell me what you want."

"Don't you know?" she asked, her hands coming to his wrists, trying to control his movements.

He shook his head. "I want the words, Bella."

"I want…" she blurted.

He realized then that there was something very fragile inside this ultracompetent and professional woman. He pulled her more fully into his arms. Cradled her to his chest. She closed her eyes and buried her face in his neck. Each exhale went through him. God, he wanted her.

He was so hard and hot for her that he could come in his pants. But he was going to wait. He felt the minute touches of her tongue against his neck. Her hand slid down his chest and opened his belt, unfastening the button at his waistband and then lowering his zipper.

*Hot damn.*

Her hand slid inside his pants and his boxers. Smoothly her touch traveled up and down his length. He tightened his hands on her back. He glanced down his body to watch her working him with such tender care and he had to grit his teeth not to end it all right then. But he wanted to be inside her the next time one of them climaxed.

She smiled up at him. *Little minx.*

"I want you, Jeremy. All of you, deep inside me."

"You're going to have me," he said, his voice raspy.

She pushed the rest of her clothing away. His breath caught in his throat. She was exactly as he'd dreamed she'd be. Nipped-in waist, long slender legs and full breasts. He nudged her over on her back.

He leaned down, capturing her mouth with his as he shoved his pants farther down his legs. She opened her legs and he settled between her thighs.

The humid warmth of her center scorched his already aroused flesh. He thrust against her without thought. Damn, she felt good.

He wanted to enter her totally naked. At least this first time. But that was a huge risk and one he knew better than to take.

He pushed away from her, fumbled with his pants, taking them all the way off along with his boxers, then found the condom he'd put in the pocket earlier today.

He glanced over at her and saw that she was watching him. The fire in her eyes made his entire body tighten with anticipation. He put the condom on one-handed and turned back to her.

"Hurry."

"Not a chance. I'm going to savor you."

"Betcha can't," she said.

"You really want—"

"I really want you, Jeremy. Come to me now."

She opened her arms and her legs, inviting him

into her body. He lowered himself over her and rubbed against her. Shifted until he'd caressed every part of her.

She reached between his legs and cupped him in her hands, and he shuddered. "Not now. Or I won't last."

She smiled up at him. "Really?"

He wanted to hug her close at the look of wonder on her face. "Hell, yes."

He needed to be inside her *now*. He lifted her thighs, wrapping her legs around his waist. Her hands fluttered between them and their eyes met.

He held her hips steady and entered her slowly until he was fully seated. Her eyes widened with each inch he gave her. She clutched at his hips as he started to move.

He leaned down and caught one of her nipples in his teeth, scraping very gently. She started to tighten around him. Her hips moving faster, demanding more, but he kept the pace slow, steady, wanting to feel her climax again before he did.

He suckled her nipple and rotated his hips to catch her pleasure point with each thrust. Her hands clenched in his hair and she threw her head back as her climax ripped through her.

He leaned back on his haunches and tipped her hips up to give him deeper access. Her body was still clenching around his when he felt that tightening at the base of his spine seconds before his body erupted into hers. He pounded into her two, three more times then collapsed against her, careful to keep his weight from crushing her. He rolled to his side, taking her with him.

He kept his head at her breast and smoothed his hands down her back, realizing he'd just made a colossal mistake.

Having sex with Bella hadn't lessened his obsession with her. It had deepened it.

Jeremy got out of the bed and padded into the bathroom. Bella stared up at the ceiling, her entire body tingling from his lovemaking. She'd never expected it to be like this. *This* was beyond anything she'd experienced. She was pulsing.

He came back into the room and climbed back in the bed, then propped the pillows up at the head and drew her into his arms, not saying anything.

She had no idea what to do now.

"What are you thinking?" He finally broke the silence.

"That you are incredible."

"Incredible, eh? I like the sound of that."

"Great, just what you need. Another reason to be arrogant."

He tipped her head back and lowered his mouth to hers. His kisses overwhelmed her. They should both be sated and not interested in making love again. Yet as his tongue played in her mouth, she felt the rekindling of her own desire. She wanted him again. She tried to angle her head to reciprocate, but he held her still.

This was his embrace and she felt the fierce need in him to dominate her. To remind her that she was his. She'd found the proof she was searching for that Jeremy was different from every other man she'd ever met.

His biceps flexed as he shifted her in his arms, rolling her under him and then running his hands over her body.

His mouth moved down the column of her neck, nibbling and biting softly. He lingered at the base of her neck, where her pulse beat frantically. Then he sucked on her skin. Everything in her body clenched. Not enough to push her over the edge, just enough to make her frantic for more of him.

She scored his shoulders with her fingernails before skimming them down his chest, caressing his flat male nipples as he held himself above her on his strong arms. She liked the way she was surrounded by him, feeling very feminine as she lay there under him. His skin was hot to the touch and she wrapped her arms around his body, pulling him closer.

He pulled back, staring down at her. Then he traced one finger over the full globes of her breasts. She shifted her shoulders, inviting his caress. He took one of her nipples between his thumb and forefinger, pinching lightly.

She shook with need. Couldn't wait for him.

She reached between their bodies, but he shifted his hips out of her reach. His mouth fastened on her left nipple, suckling her strongly. She undulated against him, her hips lifting toward him. He drew his other hand down her body, his fingers tangling in the hair at her center.

He caressed her between her legs until she was frantically holding his head to her breasts, trying to find a release that remained just out of reach. She skimmed her hands down his body.

His breath hissed out as she reached between his legs to cup him and caress his length.

"There's a condom in the nightstand."

"Hmm…mmm," she said, too busy exploring him to really pay attention to what he said.

"Bella, baby, you're killing me."

She liked the sound of that. The way his breath caught whenever she gently scored him with her nails. He shifted over her, opening the nightstand drawer and pulling out a condom.

"Put it on me."

"With pleasure."

She opened the package before she remembered she hadn't done this before. But it wasn't that hard to figure out. He groaned as she covered him, and she thought maybe she'd done it right.

She started to reach lower again but he caught her hand and stretched it over her head. He lifted her leg up around his hip, shifted his body. She felt him hot, hard and ready at her entrance. But he made no move to take her. She looked up at him.

"You're mine."

She couldn't respond to that. "I…"

"Watch me take you, Bella, and know that this means that you belong to me."

He thrust inside her then. Lifted her up, holding her with his big hands as he repeatedly drove into her. He went deeper than he had earlier. She felt too full, stretched and surrounded by him.

He bit her neck carefully and sucked against her skin and everything tightened inside her until she felt another climax spread through her body. Her skin was pulsing, her body tightening around him. A moment later he came, crying her name and holding her tightly to his chest.

She rested her head against his shoulder and held him. Wrapped completely around his body, she realized the truth of what he'd said. She was his.

# Eight

The phone rang just after lunch and Bella hesitated to answer it. Shelley had been in her office twice trying to pump her for more information on her date. And Bella didn't want to share those details with anyone. She wanted to hold them close.

Plus, despite their synchronicity in bed, there was still tension between her and Jeremy.

She struggled to keep that romantic dinner under the Chihuly glass in her mental scrapbook as one of the best meals of her entire life. There were so few in that category. And most of them had happened a long time ago, when both of her parents were still alive.

The phone stopped ringing and then the intercom buzzed.

"Yes, Shelley."

"Dare's on the line. Why didn't you pick up?"

"I'm working on a proposal," she said, which was partially true. She'd spoken to Jeremy's personal chef, Andy Conti, earlier and she was in the process of planning the details of his yacht party as a surprise to him. He'd given her so many gifts and she thought this would be a nice way to give back to him.

Andy said it was a casual event. But from their discussion, she knew it wasn't her idea of a casual event, where she offered to grill chicken and her friends brought over side dishes and bottles of wine.

She wanted every detail of Jeremy's party to be perfect. She knew Lucinda would be there. Bella figured this was her chance to show how well she fit in Jeremy's world.

"Hey, sis." She heard old-school Beastie Boys playing in the background. "No Sleep Till Brooklyn." She loved that song and had introduced her brother to the group when he'd come home with a Tupac CD.

"What's up? And can you turn the radio down?"

The volume immediately was lowered. "I'm coming home this weekend with a few friends and I'm planning to crash at your place. Is that okay?"

"Dare, it's your place, too." She liked that he

asked, but he didn't need to. She still missed him around the house. Even though he'd only lived with her off and on since she'd moved to her current place, she was still used to thinking of it as their home.

"Not anymore. I'm subleasing a place in Manhattan."

"Can you afford it?" she asked, but she knew he could. He had matured so much in the last few years. She didn't like the thought of him living so far away. She'd always had Dare close by. And New York wasn't close.

She was alone. Really alone, she thought.

"Yes, sis, I can. I'm going to be making big bucks at my new job."

"Don't spend it before you've earned it," she warned him. She'd taken several money management classes after her mom had declared bankruptcy. She hated that feeling of having nothing. Of watching strangers come in and take everything they'd owned and sell it to pay their debts.

"I'm not. We both learned that lesson the hard way, didn't we?"

She took a deep breath and smiled to herself. She still thought of him as a rebellious boy even though he'd straightened up his act. "Yes, we did."

"I want you to plan a trip to the city to visit me this fall after I've settled in."

"I will."

Dare really had turned out okay. There had been

a time—well, three and a half years ago—when he was running wild and getting arrested, that she'd thought she was going to end up visiting him in jail.

"I've got something on Saturday. Do you still have your key?"

"Yes. What are you doing?"

For some reason she didn't want to mention Jeremy's name. "A yacht party."

"One of your wealthy clients again?"

"Um…not exactly."

"A date? Bella, who are you dating?" He was teasing her and she wanted to laugh with him but wasn't sure how he'd react.

"Jeremy."

"Mr. Harper?"

"Do we know any other Jeremy?" she asked a little sarcastically, because she was nervous.

"No. Are you sure you know what you're doing?"

No, she had absolutely no idea what she was doing. But at this point she wasn't going to back out. And after last night, she'd confirmed that she wanted a lot longer with Jeremy than a mere six months.

"Sis?"

"What?"

"Be careful."

"I've been taking care of us for a long time."

"Yes, you have, and now that I'm older it's time I stepped up and watched out for you."

"Jeremy's not a bad guy."

"I'm not saying that. But he is a smooth operator and you're not his normal type of woman."

"What's that supposed to mean?" she asked, not exactly sure where her brother was going with this.

"Just that you've been busy taking care of me and haven't done a lot of dating. He's a pretty experienced man, remember that."

"I will."

"I like him. He's done a lot of good things for us, but that doesn't mean he's family."

"I know that, Dare. I don't think he understands how to let anyone close."

"And you don't know how to keep anyone at arm's length once you get to know them."

"What time will you be here on Saturday?" she asked, forcibly changing the subject.

"Sometime after lunch. Don't forget what I said."

"I won't."

She couldn't believe Dare was giving her advice. But it warmed her heart in ways she'd never be able to articulate. For so long they'd struggled and now…now she felt that they were both going to make it. And she knew they both had one man to thank…Jeremy Harper.

Jeremy wasn't sure what to expect when he arrived at Bella's house. She'd sent him a text message earlier saying that she had a weekly dinner she couldn't cancel. Since they'd spent the last two nights making love, he figured they were due for more socializing.

And it would do him good to be around other people. His focus on her was becoming too narrow. He kept feeling like he was never going to get enough of her, which wasn't helping his obsession at all. No matter how often he made love to her, he still wanted her. No matter how many hours he held her in his arms, he still felt like six months wasn't going to be long enough.

She'd told him to bring a bottle of wine and to dress casually. He heard the sound of voices and music coming from the backyard when he arrived. He recognized Kenny Chesney's song, "No Shoes, No Shirt, No Problems."

He walked around back carrying the wine he'd picked up in France when he'd been there on business two weeks ago. As soon as he came around the corner he saw a group of ten or so people sitting around the pool.

He hesitated, remembering Kell and Lucinda's reactions toward Bella. His friends hadn't been exactly welcoming. How would her friends react to him? Did he want to know her outside of their agreement? He was a step away from turning around when she stepped out of the house onto the patio and saw him.

She smiled and it lit up her entire face. He wasn't

leaving, no matter how much he might want to. This was definitely crossing the line beyond what he'd outlined in their contract. But when she waved at him, he simply walked toward her.

Everyone stopped talking and he felt like he was on display, but that was nothing new. He ignored it as best he could.

"I'm so glad you made it," Bella said, wrapping one arm around his waist and leaning up to give him a kiss on his cheek. He turned his head and captured her lips.

Then stepped away. "Where do you want the wine?"

"Over there. Charlie is manning the bar. Let me put this down and I'll introduce you to everyone."

He handed the bottle of wine to Charlie, who shook his hand. She introduced him to the rest of her friends and he found them to be an inviting and eclectic group, ranging from business professionals such as an accountant and a stockbroker to a romance novelist and her animator husband to a couple who ran a tourist sailing operation.

Jeremy was comfortable with the group and found himself falling easily into the role of host by the time the evening ended and everyone left. But despite the fact that he was enjoying himself, he didn't like the fact that he and Bella were clearly a couple here.

Bella smiled and held his arm as the last couple walked to their car. "That was fun. Next week we're supposed to go to Charlie's house. Will you be available?"

"Ah, I don't know. I'll have to check my schedule," he said. He didn't want to isolate her from her life and her friends, but he was struggling to keep her in the box labeled *mistress,* and hanging out with her friends wasn't going to help.

"Okay. Just let me know if you can make it."

"It seems like an odd group."

"Kind of. We've been meeting for about two years now. It started out being just a few of us, hanging out at Chili's, but then we decided we could hear each other better at home."

"You're not much for going out, are you?" he asked, realizing that she always suggested something in.

"No."

"Why not?"

She shrugged and turned aside to gather up some empty wineglasses.

"Tell me, Bella."

"For a long time people used to stare at us. Dad's death was front-page news."

He couldn't imagine what that had been like. "I read some articles about him."

"He wasn't like they said in those articles. He really loved our family and he was such a dreamer. He just had no head for business. Eventually he lost all he'd inherited."

"What do you remember most about him?"

"He hated to be away from us. When he'd come home, the first thing he'd do was give Mom and me a big hug and then we'd all sit around the table and talk."

"Was he gone a lot?"

"Yes…more and more that last year."

"I'm sorry."

"It's been a long time."

"But it doesn't go away, does it?"

"No, it doesn't. And people don't stare anymore. I just got used to staying home."

He looked around her house. It was smaller than his, and not decorated with designer furniture, but it was warm and cozy. He liked the looks of the overstuffed sofa and could easily imagine sitting there with her.

"I think the Heat are playing tonight. You can probably catch the end of the game if you want to."

"Do you want to watch it?"

"After I'm done cleaning up. Dare and I try to watch all the games. He e-mails with his highlights and asks for mine."

"I'll help you," he said.

"You don't have to help. You're my guest."

He didn't say anything to that, just started gathering plates to clear the table. "Have you been to a Heat game?"

"Yes, a few. But my business is unpredictable, so I don't have season tickets."

"I have tickets with Kell and Daniel. The next home game, we'll go."

"I'd like that."

He gathered up the plates from the table on the patio and loaded them into the dishwasher. She didn't say anything as they worked and soon they had the place clean. They put on the game and finished the bottle of wine he'd brought. He wrapped one arm around her and held her close to him.

She fell asleep before the game ended and he shifted her into his arms and carried her down the hall to her bedroom. He didn't want to think about tonight or the feelings she evoked in him. So instead he took off her clothes, waking her up. He took off his own and joined her on the bed, making love to her.

She fell asleep in his arms and he stared at the wall for most of the night, wondering how his carefully crafted plan had gone so wrong.

The next few weeks flew by and Bella felt that each step she took toward making Jeremy view her as more than a temporary mistress was countered by an obstacle either from her past or his friends. She carefully avoided Lucinda at any events where she and Daniel were in attendance. And Jeremy's cousin Kell spent a lot of time talking to her about prenups and the advantages on both sides.

Which made her sad, because it was clear that he thought she was only after Jeremy for his money. If he knew how well Jeremy had protected himself against that, she suspected Kell would back off. And that made her more emotional, because she sensed that Jeremy cared enough about her to keep quiet about the mistress contract.

Yet he didn't care enough to say that they didn't need a contract between them any longer. Honestly, that was what she really wanted. She reminded herself of the contract to keep a certain distance between them. To protect herself from allowing her emotions to get the better of it. But it wasn't working.

She glanced around the elegant ballroom, no longer feeling out of place. Lucinda had cornered her once and Jeremy had rescued her. It was one of the most heroic things he'd done for her. But now she was alone again, in a beautiful Oscar de la Renta gown that Jeremy had given her.

"Somehow I didn't expect to find you hiding out on the terrace."

Kell walked over to her. He looked very elegant and sophisticated in his tuxedo. Handsome, but not as attractive to her as Jeremy was.

"Jeremy asked me to wait here." She was situated behind large potted trees that had been filled with twinkling lights. From her vantage point she had a view of the entire room, but no one else could really see her.

"Now it all makes sense," Kell said. "This is one of our favorite spots."

"Favorite spots for what?" she asked.

"Hiding out," he said with a wry grin. Kell could be charming when he tried.

She opened her small handbag and took out an article on prenups she'd clipped from the *Wall Street Journal* a few days ago. "I saw this and thought of you."

He took the article, glanced down at it. A brief smile touched his lips. "You're not what I expected."

She still hoped that her relationship would outlast the three months remaining on the mistress contract. And if it was going to have a chance to survive, she knew she needed to make more of an effort with Jeremy's friends. He didn't do a lot with them but she knew they were important to him—especially Kell.

"Well, I think all of us gold diggers are a little bit different."

He arched one eyebrow at her. "Jeremy doesn't see you that way."

"Then why do you?" she asked.

"Let's just say I've been there."

She finally saw more than a good-looking, successful man in Kell and it was more than a little disheartening to realize she'd been so shallow. "I'm sorry. I care about Jeremy."

"I've noticed that."

"Why did you think I was a gold digger?" she asked.

He shrugged.

She knew that she should stop this line of questioning, but she had to know. What had he heard about her? Please don't let it about the mistress contract, she thought. She'd absolutely die of embarrassment if all of his friends knew that they weren't in a real relationship.

"Tell me. It can't be anything I haven't heard before."

"It wasn't anything about you," he said. "Jeremy would kick my butt if he heard me talking to you about this."

"Well, he's not here," she said carefully. She was almost a hundred-percent positive that whatever Kell had heard he'd mentioned to Jeremy. So he already knew whatever damaging gossip Kell had told him about her. And it had to be gossip, because she hadn't done anything for money that she regretted.

"You'd keep secrets from him?" he asked. Immediately he lost his charm and she saw the barracuda look in his eyes. She'd heard he was a corporate attorney who never lost a case and she could see why. There was an utter ruthlessness in his gaze.

She sighed. "No, I wouldn't."

"Of course she wouldn't, Kell. What are you two talking about?"

She accepted the Bellini from Jeremy and

took a sip of the smooth peach-and-champagne drink. Jeremy wrapped an arm around her waist and pulled her firmly to his side.

"Um…"

"Gold diggers."

"Not that again," Jeremy said under his breath.

"I wanted to know what he'd heard about me to make him believe I'd be after your money."

"It was old news about your family," Jeremy said.

From Lucinda. She was the only one who would have known all the sordid details. The papers had reported that a business deal had gone wrong and her father, distraught from it, had killed himself. But the truth was a little darker. Her father had somehow gotten involved with the mob in a shady deal that she didn't know all the details of. She could only imagine how desperate he must have been. The day after her father's suicide, the DEA had arrived at the door to seize all of their property in connection with her father's business dealings.

Even the papers hadn't gotten all the details. But her dear friend Lucinda had, because Bella had told her.

Tears burned in the back of her eyes. She didn't think she could still feel betrayed from that long-ago friendship. But of course she could. At one time, Lucinda had been like a sister to her.

"Thanks for telling me. Does anyone else know?"

"Just Daniel, and he won't repeat it," Kell said. "Neither would I. It's not anything personal—"

"I know," she said, putting her hand on his arm to stop him. "You were just looking out for Jeremy."

"I can look out for myself," Jeremy said wryly.

Kell didn't say anything, just kept watching her with that stare of his. Finally she sighed and said, "I can't blame you there."

Kell nodded at her and then left. Jeremy drew her back against his solid frame, not saying another word. She let the strength in his body surround her and soothe the wounds left over from Lucinda.

# Nine

Jeremy watched Kell walk away. He'd known that Kell didn't trust Bella, but he had no idea that the two of them had spent so much time chatting alone. He knew that Bella could handle herself, but he should have paid closer attention to Kell.

"Sorry if he was being a pain."

She took another sip of her drink and glanced sideways at him. Her hair slid along the sleeve of his tuxedo jacket and he wished they were home alone so he could feel her hair on his skin. She had the softest hair.

"He wasn't. It's sweet the way he tries to take care of you."

"*Sweet?* I don't think anyone would describe Kell that way."

They watched as Kell stopped to speak with his sister, Lorraine, and her group. Her women friends all moved subtly, trying to attract his attention. One woman tossed her hair, another touched his arm.

"He does have that barracuda smile—you know, all teeth—that makes you feel like you're about to be eaten, but underneath that…he watches out for you. Why is that?" she asked.

His relationship with Kell was deep and complex. He doubted that either of them would know how to explain it. But they'd been alone a lot with the same lazy nanny and they'd spent a lot of their time escaping her. "He's six months older than I am. And his mom used to make him promise to watch me."

Almost absently he remembered the long days of summer when their mothers would spend afternoons on the beach drinking fruity concoctions and gossiping while he and Kell ran free like wild boys.

"I remember you mentioning that his side of the family was goofy."

He grimaced at his old joke. He shouldn't have said that. Most people were unaware that Kell's mother was a recluse, prone to depression. For as much as he had happy memories of his childhood, it was also tinged with memories of Aunt Mary's "sadness," as his mother called it. They'd often rushed to her house so that his mom could cheer her up.

He suspected his mother used Aunt Mary's illness to ignore the fact that Jeremy's dad spent more time with his mistress than with them.

It didn't always work. His childhood memories were clouded with the secrets of his aunt Mary's depression and Kell coming to live with them for months at a time. He wouldn't share that with Bella. Some secrets weren't his to tell.

Just as Lucinda should have kept quiet about Bella's family. He'd said as much to Daniel.

"That's because my branch of the family isn't crazy," he said.

She looked steadily at him. "I think there's more to it than what you just said."

Jeremy shrugged, not really comfortable talking about Kell or his relationship with him. But there were some things he wanted to share with Bella. She quietly accepted everything about him. Even his flaws.

Whenever he was with her, he felt…complete. Which made no sense to him. He'd been happy with his life before they'd become lovers. Now he didn't like to think about what going back to life without Bella would be like.

"Tell me," she said. She wrapped one arm around his waist and glanced up at him expectantly.

"He saved my life one time."

"Literally?"

"Yes." A sailing accident that had surprised Jeremy. He'd always been at home on the water. But he'd been hit by the boom as they'd changed direction and been knocked overboard. One minute he'd been on the yacht, and the next thing he remembered was Kell's hand on his wrist, pulling him to the surface.

She cupped his jaw, bringing him back to the present. He glanced down into her honey-brown eyes. There was such a well of caring there that he felt like he'd taken a punch to the gut.

"I'm so glad he saved you," she said, raising up on tiptoe and kissing him. It was a soft and sweet kiss. The kind that made him glad to be alive and holding this woman in his arms.

"Me, too," he said. Never more so than this moment.

From the first time he'd met Bella, he'd sensed she was different from other women. At first he'd thought it was because she was no longer part of the moneyed set he ran in. But the more time he spent with her, the more he realized that she had an innate innocence that drew him to her.

He knew she wasn't innocent, that her life had been carved out of emotionally tough events. But she'd retained a certain sweetness that she showered on those around her. And he thanked God that he'd been fortunate enough to bind her to him when he had.

They only had three months left on their contract. His gut tightened at the thought of her leaving him. He needed to start planning for the next phase of their relationship, but he had no idea what that would entail.

"You ready to get out of here?"

"You did promise me a dance."

And he realized, as he deposited their drinks on a tray and led her to the dance floor, that he never wanted to break a promise he made to her.

She and Jeremy stayed for another half hour before they left the party. Twice Lucinda had made eye contact with her and indicated she wanted to talk. But Bella's evening had been perfect and she hadn't wanted to ruin it, so she'd ignored her onetime friend.

Jeremy put the top down on the convertible and drove them to the beach. It was a Saturday night and luckily she didn't have to work tomorrow. He held her hand loosely on his thigh.

Everything felt just about perfect, and that worried her. Because whenever she got too comfortable, something bad happened. And she was depending a lot on Jeremy—more than she wanted.

When she'd signed the contract with Jeremy she hadn't been too sure what she expected. Maybe a chance to reclaim something that had been stolen from her as a young woman. But she'd found so much more.

Did he feel the same? Sometimes she sensed he did, though it was true that he kept part of himself from her. He didn't speak of emotions or longevity—but neither did she.

Part of her was afraid to rock the boat. She was used to her life being constantly in flux, never taking anything for granted, but there was something very solid and reassuring about Jeremy and his presence in her life. And she wanted to believe that he was going to be a permanent addition to it.

She'd never been in love before, but she was falling for Jeremy.

"Deep thoughts?" he asked.

She shook her head, frantically trying to think of something to say that wouldn't leave her vulnerable to him. "Just enjoying the night and the wind in my hair."

He lifted her hand to his mouth, brushing a kiss along her knuckles. She liked that he was accepting of the limits she placed, that he didn't push her past them. Of course, it was different when they were in bed. There he would stand no barriers between them.

He'd pushed her further than she'd ever expected to go with any man. He made her give him everything she had, and never let her hide behind her own inhibitions.

"Then you're going to love what I have planned for us."

"What is it?" she asked. This was yet another instance that gave her hope. He was being very romantic and not at all businesslike about their relationship. After he'd offered her the town house, she expected him to focus on just the sexual side of things. Instead, he was always romancing her, planning evenings that fulfilled secret dreams she'd scarcely realized she had.

"A surprise," he said, slowing the car as they turned into the yacht club.

"I don't like surprises." But she did like going out on his yacht. She'd realized fairly early in her relationship with Jeremy that he was most at peace at sea. He liked to entertain on his boat, sleep on his boat, hold her on his boat. He never said much about it, but she could see a difference in him as soon as they motored out to sea.

"Or gifts," he said.

"I like your gifts. It's just that they're so extravagant." He'd overwhelmed her with the gifts he'd given her during the last three months. Some of the gifts were jewelry, which she half expected, but others were sentimental. Such as her mother's classic '69 Mustang, which had been sold to a collector to pay off some of their debts years ago. The collector had put it in storage and left it intact; their mom had been the last one to drive it.

She had so many memories of that car. Sometimes she just sat in the backseat and felt a little closer to her mom. Even Dare had been rendered speechless by the car.

He rubbed the diamond tennis bracelet that he'd given her earlier this evening. "I like you in diamonds."

"Is that why you insisted I wear the choker tonight?" she asked, lifting her free hand to touch the band of diamonds around her neck.

"Yes," he said, parking the car in his assigned spot. "Now, tell me what you were really thinking about."

She sighed. They were getting too close to each other. He saw parts of her that she normally hid away.

"You know me too well."

"Not yet. But soon I'll have all your secrets figured out."

"I'm not sure I like the sound of that."

"Why not? Don't you trust me?"

She did trust him on one level. She knew that, unlike Lucinda, Jeremy would never reveal anything personal about her to the world. But that didn't mean that he was planning to stick around for the long haul. And if he still left after three months, she was going to have to deal with the fact that her trust in him had been misplaced.

"Ah, that's a telling silence," he said. It was impossible to tell what he was thinking from his tone. He was a master at hiding his emotions. She wished she had that same ability. Everything she felt seemed to be broadcast like a twenty-four-hour news channel.

"It's not so much that I don't trust you."

"Then what is it?"

She took a deep breath. How could she say that every day they spent together made her wish time could stand still? "I'm afraid of what will happen when you're gone."

"Your secrets will always be safe with me."

"Yes, but I won't always be with you and I'm not sure I'm ready to think about that."

He pulled his hand free and got out of the car without another word. She watched him walk away from her. His stride was angry and she couldn't blame him, but they both had to acknowledge that there was a clock ticking as far as their relationship was concerned.

And so far he hadn't made any overt indication that he was interested in keeping her around any longer, despite their growing closeness. She wasn't going to pretend that her life was one thing when she knew it was something else.

Jeremy heard her footsteps behind him and turned to make sure her heels didn't get caught in the tiny cracks between the boards on the dock. He shouldn't have left her alone in the car. The flash of anger had surprised him.

Even as a child he'd always been even-keeled.

But with Bella so many reactions were unexpected. Even their lovemaking, though satisfying, always made him yearn for her again.

"Jeremy…"

There was a sadness in her voice that he couldn't stand hearing. He knew that she'd only given him the truth he'd asked her for. He had the same fears. Sharing so much of himself with her was bound to leave them both hurting when the relationship ended.

"No more talking tonight."

"I didn't mean to ruin the evening."

He was being an ass and he knew it. "You didn't. I'm just not ready to talk about our relationship being over."

"Me neither," she said softly.

He walked back to her. "Wait here."

He went back to his car and grabbed their overnight bags from the trunk, then locked it. Bella stood on the dock looking out to sea. She was good at keeping her true feelings and thoughts to herself. Too good.

The only time he felt her guard drop was when he made love to her.

He didn't say anything, just walked with her to his slip and lifted her aboard his boat. He untied the lines that held the boat in place and then climbed aboard. She took their bags to the stateroom as he prepared to leave the marina.

"Do you want a drink?" she called from below deck.

"No," he said. What he wanted he doubted he could ever have. He wanted everything she had to give. He wanted it from the safety of the relationship they had.

He knew that wasn't fair. But he'd designed this relationship so he'd have all the advantages. He was only now realizing he'd forgotten a few things.

"Are you going to stay mad at me all night?" she asked from right behind him. Her hair blew around her face and shoulders in the light breeze. The skirt of her dress swirled around her legs.

"I don't know," he said honestly, because watching her standing there brought home to him how far out of reach she really was. He could hold her and make love to her, but it was temporary.

"I'd rather go home than spend the night with you acting like this."

Screw that. He wasn't going to waste one night of the three months they had left together. He wanted her by his side for all of them. "I don't want you to go home."

She smiled at him, that fey little grin that he never could read, and took a few steps closer to him. "I don't want you to be sulky."

"I sound like an eight-year-old when you put it that way."

"Well…" She stopped in front of him, placing her hands around his neck. She rested her body against his and spoke softly against his skin. He felt each word the instant she said it. "You don't resemble an eight-year-old."

He wrapped his arms around her, lowering his head to the top of hers and just breathing her in. He rested his hands at the small of her back, nestling them together until not an inch of space separated them.

"I'm acting like one?" he asked, brushing his lips along the column of her neck. He traced the line of the choker with his tongue. God, she was beautiful. If she ever had an inkling of how he felt toward her...fear gripped him. He didn't want to let her go. Not tonight. Not in three months. Not ever.

"I guess I was being pretty childish, too, keeping secrets," she said, tipping her head back so that their eyes met.

But she hadn't been. He knew how hard it was for her to let anyone close to her, despite the fact that she had a large circle of friends. There were very few people that she actually let know the real woman.

And he wanted to be one of those few.

She trailed her fingers over his jaw, then down his chest. She laid her head there, right over his heart. He tightened his arms around her. Held her as close as he could without saying a word.

He didn't want to talk anymore. Why had he started a conversation that went where he didn't want it to go?

"In the car, I was thinking about this."

"Making love?" he asked, leaning down to kiss her. Sex was on his mind most of the time when they were together. Hell, even when they were apart he was thinking about how it felt to have her in his arms. The soft sounds she made when he thrust into her body and how she wrapped herself around him when they finished.

He lifted his head, brushing his lips along the curve of her cheek down to her neck. He suckled at the smooth, soft skin, wanting to leave his mark there. Wanting in some way to brand her as his so that everyone she met knew she was taken.

Taken by him. His, he thought. Really his, and not just for a few months.

She smiled up at him. "In a way."

She took a step away from him, wrapping her arms around her waist and staring out at sea. He hated how she could isolate herself from him in one movement. He stepped up behind her, pulling her back against him.

"What way?"

"I was thinking about how quickly the last three months have gone by, and wishing that the next three months never had to end."

Jeremy smiled at her, but words stuck in his throat. Could he risk being that honest and open about wanting her?

# Ten

Jeremy woke the next morning, scrubbing a hand over his face and staring at the woman lying curled so close to him. Her confession last night had set a fire in him he hadn't been able to put out. Something had started winding its way unexpectedly into his life.

She'd organized a couple of parties for him, acting as his hostess. He knew she did some business at the parties, drumming up new clientele, but mainly she acted the way his mother always had at his father's business functions. And that unnerved him.

He wasn't ready for their relationship to end, yet at the same time those three months couldn't come fast enough. He felt like this relationship was unraveling, and he had no idea how to get it back on the track he'd planned.

He pushed himself out of bed—because he wanted to linger.

"Jeremy?"

"Right here," he said, sinking back down next to her. If he wasn't careful they'd spend the rest of the weekend together on the boat, in bed.

"Is it morning already?" she asked, leaning over to kiss his chest. He shifted so that he lay next to her, his morning hard-on pressing against her hip. He shouldn't want her again so soon. He'd had her three times last night.

"Yes." He took her mouth with his, letting his hands wander over her body.

Her stomach growled and he laughed. "Hungry?"

She buried her red face against his chest. "Yes. I didn't eat at the party last night."

"Maybe that's because you kept trying to avoid Lucinda." He pulled the sheet back from the bed and reached for one of the silk bindings he'd used to tie her to the bed the night before, trailing it over her torso and breasts.

She shivered with awareness and her nipples tightened. He arranged the silk binding over her breasts. "I wish you hadn't noticed that."

He leaned down to lick each nipple. Then he blew gently on the tips. She raked her nails down his back.

"Are you listening to me?" she asked.

"To your body," he said.

He knelt between her thighs and looked down at her. "Open yourself for me," he said.

Her legs moved but he took her hands in his, brought them to her mound.

"Lift your hips, honey."

He leaned down, blowing lightly on her. She lifted her hips toward his mouth.

He drew her flesh into his mouth, sucking carefully on her. He pushed his finger into her body and lifted his head to look up at her.

Her eyes were closed, her head tipped back. Her shoulders arched, throwing her breasts forward with their hard tips, begging for more attention. Her entire body was a creamy delight.

He lowered his head again, hungry for more of her, using his teeth, tongue and fingers to bring her to the brink of climax, but held her there, wanting to draw out the moment of completion until she was begging him for it.

"Jeremy, please."

He slid deep into her. She arched her back, reaching up to entwine her arms around his shoulders. He thrust harder and felt every nerve in his body tensing. Reaching between their bodies, he touched her between her legs until he felt her body tighten around him.

He came in a rush, continuing to thrust into her

until his body was drained. He then collapsed on top of her, laying his head between her breasts.

He turned his face away from her, afraid to admit that something had changed between them overnight, but knowing that he wasn't going to let her go. He was going to find a way to keep her at his side.

The next few months flew by. Jeremy became a part of her life in a way she hadn't predicted. After their intense night together, neither of them had mentioned the contract or the fact that they didn't want to end their relationship after six months.

But that didn't bother her. Jeremy was everything she'd always wanted in a man and more. She didn't know when her dreams for the future had been reborn. But she found herself thinking of long-term plans instead of dwelling on what had been taken from her.

This afternoon was a perfect example. It was Jeremy's birthday and she'd planned a surprise party for him. Kell, despite his initial misgivings about her, had warmed considerably in the last few weeks and had helped her with the guest list. The party was going to be at her home.

She'd never have been able to do this with his circle of friends even a month ago. But it had felt right for this event. Jeremy seemed to like her house, and catering a party for him at his place felt too presumptuous. She really wanted this to be a special day.

He was turning thirty-five, a milestone that he'd mentioned to her one time and then let drop. His parents were flying home early from Europe to come to the party. They had been surprised when she'd called. Apparently Jeremy hadn't mentioned her to them.

She was a little nervous about that. She'd never met his parents, and she knew she and Jeremy weren't really dating.

"This place looks great."

She glanced at Dare. She was always a little startled to see him looking like a man. For so long he'd been that half-wild boy with eyes that broke her heart. Now she saw wisdom and maturity in him. "Yes, it does. Did you get those extra bags of ice?"

"Yes. And I made another run to the liquor store, so the bar is overstocked. Quit worrying, sis. You've thrown thousands of parties." He put his arm around her shoulder and they stood together in the living room of her home.

"But this one is different," she said. She'd never really hid anything from Dare. Not this Dare anyway. The teenage rebel he'd been hadn't been interested in anyone except himself.

Dare looked at her like she was crazy. "You really like Mr. Harper?"

"Yes, I do."

He hugged her close and then went over to the mantel to adjust a framed picture of the two of them from last summer. "I'm glad, Bella. I'm really glad."

"Why?" she asked. It wasn't like Dare to adjust anything.

"It makes it easier to take that job in New York."

She had an inkling of where Dare was going with this conversation. "Why would it?"

"Because you won't be alone."

She shook her head at him. "I'm never alone. I have a very busy life."

"Yes, you do. But you didn't have anyone to take care of while I was gone, and now you do."

His words gave her pause. Was that the main attraction she felt toward Jeremy? The fact that he let her take care of him, and she'd been searching for a long time for someone who would? "He's good to me, too."

"Glad to hear it."

The doorbell rang and soon the party guests started arriving. Daniel and Lucinda arrived in the midst of her friends from her weekly dinner. She didn't have to greet them individually, but Bella was tired of avoiding her childhood friend. Tired of running from the lies and the hateful things they'd both said.

Lucinda was standing in a mixed group of some

of her friends and Jeremy's business partners. Bella started over toward the crowd. Lucinda glanced up at her and excused herself from the others to meet her halfway.

"Bella, thank you for inviting me."

"You're welcome. I…well, I'm sure you noticed I've been avoiding you."

Lucinda laughed, and it was a kind sound. It reminded Bella of their childhood and how much fun they'd once had together.

"Yes, I have. I think I had something to do with that. I'm sorry for telling Kell and Daniel the details about your dad."

"I wish you hadn't," she said. But Bella was surprised that she didn't feel that knot in the bottom of her stomach that she always had when she thought of someone finding out about her past.

"Well, I did. It was in bad taste and I have no excuse except that I was so shocked to see you. Last time I saw you, you and your mother were cleaning my house."

There was something in Lucinda's voice that Bella had never noticed before. It sounded almost like anger. "Why does that bother you?"

She shrugged. "I hate what your dad did. He stole my best friend from me. And I'm still mad at myself for not being a better friend to you."

"I don't think I could have handled it then. I felt so destroyed and unsure of myself."

"I'm sorry. I'm really sorry for how I acted back then and for bringing it up again."

Bella forgave her friend, knowing that a portion of the blame sat on her own shoulders. "Don't worry about mentioning it to Kell. He researched me on the Internet anyway."

Lucinda started laughing and Bella noticed Daniel glancing over at them. "He did the same thing when Daniel and I started dating."

"I guess we can't fault him for caring about the men we like."

Lucinda took her hand and drew her into a corner away from everyone else. "I'm glad you're with Jeremy, but…"

"What?" she asked, almost afraid to hear what Lucinda might say.

"Be careful with your heart, Bella. Jeremy always moves on."

"I know that. But I think maybe I'm changing his way of thinking."

"I hope so. I'm looking forward to having my old friend back in my life. Even if things don't work out with Jeremy," Lucinda said.

Bella was, too. She'd renewed many acquaintances from her childhood these past few months and it had felt right to be back in that circle. Some of the people she had nothing in common with, but others were turning into good friends. It had made her realize how much she'd missed the social part of her old life.

The door opened before she could respond and Jeremy walked in. She saw the surprise on his face as everyone broke out into a chorus of the birthday song. He didn't greet his parents or his friends first but made a beeline to her side, pulling her into his arms and kissing her.

Everyone broke into applause and Bella felt like she'd found something that she'd spent a lifetime searching for. And she was certain that Jeremy realized it, too.

The party lasted until after midnight. Kell's and Jeremy's mothers were the last to leave. His dad had left early for a meeting, which Jeremy knew meant he was going to see his mistress. His mom really liked Bella and had taken him aside three separate times to tell him so. Finally the last guest left and he and Bella were alone.

"Thank you," he said when they'd finished cleaning up and were sharing a glass of wine on her patio. He pulled her down on the glider next to him, keeping her tucked close to his side.

"Were you surprised?"

"Yes," he said.

"Good. I know how much you like surprises."

"I like surprising you," he said quietly.

"I think I know why. It was so much fun planning this and waiting to see how you would react to it."

He didn't say anything else, realizing he didn't

want to talk. He tipped her head back against his shoulder and leaned down to kiss her. She tasted of the sweet wine they were drinking and of something unique to her. He loved that taste. Couldn't ever get enough of it. He shifted around until he could place the wineglass on the floor and then maneuvered her sideways on his lap so he could caress her while they were kissing.

He'd never let anyone be a part of his life the way he had with Bella. Tonight had brought that home in many ways. His mother liked her. Even Kell, who was leery of all women and treated most of them with disdain, was starting to soften toward her, though he still seemed wary of Jeremy getting suckered in.

He lifted his head, rubbing his thumb over her lower lip. It was moist and swollen from his kisses. "What were you and Lucinda talking about?"

She shrugged, laying her head on his shoulder. Her fingers traced a random pattern on his arm. "Nothing really. Just making peace."

"Everything cool between you two now?" he asked. His instinct had been to go over and pull Bella away from Lucinda.

"Yes. This is going to sound kind of silly, but I think a lot of the blame was mine. I felt so…naked when it happened that I didn't really give Lucinda or my other friends a chance to reject me. I just shut down. And then my mother ended up working for some of them, which was very awkward."

He held her closer, rubbing his hand up and down her back. He loved how fragile she felt in his arms. It made him feel that he could protect her. And he wanted to do that, he realized, not just physically but also emotionally. He didn't want anyone to snub her or make her feel less than worthy.

"I can understand that. What changed now?"

"You changed me," she said softly. Her fingers moved from his arm to the buttons of his shirt. She toyed with the open button at his collar and then opened a second one, slipping her hand under the fabric to caress his chest.

He arched one eyebrow at her. "How did I do that?"

He was trying to keep his mind on the conversation, but his blood seemed to be flowing heavier in his veins.

"I think it was the way you accepted me and Dare. The way you were never condescending to us." She circled his nipple with her fingertip, scratching her nail around it. He groaned deep in his throat.

"Money doesn't mean everything," he said, but a part of him knew that wasn't what he really believed. Their entire relationship was based on finances. He'd given her his contacts and entrée back into the world she wanted to belong to.

She shifted on his lap.

"It does to some people," she said.

He didn't want to talk any longer. He wanted her naked, he wanted to open the birthday present he'd been planning on savoring all day long.

He tugged at the hem of her camisole top, but she caught his wrists in her hands. "Not yet."

She hopped off his lap. When he moved to stand she pushed him back to the glider.

"Wait here. I have a present for you."

"You don't need to give me anything else. I'll be happy to undress you and count that as the best present I've received."

She smiled at him with her heart in her eyes and he had trouble swallowing. "You can do that after you open my other gift."

She left him alone on the porch while she went inside. A few minutes later he heard the sound of a Jimmy Buffett ballad—"Stars Fell on Alabama"— and then she reappeared. She held a small box in her hands.

He took it, recognizing the blue box with the white ribbon. He knew she was on a budget and worried that she might have given him something too extravagant.

"Open it," she said.

He did, and saw a pair of silver fish cuff links. Masculine, understated. He looked up at her. Perfect.

"I know how you love the sea and being out on your boat," she said.

He realized then that he'd fallen for her. And he didn't like it. Didn't like the power she had over him. The intense vulnerability that feeling brought with it.

He suddenly felt unworthy of her. Everything he had in his life had been given to him due to the lucky circumstances of his birth. Bella had lost everything, then carved a life and a place for herself in the world through sheer determination.

If he'd learned anything tonight, it was that he couldn't let her go. And watching his parents had strengthened his resolve to never ruin his relationship with Bella by marrying her.

# Eleven

Bella's day wasn't going according to plan. Tomorrow was the official last day on her contract with Jeremy and she wanted to put the finishing touches on the private event she'd been working on for the two of them.

But instead of focusing on Jeremy, she had to turn her attention to her business. And for the first time, she really resented it.

Her business had always been the center of her life, the thing she used to keep herself on track and balanced.

But now Jeremy filled that need.

They'd had brunch with his mother and aunt

Mary on Sunday, merging their lives even more closely together, and she'd found that she liked that. She'd arrived at work today feeling hopeful.

Now Shelley had been in a minor fender bender and was late for work. One of Shelley's clients had shown up early, while the client Bella was supposed to be meeting with was late.

She smiled at Huntley Donovan of the Art Council Guild as she showed her to the conference room and left to get her something to drink.

Randall, one of her event managers, walked in the door. Bella pounced on him. "Thank God you're here. Shelley was in an accident. She's fine, but she was supposed to be doing a precontract bid for the Art Guild this morning."

"I know. That's why I'm here. She called me before she called her insurance agent."

Randall was one of her best employees. He'd joined her staff only three months earlier and had proven himself invaluable. He was a tall African-American man with an easy smile and affable charm as well as a sense of calmness that put even the most temperamental clients at ease.

"I think it's time I gave her a raise," Bella said with a smile.

"Where is Ms. Donovan?"

"In the conference room. She'd like a cup of Earl Grey tea, and the file is somewhere on Shelley's desk," she said, gesturing toward the messy stack of paper.

Randall walked over to the desk and started going through the piles there. "I've got it."

"Thanks, Randall. I'm expecting a new client any minute."

Her phone was ringing when she entered her office and she was almost afraid to answer it and have one more thing go wrong.

"Good morning, this is Isabella."

"Hey, honey. Got a few minutes?" Her pulse sped up just at the sound of his voice. Oh, man, she had it bad for him. She propped her hip on the edge of her desk so she could keep an eye on the front door for her client.

"Yes. My client is running a few minutes late," she said, trying to reach her coffee cup while they were talking. It was too far away. With anyone else she'd put the phone down and grab her coffee but she didn't want to miss anything that Jeremy said.

"I want you to clear your calendar for tonight and tomorrow."

That arrogance of his was going to get him in trouble someday, but not today. She did like the way he was so confident in everything he said and did with her.

"I'll try," she said, adding that task to the growing to-do list in her head. Frankly, after this morning, she wanted to take a few weeks off and just hide away.

"Don't try. I need you to do it."

"Is this more than mere bossiness?" she asked.

There was a tone in his voice that she'd never heard before. Something she couldn't place.

"Yes."

"What's up?" she asked. "Is everything okay with your family?"

"Yes. I have something special planned for tonight and I think we're going to want to spend the day together tomorrow."

"What do you have planned?" she asked. She should have realized that he'd be as aware as she was that they were nearing the end of their contracted time together.

"Something special that's just for you," he said. There was an odd huskiness to his voice.

"Another surprise? I think I'm beginning to like them." And she was. Before Jeremy, she'd liked to know every detail of her day and any variation would immediately send her into crisis mode. But she'd learned that not every upheaval was a bad one. Not every surprise was to be dreaded. In fact, most of the ones he'd sprung on her were to be embraced.

"You'll like this one."

"Promise?" she asked, knowing that was just her knee-jerk reaction. Her conditioned response to anything unexpected.

"Guarantee it, honey."

"I'm going to hold you to that."

"You do that. I'll pick you up around six tonight."

"Where are we going?"

"Out on my yacht."

They hadn't been out on his yacht since the night they'd had that argument and he'd said that he didn't want their time together to end. She told herself not to get her hopes up, not to expect more than he'd promised her. But she felt a tinge of excitement.

"What are we going to be doing?"

"Having dinner and discussing the future."

A surge of joy went through her and she could hardly speak as he said goodbye. She hung up the phone, her mind alive with the possibilities of what the future held for her and Jeremy.

Jeremy checked every inch of the yacht before leaving to pick up Bella. Andy had prepared Bella's favorite meal and left him explicit instructions for heating it up. He'd had the housekeeping staff ensure that the dining room was set to Jeremy's exact instructions.

The bed was made up with the new Egyptian cotton sheets he'd ordered that would just match Bella's honey-brown eyes.

He had her favorite white wine chilling in the fridge, her favorite songs queued up on his Bose stereo. In fact, everything was as perfect as he could make it. He adjusted one of the blooms in the vase of purple tulips before he climbed the stairs two at a time and vaulted from the boat to the dock. He could probably run all the way to her house and not get rid of the excess energy that was dogging him tonight.

Seldom was he nervous about anything, but he was about tonight. He had played the scenario in his head a million times during the last few days. He'd gone over every possible answer she could give him and had a contingency plan worked out for each one.

He forced himself to stand still and calm the nervous energy. This was the same as closing a big deal at the office. Except a big deal never affected him this way. He had a lot invested in the outcome of this evening. He'd done everything he could to ensure he got the outcome he wanted.

Then why the hell was he so nervous?

He shook his head at his own stupidity and walked to his car. Once he had Bella on his boat out at sea, everything would fall into place.

He knew she wanted to be with him. She'd said as much the last time they were here. And he knew she needed some kind of stability, so his plan was absolutely perfect.

He drove to her home and parked out front, waiting for a few minutes before getting out. He refused to give in to the urge to get to her sooner. He had to manage his emotional response to her and so far, tonight, he was doing a piss-poor job of it.

He rang the bell instead of letting himself in with

the key she'd given him. He liked her quiet neighborhood more than he'd expected to. One of her neighbors waved at him as she backed out of her driveway. It seemed like a good sign. A sign that things were meant to be between him and Bella.

The door opened with a rush of cold air. He glanced at Bella, his words dying on his lips. She was breathtaking in her simple silk sundress. The halter top dipped down in the front between her breasts.

"Aren't you going to say anything?" she asked, looking like a femme fatale.

"Uh-huh," he said, but he couldn't get his brain to work. Her hair was pulled up on top of her head and a few tendrils fell around her face.

She had on some kind of dewy lip gloss that made him ache to lick her lips. To taste them. He skimmed his gaze higher and saw the amusement in her eyes. He knew he was a goner.

He stepped forward, put his hand on the back of her head and tilted her head up to his. He leaned down and licked at her lips. They tasted sweet but when he thrust his tongue into her mouth, he realized he liked the way she tasted more. Craved her on his tongue.

His body stirred. He thrust her away from him, turning his back to her before he did something crazy like make love to her on the front-hall table.

"Jeremy?"

"Bella…dammit, woman, I have plans for this evening."

"Ah, sorry?"

He shook his head and cleared his throat and then turned around again. "Good evening. You look gorgeous tonight."

"Thanks. You look very nice as well," she said. There was a lightness about her tonight that he'd never seen before and as soon as he recognized it, he was at ease. She wasn't on her guard around him.

"I hope this is okay," she said.

"I have no idea what you're talking about," he said.

"My clothes. You said it was going to be a special evening, so I thought I'd dress up."

"I like you dressed up," he said. The only thing he liked more was her naked. But her clothing tonight was perfect for what he had in mind. He was glad she'd picked up on the vibe he'd sent her. Glad to see that she, too, was ready for a special night.

When he'd asked her to be his mistress he had no idea how important she'd become to his life.

"I thought you would. Do we have time for a drink before we leave?" she asked.

"We're going out on the boat so we have all the time we'd like."

"So, do you want a drink?" she asked.

"I want this evening to be perfect for you, Bella."

"I think it will be," she said, pushing the door all the way open. "Come on in."

He followed her into her home and saw she'd taken the time to prepare for this drink. She had all the ingredients for his favorite cocktail on her bar. She mixed him a Grey Goose martini and poured it neatly into a glass, then garnished it with a cocktail onion instead of an olive. Then she poured herself one as well.

"To the future," she said with a faint smile.

"The future," he said, tapping their glasses together.

He watched her take a sip of the cool drink and tip her head to the side to watch him. He knew there was no such thing as a sure thing, but he felt very sure of Bella.

Very sure that he'd made the right decision as far as tonight went.

The sun was setting as they left the marina behind. Bella relaxed against the padded bench at the back of the yacht while Jeremy piloted the boat. Her entire body was buzzing from the way he'd kissed her when he'd shown up at her door.

They'd talked on the way to the yacht club, but not about anything important. Just the day's events. And it was nice to be able to share that with someone. She'd never really had that before Jeremy. Dare asked how she was, but he didn't really listen unless something was wrong that she needed him to attend to.

It was so different with Jeremy. She had given up cautioning herself about expecting too much from him. She was filled with the love she felt for him. It made her nerves tingle.

She wanted him. Needed him. Needed to be by his side.

Kicking off her high-heeled sandals, she walked across the deck to him. The breeze tugged at her hair and a few more strands escaped her clip. She felt them curling over her bare shoulders. Finally she reached him and she wrapped her arms around his back, resting her head between his shoulder blades.

He turned in her arms, lowering his head to hers. She lifted her face, meeting him halfway. The kiss was everything she wanted, yet left her wanting more.

She framed his face with her hands as he moved his mouth over hers, skimming his tongue along the seam of her lips and then pushing inside. He tasted wild and untamed, like the sea surrounding them. He groaned and angled his head for a deeper penetration of her mouth.

He pulled her body more tightly against his. She felt the weight of her breasts against his chest and his big hands wrapped around her waist. She stroked his face and neck with her hands. He lifted her more fully into him.

His kiss left room for nothing but thoughts of

Jeremy. His hands slid down her back, pulling her closer. He nibbled on her mouth and she felt like she was completely at his mercy.

Exactly where she wanted to be. She dug her nails into his shoulders as she leaned up, brushing against his chest.

She glanced down and saw her nipples pressing against the thin bodice of her dress. Jeremy skimmed his thumbs over her breasts before he slid his hands beneath the fabric.

"Baby, you are playing hell with my plans."

"Should I go sit back down?"

"Oh, hell, no," he said, caressing her back and spine.

She had a feeling she was going to remember this night for the rest of her life.

Jeremy dropped anchor when they were in the middle of nowhere. They were out of shipping lanes and away from other boats. The moon had risen and the sky stretched forever, enveloping them both in the night.

His body still pulsed from making love to Bella, and he wanted her again. He wanted to take her down to his bed and have her again and again until she forgot every name except his.

But first he wanted to ask her to stay with him.

She'd gone down to the master stateroom a few minutes earlier to touch up her makeup. He hoped she reapplied that slick lip gloss. He was looking forward to kissing it off again.

He went into the galley and readied their meal, then took out the presents he'd purchased for her, setting them in the different areas where he needed them.

He took a deep breath. He was a little nervous about her reaction no matter how well he thought he'd planned for it. He wanted her in his life for a long time. This was what he needed. What they both needed.

He opened the bottle of wine and left it to breathe and then checked the drawer where he'd left the paperwork he'd need later if she agreed to his proposition.

"What's that?"

He shut the drawer and turned to look at her. She'd taken her hair down and it hung in waves over her shoulders. She had reapplied her lip gloss and her dress was refastened. In the center of the V-neck he noticed a mark he'd left on her.

He took a box off the counter. "This is for you."

She glanced again at the drawer but took the gift and let the other matter drop. He poured her a glass of wine, then leaned one hip against the counter and just watched her.

"You're making me nervous."

He shrugged, taking a sip of his wine. "I like looking at you."

"I like having you look at me," she said, a hint of shyness in her voice.

"How can you be shy with me after all we've done together?" he asked, coming over to stand next to her.

"I don't know. It's different when we're together. I forget about everything else."

"Good. Now open your present so we can have dinner."

She opened it. He heard the gasp of surprise in her voice and he was pleased. He took the diamond and sapphire pendant necklace from the box.

"Hold your hair up," he said.

She lifted her hair and he fastened the necklace. Keeping his hands on her neck, he leaned down and kissed her. He wanted to find a way to tell her everything that was inside him even though he knew he couldn't.

He lifted his head slowly and took her arm, escorting her to the dining area. He picked up the gift-wrapped box by her seat.

"Open this one while I'm getting our dinner."

"Jeremy, you spoil me."

"It's about time someone did," he said. He ached for her past and her childhood. The way it had been torn away from her. He wanted to make sure that she had a safe cocoon for the rest of her life. That she never again had to face financial insecurity or worry about being left alone.

That's why his plan would work for both of them. It was a safe way for them to be together and not have to worry about the unexpected things that life sometimes threw at them.

He dished up their food and brought the plates over to the table. She'd opened the second present, a bracelet that matched the necklace he'd just given her.

She fastened it around her wrist and glanced up at him. There was so much hope in her eyes that it was almost painful to glimpse it.

He knew he had to do this right. He couldn't screw this up for her. Her trust was a precious gift and he didn't want to abuse it.

"Thank you for the bracelet, Jeremy. I wish I had something to give you."

"You already did."

"Sex?"

"No, Bella. So much more than that. Ralph Waldo Emerson once said that 'the only true gift is a portion of yourself.' You've given me a gift that I can never reciprocate. Bringing me into the circle of your friends. Welcoming me into your life and into your bed."

Tears glittered in her eyes and he thought, yes, this was right. For once he was doing what he needed to do. He wasn't betting on charm to get him through, but speaking straight from his gut.

"That is the sweetest thing anyone has ever said to me."

"It's only the truth."

The conversation ranged over many topics as they ate, and soon Jeremy was clearing the dishes away. He brought out a fruit-and-cheese tray with a small box nestled on it.

He handed her the box after he seated himself.

"I have something I want to ask you, Bella. But first please open this last present."

Bella held her breath as she opened the box. She could hardly concentrate on the gift, wanting instead to know what he was going to ask her. Would it be to marry him?

After brunch last Sunday with his family, she suspected he had something permanent in mind for the two of them. And she wanted that. She'd already made up her mind to ask him to move in with her after their contract was up.

"Bella, open the box," he said.

She did and found a pair of teardrop earrings that matched the necklace and bracelet he'd already given her. Jeremy was at his most romantic tonight. And she couldn't help falling more deeply in love with him.

He was everything she'd ever wanted in a man. Caring, attentive, supportive and the kind of lover every woman dreamed of having. She glanced up to find him watching her. She removed the silver hoop earrings she had on and put on the ones that matched her necklace and bracelet.

Was a matching ring soon to follow?

"Thank you."

"You're welcome, honey."

She didn't want to rush him but he didn't say anything else, and finally she couldn't stand it any longer. "You said you had a question."

"I do. I'm not sure how to ask it."

"Whatever it is, just ask."

He leaned forward. "Do you remember when we met?"

How could she forget? Her secret crush noticing her at a party where she was working, taking the time to talk to her and flirt with her and then offering her something that could never be repaid. "Yes."

"From that moment, you've been like an obsession for me. The last three and a half years I've been consumed with thoughts of you."

"Oh, Jeremy," she said, unable to keep her emotions from her voice. It was like he had glimpsed inside her heart and knew what she felt for him. "Me, too."

He smiled at her then. It was a sweet expression and not one she'd ever seen before on his fierce face.

"Obsessions aren't healthy things because they are all or nothing. Our relationship was nothing at first, just a piece of paper that was kept in a file. But then it became…well, I think you'll agree it became more than either of us ever anticipated."

She'd never been a man's obsession before and

was flattered he'd thought about her so much. It made her feel a lot less vulnerable. It reminded her *that Jeremy was invested in this relationship, too.*

"I'd definitely agree to that," she said. She'd never expected to fall so completely in love with Jeremy. In the beginning she might have even intended to use him to get back into the crowd that had once been her own, but that had quickly faded. She wanted *him,* and it didn't matter if he was part of her old social set or not.

"I was hoping that you'd feel this way, Jeremy. For the last few weeks I've been dreading this day. Knowing that it would mean an end to our contracted time together."

He reached across the space between them and took her hands in his. She liked the way his big hands enfolded hers.

"Me, too. I've been thinking our situation over. Trying to come up with a new relationship that would suit us both."

"Anything where we can be together will work with me. I don't think I can take living apart now. You really have become so much a part of my life."

"I hoped you would say that."

He tugged her to her feet, drawing her to him. He led her upstairs. He hit a button and low-level lighting illuminated the deck. She saw that there were a bunch of pillows on the bench where they'd made love earlier.

"What are we doing up here?"

"I wanted to hold you in my arms," he said. He pushed a button and music came from the speakers. Not pop music, but Ella Fitzgerald, her evocative voice singing about love and heartbreak in a way that made Bella believe that the woman had experienced them. She rested her head on Jeremy's shoulder as he danced them around the deck.

In this moment everything felt perfect. The anticipation of his question hung between them, sweetening the moment. For the last few months she'd been so aware of the contract and the expiration date of their relationship, and now she felt something so magical she could scarcely comprehend that this moment was here.

When the song ended he pushed a button and the music stopped. He led her toward the railing of the boat and turned her in his arms so they both faced the distant horizon. He wrapped his arms around her and pulled her back into the cradle of his body. He surrounded her completely.

She took it all in—the moonlight on the water, the softly blowing salt-scented breeze. The rocking motion of the boat and the heat of the man standing behind her.

He took a deep breath. "This is so much harder than I thought it would be."

Suddenly she was afraid. But she took a deep breath and turned in his arms. "Whatever it is,

Jeremy, if it involves the two of us staying together, then my answer is going to be yes."

He crushed her to him in a hug that made her feel like he'd never let her go. "I'm so glad to hear that. I've had a new contract drawn up and it is more generous than our last agreement."

She pulled back to look at him. "What kind of contract? I thought we'd moved beyond needing some legal paperwork between us."

"Honey, I want to make sure that you're protected. That you have everything you've ever wanted."

That sounded so nice that she cautioned herself from letting her temper get the better of her. Maybe it was some kind of prenuptial agreement. The kind that Kell had been talking about these last few months. "Do you have the contract with you?"

"Yes, I do."

"Let me see it."

Bella heard Jeremy talking and knew he was saying something important, but for the life of her she couldn't understand what the heck it was. She followed him down the gangplank back to the dining room where the remains of their dessert still sat on the table.

The last five minutes had been so bizarre she was sure she'd entered some kind of twilight zone. He seemed normal, but maybe there'd been some kind of break in the time-space continuum that had put her in an alternate universe where the man she loved would offer her a contract to stay with him.

"Here's the contract," he said, handing her a folder with a thick sheaf of papers inside.

She took the folder from him and drifted over to the table. Sitting down, she opened it up and saw the words at the top that stopped her. This was the same shell agreement as the original mistress contract she'd signed three years ago.

Anger began a slow churning deep inside her and she used that anger to help stem the tears that wanted to flow. How could he have completely missed the point?

"I think you'll agree that the new contract is more generous than the first one was. I've recently started doing business with an international firm that I think will net you a lot of new contacts. I've offered that as well as an exclusive arrangement with my company to be our only party planner."

"Please don't say anything else," she said, forcing the words out in a reasonable tone. But inside she was screaming and she didn't think she was going to stop for a long time. This evening that had been picture-perfect had shattered into a million little pieces. Pieces that cut deeper than she would have thought they could. And hurt so badly she didn't feel like she was going to recover.

But she'd deal with that later. She just wanted to

keep it together until she could get away and be by herself so she could lick her wounds in private.

Once again she'd fallen for an illusion. Something she knew didn't exist for her. She wasn't one of those women who was meant to have a stable, happy future. She was meant to live one day at time.

"Bella? What's the matter, honey?"

She glanced up at him and realized that he meant this to be in both of their best interests.

She took a deep breath and fought to find the words she needed. "Why do you still want a contract?"

"It's the only way to make sure we're both protected. I know that you need financial security and I need…"

"What do you need?"

He shrugged and looked away from her.

"Jeremy, I don't want to be your mistress anymore."

"Is it that you doubt the business I can generate for you? I can add an addendum that guarantees at least a million dollars a year in new business for the length of the contract."

She shook her head and got to her feet. "I think you should take me home."

"Not yet. Talk to me, Bella. I'm willing to sweeten the deal."

Was he really? Was he just afraid to admit he cared for her without knowing where she stood? For a minute she stood there, undecided, afraid to take a chance. But then she remembered that life was precarious and changed on a dime. And this might really be her only chance at love.

"I don't want you for your contacts or the amount of business you can generate. I want you for you."

He frowned at her and rubbed the back of his neck. Crossing to the bar he poured himself a shot of whiskey and downed it in one gulp.

"Jeremy, don't you feel anything for me?"

"Obsession," he said, the one word bit out between drinks as he refilled his glass again.

His earlier words circled in her mind. She'd thought he was joking, but saw now that he viewed her as something unhealthy for him and his life. Less than worthy, she thought. Still not worthy of someone in that social set.

"You're an obsession for me, Bella. This is the only way I know how to control our relationship. I have to know the parameters."

"Why would you want that? We could have a really great relationship. The kind that most people only dream of. Why can't you see that?"

"These last six months haven't been realistic," he said. "We have the illusion of a relationship. Because we both know that it can't end until the contract runs out."

She couldn't believe what she was hearing. "Do you really think that what I feel for you is some by-product of the contract?"

He shrugged. "I don't want to analyze it too closely. Whatever you feel for me…whatever you tell yourself, that's all immaterial to the contract. I think we've both proven that we're trustworthy."

She felt tears stinging her eyes and this time had no anger to assuage them. She tried to say something else, but her mouth trembled and she couldn't make herself talk.

She'd thought she'd been hurt in all the ways a person could be. That her heart had been thoroughly broken. But until this minute, when she stood in front of the man she'd given her heart to and heard him describe her as contractually trustworthy, she realized she hadn't known how deeply love could hurt.

"I can't believe I fell in love with you."

"You aren't really in love with me," he said. "It's obsession, honey."

"I think I know the difference between love and obsession, Jeremy."

He didn't say anything else and finally she couldn't stand the silence between them for another second. "Please take me back to shore. I want to go home."

# Twelve

Bella ignored the phone and her friends and concentrated only on business. But at the end of two weeks, even though she was utterly exhausted, she still couldn't sleep through the night. She'd gotten used to Jeremy's presence in her bed and in her life, and she missed him.

Even though he was a huge jackass with some stupid ideas about her and their relationship, she still missed him. That really ticked her off because it made her feel like an idiot. But in the middle of the night, when she stared out her window at the waning moon, she couldn't help but remember their last night together and how perfect it had been. Until he'd brought out the contract.

Her lack of sleep made her cranky at the office. Randall and Shelley had insisted she go home early. So here she was in the middle of the afternoon, sitting on her porch on the glider, Jack Johnson playing on her iPod and a cup of blueberry tea at her side.

She was putting together a bid for another event at the Norton and wanted to double-check the images from the last event. She absolutely refused to think of Chihuly glass ceilings or the exquisite sculpture that was now in her backyard.

She uploaded a batch of pictures from her digital camera, forgetting that she'd used it the night of Jeremy's thirty-fifth birthday until the images starting popping up on her computer screen.

She stared at them. At him. At the picture she'd snapped of him with Kell, both men looking intense and serious just standing in a corner talking.

"Jeremy," she said, hearing the heartache in her own voice.

She cropped the picture down so that it was just him. Soon his face filled her screen and she traced his eyebrows and the sun lines around his eyes. God, she missed him.

Maybe she should go back to him. Swallow her pride and say yes to his contract. Except she knew she could never be happy as his mistress. She wanted to be his wife. That was the truth of it.

She wished she'd had a friend who could have

offered her a bit of advice at the beginning of the original mistress contract—*don't fall in love.*

"Too late."

Lucinda had called her twice. Each time the messages had been short and to the point, just saying that she was there for Bella.

Her doorbell rang and she minimized the screen she'd been working on, setting her computer on the glider seat before going to answer the door.

She checked the peephole first and scowled as she recognized Kell. She opened the door and he frowned at her and then cursed under his breath.

"You look like hell."

"Uh, thanks." She pulled the jacket of her sweat suit closer together before crossing her arms over her chest. Randall and Shelley had pretty much said the same thing when they'd sent her home this afternoon.

"Damn, this is a mess. I thought I had everything figured out but I think I'm missing something here," Kell said, running his hand through his thick blond hair.

"What are you talking about? It's really too early in the day for you to be drunk."

"I don't drink. Listen, can I come in?" he asked, taking a step toward her before she could even move.

"Sure."

She wanted to pretend he was the last person she wanted to talk to but the truth was she was starved for news on how Jeremy was doing. She had even tried to delicately pump her brother for information, but Dare hadn't heard from Jeremy, either.

She led the way into her house, stopping in the middle of the living room. "What's up?"

He paced around the room like a caged tiger. There was a grim set to his mouth. "That's what I want to know."

"What did Jeremy tell you?" she asked, knowing that no one was going to be able to help them. Over the sleepless nights she'd spent alone in her bed, she'd rehashed everything a million times. She knew she couldn't force Jeremy to love her, and she didn't want to be with him without love.

"Nothing. He hasn't said a word about you in two weeks. All he does is work."

She shook her head. She wished he was getting on with his life, but by the same token a part of her was happy to hear she wasn't the only one suffering. It made her believe that maybe he had cared for her. "I'm sorry to hear that. I don't think it has anything to do with me."

"It has everything to do with you. It's clear to me that you two have had a fight. Whatever it was about, you need to go to him and fix it."

"It's not that easy."

"Yes, it is. No problems are that insurmountable."

"Some of them are, Kell. This isn't just a fight or a difference of opinion. We want different things from life."

Kell sighed. "I pushed him to offer you a prenup. Don't hold that against him."

"It wasn't that. I would sign one if he asked me to."

"Then what is it? He's so into you."

"He's not into me. At least not the way you mean. I'm an obsession that he's trying to exorcise from his soul."

"He said that?"

"Yes, he did. And I don't know how to convince him otherwise. I'm not sure what you want from me, but I can't just go back to him and pretend to be whatever he wants until he gets tired of me."

Kell stared at her for a long time. "Because you love him."

She nodded.

Kell paced over to the front door and opened it. Glancing back at her, he said, "Just think about talking to him."

She nodded and watched him leave, knowing that she'd think of little else other than Jeremy.

Jeremy watched the sunset from his multi-million-dollar home. He glanced around at the luxury furnishings and the life that was full of the best things money could buy. But it felt empty. It felt the way it had before he'd met Isabella McNamara and his life had changed.

Obsessions had a way of doing that.

But the thing was, he no longer believed she was only an obsession. Her words that last night on his boat haunted him. A million times he replayed them. Heard her say she loved him and then quietly ask to go home.

He'd broken her heart and he had no idea how to fix it. For a while he hadn't even contemplated fixing it. He'd wanted to find another woman and prove to Bella exactly how desirable he was to other females. But he'd been disinterested in any other woman.

Then this last week he'd realized how much she'd brought to his life. Not just her presence in his bed, but the way she'd brought his circle of friends together with hers. The effortless way she had of making connections between people and ensuring no one felt inferior.

The way she had long ago. And he'd offered her a contract to stay in his life. In retrospect, he understood perfectly where he'd gone wrong.

His gut said to go back to her and make another offer. One where she set the terms and he'd do whatever she wanted. Be her love slave or whatever else she'd have from him.

But another part, a bigger part, was truly afraid of what she made him feel. He'd hurt this past week in a way that he'd never felt before. His life had been a gilded one of privilege where no one denied him anything.

Until Isabella. His Bella. He wanted her back. He wanted her happy.

There was a knock on his study door before it opened. He glanced over his shoulder to see his butler standing in the doorway. "Are you receiving, sir?"

"Who is it, Thomas?" he asked, hoping against hope that it would be Bella. If she came to him, he'd take her back and throw out the contract.

"Kell, sir."

The last thing he wanted to do was talk to Kell, who kept trying to take the blame for his breakup by pointing out that some women found prenups offensive. If only he'd offered her a prenup, he had the feeling she would have signed it with no qualms. God, he'd been a total ass.

And Bella wasn't going to come back. She deserved a man who loved her the way she loved him.

She loved *him*. That's what she said. What if she'd been mistaken?

"Sir?"

He rubbed the back of his neck and glanced around the study. His desk was littered with files and he'd closed more deals this week than he had in the previous three months. He'd been working nonstop, jacked up on coffee and adrenaline. Afraid to close his eyes because he dreamed of her in his bed and woke aching and hungry for her.

"Yes, send him back."

Jeremy logged on to his e-mail while he was

waiting for Kell and saw that he had a message from Bella. Before he could open it, Kell came into the room and headed straight to the bar, grabbing a bottle of Perrier. "What the hell did you say to Bella?"

"Why?" he asked, distracted from her message for a moment by his cousin. Damn, he should have refused to see Kell—then he could have read her message in private.

"Because I went to see her to apologize for putting you up to asking for the prenup and…"

"And what?" He was surprised by Kell's actions, but he shouldn't have been. Kell had spent the last week telling him that just because he'd screwed up by trusting the wrong woman, Jeremy shouldn't screw up by not trusting the right woman.

"She looked like hell. I don't think she's slept in a week."

Dammit, he thought. He'd wanted to be her hero and to protect her. Instead he'd left her and she was worse off for having known him. "Leave it alone, Kell. I told you to stay away from her."

Kell didn't respond to that, just scooped some ice from the ice bucket and poured his Perrier into a glass. "You're miserable, too."

"And your point is?" he asked, trying not to look at his Outlook inbox, but failing. Why had she e-mailed him?

"You've never been stupid about anything. Not women, not business. Don't let her be the first."

"Why is this so important to you?"

"I want to believe that you and I can be happy."

"I'll take that under consideration," he said, glancing at his computer screen again.

"What's so important on your computer?"

"Bella sent me a message."

"Did you open it?"

"No, I'm waiting for you to leave."

"Are you sure you don't need me?"

He nodded. Kell walked toward the door. "I'll call you tomorrow."

Jeremy watched him go before finally clicking on the icon to open the e-mail message. It was brief and to the point. No smiley face after her name. Just a listing of JPEG file names.

Pictures from his birthday party. He opened them up one by one and felt like he'd been punched in the gut. In front of him in full color was the life he'd been afraid to imagine for himself and Bella. A life that was full of friends and family. One that they shared together.

And he knew then that there was a small chance that she still loved him. A woman who'd go through all this effort for her lover wasn't someone who could walk away easily. And he remembered other things she'd said that last night. Remembered that she, too, wanted a life together. Just not as his mistress.

Finally he got it.

He pushed away from his desk, grabbed his keys and walked out of his house. He didn't realize he was running until he reached his car.

The knock on her door just after dinner startled her. But a part of her had been hoping, ever since she'd e-mailed the pictures, that Jeremy would come. She was almost afraid to look in the peephole and see someone other than him.

But there he was. Wearing a pair of faded jeans and a faded college T-shirt. His hair was unkempt and he scarcely resembled the fashionable man she knew him to be.

She opened the door and stared at him. He didn't say anything to her, either. He shifted from one foot to the other.

"I got your e-mail."

"Oh. Did you like the pictures?"

"Yes. They turned out really nice," he said.

God, had he really come over here just to thank her for the pictures?

"I don't have any other ones."

"That's okay. Thanks for the ones you sent."

"You're welcome," she said, waiting for him to say something else, but minutes dragged by and he said nothing. Finally she realized that he wasn't going to say anything and a part of her was ready to beg him to take her back. But then she remembered how hard she'd struggled to rebuild her life. And she knew she couldn't. He had to meet her halfway.

"Goodbye, Jeremy," she said, starting to close the door.

His hand shot out and he blocked the door from closing. "Can I come in?"

"Why? To talk more about the photos?"

"No," he said, thrusting his hands through his hair. "I didn't come over here because of the pictures. I'm here because I'm an idiot."

"No, you're not."

"Yes, I am," he said, stepping over the threshold and closing the door behind him. "I want you in my life. I can't live without you."

"I want those things, too, but I don't want to be your mistress."

"I don't want that, either, not anymore. I was afraid to admit how much I need you, but that doesn't change the fact that I do need you, Bella. I'm asking you to take me back on your terms. I don't have a contract or gifts. I don't have anything except myself."

"Someone once told me that the best gift was one of yourself."

"A wise man."

She was almost afraid to hope that he meant what he said. "What if I said my terms were marriage and a family?"

"That offer would be more than I deserve," he said, drawing her into his arms and holding her so tightly she knew he'd never let go. "But I'd say yes before you changed your mind."

"I'm not going to change my mind."

"That's good." He buried his face against her neck. "I love you, Bella."

"I love you, too."

He lifted her in his arms and carried her into her bedroom. He made love to her and then cradled her *to his chest. They talked about the future and made* plans. Permanent plans. Plans for their life together.

\* \* \* \* \*

# HIGH-SOCIETY MISTRESS

BY
KATHERINE GARBERA

This book is dedicated to all the readers at katherinegarbera.com. Thanks for always playing with me at Chatty Kathy!

# One

Tempest Lambert, the tabloid's favorite party girl extraordinaire, stood quietly in the foyer of her condo building, dressed conservatively and trying not to be nervous. It was silly really. She'd charmed heads of state and celebrities. She'd made the world her oyster. But one man still had the power to reduce her to a nervous wreck.

Her father's chauffeur-driven car arrived promptly at 7:35 p.m. Tempest normally would have driven herself to the Leukemia Foundation Gala dinner and silent auction but her father had wanted to speak with her in person. And this was the only time he had in his schedule.

So here she was trying to smile and pretend that

this wasn't a big deal. And when her father didn't get out of the car to greet her she had her first inkling that it really wasn't a big deal to him.

"Good evening, Ms. Lambert."

"Good evening, Marcus." The elderly chauffeur had been with her father for almost twenty years. He gave her a quick smile. "You look beautiful tonight."

"Thanks," she said, her nerves melting away at the compliment. This was her night. She'd just handled a rather messy PR problem for Tempest's Closet. Her father had even e-mailed her a note that said good job. The only note he'd ever sent her.

She slid into the car as the chauffeur held the door open for her. Her father was on the phone and didn't glance up as the car door closed behind her.

She tried to relax against the plush leather seat of her father's Mercedes-Benz E63 AMG Sedan. The driver sat in the front facing forward, all but invisible to them. She wasn't nervous. Well, maybe a little. It had been so long since she'd allowed herself to want her father's approval. At twenty-eight she was well on her own.

August Lambert, the CEO of Tempest's Closet, was an imposing man. Well over six-feet tall he'd always seemed bigger than life to her when she'd been a little girl. He'd revolutionized the way Americans thought about and purchased clothing with his line of high-end retail Tempest's Closet stores that he had started back in the 1970s and named for her after her birth.

He finished his phone conversation and made a

note in his day-planner before looking over at her. Silence grew between them as he studied her face. She wondered what he saw when he looked at her.

Some people said she looked like her mother but Tempest had never really believed that. Her mother had been one of the most beautiful women Tempest had ever seen. And what she saw reflected back in the mirror was never…beautiful.

"Thank you for meeting with me," he said.

"No problem. What did you want to see me about?"

"I'm promoting Charles Miller."

No small talk or chitchat from him. Just the blunt news that she…well, she hadn't expected.

"Charlie Miller? You've got to be kidding me." Dammit, she'd meant to be calm and cool.

"He's the right man for the job."

She gave her father a hard look—one that she'd picked up from him. "Please tell me you didn't promote him over me because I'm a woman."

"Tempest, I'm not a sexist."

She knew that. She was grasping at straws trying to find a reason. "I'm not so sure, Father. I have more experience than Charlie and am better qualified."

August sighed and rubbed the back of his neck. He stared at the car window watching the Lake Shore Drive scenery pass. She loved Chicago. Sometimes she wished she didn't because then she could simply leave her father and Tempest's Closet far behind.

Her father seemed so unapproachable, so alone. Even though only a few inches of space separated them.

And she felt the distance between them widen. No matter what she tried, she could never get his approval. His respect. A few crazy stunts when she was in her late teens and early twenties and he was going to hold that against her for the rest of her life.

"I haven't done anything to draw attention to myself lately," she said, quietly. This job had become the driving force in her life—no longer a party girl, she'd become a businesswoman. Something she was sure her father would notice.

"There was an article in *Hello!* not a week ago about you and Dean Stratford with pictures of you in your love nest."

"Father, please. You know there's nothing between Dean and me. He's recovering from a serious addiction. He needs support from his friends."

He glanced over at her. "It doesn't matter what I know. The world believes you're a party girl."

She couldn't believe what she was hearing. "The board knows I'm not."

He rubbed a hand over his heart before he put his hands in his lap, linking his fingers together. "I'm more concerned with what the public thinks."

Tempest couldn't argue that point. She almost regretted it but she'd made herself a promise long ago not to apologize for her actions. Though they were most times misconstrued she knew that she always only had the best of intentions where all of her escapades were concerned.

"I think we can overcome that. I've been working with the children's foundation, which is helping my image."

"It's not enough, Tempest. Tempest's Closet is facing some tough times."

"What kind of tough times?" she asked. Being in PR, her focus was more on image than on the company bottom line. But she hadn't heard any rumblings of trouble.

"Nothing you need to worry about."

"I'm an employee, Father. Of course I worry about the stability of the company. Tell me what's going on." She worried more about her father. It had always been one of her biggest fears…losing him. And if anything happened to Tempest's Closet he'd have nothing left to live for.

"It's Renard Investments."

*Again?* Gavin Renard had been gunning for Tempest's Closet since he'd come onto the investment scene some ten years earlier. He was always trying to man some kind of takeover.

"And Charlie will be a better VP to help you out?" she asked carefully.

"Yes. I need a public relations vice president who can get out there and give us some good spin."

"I think the articles about me should prove I know something about spin," she muttered.

"That's not the kind of spin we want."

"Father, please."

She'd spent her entire life trying to make sure that no one in the world pitied her. Poor little motherless rich girl. Instead she'd made life her party and now she had the feeling she was paying for it. She'd gone to Vassar and gotten her degree. Though she'd heard rumors that her affair with the dean of students was the only reason she'd passed, she knew she'd done the work and Stan had no control over her grades.

She crossed her legs, feeling the smooth silk of her Valentino gown against her skin. She glanced at him out of the corner of her eye.

He sighed and she had her answer. Why she was surprised, she couldn't understand. She hated that she always wanted something from him that he could never deliver.

"I'm sorry, Tempest. My mind is made up."

"Unmake it," she said, starting to lose her temper. Though she desperately wanted to hang on to it. Desperately wanted to find the cool and calm front that her father always presented. Why hadn't she inherited that?

"I think we're done here."

"Not yet. I want you to tell me exactly why I wasn't promoted."

He looked her square in the eye. "You're not responsible enough. I don't trust you to do the job."

The words hurt worse than she'd expected. And she felt the sting of tears in the back of her eyes but refused to cry in front of him. She had, in fact, never cried in front of him. She knew he considered it a cheap feminine ploy used to manipulate men.

"I don't think I'm going to be able to continue to work for you."

"That's your choice, Tempest."

"No, Father, that's yours."

From across the crowded ballroom Gavin Renard caught a glimpse of Tempest Lambert. The socialite was surrounded by a group of people and didn't look the way he'd expected her to. They'd never met, though they attended many of the same functions. To be honest he never really paid that close attention to her until tonight. Maybe it was the way she'd split from August as soon as they'd entered the room.

In her photos she appeared too thin and her mouth was always set in a pout. Her eyes usually held a vacuous expression. As he maneuvered around for a closer look, he noticed that her wide-set blue eyes weren't vacuous tonight. They seethed with something that was either passion or anger.

She wasn't as scary thin as she appeared to be in her photos. He'd thought her an attractive woman when he'd seen her on the cover of *People* magazine but in person she radiated a kind of beauty that left him speechless.

She was his enemy's daughter. So he knew the details of her life. That her mother had died when she was six of complications due to breast cancer. He knew that Tempest had been shipped off to a boarding school in Switzerland and, from all reports, been an excellent student until she turned eighteen and came into the fortune left her by her grandparents.

She'd dropped out of school and joined Europe's party set and never looked back. For six years she partied hard and with little regard for others. There were rumors of affairs with married men, scandalous photos of her in every paper on the continent and occasionally in the U.S.

Then she'd dropped off the party circuit and returned to the States to go to college. The report he'd read of her transcripts had indicated she was an excellent student. But once again she found herself embroiled in a scandal just weeks before graduation when pictures of her and the dean of students surfaced in a local paper.

She glanced up catching him staring. He arched one eyebrow at her, but didn't look away.

"What are you doing?"

Gavin didn't take his gaze from Tempest as he replied to his brother Michael's question.

"Flirting with a pretty lady."

"She's off limits, Gav. Unless you've changed your mind about…?"

"I haven't." He would never change his mind about going after August Lambert's business. August was the reason that Gavin was so successful. The reason he'd driven himself and his employees to take his company to the top. The reason he was here tonight.

Since he'd been old enough to understand the business world, he'd known who August was. At first Gavin had been in awe of what the man accomplished but seeing his methods up close and personal had changed the admiration to disdain.

He'd never forget the excitement he'd felt when he'd heard that August Lambert was opening one of his innovative Tempest's Closet stores in his home town. But he hadn't understood his father's quiet anger toward the man, and had felt a wave of distain for his father and his small-town mind-set in a way only a twelve-year-old boy could.

But in a short while, as the life his father had provided for the Renard family had fallen apart, Gavin had come to understand why his father hated Lambert. Soon Gavin felt hatred for the man, too, slowly turning to a need for revenge that had never left him. The opening of Tempest's Closet had slowly driven all the Main Street shops out of business. Gavin had watched his father struggle to keep the downtown area vital, even going to August Lambert for help. But Lambert had refused.

"Of course you haven't."

"What's your point?"

"Just that you don't want to get involved with someone who works for a company we're going after."

He glanced at Michael. "Since when do I need advice?"

Michael punched him in the arm. "Old man, you always need advice when it comes to your personal life."

"Yeah, right. I think I see Melinda trying to get your attention."

Michael groaned under his breath but turned toward the woman he'd been dating on and off for the last four years. "When are you going to marry her?"

"When you start taking my advice."

"Never?"

"I don't know," Michael said, but the comment felt as if it were directed more at himself than to Gavin.

"Catch you later, Gav. Remember what I said."

"Later, Michael."

As his brother left, Gavin realized that Tempest was no longer talking with the group. The doors opened for seating in the main banquet room. Gavin held back, hoping for one more glance of Tempest.

He felt a hand on his shoulder. Long manicured fingernails rested on the black fabric of his dinner jacket. A sweet sultry scent perfumed the air and he glanced over his shoulder at Tempest.

"Well, hello," he said.

"I saw you watching me."

"Good."

"In some cultures it's considered impolite to stare."

"Your point is?"

She walked around in front of him, staying close

in the crush of people trying to enter the banquet room. "My point is I don't believe we've met."

"Gavin Renard."

"Ah."

"So you've heard of me."

"Vaguely," she said, with a twinkle in her eye. She took another sip of her drink. "I'm Tempest Lambert."

"I know who you are."

"Because of your business interest in Tempest's Closet?" she asked.

Her boldness surprised him. And he wasn't sure why. "Among other things."

She took a sip of the drink in her hand, tipping her head to one side. "Don't believe everything you read about me, Mr. Renard."

She was an enticing bundle of femininity. "I don't."

She reached up and touched his chin. Just her fingertips against the stubble on his face. "That's good because I have a proposition for you."

"I like the sound of that."

"Not that kind of proposition."

"A man can hope."

She turned away, but not before he saw a flash of desire in her eyes.

Interesting.

"What's your offer?" he asked.

"I'm in the market for a job, Gavin," she said.

Just the sound of his name on her lips made everything male in him come to point. He wanted to hear her say his name, but from the tangled sheets of his bed after they'd had wild sex. Not in the middle of this crowded function while he was trying to follow Michael's advice to keep his hands to himself. "No."

She sighed. "I'm very good at PR and I think I can be an asset to your company."

"I can't hire you." He wondered if August had set his daughter up to come to him for a job—maybe with the intent of using her as a corporate spy.

"Don't say no. Not yet. Let me come to your office tomorrow and talk to you. Once you see my resume you might reconsider."

He took her arm. God, her skin was smooth and soft. Softer than a woman's arm should be. He drew her away from the flocks of people and into a quiet part of the hallway. She didn't hesitate to follow him.

He stopped when they were alone and she leaned back against the wall watching him the way a woman watches a man she wants.

"Don't play with me, Tempest."

"I'm not," she said, quietly.

But he knew she was. Gavin hated to think that he might be falling in lust with the daughter of his enemy. Hated that August might have found the one chink in his otherwise impenetrable façade. But then what kind of man would use his daughter like that?

Suspicion and desire warred inside him and he finally gave into desire. He leaned in over her. So close he could see that her blue eyes weren't a pure color but a combination of several different shades.

And that her lashes were thicker than a mink stole. And her lips, ah, hell, her lips were full and wide and as she drew her tongue over the bottom one he remembered exactly how long it had been since he'd held a woman in his arms.

And he couldn't trust her. His best bet would be to scare her off with a bold pass. From what he'd read of her, she was used to pampered boys who lived off their family's fortunes.

"Gavin?"

"I don't need you in my PR department… but…" he said.

"Don't say it," she warned him.

He didn't voice his request, just tugged her a little closer and brought his mouth to her ear. She shivered as his breath brushed over her and he felt an answering spread of sensation. He felt the first tingling of arousal in his loins.

"It's obvious we're attracted to each other," he whispered.

She pulled back from him. "I am attracted to you, which makes no sense at all."

Hell, he knew that. But he wanted her. More than he should. This wasn't logical or rational but she felt so right.

Too right. It reminded him that the deep freeze he'd carefully existed in while focusing on his plan of revenge was starting to thaw. In her gaze he saw a hint of sadness and the kind of determination that played havoc with his control.

She closed her eyes. He saw her skin flush at his words and her shoulders sank back, lifting her breasts toward him.

He caressed the long line of her cheekbones. Her skin was softer than the sea mist. Her lashes drifted down as he explored the angles and curves of her face. He traced the lines of her lips as they parted under his touch. He stroked his thumb over her full lower lip, watched the natural pink color of her lips darken.

She tipped her head back and leaned the slightest bit toward him. There was a bit of haughtiness in her that intrigued him. He wanted to take her in his arms and see how haughty she looked after he ravished her mouth with his kisses.

She shrugged her shoulder. "I'm not looking for an affair, Gavin. I'm looking for a job."

He knew he'd never hire her but he didn't want to just let her walk away from him. And he knew that was her intent. "I can see you tomorrow at eleven."

"Great. Prepare to be amazed," she said, walking away.

# Two

Tempest had dressed for her interview with Gavin Renard with care. Her black Chanel suit was a classic and she wore it like a security blanket. She loved the feeling of the lined summer-weight wool skirt against her legs. She paired it with a pair of *ultra-thin sheer French hose* and some Ferragamos that were understated and sophisticated.

But still she was nervous. Her hands trembled as she took a sip of the coffee Gavin's secretary Marilyn had gotten for her. She hated being that betrayed by her own emotions and forced herself to rehearse in her head what she planned to say one more time.

She wasn't only thinking of a new job. She was

thinking of Gavin Renard the man, and that ticked her off. It was one thing to think of him as a way to make her father sit up and take notice of the kind of executive he let slip through his fingers. But who would have thought that this man could mess with her plans? Of course, to be honest, she hadn't had much of a plan when she walked over to him. She'd just wanted to meet the man her father was so obsessed with and get a bead on whether or not there was something there she could use to make her father reconsider her for the promotion. Those plans had gone out the window when she'd realized how attracted she was to Gavin.

"Ms. Lambert?"

"Yes?"

"Mr. Renard will see you now."

She smiled her thanks at the secretary and put her *coffee cup on the* end-table. She took a deep breath before getting to her feet. Her mother had always said to take her time. That it was better to arrive late and prepared for an event than on time and unrehearsed.

In her mind she cranked up "Welcome to the Jungle" by Guns 'N' Roses. Then she picked up her briefcase and walked into his office.

Gavin stood when she entered. His shirt was a deep blue that made his gray eyes seem even more brilliant in the office lighting. He was taller than she remembered and she realized her heels the other evening had given her an extra inch of height that these didn't. She smiled up at him as the soundtrack in her head changed from energizing rock to Sade's "Smooth Operator."

He smelled really good, too. The spicy male scent enveloped her as he held out his hand. The slow sensuous music in her head made the office background drop away.

"Good morning, Tempest."

She shook her head. His big hand totally engulfed hers. She held on longer than she should have before pulling back and nervously clearing her throat. No, she thought. She wasn't nervous. She was calm, cool, totally collected and together.

"Good morning, Gavin. Did you enjoy the benefit last night?"

"Yes. Please have a seat."

So much for small talk. It was clear to her that Gavin wasn't interested in the social niceties that she'd built her life around. She made a mental note to remember that. She sat down and pulled her resume from her briefcase.

"Thank you for agreeing to this meeting."

"I'm still not sure why I did," he said.

For a minute she thought this was a big mistake and then their eyes met and she realized he'd agreed for the same reason she'd asked. *Mutual attraction.* She knew this was an impossible situation. He'd never be able to forget she was her father's daughter.

But she wasn't one who backed down. She'd

made it her life's goal to always keep moving forward. Never looking back. She wanted Gavin to see her as a prospective employee first and a woman second. And to totally forget she was a Lambert. Today that seemed really important. She was just another out-of-work businessperson.

"Because you're a shrewd businessman who knows a good thing when he sees it," she said, handing him her resume. Stay cool and confident, she reminded herself.

"I definitely liked what I saw the other night."

She smiled at him. This might be easier than she'd expected. She could play on the attraction flowing between them like a high-voltage current.

"Me, too."

He gave her a half-smile. It was an arrogant expression from a man who was confident of his appeal to the opposite sex. But then she wasn't lacking in confidence herself. She crossed her legs letting the hem of her skirt ride up the slightest bit. His eyes tracked the movement.

"What exactly is it that you do, Tempest?"

"I'm in PR. I've been responsible for most of the press you've seen about Tempest's Closet for the last three years."

"What makes you think I've been watching your press?"

"Please, Gavin. I think we both know that you are aware of every move that Tempest's Closet makes."

He shrugged one shoulder and leaned back in his chair. "I am."

He said nothing else, letting the silence build between them. She couldn't stand it because she knew he was building the case against her in his head. Finding the words to tell her to take her briefcase and walk out his door.

And this was her only option. Her only chance to really make sure her father realized that he'd let her slip through his fingers…for good this time.

"Just look at my resume. I think you'll see I'm more than you expected."

"You already are," he said.

She was a little startled by that. She handed him her resume and sank back into the chair.

Her resume was more impressive than he'd expected it to be. He didn't know why he was surprised. He'd made a few phone calls this morning and found out more information on his enemy's daughter than she'd probably be comfortable with him having.

Everyone he spoke to mentioned her keen intelligence and her ability to put people at ease. She had a knack for finding the morsel of good news in the worst situation and spinning it out until the media was running with the idea she fed them.

In short she'd be the perfect addition to his team if she weren't August Lambert's daughter. But she was. And nothing could change that.

He hadn't been able to get anything from his Tempest's Closet source on why Tempest was job hunting. But he'd figure that out today. See if there was anything in her leaving Tempest's Closet that he could use to his advantage.

She shifted her legs again and he tracked the movement with his eyes. She had dynamite legs. All he could think of was how smooth they'd feel to his touch. The few glimpses he'd had of her thigh were enough to make his fingertips tingle.

He frowned and forced himself to study her resume. He wasn't getting involved with her. He wasn't doing the lust thing with this woman. It had nothing to do with the advice of his brother and everything to do with focus. He couldn't afford any kind of distraction now that he was so close to his goal. Ten years of walking the path of revenge and he wasn't going to lose it this close to the finish line.

"Why did you leave Tempest's Closet?" he asked. No one knew the answer to that.

"I had a differing opinion with my boss."

"You mean your father, right?"

She sat up straighter in the chair and put both of her feet on the floor. Staring him straight in the eye. "I didn't get the job because of nepotism. I worked hard to prove myself within our charitable foundation before making the move to Tempest's Closet."

"Of course you did." He knew she'd gotten the job the same way every other employee had. Through her qualifications and skills. In fact, she'd probably had to work harder.

He knew how contentious her relationship was with August. He also didn't want her to leave his office until he figured out if there was a way that he could exploit that. There had to be something here he was missing.

"I'm not going to argue the point. If you can't see what an advantage I'd be to your organization then you're not the man I thought you were."

He glanced up at her then and realized he felt a grudging respect for her. She fought dirty…well she fought to win. And he always respected winning except when August Lambert won.

And somehow this daughter of his had to be the key to bringing him down. No, she was the key to twisting the pain of losing when August fell. And the old man was going down.

Right now, though, he needed some answer from her. He should be treating this like an interview. Keeping his eyes off her legs and focusing on what she was doing here. "Why did you go into PR?"

She relaxed in her seat, crossing those long legs again. "It seemed like the right fit for me. I know a lot of people in the media."

*"Is it only because of your contacts?"* he asked. There had to be more. She'd been hounded by the press for years before she'd started working in PR. He thought it was a very shrewd move on her behalf to turn that around. To make dealing with the press her career.

She swallowed hard. "I just wanted to give them something real to print. To move the focus off of me and onto something else. That's why I started with the charity. I knew no one would take me seriously until I changed my reputation in the media."

He respected what she'd done. To some extent he'd made a similar decision when he'd entered the investing world. His family had started with nothing and he'd turned that around. Taking the very thing that had ruined his father and making it his own strength.

"Good move."

"Thanks," she said, flashing him a grin that stopped him in his tracks. She had a wonderful smile.

"Okay, as impressive as your qualifications are, I can't hire you."

Her smile disappeared and she blinked a few times. "Is it because I'm a Lambert?"

Yes, he thought. She had to see he couldn't hire her. But he didn't want her to just walk out his door. He wanted to see her again. "Only partly. I don't have any openings in my PR department."

"But you said partly. Don't think about who my father is."

"It's a big part of who you are, Tempest. Even if I had an opening, I wouldn't hire you."

"You're missing out on one hell of a PR exec, Gavin," she said, standing up and gathering her briefcase.

He stood as well and walked over to the door, blocking her from leaving.

"I think if I hired you, I'd miss out on a hell of a woman, Tempest."

Her eyes widened and he knew she was debating the next move to make. He wondered then if he wasn't the only one fishing for information. If he wasn't the only one who was dealing with emotions he didn't understand exactly.

That's what he wanted to find out. He'd never be able to trust her in his office but in his bed…that was something all together different.

"Are you saying you want to date me?"

He thought about that for a long minute. Dating her really wasn't any different than hiring her. She was still his enemy's daughter…but he'd been focused on revenge for too long.

Barely an inch of space was between their bodies. He smelled even better up close than he had when she'd shaken his hand. He crowded closer to her and she fought not to back up. But in the end her need for personal space won out and she inched away from him.

He was all arrogant male. Totally sure of himself and his impact on her. And she wished she could prove him wrong. Wished she could take a step away from him and dismiss him with a snooty comment that would put him in his place. Remind him that she was the daughter of August Lambert.

"You're crowding me," she said carefully. She was completely out of her element with this man.

She didn't know him well enough to know the best way to deal with him. She only knew one thing for certain. She wasn't leaving this office without some kind of offer. Her pride was on the line, and to be honest, pride was the only thing she'd ever really had that was her own.

"Good."

"Why good?"

"I like it when you get your back up."

"I don't *get my back up*. I'm a well-bred young lady." No one had ever said anything like that to her before. He treated her like he wasn't impressed by her pedigree, which of course he wasn't. He disliked her father. Did that feeling transfer to her, as well?

"I'm not a well-bred man," he said.

*She realized she knew practically nothing about* Gavin. There was something in his tone that warned her that he hadn't had the same privileged upbringing she had. "Well, for future reference, I get haughty."

"I'll make a note."

She couldn't believe their meeting had come to this. Flirting. She was flirting with a man who had pretty much said he wasn't going to do what she wanted him to. And for some reason that didn't hurt as much as she'd thought it might. But then she was a master at hiding the hurt inflicted on her by the men in her life. And Gavin technically wasn't in her life.

Gavin was a long shot for a job from the beginning. But she wasn't ready to throw in the towel yet.

"I've got a deal for you," she said.

"I'm not interested in making deals."

"You're kidding. Your entire career is based on *making deals*."

He leaned closer to her, bracing his arms on the wall on either side of her head. Just like that she was trapped. He brought the heel of his hand down on her shoulder and tangled his fingers in her hair.

"Is it a business proposition?" he asked, using his grip on her hair to tip her head to the side. His thumb traced the line of her jaw.

He touched her so carefully. Like she was something fragile and breakable. It wasn't the way people usually treated her. Everyone knew she was tough as nails. Ballsy and brash and haughty. No vulnerabilities.

"Tempest?"

What the heck was he talking about? Then she remembered. She wanted to make a deal with him. She wanted to convince him to hire her. And she'd use whatever she had to get his attention. If that meant playing up the attraction between them then so be it.

"Kind of."

"Kind of?"

She thought quickly, trying to blunt the impact of his body next to hers. She closed her eyes so that she wouldn't have to look into his brilliant gaze. But that just made her more aware of his body heat and the yummy scent of his aftershave.

She cleared her throat. "You give me one media event to handle and if I do a good job you hire me."

He looked her straight in the eyes and she saw his answer before he said anything. She put her finger over his lips. Traced the lower one when his lips parted.

"Tempest…"

"Don't say no."

He leaned down so that when he spoke his breath brushed her ear. She shivered in awareness and had *the feeling that Gavin knew exactly what he was about* when it came to seducing women. And it had been so long since she'd been with a man. Three years to be exact. Three long years while she'd focused on her career. And look where that had gotten her.

"Tempest…"

"What?" she asked, cocking her head to the side so that her mouth was angled right next to his—a breath away. She wet her lips and watched his eyes following the movement of her tongue.

"I can't hire the daughter of my enemy."

She was afraid he'd say that. She had known this was a long shot, but she'd spent her entire life battling against a man who was resolved to feel nothing for her. She didn't give up easily and she wasn't going to now either.

"I'm not your enemy," she said. "This could work to your advantage."

He shook his head.

"Gavin, this is my last chance to prove to him that he's made a mistake. I'm not leaving your office unless you change your mind."

"An ultimatum?"

"A promise. I'm not the flighty-flirty heiress you've read about in the papers. I'm a well-educated asset that could be working for you."

He sighed and moved back from her. "I'm not making any promises, but I'll consider you if there is an opening."

"That's all I ask."

"Until then…"

"Yes?"

"Dinner?"

"What about it?" she asked. She wasn't going to accept an invitation like that. She was, after all, Tempest Lambert.

"Would you have dinner with me tonight?"

"I'm busy."

"Liar."

"I do have plans. You can join me if you want. I'll pick you up here at seven."

# Three

Gavin had been surprised when he'd gotten the e-mail from Tempest asking him to meet her at the Gillock Gallery on north Ravenswood Avenue. He'd worked later than he'd planned to and then made his way across town to the gallery opening for an artist that Gavin had never heard of before, Pablo Montovan.

He mentioned Tempest's name at the door and was told to go right in. He got a glass of wine from the waiter and walked through the room stopping to study the art. He'd never taken time for the niceties in life. Michael collected sculptures and their mother had an affinity for photography. But Gavin wasn't interested in anything unless it brought him closer to his goal of bringing down August.

For the first time he realized how one-dimensional his life was. How work-centric he was. He took a sip of the California chardonnay and studied the portraiture. It depicted a crowd of people in the center of the canvas on a solid block of color. As he stood there he realized how alone each person was. Isolated in a sea of many.

He glanced back and came face-to-face with Tempest.

A soft feminine hand rested on his shoulder. "Like it?"

"I'm not sure."

"Why not?" she asked. She wore a simple cocktail dress in black and white. But the dress was anything but simple on her.

He shrugged, not planning on answering that.

"This piece—Waiting #7. Makes me feel kind of sad. Not a good feeling of expectation. But like they are all waiting for something they don't want."

He took another sip of his wine.

"Come on, Gavin, tell me what you see."

"I'm not really into art," he said, afraid any comments he made would reveal too much of his own inner turmoil.

He saw the disappointment in her eyes and told himself it didn't matter. He'd only come tonight out of curiosity. Not about the art but about the woman he couldn't figure out.

"Nice turn out," he said.

She sighed and then smiled at him. But it wasn't her usual brilliant expression.

"Yes, it is. I was worried that Pablo wouldn't get the crowds he does in Europe."

"You're a friend of the artist?" he asked. There seemed to be few circles where she didn't know someone. He knew that would be a great asset in a PR director. For a minute he wondered if she had been legit in his office. Was she really just looking for a job? Or was he right to suspect that her father might be using her as a pawn?

"Yes. I want you to meet him. I noticed that the lobby of your building is a little bare. Pablo does some stunning murals."

Gavin followed her through the crowd, stopping when she did and engaging in small talk with people he had nothing in common with. Yet slowly he realized he didn't mind it. He liked listening to Tempest and the way she talked to others.

She effortlessly put everyone at ease. Finding obscure connections between the various groups and starting conversations that weren't frivolous. She introduced him as simply the head of an investment firm and when he noticed a few raised eyebrows from people who'd obviously heard of the feud between him and August, she simply smiled it off.

Was that her intent? To plant the seeds of doubt in public so that his investors would get jittery and pull back?

He pulled her to the side of the crowded room.

The noise of conversation and music filled the air but he found a quiet hallway tucked out of the way.

"What?" she asked.

"Why did you invite me here tonight?"

She lifted one shoulder and glanced back at the crowd. She was ill at ease for the first time since he'd met her, her normal boldness stifled by this quiet hallway and his questions.

"I wanted a chance to get to know you better," she said at last. "I'm not going to lie to you. I'm still hoping to convince you to give me a job."

"Why do you want to get to know me better?" he asked, completely ignoring the job thing. He'd already made up his mind not to hire her, nothing would change it. "Are you spying on me for your father?"

She wrapped her arm around her waist and took two steps away from him. There was such hurt in her eyes that he wanted to apologize but he didn't. He'd made a plausible assumption.

"I'm not like that, Gavin."

She waited and he sensed that she wanted him to say something that would make things right between them. But he didn't have the words.

She turned away but he stopped her with his hand on her elbow, tugging her to a stop. "Don't be offended. It was a logical theory."

"And you're always logical, aren't you?"

"Yes. I don't understand you." He'd learned from watching his father that emotion had no place in the decision-making process.

"What's to understand? I want a chance to work for you and I'm attracted to you. I thought we agreed to at least explore the attraction."

Did they? He wasn't sure now what he'd agreed to. Her skin was ultra soft and he ran his finger over the flesh of her inner arm. He knew he should stop, that the touch was too intimate for a public place, but she felt so good. No one should have skin that soft.

Goose flesh spread down her arm and she turned to face him. "You can't argue the attraction."

"I don't want to," he admitted. Though it wasn't logical, it made no sense to confess to feelings that he knew weren't sensible.

"But you don't exactly want to embrace it, either," she said.

"True."

She turned away from him and this time he let her slip free. He'd seen the hurt in her eyes. What had it been like growing up with August as a father?

Tempest was the first to admit she didn't always handle herself well with men she wanted to impress. But normally she was able to insulate herself enough from them that she didn't allow any of their comments to hurt her.

Gavin was different. She really wanted to make a good impression on him. Yet everything she did he saw as a move in the ongoing business of one-upmanship he had with her father.

"Let me introduce you to Pablo and then we can say our goodbyes," she said. She had the feeling no matter what she did to show him she was qualified to work for him, he wasn't going to change his mind.

"I don't want to meet Pablo."

"I promise you won't regret it."

He wrapped his hand around her neck and drew her back against his body. Lowering his head he inhaled deeply and she held herself still in his embrace, afraid to move.

"I regret everything about this night."

There was a finality to his words that she wished she didn't understand but it was too late. He was saying goodbye. She swallowed and stepped away from him, felt his fingers in her hair until she moved far enough away that the strands fell to her shoulders again.

There were a million thoughts rushing around her head. Regret of her own that she'd never get to know this man she was attracted to. Some anger at her father because if not for him…well, if not for him she wouldn't have approached Gavin so she knew that anger wasn't justified. It was just…oh, man, she wanted him. Him, not any other man, and it had been a long time since that had happened.

How had that happened? She was careful not to let anyone too close to her.

"Tempest?"

She shook her head, realizing she'd been standing there staring at him. "You really need something to soften the austerity of the lobby. Art puts people at ease." She needed to keep talking about his business. To somehow keep that knowledge in the front of her mind. If she stopped and let herself think about the fact that she'd been rejected again, she might break down.

"Okay," he said quietly.

She led him out of the hallway and back into the main gallery room. A buffet table was set against the windows that looked out on the street. There was a small jazz combo in the corner and a postage stamp-sized dance floor.

She moved into the crowd away from him. Trying to not be hyper aware of where he was but it was impossible. As she moved through the room she realized the truth of her life.

People smiled at her, air-kissed her cheek. Complimented her haute-couture outfit and made references to events they had attended together in the past. And the truth of the evening kept circling in her head. She kept hearing that voice that she hated listening to, the one that never let her flinch from the truth. The one that made her want to cry.

The truth was that she had a life filled with things just as her father did. A life filled with acquaintances instead of friends. A life empty of any real joy or real emotions.

And for one moment she'd come close to finding someone who'd maybe fill that emptiness.

She finished her Bellini in one long swallow and deposited the glass on the tray of a passing waiter.

Good God, she was getting depressing. She needed to get out of Chicago for a while.

Chicago was the place where her greatest hurts were. It was the city she'd been living in when her mother had died. And now she had this new one.

"Got a minute, Tempest?"

"Sure," she said, surprised to see Charlie Miller at this event. Though he was a crackerjack PR man, he didn't move in the same circles she did.

"Um, first I want to say, I'm sorry you didn't get the promotion."

She genuinely liked Charlie and with a few more years experience he was going to be exactly what her father needed. He was smart and savvy but a little young and inexperienced.

"As my father said, 'the best man got the job,'" she said.

He flushed. "I hope I can live up to that expectation."

"Of course you will. So what did you want?"

"I was hoping you'd have some time in your schedule to sit down and talk about some of the projects that were pending when you left. Kind of get me up to speed."

She had left abruptly. Like a spoiled child when she'd realized she'd once again let her father disappoint her. "Yes, I can. But I can't come by the office. How about Starbucks on Michigan tomorrow?"

"Fine. Ten would be good for me."

The small talk continued for a few more minutes before Kali interrupted them. Grateful for the rescue,

Tempest smiled at her friend. Kali Trevaine was one of Tempest's oldest friends. Kali's mom, Talia, had been a supermodel, one of the first that Tempest's Closet had used in their American marketing campaigns. In those early days her mother had been very active in the company and had brought Tempest to all the photo shoots.

She and Kali had bonded young. Playing in the clothes and getting into mischief. When Tempest had been a teenager and her father had wanted her to stay at school for the summers, Talia and Kali had invited her into their home. Kali was the closest thing Tempest had to a sister.

"What was that about?"

"He's the guy my father replaced me with."

"Ah, the competition. I think you could have taken him in a physical match."

Tempest laughed as she knew Kali wanted her to. It was true that Charlie was a small man, only five-seven and slim. She probably could take him if she were given to doing such a thing.

"Is that your new reality TV show idea? A corporate version of *Celebrity Death Match?*"

"Ah, no, I hadn't thought beyond you. But that thought has merit."

"Please, I was kidding. I don't want to see something like that on TV."

"Maybe America does," Kali said.

"Excuse me, ladies."

Tempest was surprised Gavin had sought her out

again. But maybe he wanted to meet Kali. At five-nine she was thin and stunningly beautiful. Her coffee-colored skin and exotically shaped eyes drew men to her like bees to honey. But Tempest was also disappointed that she'd been so strongly attracted to a man who could go so quickly from wanting her to wanting her friend.

"Yes, Gavin?"

"Dance with me," he said.

He nodded to Kali as he drew Tempest through the crowd to the dance floor.

"I thought we'd said goodbye," she said, as he drew her into his arms.

"Not yet."

She rested her head on his shoulder as the band played a slow jazzy number. She knew this wasn't real and wouldn't last, but for this instant she felt at home in his arms.

There was no way in hell that this woman belonged with him.

She could never be more than a means to an end. But it didn't feel that way and for just one moment he shut down the logical part of his mind and just held her.

The music swirled around them as did the other couples on the small dance floor, but when Tempest lowered her head to his shoulder the rest of the world disappeared.

He knew this was an emotional reaction. Tried to

justify the feelings with the knowledge that anything he started wouldn't go any further than this dance floor.

And that made the need sharpen inside him. He wanted her. His skin felt too tight and his blood flowed heavier in his veins. He'd been jealous when he'd seen her talking with that skinny man earlier. And he didn't like that.

He wasn't a jealous man—he just never permitted himself to connect to any of the women he'd dated. He reserved those emotions solely for his mother and his brother.

But with Tempest everything was different, dammit. He didn't like it. He wasn't a possessive man but each time Tempest had stopped with a group to chat he'd found himself resentful that he wasn't in the group.

"Did you talk to Pablo?"

"Yes," he said, not interested in discussing another man with her. This covetousness was unfounded. She wasn't his. He shouldn't feel so possessive but he did.

"Did you ask him to do a mural—"

"No, Tempest. I don't want to talk about art tonight."

"Then why did you come to a showing?" she asked. There was something in her voice that stopped his impatient answer. That hint of vulnerability he'd noticed before. It roused more than his possessiveness—it made him want to protect her. To ensure that she wasn't hurt.

"Because *you* asked me to," he said, quietly.

She rubbed her cheek against his shoulder and he

wished they were both naked so he could feel the softness of her skin against his own.

"I think there is more to it than that," she said.

Of course there was more to it. Nothing with Tempest was easy. It was complicated by matters that had been a part of his life for too long now. He almost wished they'd delayed their first date until after the November board meeting of Tempest's Closet. After he'd dismantled her father's empire and finally had the revenge he'd spent years working toward.

He knew that she'd never have anything to do with him once he took over her father's company. Sure, the relationship with her father was strained, but August was all that Tempest had. Though a boy at the time, Gavin could remember the stories of Tempest Lambert…poor little rich girl. The Lambert family had one of those curses that the media liked to play up. And Gavin had learned one thing from all the articles he'd read about her. She was an incredibly loyal woman.

Her loyalty to Lambert was obvious to Gavin even thought she'd come to Renard Investments for a job. She was still a Lambert and still passionate about Tempest's Closet.

He wondered what that felt like. He wondered if August had any idea how lucky he was to have someone so loyal to him that no matter how cruelly he treated her, she'd still be there. And for just a moment he wanted to shake Tempest for always allowing her father to hurt her.

"We already discussed this."

"Yes, we did and I thought we'd found closure but somehow I'm back in your arms again."

His gut clenched at her words. He wanted her in his arms. Really in his bed. Naked and willing under him. Only then would he be able to find any closure to the relentless need that kept hammering through his body.

He tightened his grip on her back, slowly sliding his hands to her hips. His fingers flexing and sinking into her soft curves. He drew her nearer to him until her breasts rested against his chest.

Her breath caught in her throat and she tipped her head back, looking up at him with those wide blue eyes of hers. He saw the answering need in her gaze. Saw that she wanted him with the same insane passion. Saw that this wasn't going to be easy for her to walk away from either.

And strangely that was just what he needed to justify lowering his head to hers right there on the crowded dance floor. He forgot that public displays of affection were taboo for him because they made the public and the stockholders doubt his ability to run his business. He forgot that she was the daughter of his rival. He forgot everything except the fact that he hadn't tasted her lips and he wanted to.

Needed to. He wasn't going to last another second until he knew if her kiss was as flat-out hot as he expected it to be.

He lifted one hand from her hips, tangled his fingers in her softer-than-sable hair and tilted her head back.

She gasped as he lowered his mouth over hers and he wasn't tentative in taking her. He thrust his tongue deep into her mouth. He gave her no chance to respond, just wielded his will over her.

She tasted of the slightly sweet drink she'd had earlier and raspberry lip gloss. She wrapped both her hands around his shoulders and shifted in his embrace, her tongue sliding against his. Her hands tangling in the hair at the back of his neck.

Blood roared in his ears as he rubbed his hand up and down her back. He felt the fragility of her spine, the fineness of her slim body. He lifted his head and rubbed his lips along the line of her jaw and down to her neck.

She tasted again of that essence of woman that he was coming to associate only with her. She moaned deep in her throat as he thrust his tongue into her mouth. Her tongue stroked tentatively against his.

Sliding his hands down her back he cupped her hips and pulled her more firmly against his body. He'd meant to keep the embrace light because they were in the middle of the dance floor.

He rubbed his growing erection against her and she made a soft sound in the back of her throat. Her nails dug into his shoulders through the layer of his shirt. She undulated against him.

He lifted his head. Her eyes were closed and face was flushed with desire. He knew that it would take very little for him to persuade her to have sex with him tonight. And part of him wanted to do that, to take what he needed.

His heart beat too quickly in his chest and the lust that had taken entire control of his body abated at the fear that was slowly creeping through him. He wanted her more than he should.

He had to stop this insanity and leave. He rubbed his finger over her wet lips and took a step back.

"Goodbye," he said, knowing that he was going to have a hell of a time forgetting her.

She lifted her hand toward him and he was tempted to stay. Tempted to say the hell with the inappropriateness of their relationship and take something he wanted even thought it didn't fit into his plans.

A camera flash went off to his left. He caught a glimpse of a man running through the crowd. This is what a relationship with Tempest would be like, he thought.

"Gavin?"

He shook his head and walked away without looking back. And it was one of the hardest thing he'd ever done.

# Four

Tempest was tired, cranky and out of sorts when she left her condo the next morning for her meeting with Charlie. And she wasn't very well prepared. She hadn't gone back to the office after she'd decided to quit working for her father, so she had no notes other than the things she'd kept in her head.

And this might not be the best morning for a meeting because all she could think about was Gavin. She hated the fact that they'd both agreed to part ways. She knew it was the most sensible thing to do but she ached for him.

That kiss last night had made it impossible for her to do anything other than moon over the man. And that ticked her off. The only man who'd had the power to completely make her crazy before had been her father. Of course that was an entirely different thing.

All conversations stopped when she entered the Starbucks on Michigan Avenue. She tried to pretend that she hadn't noticed. But she felt like a huge spotlight was on her. She glanced around the barista trying to find something else to engage her attention when she saw a discarded newspaper. She snagged it from the table while she waited to order her coffee.

She skimmed the headlines and then flipped to the society page, hoping her presence at Pablo's opening got him some additional press. Her jaw dropped as she saw the picture of her and Gavin. She hadn't even noticed the flashbulb when he'd been kissing her.

But there they were in the middle of the dance floor. Totally wrapped up in each other. She touched her own lips as they started to tingle. There'd been so much passion in that kiss. She could still feel his body pressed against her. She glanced at the caption and felt the blood drain from her face.

*Sleeping with the enemy? Tempest Lambert never shies away from scandal but cavorting with Gavin Renard the CEO of Tempest's Closet's fiercest competition is a little over the top even by her standards.*

She fumbled in her purse for her sunglasses and donned them quickly. It was too late to really disguise herself but the glasses provided a shield that no matter how false, she needed.

She dug around her bag until she found her cell

phone and dialed Kali's number. She didn't know what to do and needed her friend.

A call beeped in before Kali answered and she glanced down at the caller ID wondering if it would be her dad. It wasn't. The number was one she couldn't identify. She let it go to the voicemail and switched back to Kali's line.

"Hello?" she asked when she heard silence on the open line.

"Tempest?"

Thank God, Kali was home. "Yes, did you see the paper?"

"No. What's up?"

The man in front of her glanced over his shoulder at her and she realized this was not a conversation she wanted to have standing in line at Starbucks. She walked out of the coffee shop and down the sidewalk to a quiet area.

"There's a picture of Gavin and I."

"From last night?"

"Uh…yes."

"From the dance floor?" Kali asked again and the speculation in her friend's voice made her want to cringe.

She'd openly courted the press for years after she'd graduated from finishing school. Used them as a way to make her father notice her even though he'd always made it a point to ignore her. And she'd regretted it for the last few years but it was, of course, too late to go back and change things. But this picture she resented the most.

"Yes," she said to Kali. "What am I going to do? Gavin didn't want to date me for precisely this reason."

"He wasn't exactly an unwilling participant."

"Kali!"

"Well, that's the truth."

"I know. I was just hoping…" she stopped before she said any more. She'd been hoping that Gavin would have a change of heart, but now she doubted he would.

"Oh, honey. I was hoping, too, that this guy would be different."

Sometimes she wished Kali didn't know her as well as she did. But right now it was nice to know she wasn't alone. That she had someone in her corner. "There's no way the tabloids aren't going to pick this up."

"You're right. So what's the plan?"

"I don't know. I have to think this through."

"I don't like the sound of that," Kali said.

"Maybe there's a way to make this a win-win."

"For who? You?"

"Me and Gavin."

"Be careful."

"I will be." She hung up the phone and waked slowly back to her car. Her mind was moving swiftly over the possibilities. There had to be a way for this to work to their advantage.

With the press playing up the fact that they were

involved, she might be able to convince Gavin to make their relationship real. She made a quick call to Charlie to cancel their appointment.

She didn't have Gavin's number but knew where his office was so she drove there. She parked and walked into the building wondering what she was going to say to him. But it was nerves ruling her now. It was excitement and the thought that she'd found a way to spend more time with him.

She still wanted a job. A job for her father's rival would anger her father but it was more than that. She wanted the job to prove that someone else had thought her worthy.

She stopped for a minute near the bank of elevators. Nerves simmered again as she realized that Gavin might have had the same thought that the newspaper did. That sleeping with his enemy's daughter would be a nice twist. And she had some doubts for the first time since she'd decided to come to his building.

Then again she'd planned to use him to make her father angry. Could she really begrudge him the same thing?

Tempest heard someone come up behind her near the bank of elevators. Her gut instinct was to try to make herself smaller so she wouldn't be recognized, but instead she put her shoulders back and stood taller

"Tempest?"

Gavin. "Hi. Have you seen the newspaper?"

He nodded. "Let's talk in my office."

\* \* \*

Gavin focused on the fact that he'd correctly predicted that Tempest would come to his office when she saw the photo instead of on the fact that they were alone in the elevator and he wanted to hit the emergency stop button and pull her into his arms.

Only the knowledge that Michael was waiting in his office stayed his hand. He had a vague idea that seducing Tempest wasn't off limits now. Everyone was going to believe they were involved anyway. But the way he felt about her was too intense. Could his logical side stay focused on business if he was involved in an affair with her?

His libido said who the hell cared. But he knew better than to let his groin make a decision.

"Why are you staring at me?" she asked.

There was none of the ballsy attitude she'd had the first time she'd visited his office. "Probably because you're wearing your sunglasses inside."

She flushed a little and shifted her brown Coach bag from her right shoulder to her left. "Oh, I'd forgotten them."

He leaned against the walnut paneling in the elevator and tried to look like he was at ease.

"Why do you have them on?" It was an overcast morning, no sun in sight.

She straightened the large dark glasses on her face and then glanced up at him. "I was in Starbucks when I saw the paper."

"I don't understand."

"Of course, you wouldn't."

He just waited and she sighed and wrapped an arm around her waist. "People stare at me when I'm out. And after I saw that picture of us in the paper I felt…well, I just put the glasses on because it gives me the illusion of hiding."

In that instant he knew whatever else happened between them he wasn't going to be able to just let her walk back out of his door. He wanted to pull her into his arms and hold her tight to his side. But dammit, he wasn't a protector. He was a destroyer. He knew that. Even his success in business had come from buying up failing companies and taking them apart.

He took her sunglasses off and folded them in his hand. She stared up at him and he saw the truth in her gaze. The vulnerability that she never let the world see.

He cupped her face in his palm and tipped her head up so that she could see the truth in his eyes.

"You don't need to hide from me."

She chewed on her lower lip. He lowered his head and brushed her mouth with his. He wanted to deepen the contact but restraint was needed now. Later when they were alone in his office…

"I think I need to hide most of all from you."

"Why?"

"Because you see me in ways that no one else does."

The elevator doors opened before he could respond and his brother stood there in the hallway waiting for them.

"We'll finish this discussion later."

"Will we?" she asked in that sassy way of hers. She was getting herself back from the shock of seeing that photo. He was glad for it. He could deal with the ballsy woman better than the vulnerable one.

"I just said we would."

"Well then I guess your word is law."

"Yes, it is," Michael said.

Gavin gave his brother a hard look but Michael just grinned at him. "Trust me. You can't win when you go up against Gavin."

"I'm not so sure that's true," Tempest said.

"I don't believe we've met. I'm Michael Renard."

"Tempest Lambert."

She shook hands with Michael and made small talk as they walked down the hallway to the executive offices. Gavin envied his brother many things but in this moment he wished he had the ability to loosen up the way Michael did. Then again, Michael lacked the focus and intensity that were so much a part of his own make up.

As they entered his office, Gavin told his secretary they weren't to be disturbed. Tempest and Michael fell silent as they took a seat in the guest chairs.

Gavin walked over to the windows that looked out over Lake Michigan. He'd spent the morning going over different courses of action, trying to find the one that would best suit this situation. The one he could use to his advantage.

For once he didn't trust his own logic. Didn't trust the plan he'd settled on. All because of the one variable he couldn't control—Tempest.

Tempest cleared her throat and he turned around to face her.

"I'm sorry," she said. "You shouldn't have to pay the price just because my life is one big goldfish bowl."

"You don't have to apologize. I'm the one who kissed you."

She flushed and glanced at his brother.

"Um…I'll leave you two to discuss this. Let me know when you need me."

Michael left the office closing the door behind him. Tempest stood up.

"I'm not sure where we go from here, Gavin. Short of me finding another man to go out with— that might draw the press away from you, but I'm not interested in anyone else."

She wasn't going to date anyone else if he had anything to say about it. "That's not necessary. I think the best thing to do would be for us to have an affair. See where this attraction leads."

Gavin stared at her for a moment and realized that the only plan he wanted to enact was one where they were together. There was the added bonus that the press from any type of relationship they had would drive her father crazy.

He wasn't the kind to talk about business outside of the office so even if she were some kind of corporate spy—which he doubted—there was no information she could take back to her father from him.

He didn't allow himself to think of Tempest except in terms of an affair. He hoped like hell that the attraction he felt for her was only a sexual thing and once it ran its course they could both move on.

*An affair*. She wanted one with him but he was so cold when he suggested it. She hesitated. Was she really going to start a relationship with a man who could be so aloof?

"That sounds so romantic," she said hoping she didn't sound too sarcastic. But not really caring if she did.

"It isn't meant to be romantic. We're both attracted to each other. The media will make our lives hell no matter what the circumstances…it's rational."

"Rational? Was that what you felt last night?"

He walked around his desk in long measured strides and she fought to keep her ground. Because there was something about him that intimidated her. Something about his large frame and his stern countenance that made her want to back down. Except she didn't back down for anyone.

He put his hands on her waist, pulling her against his body. "There was nothing sensible or sane about last night. I wanted you and I didn't want to let you go without tasting your kiss at least once."

"Oh."

"I'm not romantic, Tempest. I'm a businessman and for the better part of my adult life I've been focused on only one thing."

"Ruining my father."

He nodded. He didn't even try to deny it which made her respect him just a little more.

"If we decide on an affair, don't expect romance."

"What should I expect?" she asked. No one had ever been as forthright with her as he was now. And in that moment she realized she could really fall for Gavin Renard. She realized that he was the kind of man that she'd been searching for all her life. He was solid and straight forward and he didn't care that she had more money than any one person needed.

"I'll treat you the way that you deserve to be treated in my bed and out of it."

She shivered at his words. She wanted what he'd described but if she said yes to this she'd be little more than his ornament—his date at functions until he tired of her. And a man like Gavin would tire of a woman who allowed herself to only be his bedmate.

"I want you to give me a chance to work for you, too."

He dropped his hands from her and stepped away. "I can't."

"Just let me come up with a PR plan for you. No promises of employment—just a test run to show you what I can do."

"Why is this important to you?" he asked. "You don't need the money."

"No, I don't need the money. But I want to prove to my father that he's wrong."

"What was he wrong about, Tempest?"

Me, she thought. But she'd never said that out loud in the past and she wasn't about to say it to Gavin. She didn't want him to realize that her own father thought she was little more than an ornament for men to use and display.

"That I'm not qualified to run the PR department of a large firm."

He leaned back against his desk, crossing his legs at the ankle. "Why Renard Investments?"

"Because you are rivals," she said, and then wished she hadn't.

"And that will make your success sting a little, right?"

She shook her head. "I know that makes me sound mean and petty but..."

She couldn't go on. Her father did make her want to be petty. Made her want to do ridiculous over-the-top things. Anything that would get his attention. And she was too damned old to still crave his approval. But she'd never had it and would always want it.

"It doesn't sound small at all," he said. "I imagine your relationship with your father is complicated."

"It is. What about you and Michael?"

"We're nothing like you and your dad. Michael knows that I'm here for him. So are we in agreement to an affair?"

"No."

"Why not? It's just the sort of thing you can use to get back at your father."

"He doesn't care who I sleep with."

"I'm not sure about that."

She was. "Trust me. I have it straight from the source."

He'd told her that her cheap escapades were of little consequence to him as long as she didn't bring any of the men home. And she doubted that Gavin would want to come to August's Lake Shore Drive mansion.

"He really said that to you?"

She nodded and shrugged it aside. "Let me do the PR plan…it's obvious to me that your job is your life and it will give us something to do together."

He rubbed the back of his neck. "I could never share any proprietary information with you."

It hurt a little because she knew he was trying not to say that he didn't trust her. But once he got to know her, she was sure she could change his mind.

"I can do something about your reputation as a cold-blooded shark. Someone who goes in for the kill when a company is floundering."

"I like that rep."

"Maybe I can come up with a plan to humanize you."

He stared at her for a long moment and then he shrugged. "Okay, but I'm not hiring you."

"We'll see."

# Five

Tempest was thirty minutes late to her meeting with Charlie. She wasn't exactly sure of what she'd agreed to in Gavin's office but she knew they'd discuss it further when he came to her house tonight for dinner.

She called her housekeeper and informed her she'd have a guest for dinner. Then she stopped in front of the Tempest's Closet corporate offices. Since their earlier meeting at Starbucks had been delayed, Charlie had suggested they try for lunch. He was lounging against a low railing that lined the handicap ramp leading to the entrance, cigarette in one hand, cell phone in the other.

The wind blew his short hair and he stubbed out

his cigarette as he saw her. As he walked toward her, she realized that there was more to Charlie than she'd first thought. He opened the door to her Aston Martin convertible and slid onto the leather seat.

"Sorry I'm late," she said as he slid into the car. He smelled of the summer air and cigarettes. She'd quit smoking almost three years ago but she missed it.

"You're doing me a favor," he said, putting on his seat belt.

"Where to?" she asked, as she eased the car out into the light traffic. It was the middle of the afternoon so they wouldn't have to worry about the lunch crowds.

"Some place quiet so we can talk without worrying if we're overheard."

She chose a small restaurant in the Art Institute that was quiet at this time of the day. They sat in the back corner and she gave him all the information she had on the projects she'd been working on. The part that would be more difficult for Charlie would be using her contacts.

She wrapped things up quickly. "Well, that's it then. Good luck, Charlie." She put her notebook back in the large Coach bag that she'd brought with her and made a move to get up.

"Thank you, Tempest. There's one more thing," Charlie said. His tone of voice made her leery. What else could they possibly have to discuss?

"What?" she asked. She sat back in her chair

almost afraid of where this was going, which was ridiculous because Charlie had nothing over her. He had nothing she wanted, except her father's respect.

"The picture of you and Gavin Renard from today's paper."

"What about it?" She tried not to sound defensive. But she didn't think that Charlie was the right guy to be talking to her about her personal life.

Charlie glanced away from her. "Your father has made that our number one priority."

"I don't see why it's any business of his. I am no longer employed by Tempest's Closet."

"You are still a major shareholder."

Tempest rubbed the back of her neck and really wished she'd stayed in bed this morning. "I always let my father vote my shares. If he has a problem with me he knows how to reach me."

Charlie didn't say anything, just leaned back in his chair. "He's put you back on the payroll. There was an article in the business section tying your departure and your relationship with Renard together."

"No. Tell him no."

"I can't, Tempest. He's not listening to me on this subject."

"Who is he listening to?"

"I have no idea. I got an e-mail from Jean this morning and tried to call him."

Jean was her father's secretary. "I'll take care of it."

"Thanks," he said, getting to his feet. "If it turns

out you're still in my department, I'd like you to handle the new store opening in Los Angeles."

"Better have a back-up plan because I'm nothing more than a shareholder now."

"I do," he said. She followed him out of the restaurant, trying to numb her mind. But it wasn't working. Just when she thought there was no way for her to feel more insignificant to her father, he did something like this. But she'd moved on and was trying to win Gavin's trust. That meant there was no way she could return to work for Tempest's Closet.

She tried to tell herself that it didn't matter what he did, that she'd moved on. And a part of her had moved on. A big part of her was looking forward to a new relationship with Gavin and the new opportunities he offered.

Charlie said nothing as she drove him back to his building. The entire time she stewed over her father and the fact that he thought…who knew what he thought.

"I'm not coming back to work at Tempest's Closet, Charlie. As far as I'm concerned I resigned and no one from HR has contacted me."

Charlie smiled at her as he opened the door. "I understand."

"It's nothing against you," she said, realizing that he might think she'd quit because he'd gotten the promotion she wanted.

"I never thought it was. Take care of yourself."

He eased out of the car. She grabbed her cell phone

thinking she should call her father but she didn't want to give him the pleasure of doing that. Yet this was one time when she couldn't let him ignore her wishes. She dialed his office number and got Jean.

"Is my father available?" she asked.

"I'm sorry, Tempest, but he isn't. Can I take a message?"

He was playing this through third parties and she'd be happy to let him continue on that way.

"Yes, Jean, please tell my father that I'm not coming back to work for him. Also please advise the HR department to take me off the payroll."

Jean sighed. "Umm…"

"Jean, he can't rehire me without even asking me to come back to work for him."

"You have a point. I'll make sure he receives your message."

"And the HR department?"

"Yes, I'll do that, as well."

"Thanks, Jean," she said, hanging up the phone. It occurred to her that she'd probably had more conversations with Jean than her father over her lifetime. But she refused to dwell on that.

Instead she thought about the coming evening. Staying in was out of the question. She wanted to go public with Gavin in a big flashy way. In a way that would garner the attention of every media outlet. She wasn't just doing it to annoy her father, this would help Gavin, too.

* * *

Tempest e-mailed him a PR plan for changing his image within the local community. He glanced at the first few items then put the plan out of his head. He was a businessman who focused on the bottom line and didn't give a damn what anyone thought of him.

The first thing on the list was to buy art for the lobby of his building. She'd put a little smiley face after that one and a note that said just kidding.

She was the only one who did that. Joked with him, well except for his brother but that was simply because he and Michael had relied on each other and only each other for the majority of their lives.

"What's that?"

"Nothing," he said, fighting the urge to minimize his Outlook e-mail box. He hadn't heard Michael enter but then the door between both of their offices was often left open.

"Nothing?" Michael leaned over his shoulder for a closer look. "It looks like an e-mail from Tempest Lambert. I thought you said there was nothing going on with her."

"Who are you, Katie Couric?" he asked, taking the mouse from Michael's hand before he could open the e-mail.

"Ha, very funny. Why is she e-mailing you a PR plan?"

"Michael, did you come into my office for a specific reason or just to be a pain in the ass?"

"I did have a reason. Being a pain in your ass is just something I throw in for fun."

"I'm pretty sure Mom wouldn't miss you if I relocated you to our Alaskan office."

"We don't have an office in Alaska," Michael said with a small grin.

"We will if you don't get to the point."

Michael leaned against the desk, crossing his legs at the ankles and his arms over his chest. "Our inside source at Tempest's Closet said there was a lot of rumbling going on today in mid-to-executive level management. Did you know Tempest no longer works for Tempest's Closet?"

"She mentioned it." She'd come to him for a job as soon as her father had shown her the door. He was beginning to believe there was more to her unemployment than met the eye.

"Well the inside dirt is that she quit when Charles Miller was promoted to the PR vice president opening," Michael said.

Gavin leaned back in his chair away from his brother and the desk. He hadn't asked about why she'd left Tempest's Closet. Hadn't really wanted to know the details because then he might sympathize with her. Might have a real reason to trust her and then he'd have no barriers to keep between them.

"Who's Charles Miller?" he asked. He was as familiar with the Tempest's Closet organizational chart as he was with his own. He knew all the players in the company and the name Charles Miller wasn't ringing any bells.

"We're checking him out. Seems like that picture of the two of you caused a stir, as well."

He didn't give a crap what people thought about him. He had made himself stop caring the day his parents had moved them out of their large family home just off of Main Street and into a mobile home park. It was the same day that the local Tempest's Closet announced record sales and plans to double the size of their store.

But he didn't like the fact that anyone was speculating on what was between him and Tempest. What he felt for her was too raw. Too protective and possessive for him to want to share it with the world.

"We dealt with the picture, too," Gavin said, not wanting to give the situation too much weight.

"You didn't give Tempest an ultimatum, did you?" Michael asked.

"No. Why would I do that?" Then again, she'd left his office to go to a meeting. One with her father? Tempest didn't have it in her to be a corporate spy, did she?

"August wants her to come back to work for him."

Gavin didn't want to ask if she'd said yes. A minute ago he'd been certain she'd say no to anything her father asked of her. Now he wasn't. He realized steamy hot attraction and one kiss weren't nearly enough to constitute a working knowledge of her.

"Don't you want to know what she said?"

"How does your spy get this information so quickly?"

"We pay him really good money and he's highly placed."

Seriously he wondered if they had any property in Fairbanks that would make a nice office. They didn't do a lot of business in Alaska but Michael would be out of his hair for a while. "You're on my last nerve."

He chuckled. "But we're blood so you'll forgive me, right?"

He shrugged. "What'd she say?"

"She told him no."

Relief and a kind of sadness moved through him. He was glad she hadn't gone back to work for her dad but the sensitive woman he was coming to know had to have been hurt by that situation.

He would look at her PR plan and see if she really knew her stuff. If she did, maybe he'd find a way to hire her in one of their subsidiaries. She couldn't work in the corporate offices or he wouldn't get any work done from lusting over her.

"Was that it?"

"No. The Tempest's Closet stockholders are antsy and several of them put out feelers to sell blocks of shares."

Tempest had been more of a help to him than she could ever guess. Not just because she'd acted the way he'd hoped she would with her father today.

"Did you make an offer?"

"Yes, I'll know something tomorrow."

"Keep me posted," Gavin said reaching over to turn off his laptop.

"I will. Where are you going?"

"What are you my social secretary?"

"You never leave the office before eight."

"Then maybe it's time I started."

Michael didn't say anything as Gavin pulled on his coat and gathered his briefcase.

"You okay, bro?"

"Yes," he said and walked out of the office. But he wasn't so sure that he was okay. Everything in his life was changing. And it was all to do with one woman. The daughter of his enemy.

Tempest wanted nothing more than to stay in for the evening but she knew it would be construed as hiding out so she got dressed for her date with Gavin. He hadn't responded to the e-mail she'd sent him earlier. She'd left a message with his secretary letting him know that she was expected at a new club downtown later tonight.

The celebrity deejay was the brother of one of her oldest boarding school friends and she wanted to lend her support to him. But she was tired and deep inside where she didn't lie to herself she was one mass of aching hurt.

She didn't know what Gavin expected from her other than sex. She didn't know why she still allowed her father to hurt her. And she knew that going back to work for Tempest's Closet would change absolutely nothing. Her father would still treat her with the same disdain he'd held her in for her entire life.

She reached for the pitcher of margaritas that her housekeeper had left sitting on the bar. Getting drunk or a least a little buzzed seemed like just the thing to insulate her from the worries in her head and the aching loneliness in her heart.

But she thought of Dean struggling to stay sober in a safe house in Italy. And knew that too easily she could slide back into the party lifestyle that had almost killed him.

The doorbell chimed and she sank down in one of the gilt Louis XIV chairs that faced the fireplace. She set her margarita on the end table, then reconsidered, thinking it might look as though she'd been waiting desperately for him. She heard his footsteps in the hallway leading to her sitting room a second before she decided to pick up the drink. She took a sip and tried to look…

He was gorgeous. He stood in the doorway in the light of the setting sun and she forgot about the worries in the back of her mind. Forgot that she wasn't sure she trusted him. Forgot everything except the slow physical awareness that was spreading through her body.

Her pulse picked up and her breathing became a little shallower. He still wore his suit jacket but his collar was open and she saw that he didn't wear a T-shirt underneath. His skin was tan and she wondered if he was muscular. She wanted to see what was beneath that shirt.

"Good evening, Tempest," he said.

Just hearing her name on his lips was enough to make her stand up. She had to stop this. This was ridiculous. She wasn't even sure she trusted the man; was she really going to let this attraction take control of her life?

"Can I get you a drink?"

"What are you drinking?"

"Margarita."

"I'll have one."

She fixed his drink a little nervously. She knew what she wanted and had no qualms about going after it. But the scene with Charlie this afternoon when he'd told her about her dad kept replaying in her head. What if Gavin found out and thought he couldn't trust her?

She handed him the drink but his fingers lingered on hers. Trapping her hand in his grip. She glanced up at him and felt the world drop away. Felt it narrow to just the two of them. She no longer heard the sounds of Maria in the kitchen or the ticking of the grandfather clock in the hallway.

It was just her and Gavin and nothing else mattered. And she wanted life to stay that way. Suddenly it didn't seem like a good idea to go out tonight—she wanted to be all alone with this man, with no outside interference whatsoever.

"That's a big pitcher for one person."

She knew that. She'd never had a problem with alcohol so she used it when she needed to. But now that Gavin was here she realized how it might look to him. "I was hoping to have help drinking it."

"Not getting drunk?" he asked.

"I did think about it," she admitted. There were so many rumors about her that she tried to never tell lies. Not even ones that would help her.

He raised one eyebrow at her.

"It hasn't been the best day for me," she said reluctantly.

"Because of the picture?" he asked.

"Sort of." No way did she want to go into all the sordid details of her pathetic relationship with her father.

"Want to talk about it?"

"No—yes."

He drew her over to the loveseat and sat down, sprawled his large frame on the piece of furniture. It made her realize how big he was as he settled in next to her.

"Talk."

She stared up at him wishing she'd never opened her mouth. He seemed so immune to the doubts that plagued her, above such petty worries as what someone else thought of him.

"How do you do it?" she asked, taking an absent sip of her margarita.

"Do what?" He set his glass down on the table, stretching one long arm along the back of the loveseat.

She stared at his hands instead of at him. No lies, she thought. Realizing that with Gavin that rule was going to be much harder to keep. He made her feel so vulnerable and she hated that.

"Stay so cool," she said. She really wanted to know. She could fake it for a while and people never seemed to notice the falseness of her smile but inside she died a little each time. And she was so incredibly tired of feeling empty.

When she was with Gavin she felt more than she wanted to, which was a double-edged sword. She craved the attention and the emotions he effortlessly brought to the fore but at the same time she was afraid of him.

He reached for his glass and took a sip of his margarita. "I don't"

"It looks like it."

"Appearances can be deceiving."

"Yes, they can."

Tempest tried to push it from her mind but the thought weighed heavily there. Appearances could be deceiving. What was Gavin hiding, and was she really going to try to figure it out?

# Six

Appearances were a tricky thing, Gavin thought as he watched Tempest move through the crowded club. Anyone seeing her now would never have guessed at the vulnerability he'd witnessed in her home earlier.

He'd ached to draw her into his arms and just hold her but he knew he was just as much to blame for her current troubles. He'd been thinking about it all night how the one that'd come out looking bad in the entire photo-lost-job situation was Tempest.

Her father had gotten the sympathetic he's-done-everything-for-her treatment and Gavin himself had gotten the businessman-led-astray-by-a-beautiful-woman thing. It wasn't fair, he thought.

But then he'd learned early on that life wasn't fair. And usually he didn't dwell on that.

She was incandescent tonight, glowing with a light from within, as she moved among her high-society friends, the groupies who followed the deejay from club to club and the paparazzi that seemed to follow her everywhere she went.

Gavin leaned against the wall in the VIP section and just watched her. He still had absolutely no idea what he was going to do with her other than take her to his bed. He knew that if he wanted her there tonight he should be a little more sociable but night-clubs like this left him cold. And pretending to be something he wasn't simply wasn't his way.

"Are you going to stand here all night?" she asked, coming up to him. Her hips moved in time with the driving beat of the music.

"Probably."

"Why?"

"This isn't my scene."

"No kidding. Why don't you give it a try?"

"I'm not really social."

"I am."

"I've noticed."

She glanced up at him. He wished he could read what was going on inside her head because he knew something was off but had no idea how to fix it.

"Why don't you like this scene?" she asked.

"There's no point to this."

"The point is to have fun…is that something you've heard of?"

"Ha, ha, smart-ass. Of course I've heard of fun, *it's just so pointless to hang out in a club when you* know there are people waiting to take your picture and write down everything you've done."

She pulled him further into the VIP section to a small booth in the back that was shrouded in shadows. She scooted in and then glanced up at him. "Sit down."

He slid in next to her. Giving into the temptation to put his arm around her shoulders and tug her up against the side of his body.

"Why are we back here?" he asked.

"No one can hear us back here or see us."

"If you wanted privacy, why'd we come here?"

"Because my doorman at home is on the payroll of at least two tabloid newspapers. He always tells them when I have visitors of the opposite sex and how long they stay. This way he won't have much to report."

He took a strand of her hair in his hand swirling it around his finger. "How do you stand it?"

"It's my life."

He added this complication to the matrix running in the back of his mind. It wasn't enough that she was August's daughter. She was someone who was used to living in the spotlight.

"Seriously, Tempest, how do you stand it?"

She stared down at the table. "I'm one big fraud.

I smile at strangers and chat up acquaintances and pretend that they are friends."

He heard more than her words and knew that deep inside these kinds of situations took a toll on her. And he wasn't going to add to it. He had the money and the manpower to shield her.

He let his fingers slide down her neck, tipping her head back so that she rested on his arm. He traced the lines of her face, trying to ease the stress that he saw there. Then he leaned down and brushed his lips over hers. Just felt her in his arms, where he'd wanted her since she'd left his office hours ago.

She opened her lips and he felt the brush of her tongue against his. Her hands caged his face and she lifted slightly so she was pressed more firmly against him.

Deep inside where he'd been hiding for the majority of his adult life he felt something melt. Some part of him that he planned to ignore, but all the same that part knew that this woman was his.

*His.*

He took control of the kiss, changing it from a sweet gentle meeting of mouths, to an all out claiming of the woman. He wanted to make sure there was no doubt in Tempest's mind that she belonged to him.

A flashbulb illuminated them and he lifted his head, pushing to his feet, but Tempest stilled him with her small manicured hand on his arm.

"Want to dance?"

"No."

"Gavin…"

He stopped walking toward the velvet ropes and the photographer who'd snapped their picture.

"What?"

"I'm sorry my life is like this."

He glanced back at her, turning to face her. "I am, too. Let's get out of here."

"I wanted one dance with you," she said.

"Ah, hell, you know that guy is still out there," he said.

"Yes, I do."

He wasn't much of a dancer but couldn't pass up the chance to hold her in his arms. She'd changed into a skirt that was so tight and short, he couldn't keep his eyes off her legs, which were long and slim, accentuated by the heels she wore.

"Why don't you have a bodyguard?"

She shrugged but he wasn't going to let her evade the question.

"Tell me," he said.

"I did have one but he worked for my father. When I left finishing school my dad and I had a falling out so he cancelled the contract with the company that provided my bodyguard. My father said if I was going to court trouble then I deserved to get myself out of it…I've just kind of never wanted to give him the satisfaction of knowing I couldn't take care of myself…so no bodyguard for me. I can handle the paparazzi without one."

"Give me a minute," he said.

"What are you doing?"

"Hiring a bodyguard. And it's not because I think you can't handle yourself."

"Why then?"

He didn't answer her, refused to say out loud that he needed to protect her. Instead he dialed the private investigating firm that he used in researching company CEOs before he decided to invest in their businesses. He had a short conversation with the owner and the promise that a bodyguard would be along shortly to ensure their privacy.

She grabbed his hand, tugging him toward the dance floor. He pulled her into his arms and realized dating this woman was more complicated than a million different mergers but that didn't deter him from going after her.

Tempest watched the street lights and shadows go by as Gavin drove. He wasn't going in the direction of her condo and she was pretty sure she was going to get an up-close and personal tour of his place.

The bodyguard he'd summoned to the club was following behind them making sure they weren't followed too closely. She wasn't sure that the press would stay away from her, but it was nice for tonight to have this sense of anonymity. It was something she'd never had

"Thanks," she said, at last. Needing to talk, needing to get out of her own head before she started crying about her life. God, how pitiful was that? She had a nice home, food in her kitchen and a roof over her head. There was nothing to be so sad about.

"For?" he asked, his voice low.

She shrugged, wrapping one arm around her waist as a chill spread through her body. "The body-guard thing."

"It was nothing. Cold?"

She shook her head but he adjusted the air conditioning making it warmer on her side. But it wasn't nothing to her. Her father always said she brought the intense scrutiny on herself. That if she'd acted like a lady they would never have been interested in her. Ironic that when she cleaned up her act and started behaving like a lady, he was the one who became more indifferent in her.

Gavin wasn't indifferent. But he was still holding a part of himself back from her. Not that she necessarily blamed him. She'd read the *Page Six* dirt on herself and knew without a doubt that anyone with a nice normal life would think twice about getting too involved with her.

But Gavin didn't have a normal life. He had a life where he was gunning for Tempest's Closet. Why? Even her father had never said exactly why.

"Can I ask you a question?" she asked into the silence. She wanted to unravel Gavin and figure out what made him tick. And a big part of who he was, according to rumor, involved the take over of her father's company.

"You just did," he said wryly.

"Are you trying to be funny?"

"I don't know, is it working?"

"No."

She turned in her seat to face him. His stark features were illuminated by the dashboard lights making him seem more of a stranger than she wanted him to be.

"Why are you fixated on taking over Tempest's Closet?"

He glanced over at her and then back to the road. "It makes good business sense."

"There seems like there is more to it than that."

He turned off the highway and entered an exclusive neighborhood. "Maybe there is."

"If you don't want to say then just tell me it's off-limits."

"I don't want to say anymore about it," he said, pulling into the garage of a large McMansion. There were two other cars parked in the three-car garage. One low, sexy sports car and an SUV that looked like it had been taken off-roading.

"Why not?"

"Tempest, it's private."

"And I'm only allowed to fall into a certain part of your life?"

He shrugged.

"I'm not into anonymous sex."

"Neither am I. I like you and I'll share parts of my life with you."

But just the parts that he wanted to share.

"I can't do this," she said. She'd had affairs in the past that were short and frivolous but she couldn't do that with Gavin. She wanted to know more about him. He made her feel safe and real.

And she was so afraid that if she slept with him, she'd be in over her head.

He glanced over at her his features illuminated this time by the garage lighting and she knew this was a crossroads for them. Either they'd continue on in a relationship or they'd part ways.

Gavin rubbed the back of his neck, He had known this moment was going to come—he should have been better prepared for it. And he'd already decided she was not a corporate spy. Was it possible that August didn't know why he was coming after him? Or was it only his daughter?

"Come inside and we can talk. If you still want to go home…I'll take you. The bodyguard is yours no matter what choice you make. Everyone deserves privacy."

"Thanks for saying that. A lot of people believe I deserve the attention. That it is some kind of punishment for my actions."

"People?"

She shrugged and he knew that she meant her father. She'd said as much earlier but now she wasn't going to say anymore. He opened his car door and pocketed his keys. He escorted her into his house.

As the door closed behind them he felt a sense of rightness. She belonged here.

He could talk her into anything on his home turf. But he didn't want to persuade her to stay. He wanted her as hot for him as he was for her.

He led her into the living room with the plasma screen TV on one wall and the tropical fish tank on the other. There was expensive art hanging on the wall that his decorator had purchased and the floor was made of marble he'd had imported from Italy. He didn't want to acknowledge it but he knew that he'd been working hard his entire life for a moment like this one.

He wanted her to know that he wasn't some poor kid who'd lost everything and lived on government subsidies. He didn't want to acknowledge that part of him, not in front of her. But he was going to have to. There was no way to talk about his focus on acquiring Tempest's Closet without talking about the past.

And standing in this opulent room even he felt the distance between who he'd been and who he was today.

"Can I get you a drink?"

"No, I'm good," she said, drifting around the room and settling on the couch.

He walked over to the well-stocked bar in the corner and poured himself two fingers of scotch before turning back toward her.

She looked like a sexy angel in the dim lighting. And he didn't want to let her go. Even though he knew deep inside that he wasn't going to get to keep her. The past was too much a part of the man he was today for her to every really be a part of his life but he wanted whatever time they had.

"Am I pushing too hard?" she asked. "I know what it's like to feel like you're being hounded."

"Ah, honey. You humble me." And she really did. She was selfless in a way that he knew she wouldn't recognize. She was constantly thinking of others and though she had a reputation for being a party-girl and going after only what would make her feel good, he was coming to realize that making others feel good was what did it for her.

"Come sit with me, Gavin."

He sank down on the sofa beside her and she turned toward him, slipping off her shoes and curling those long legs under her. The hem of her skirt rose to a dangerous level. He couldn't tear his gaze from her thighs until she put her hand on his forearm. Stroked her fingers up and down his arm.

She stared up at him with those wide-blue eyes of hers. Seeing past the successful man he was today and straight into the heart of him. Straight to that little boy he'd all but forgotten about.

He tugged her into his arms, until her back rested against his chest and she faced away from him. He wrapped his arm around her waist and lowered his head to the top of her hair. Breathing in that sweet clean scent that he associated only with her.

"Tempest's Closet industries took my life from

me," he said, softly. And realized he wasn't going to be able to do this. He didn't want to sound like some kind of sap whose life was ruined. Because he really couldn't imagine living another way. He was happy being the man he was today. And grudgingly he realized he owed that to August Lambert.

"How?" she asked, tipping her head back on his shoulder. Her silky hair slid against his skin.

"The same way they did so many lives in this country. Tempest's Closet came to my home town and the small merchants in the town slowly went out of business."

"Tempest's Closet brings a lot of money into the communities that it develops in. You know a lot of local governments solicit Tempest's Closet to get them to come to their towns."

"I thought you stopped working for Tempest's Closet."

"That doesn't mean I'm not still proud of what my father has done."

He pushed to his feet and walked away from her. This wasn't something he could ignore. "For every job that Tempest's Closet brings into a community at least five are lost. And a way of life is compromised."

She sat up. "A way of life? Tempest's Closet isn't going in and making these communities into company towns that they run. They bring fashion and style to places where such things weren't even talked about before."

"We're never going to agree on this."

"I know," she said, quietly. She studied him for a long moment and then stood and walked over to him.

"Did your family lose everything?"

He nodded.

"We owned the general store. You know one of those small old-fashioned ones that carried everything from clothes to hardware to groceries."

"Tempest's Closet shouldn't have affected the hardware and grocery part of your business," she said.

"No, but the other large retailers that followed Tempest's Closet to our town did."

"I'm sorry."

"Don't be. It made me who I am."

"I like who you are," she said, wrapping her arms around his waist and resting her head against his chest.

He tugged her up against him. There was no room for any other thoughts. He didn't want to dwell on the past or think about business. He just wanted to relish the feel of her.

To focus solely on her and the now. The part of his life that she could be in. He danced her around the living room. Just enjoying the feel of her in his arms.

He lowered his head to hers and kissed her again. Rekindling the desire that was never far from the surface when she was around. She responded instantly, tipping her head back and thrusting her tongue into his mouth.

He lifted her in his arms and walked out of the living room toward the stairs and his bedroom.

# Seven

Gavin's bedroom was different than she expected it to be. Done in warm earth tones with a large Ansel Adams' photograph from the Mural project but it wasn't a poster it was the real thing. She moved closer to it when he set her on her feet. The stark black-and-white photograph called to her as nothing else could.

Gavin put his hands on her shoulders and drew her back against his body. Just holding her while she examined the photograph to her heart's content. She felt the subtle movements of his body rubbing against hers. Felt his erection against the small of her back and knew in a few minutes that passion would take over and they'd be making love. But for this one moment she felt something she'd never expected to feel. Something she'd long ago given up searching for. A kind of welcome and peace.

She closed her eyes and turned in his arms, resting her head over his heart and wrapping her arms around his body. He lowered his head over the top of hers. The warmth of his breath stirred her hair before he cupped her face and tipped her head back so that their eyes met.

She tunneled her fingers through his hair, drawing his head down. Their mouths met, his lips rubbing lightly over hers. Touching her gently…so gently. She knew she'd never get enough of tasting him.

Then the dynamic of the embrace changed. His tongue thrust deep into her mouth as his hand swept down her back. He cupped her butt and drew her closer to him. His erection rubbed against her belly. She moaned deep in her throat and moved closer to him.

Her hands clutched at his shoulders, her body craving more. She felt his hands at the hem of her short skirt. Sliding up underneath it and rubbing random patterns on her skin. She shifted her legs, craving his touch higher. But he kept up the subtle caresses.

"Gavin…"

He nibbled his way from her mouth to her ear biting the lobe. When he spoke his words were a strong puff of air in her ear, felt as much as heard. "What?"

"Touch me," she said, breathing the words against his neck. Damn, he smelled so good. She wanted to close her eyes and lose herself in the sensation of him. The feel of his big hands on her skin. The white-hot tingle that followed his touch. The sweet craving for more that was permeating her bloodstream.

He moved his hand higher cupping her butt cheek and holding her in place as she undulated against him. She moaned deep in her throat, trying to stand on her toes and feel his erection where she wanted it. Needed it.

She lifted her leg trying to wrap it around his hip but he gripped her thigh in his hand, his long fingers holding her so close to where she needed his touch.

"I am touching you, Tempest."

But it wasn't enough. She shifted again in his arms but it was futile. She wasn't getting closer to him until he decided she was. "I need more."

"Not yet," he said.

She realized then that he was playing her. Not in a malicious way but in a power way. One that made her submissive to him and his desires. He'd give her what she wanted but only on his agenda. She didn't understand what his agenda was here. But she felt that he did have one.

She stepped away and looked at him. His gray eyes were cold and flat. She saw the passion in him in the flush of his skin and the erection straining against the front of his pants. But she saw that he kept a part of himself locked away from her and this moment.

"What are you waiting for?"

He reached out then, taking a strand of her hair

in his hand and drawing it through his fingers. She tipped her head toward him and his thumb found her lower lip. She knew her mouth was swollen from his kisses and it tingled as he moved his thumb over it.

"Just waiting," he said.

She couldn't follow the conversation anymore. Her world had narrowed to his hand in her hair and that thumb rubbing over her lip. She caught it gently *between her teeth, sucking him deep into her mouth* and his hand on her hair stilled. His eyes narrowed, his breath hissing out in a rush.

He drew her closer again, wrapping her hair around his hand. He pulled his thumb from her mouth and ran it across her lips and then down the side of her neck. He stroked her pulse there at the bottom of her neck before moving down the edge of her blouse. Caressing the skin left bare there.

His features were harsh and strained in the light, yet very sensual as he focused on touching her. And she realized what he was waiting for. He didn't want to rush this moment and neither did she.

He brought his mouth down to hers. His one hand burrowed deep in her hair, holding her still for his possession. His tongue delving deep, leaving no inch of her mouth unexplored.

His thumb stroked over her skin, down beneath the silky fabric of her summer weight top. Finding *the lacy edge of her bra with his thumb, moving* lower and flicking around the edge of her breast. She shivered as he came close to touching her where she needed it most. Her nipple tightened in anticipation but he just kept moving down her body. His knuckles brushing the underside of her breast.

He sucked her lower lip between his teeth and bit down delicately on her flesh before drawing his head back. "Take your top off."

She shivered again as the rough growl of his voice played over her skin. She drew her shirt up over her head tossing it to the floor.

"Now your skirt," he said.

She took a step back but his hand in her hair kept her bound to him. "Do it here."

She trembled at the command in his voice. She'd never had a man treat her this way in the bedroom. Moist heat pooled between her legs as she reached behind her back and loosened the button and then drew down the zipper. With a swivel of her hips the skirt slid down her legs and pooled at her feet.

"Now take off your underwear," he said.

She undid the bra and slid it off her arms. She leaned against him for a moment, letting the tips of her breasts brush against the crisp linen shirt he wore.

She hesitated to remove her panties. She'd be naked and he was fully clothed. He seemed to sense her hesitation and leaned down to capture her bottom lip between his teeth. He sucked on her lip until shivers ran down her body. Being naked while he was fully clothed no longer mattered. He lifted his head and she reached for her panties, sliding them slower down her legs until at her knees they fell to the floor.

Gavin stepped back to look at her. "Go lay on the bed."

In the lamp light her skin glistened and it was clear to him that she was too fine to be in his bed. In that moment, with her lying there waiting for him, he knew that he wasn't good enough for her. He was too rough—still the boy who'd had to fight for everything he owned—despite the millions he'd made.

He was too demanding and she was too…out of his league. There was the slight hint of shyness in her eyes as she settled in the center of his bed. And there was a part of him—granted it wasn't a big part—but a part of him that demanded she prove that *she really wanted him*.

"I'm here," she said, her voice soft and tentative. This wasn't the same nervy woman who'd confronted him in his office demanding a job.

He should walk away from her. Tell her to get dressed and make her leave. There was no good way for this to end, this affair they'd talked themselves into. His need for revenge was too great and as he looked at her lying there he wished…ah, hell, he wished he were a different man. The kind who could walk away from the past because he had a glimpse of what the future could be.

"Gavin," she said, lifting her arms toward him.

Walking away was no longer an option. Not when

she watched him with those wide vulnerable eyes and stared up at him like she really wanted him. Like her heart was empty without him. And God knew his heart was empty without her.

He sank down on the bed next to her hip, tracing the curves of her body with his hand. Her skin was porcelain and perfect. He traced a line down the center of her body over her sternum right between her two perfect breasts. Her pink nipples beaded as he moved his finger. He stopped and leaned over, breathing on her nipple, watching it tighten even more before he lowered his mouth and tasted her.

She moaned, the sound a symphony in his ears. Her hands moved restlessly, falling to his shoulders. Her nails scored his skin through the fabric of his dress shirt as she tried to draw him closer. But because he couldn't see a way to hold her in his arms forever, he wanted to make this moment last. He wanted to ensure that she never took another man to her bed and didn't think of him.

He caught her delicate flesh between his teeth as jealousy pounded through him. No other man would touch this woman the way Gavin would. His hands slid down her body gripping her hips as they lifted toward him. He pinched her other nipple and heard her gasp as he did so.

He lifted his head, making sure she was with him. She drew his head back to her breast. Lifting her shoulders so that the tight bud of her nipple brushed against first his cheek then his lips.

"More," she said.

He lowered his head to oblige her, working her nipple with his lips, teeth and tongue until her legs were moving restlessly on the bed. His body was so tight, so aching for the sweet release that she promised, that his entire being echoed with his own heartbeat.

He felt the blood pounding beneath the surface of his own skin. Felt the pulse pounding at the base of his spine and in the flesh between his legs. He attended her other nipple and then nibbled his way down her body, lingering over her flat stomach. He sucked the skin around her belly button and delighted when he skimmed his fingers lower to find the moist proof of her desire for him.

He traced the edge where the smooth skin met her curls and then ran his finger up one side of her and then down the other. The small bud in the center of those two lips was red and swollen, begging for his touch. But he ignored it. Shifting to his knees, he pushed her thighs apart.

She let them fall open making room for him between her legs. He looked down at her. Her skin was flushed with a slight pink tinge. She held her breath, everything in her body tensing as he lowered his head between her legs. Her hips rose toward him as he reached down and licked her once.

The taste of her was addicting. He pulled the flesh into his mouth, careful to treat her delicately.

She grabbed his head, pulling him against her as her hips rose with each tug of his mouth.

He bent lower to taste her more deeply. She was delicious and he knew that he'd never forget the sensations of this moment for as long as he lived.

She moaned and said something—perhaps his name or a demand—but he was lost in a red haze. He was surrounded by her and he could think of no other place he wanted to be.

He could feel her body starting to tighten around his tongue, and shifted back to see her at this moment. He wanted to watch her face as she went over the edge.

This was something that her money couldn't buy and her family name couldn't control. This was about Tempest and Gavin, he thought. He relished the sound of their names linked in his mind.

He pressed one finger inside her, then added a second finger, pushing deep and finding that spot that would bring her the most pleasure. He leaned down over her, taking her nipple in his mouth again, sucking her deep into his mouth.

She was panting, his name falling from her lips in between pleas that made no sense. He drew her out until finally he touched that bud between her legs and brought her to climax. She called his name and grasped his head, holding him to her like she'd never let go.

Shivers still rocked her body as she came back into herself. She couldn't believe Gavin was still fully dressed from the fine linen shirt down to his wingtips.

She shifted on the bed, reaching for him to draw

him down to her. He hesitated for a second and she wondered what was going on in his mind. She knew there was more to this than simple lust. Oh, God, please let it be more than lust.

*She'd never had a man make her forget…forget* everything except him. In the past sex was something she'd had because it was convenient or expected. But this was the first time in her life that she was with a man just because she wanted to be with him.

For the first time who she was—Tempest Lambert—was actually a strike against her. And he still wanted her.

She felt tears sting the back of her eyes and she turned her face against his chest, reaching for the buttons of his shirt. She undid them slowly, taking her time, revealing the masculine chest slowly.

Gavin wasn't waxed; she doubted it would even occur to him to do something like that. And she liked the feel of his chest hair against her fingers. She slipped her hand under the shirt and found his flat nipples. His breath caught as she scraped her nail over his flesh. She knew he wanted her.

She could feel him straining toward her through the clothing. It was a costume he wore, a façade of sophistication. She realized the real man beneath the clothing was rougher, needier and not at all sophisticated.

That very realization was exciting. She slid the shirt off his shoulders and pushed him back toward the headboard. She wanted to take her time and explore him. She wished she was brave enough to order him to take off his clothes and lay on the bed. But she wasn't.

"Why are you staring at me?"

She shook her head. No way was she going to say what she was really thinking. "You're gorgeous."

"Ha. I think we both know I'm not model material."

"No, you're not," she agreed. Because she'd been with model-type men. Men who were too picture perfect to be true. But there was something so real about Gavin. Something that made her feel real by association.

"You should at least have argued."

"Models aren't real," she said, tracing the delineated pectoral muscles on his chest. "They are airbrushed perfection."

She bent to taste his skin, licking a path over his chest. He tasted salty and his skin was warm and she closed her eyes wanting to lose herself in him again.

He turned in her arms, pinned her under his body. His mouth found hers, his tongue thrusting deep inside. The feeling of his muscled chest against her breasts was exquisite.

He reached between their bodies and freed his erection. She felt the scrape of his belt against her inner thigh as he pushed his pants down.

He hesitated as he was about to enter her body. "Are you on the pill?"

It took a second for her to understand what he was

*asking. She just wanted him to drive into her and* take her. Birth control. She'd never thought of the consequences of making love before…not really. But suddenly, staring up at his face in the dim lamp light, she did. She'd always vaguely wanted a family. A real family and kids. She bit her lower lip.

"Tempest?"

"No. I'm not on the pill. I'm not as promiscuous as the tabloids make me seem."

He cupped her face in his hands, leaning forward to kiss her. "I know."

Those few words made her wish they were different people. Or maybe that she was a different woman. One who would be strong enough to pull Gavin off his quest for revenge because deep inside she sensed that he'd never give up going after her father for her.

He kissed her so tenderly before moving away to put on a condom. He came back down on top of her and she put her hands on his chest, holding him back from entering her body.

Bending down, he captured the tip of her breast in his mouth. He sucked her deep in his mouth, his teeth lightly scraping against her sensitive flesh. His other hand played at her other breast, arousing her, making her arch against him in need.

"Now, Gavin. I can't wait."

"Not yet."

She reached between them and took his erection in her hand, bringing him closer to her. Spreading her legs wider so that she was totally open to him. "I need you now."

He lifted his head, the tips of her breasts were damp from his mouth and very tight. He rubbed his chest over them before sliding deep into her body.

She wanted to close her eyes as he made love to her. To somehow keep him from seeing how susceptible she was to him, but subterfuge had never been one of her strong suits. Gavin was essential to her in ways she was only beginning to comprehend.

She slid her hands down his back, cupping his butt as he thrust deeper into her. Their eyes met. She felt her body start to tighten around him, catching her by surprise. She climaxed before him. He gripped her hips, holding her down and thrusting into her two more times before he came, loudly calling out her name.

Disposing of the condom, he pulled her into his arms and tucked her up against his side.

She wrapped her arm around him and listened to the solid beating of his heart. She wanted to stay here forever wrapped in his arms. He made her feel safe and complete and she wished he didn't. She felt vulnerable to someone other than her father and that made her angry because until this moment, she'd been able to keep moving on and never look back. But now she was going to be looking back.

She understood Gavin so much better now than she ever could have before. And because she had her own weaknesses, she didn't want him to feel vulnerable with her. Plus, he had given her back something she wasn't sure she could have found on her own.

"Are you sleeping?" he asked.

She felt the vibration of his words in his chest and under her ear. She shifted in his embrace, tipping her head so she could see the underside of his jaw.

"No." This had been one of the most tumultuous days of her life. She felt that if she went to sleep she might wake up and find out that Gavin had really washed his hands of her and this had all been a dream.

"Thanks for taking care of the birth control. To be honest I wasn't thinking of anything but you," she said.

"You're welcome." He pulled her closer in his arms. "I want to take care of you, Tempest. To watch over you."

His words warmed the long cold part of her soul. And she knew then that she was starting to fall for him. How stupid was that? She'd spent her entire life trying to win her father's love and she was falling for the one man who'd make his acceptance an impossibility.

She propped herself up on his chest, looking down at him in the shadowy night. He made her feel safe and she knew it wasn't an illusion. He'd provided her a bodyguard and he held her in his arms tonight. She'd seen the same thing with his brother. The way he always protected those around him. What had happened to make him do that?

"What are you thinking about?"

"The way you take care of me. No one has ever…" she trailed off as she realized how vulnerable those words made her.

He slipped on a condom and rolled over so that she was under him. Her legs parted and he settled against her. His arms braced on either side of her body. He caught her head in his hands and brought his mouth down hard on hers. When he came up for air long minutes later, he said, "I will always."

She believed him. Gavin wasn't the kind of man to make promises lightly. When he gave his word he kept it and she wondered if she should ask him how he felt about her. If he thought he could ever love her enough to give up his vendetta against her father. But those kinds of words weren't easy to find and she was much too scared to find out that he couldn't love her to ever say them aloud.

Instead she lifted her hips toward his and felt him slip inside her body. Their eyes met and held again as he took her.

# Eight

Tempest glanced at the alarm clock, afraid to move in case she woke Gavin. The illuminated dial read 2:30. She had always been a bit of an insomniac.

She felt too vulnerable lying naked in his arms. She'd shown him too much of who she really was and now he had the power to hurt her. Really hurt her and she wasn't sure she trusted him not to. Oh, he wouldn't do it intentionally. He was too caring to deliberately hurt her but she was still…afraid. She tipped her head back, staring at his beard stubbled jaw in the dim light of the moon. She wanted to touch him. To explore him now that he was sleeping and not watching her. She wanted to memorize all the little details of his body so that she'd be able to *pull them out later when* she was alone and remember them. So that any time she saw him at social functions she'd have a secret knowledge of the man beneath the suit. The man behind the image.

Turning in his arms she reached up and touched his jaw. She ran her finger along the edge of it and felt his breathing pattern change. She closed her eyes and held herself still. She didn't want to disturb him, wake him up and maybe remind him that she wasn't supposed to spend the night with him.

What if he asked her to go? To be honest it had happened before and nothing made her feel worse than having to put her clothes on in the middle of the night and leave. But everything with Gavin had been different. Please, God, let things still be different.

"What are you thinking about?" he asked, his voice a sleepy rumble.

"Nothing," she said, softly.

"You're tense."

"I am," she said. No point in lying.

"Why?"

She struggled not to smile. There was no artifice in Gavin. He had no time for small talk and always cut to the chase.

She shrugged, very aware that she didn't want to reveal anything else to him.

He cupped her jaw and tipped her head back so that their eyes met. In the dim light it was easy to pretend that she saw something more in his eyes than was probably there. She wanted to believe that she really did see caring, affection and then the narrowing of his eyes and lust. But she didn't want to deceive herself.

"Tell me."

"It's nothing and everything," she said. There was no other way to say it.

He shifted on the bed, pushing the pillows behind his back against the headboard and drawing her into his arms. She liked that feeling that came as she lay there. It was safety and security but more than that it was belonging. However false it might be, for this night she belonged in Gavin's arms. And there was no place she'd rather be.

"Tell me the everything part."

"I don't sleep much at night. Never have. So that's the everything. Just my normal habits."

"Why don't you sleep?"

She shrugged, reluctant to tell a bold-faced lie and say she didn't know. Her therapist and she had gone over every detail of why she didn't sleep for years. Tracing it to the night her mother had died. Being woken up by her nanny in the middle of the night and informed that her mother was asking for her. Being rushed down the hall to her parent's big dark bedroom to hold that cold limp hand. Her father sitting in one corner not even glancing in her direction, while the machines made scary noises. The nanny watching her as if she knew more than she would tell.

"Why, Tempest?"

"My subconscious thinks bad things happen at night but I want to focus on now."

"Tonight?"

"Yes, just tonight. You and I together," she said. The words should be a reminder to her that she and Gavin didn't have forever.

"We don't have much in common," he said.

She'd like to pretend that the comment was apropos of nothing but she knew he was trying to warn her in his own way that this couldn't last. She knew that she should try to guard her heart but was very afraid that it was too late.

"I don't know about that," she said, so very afraid that he was going to use that as a reason to never see her again. She didn't want that to happen. She no longer cared if she got a job at his company, just wanted to stay with him. To have a legitimate reason to stay in his life.

"Name one thing we have in common."

"We travel in the same social circles."

He tightened his arm around her shoulder. "Yeah, but I'm a fraud there. I don't belong in high society."

"You aren't a fraud, Gavin. You earned your place in that circle. So many just find themselves there because of the circumstances of their birth." People like her. If anyone was a fraud, she knew it was her. She'd spent the first part of her adult life being exactly the kind of thoughtless heiress that gave the wealthy set a bad name.

He tipped her head back and leaned down to kiss

her. It was a sweet kiss that demanded nothing and gave everything. "You've paid a high price because of the circumstances of your birth."

"So have you," she said, shifting in his arms. Turning more fully into his embrace.

He lifted his head staring down at her and she realized they both had this in common. This past shaped by their parents. Those long ago events shaping the people they were today.

He lowered his head again. This time his kiss was demanding. She tried to caress him, to draw him over her, but he held her hands in his grip. He lifted her onto his lap and he pulled her hands up behind his neck. She let him. She hung there in his embrace, letting him control her. Hoping that he'd take her again and give her the release she desperately needed to find in his arms.

Tempest was exhausted and totally able to sleep now but didn't want to miss a moment of this night. Her skin felt as if she'd been branded by him. There was beard burn on her breasts and her neck. She fingered the base of her neck where he'd sucked on her skin the last time they'd made love.

She'd never had a man so obsessed with her body. Even now while he was sleeping his hands moved down her back. Tracing the curve of her hip and then moving slowly back up. She was drowning in a sea of sensation and didn't care to be rescued.

She'd never realized how alone she'd been surrounded by the hoards of people that populated her life. But she had been lonely and it was only now that she recognized it.

"Baby, go to sleep," he said.

His voice was a deep husky murmur that made her toes curl in a good way. She lifted her thigh over his legs, curling herself around him. More fully into his arms and into his embrace.

She felt him stir against her and shifted her hips to rub against him. He rolled her under his body, taking her wrists in his hands and stretching her arms up above her head.

"What is it?" he asked.

She stared up at him, his features barely illuminated in the dim light. She ached—pleasantly from the hours she'd spent in his arms, but inside she still craved more. She had no words for what she wanted. For what it was that was keeping her from drifting to sleep.

Instead she lifted herself up, leaning on her elbow and tracing his features in the dim light. He lay still under her and let her explore. He wasn't like the pretty boys she'd grown up with. The soft boys who'd matured into fine-looking men who graced the pages of fashion magazines and society gossip columns.

He had a scar in the middle of his left eyebrow. She traced it over and over again with her finger before bending down to brush her lips over it. She found another small scar just under his left eye and then further down on his jaw and neck. "What happened?"

"Skateboarding accident."

"Skateboarding?" she asked, shifting around to rest her arms on his chest. It was the least likely thing. She couldn't picture him doing anything other than running a multi-million dollar investment group.

"I didn't grow up in a bubble."

"I know. But skateboarding?"

"Yeah, I liked it. Skateboarders don't care about anything but your board and your skills."

He didn't say anything else but she sensed there was more to it then that. She let her mind roam over what he said and suddenly it came to her. "Is that when you realized that you could make your own dynasty?"

He shifted under her, pulling her over him like a blanket and then rolling her under him.

"I'm not into dynasty building."

He wouldn't be. Not with his quest for revenge. Revenge was focused on the past. On avenging wrongs done a long time ago. Dynasty building required a forward vision—something she realized that Gavin didn't have. "Don't you think it's time you started looking to the future?"

He took her wrists in his hands and stretched her arms over his head. Pushed one thigh between her legs until he nestled between hers. Then he held her under him.

"A future with you?" he asked.

She turned her gaze from his. She hadn't been fishing for that and wasn't even entirely sure they could have something permanent together. "I don't know. I just know that you're not happy living the way you have been."

"And my happiness matters to you?"

A day ago she would have said no. That it didn't. He was just a means to an end. A way of striking back at her father. But lying with him naked in his bed having been in his arms and felt the protectiveness that was so much a part of his nature, she knew that his happiness did matter. It mattered more than she wished it did.

She tried to free her hands, wanting to touch him but he held her in an unbreakable grasp.

"Tempest, I asked you a question."

She bit her lower lip. "Yes, your happiness matters to me. Don't ask me anything else, Gavin. A man afraid of the future won't like my answer."

"I'm not afraid, honey."

He lowered his mouth to hers. His kisses overwhelmed her. They should both be sated and not interested in making love again.

Yet as he thrust his tongue deep in her mouth, she felt the rekindling of her own desire. She wanted him again. She tried to angle her head to reciprocate, he held her still.

This was his embrace and she felt the fierce need in him to dominate her here. God, he made her feel like she belonged to him. She tried to remind herself that Gavin had made her no promises, but his body *moving over hers felt like a promise.*

# Nine

**W**aking in Gavin's arms wasn't something she was used to. Even after two months of quasi-living together on weekends and even during the week once and a while, she was afraid to open her eyes each morning. Afraid that somehow the relationship with him was another fantasy like the vivid dreams she sometimes had of her mother.

But the big warm hand drifting down her back and drawing her more fully against him wasn't a lie. She opened her eyes and realized that once again she was on top of him.

"Sorry," she said, trying to shift to his side.

"No problem," he said, holding her in place.

He stroked her back and shoulders until she relaxed against him. "Is this normal for you?"

She shook her head, refusing to look at him. The comforting sound of his heart beat under her ear. She wasn't sure she could explain to him why she always ended up on top of him during the night. She only knew that…heck, it felt more real when she held on to him.

"You're not exactly normal for me," she said, softly.

"Good."

She leaned up on her elbows again and noticed he was smiling. He rarely smiled, something she'd observed over the last few months but this morning he seemed…happy, content and she liked to think she had a lot to do with that.

"I'm starting to receive invitations for the fashion shows in New York next month. Do you want to go with me?"

"No."

"It would be a nice getaway."

"I can't. I have a project at work that I'm hoping to close then."

"What project?" she asked He never talked about work, which she suspected was because he was in a fierce competition with her father to take over Tempest's Closet.

"A big one."

"Involving Tempest's Closet?"

He rolled to his side, dumping her on the bed and sitting up. "I don't want to discuss it with you."

She bit her lower lip knowing she should just let it go, but the thing was they couldn't move forward as they were. They were lovers and the world knew it. The tabloids had taken to labeling her the high-society mistress. Sleeping with her father's fiercest competitor. And in essence that was true but she felt like there was so much more between the two of them.

"I think we have to." The last thing she wanted was to force this confrontation but she felt like his business with her father was always between them. It was the reason why the press were so interested in them as a couple. The reason why he wouldn't hire her at his company. The reason they lived together in a seclusion of sorts.

"Are you threatening me?" he asked, his voice a low rumbled.

Never, she thought. She was way too afraid to lose what she'd found with him. But she'd been operating on a level of fear for most of her life. All of her relationships had always been driven by that fear and she hated that. Everything about Gavin had been different and this had to be too. She took a deep breath.

"No. That would be silly. How could I possibly threaten you?"

"You have something I want very badly."

"What?" she asked, aching inside at the thought of what he might say.

She knew that Gavin wanted her in stark physical

terms. He told her every night. But she…oh, man she'd been hoping there was something more between them. Something…

And to be perfectly honest no one had ever wanted anything she had but her father's money. Oh, God, don't let him say her shares in Tempest's Closet. She thought she'd wither and die on the spot if he said that.

"Your body."

Oh, that hurt. It really did. In a way she hadn't anticipated. And now she felt small and alone. Where just a few minutes ago she'd felt powerful and sexy and wanted.

"I'm sure you can find another lover."

She wrapped her arms around herself wishing she could curl into a ball and disappear. Why exactly did she decide she wasn't running anymore? She'd had some brief thought that he was different. But this felt so painful and very familiar.

"Not like you."

She glanced up at him. "I don't want to fight but I think we need to find a way to move past your business with Tempest's Closet or else…"

"Are you going to ignore what I just said?"

"I don't know how to take that."

"You make me want to be a different man, Tempest. I wish there were a way for me to give up this thing with Tempest's Closet but it has shaped my life for too long."

She nodded understanding. Her outrageous press antics had been the same kind of thing. But she liked the life she'd made for herself once she'd stopped behaving that way. "The past is going to suck you down and leave you with nothing. You have to move on."

"I thought you said you liked who I was?"

"I do. But this thing with Tempest's Closet is…"

"Is what? We're having an affair."

She gave him a hard look. "Fine."

She turned and walked away going into the bathroom and turning on the shower. How could she have read him so wrong? How could she have misjudged the man he was? How could she possibly go back out there and face him without giving him a good piece of her mind?

There was rap on the bathroom door. Gavin entered, looking tired. The stubble on his chin darkened his features and made him seem almost menacing.

"I'm not good with this kind of thing."

"Let me take a shower and get dressed. Then we can talk."

He nodded and turned to walk out, stopping on the threshold. "I don't want to lose you."

Gavin's housekeeper Mrs. Stanton had Sundays off, which usually didn't bother him. He liked having the time alone with Tempest since she had started spending the weekends at his house. But this morning when things were so screwed up and he had no idea what to say to make them right he wished Mrs. Stanton were here.

Since she wasn't he busied himself making coffee and breakfast for Tempest. Cooking wasn't something he'd ever learned to do. He could work a grill and a microwave but breakfast wasn't exactly grilling time. Luckily Mrs. Stanton had left a breakfast casserole and some fresh fruit already cut-up in a bowl.

He put the casserole into the oven and tried not to dwell on the fact that he was losing Tempest. It was inevitable that she'd start to want more than he could give her. But then again he'd always been a hollow shell inside. The only time he didn't feel empty was when he was at work, and that had never bothered him before.

He suspected that Michael knew this, and that was why his brother spent so much of his time trying to involve Gavin in outside activities. Anything to get him away from the office.

Hell, he thought rubbing the back of his neck. He prayed that those few words he'd given her before he'd left the bathroom would be enough.

But he knew they'd held a tinge of desperation. How could Tempest miss it?

He turned on the music, filling the house with sound so he wouldn't feel so alone. But the Beastie Boys didn't work their usual magic. Didn't energize him and make him feel unbeatable. The music just made him realize how alone he truly was as he stood on the oriental carpet in the family room and stared at the electronics equipment that any man would envy.

He glanced around his opulent house. Seeing the things—instead of people—in his life. Even Michael was rarely a guest here. His mother had never visited him here. This was his inner sanctum. The place he hid from the world and ah, hell, he really couldn't imagine the place without Tempest.

He saw the ghost of her curled up on the couch next to him as he'd watched the basketball game last night. He heard her laughter in the hallway leading to the kitchen when he checked on their breakfast. He smelled that unique scent that was only Tempest. That blend of expensive one-of-a-kind French perfume and something else that was just Tempest.

He glanced over his shoulder to the other doorway and saw her standing there. Her hair was perfectly styled, her makeup flawless. She had on a pair of capri pants, a scoop neck sleeveless summer top and stylish sandals. She was the picture of casual glamour standing there.

And he saw them both clearly. Him with his stubbled jaw wearing only his boxers. Her so clearly perfect….

There might be a reason why he couldn't find the words to make her stay.

"I'd kill for a cup of coffee," she said.

She was trying for sassy but the sadness in her eyes made it impossible to pull off. He realized then that this was going to be his gift to her—this hollow *emptiness he* brought to all of his relationships.

Some gift. One that she'd remember long after he'd left her life. And he didn't want that for Tempest.

She should be sassy and happy. Teasing and laughing the way she'd been with him every morning until this one. But he didn't know if he could give her what she wanted.

"Gavin?"

He shook his head and pulled down the coffee mugs she'd bought for them at Starbucks, after insisting that using his company logo mugs wasn't going to cut it. They were big cups since they'd both discovered that neither of them could face the day without an extra-large-extra-strong brew. The green background with white flowers always reminded him of Hawaii.

He poured her a cup, added a splash of fat-free half and half and handed it to her. He poured his own and left it black.

"Breakfast should be ready in thirty minutes. Want to go out on the patio?"

She nodded and followed him outside. He sat down on the double-lounger and drew her down beside him. She held her coffee mug in both hands and took a tentative sip before tipping her head back against his shoulder.

She sighed but didn't say anything. His confidence rose a little when he heard that sound. She wanted to stay here with him, too. Maybe they were both in unchartered waters.

He'd always disliked August Lambert, okay, he'd

actively hated the man for years but at this moment he wasn't thinking of the past. He wanted to keep business matters out of this embrace and not let work affect his time with her.

He put his coffee mug on the table next to him and took hers and did the same. He turned and pulled her flush against his body.

She wrapped her arms around his neck and pulled herself closer to him. He held her in his arms hoping this would be enough. Hoping that somehow she'd be able to determine from his embrace that he needed her in his house, needed her in his bed, needed her in his life. Only now, when he felt like he might lose her, did he realize how intensely he wanted to keep her here.

"I can't say the words you want me to."

"I don't know what words I want you to say."

"Something about giving up going after your father's company."

She shrugged but he saw in her eyes that he was right. "Why can't you give it up?"

He didn't want to talk about that but he saw in her eyes that she did need the words and if she were any other woman he'd say "screw it" and walk away. Instead he sat up and grabbed his coffee mug, using the drink as a distraction until he could figure out what to say.

Tempest watched Gavin as he pushed to his feet and paced around the patio. A part of her really wanted to just let this go. She was used to taking only what the men in her life wanted to give her. Scrambling around for any bit of attention and then gratefully basking in it until they tired of her and moved on.

But she couldn't do that with Gavin. She was falling for him. Who was she kidding—she was already in love with him. He was the kind of man she'd always wanted in her life.

So why the hell didn't she just keep her mouth shut and let things ride? Mind her own business about the Tempest's Closet takeover, hard as it might be. She shook her head and reached for her coffee mug. Taking a small sip, she realized that settling with Gavin wasn't enough. She'd never really loved any of the men she'd been involved with before. She loved Gavin and that made all the difference. She didn't want to be a tabloid footnote to the merger or takeover with Tempest's Closet. They needed to clear the air about it to stand a chance of staying together.

"Gavin?"

He cursed under his breath and turned back to her. He watched her carefully and she saw him searching for the right words to say. That gave her hope as nothing else could. He wanted this relationship between them to work, too.

"I don't want to talk about business with you," he said.

Was it really just business? She doubted it since he'd brought it up this morning. From the beginning of their relationship he'd been careful to avoid conversations about her time at Tempest's Closet and he never talked about his own work, except to continue to turn her down when she asked him to hire her. To be honest she'd pretty much given up working for him.

"I don't think this is about Renard Investments and Tempest's Closet. There's so much more going on here than that."

"Yes, there is. But it's personal. And I don't want you to know that side of me."

She saw the concern in his eyes. The anger and the fear. Did he really think that hearing him admit to things she already suspected would make her leave?

"I'm not going to look at you differently."

"You will."

His confidence shook her own and she worried about what he might say. Maybe this would be the morning he walked out of her life. Oh, God, she really hoped it wasn't.

"Just say it. Don't worry about how it sounds, just say it."

He ran his hand through his hair and then sat down in one of the arm chairs across from her. He was muscled and lean sitting there looking for all the world like a man who had it all. The kind of man who clearly could have anything he wanted because he wasn't afraid of hard work.

"I want revenge on your father."

"Revenge?" She'd guessed there was something more to the take-over than just business. But revenge?

"Yes."

"Why?"

"He took everything from us. And I want to do the same to him."

"Does your family feel that way, too?"

"My mother doesn't. But Michael does."

Of course his mother wouldn't. A mother would know that revenge was too destructive. A mother would weep for her son and the fact that he could never have a future without letting go of the past.

Tempest felt a knot of ice form in her stomach. She'd expected something tied to pride. Something that she could combat. Something that she could find a way to fix so that they could be together.

"Tempest, just know…I wish it were different."

She saw him then. Heard the rap music still pulsating from the stereo in the family room. Saw the beautiful but empty house and the lush retreat he'd created for himself. And she sensed that he didn't know any other way to be. That he'd spent his entire life focused on one thing.

Taking over her father's company. Ruining her father. Her heart ached because her father was just like Gavin. He lived for his business, nothing could interfere with Tempest's Closet as far as August was concerned. Certainly not her.

But from the beginning Gavin had always had time for her. Granted she'd arrived in his life amid scandal but he'd always been there for her. She thought of all the things he'd done for her and how he'd filled her life in ways she'd never expected another person to.

She wasn't going to walk out on him now. She put her coffee mug down and went over to him. Sitting down on his lap she wrapped her arms around his shoulders and tucked her head under his chin.

His arms came around her and he held her so close and so tight that she knew her instincts were right. Gavin wasn't playing with her to get at her father. She imagined at first he'd had some sort of intent to that end but not now. He held her with the same intensity that she was holding him.

Both of them needed each other in a significant way. Maybe in a way he hadn't experienced before. Or allowed himself to experience before.

"There's only one question I need answered," she said, turning things over in her head until she had the kind of sharp clarity that made all the inconsequential stuff drop away.

"What is it?"

She tipped her head back and looked up into his diamond hard gray eyes.

"Do you want me to stay with you?"

"Hell yes."

"I need a commitment from you, Gavin. More than this temporary arrangement."

He buried his head in her neck and didn't say anything for a long time.

"Gavin?"

"I'm giving you more than I've ever given another woman. Can't that be enough?"

She thought about it, wanting to say yes of course she'd take whatever he had to give her. But she knew that once she started settling she'd never be able to convince him that she was worth more. That *they* were worth more.

"No, it's not."

He lifted his head, looking down at her with those startling gray eyes of his. "I don't know how to build anything," he said.

She knew that. Had seen the truth in those words more times than she'd wanted to count. "I do."

"I'll try," he said, as his mouth captured hers in the kind of kiss that left no room for thinking about anything other than Gavin.

# Ten

Michael stood in the doorway leading between their offices, clearly excited about the report he held in his hands. But this was a moment that Gavin had come to dread in his mind. He knew that it was only a matter of time until August over-extended himself far enough that Renard would be in a position of power. A position that they'd maneuvered and planned to be in for over ten years, one which would enable Renard Investments to come in and take over the company.

It was what he'd focused on for years, but now that he had Tempest in his life, he was no longer confident that it was going to bring him the same sense of pleasure he'd expected it to.

"He did it. Took the bait just like you said he would. Tempest's Closet is most definitely over-extended. I just got off the phone with Hugh Stephens in Orlando. He's going to make the loan offer."

"Great." Hugh Stephens worked for one of Renard Investments subsidiaries that was connected through so many other companies that the trail was hard to trace. And knowing how desperate August's finances were as he clung to old ways of doing business, Gavin's gut had said that Hugh could get Lambert to commit to another loan. This was the final nail in the financial coffin that Tempest's Closet had been heading toward for a long time.

"Great? What the hell's going on? You've been planning this since we opened our doors and all you have to say is 'great'?"

"It's business, Michael. We knew he'd make too many mistakes eventually and Tempest's Closet would be ours. I'm not going to dance around the office."

"Given that you can't dance that's not surprising. But something's off here, bro. I figured you'd be breaking out that bottle of scotch you've kept in the wet bar for years. This is the moment we've been working for."

"I'm happy."

"But not like I thought you would be. If this isn't enough for you, what are we going after next?"

"We'll find another company that needs us."

"Gav, talk to me."

Gavin rubbed the back of his neck and refused to look at his brother. Was he having some kind of meltdown? Was he really letting a woman affect him this deeply? Did he honestly think he had any kind of control over what he felt for Tempest?

"Hell, I'm ecstatic, Michael, you know that. Let's open the Glenlivet and drink up."

*Michael smiled at him and Gavin realized that his* brother had been waiting for this moment for a long time, too. That even though Michael always seemed so open and jovial a part of him was waiting for this retribution against the man and the company that had so altered the course of their lives.

He poured two fingers of scotch into both of their glasses and turned to face his brother. They looked into each other's eyes. Michael's were the same deep brown that their father's had been and for a moment Gavin stood frozen in time.

He remembered what his father said all those years ago—the Renard boys were wily as foxes and twice as smart as the competition.

Michael's mind must have gone down a similar path because he said, "To the Renard boys—"

"Wily as foxes—"

"Twice as smart as the competition."

They clinked their glasses together and each of them swallowed the scotch. Gavin savored the feel of it burning down the back of his throat.

There was a knock on his office door and he

glanced at his watch. He was having lunch with
Tempest today.

Just the thought of her standing on the other side
of the door tinged his happiness with something sour.
He put his glass down and excused himself from his
brother. He opened the door and she smiled up at him.

"You ready?"

"Not yet."

"No problem. I'll just sit out here and wait for you."

But he didn't want to discuss the take-over of her
father's company with his brother while she sat in
his outer office.

"Michael, can we talk about this after lunch?"

Michael's shrewd gaze didn't waver as he put his
glass on the counter of the wet bar. "Sure thing, bro."

"Hey, Michael. I'm going to fashion week next
month, do you think your girlfriend Melinda will
want to join me?" Tempest asked.

"What is fashion week?" Michael asked.

"You're kidding right?"

"No. I'm not. Will Melinda know what it is?"

Tempest and his brother continued to banter back
and forth about fashion and men's ignorance of such
things as Gavin turned back to his desk and logged
off the network.

It felt strange to know that the end of his quest to
take over Tempest's Closet was in sight. That finally
the company that he'd lusted after for all these years
was going to be in his hands.

Tempest's cell phone rang and she excused

herself to take the call, going out of his office. Michael closed the door behind her, pivoting to face him.

"Have you changed your mind about Tempest's Closet?"

The question was unexpected coming from Michael. "Why would you think I have?"

"Because if we go through with this take-over you're going to be destroying the company that her father named after her."

"August barely pays any attention to her."

"It doesn't change the fact that he's her father."

"My personal life is none of your business. Our company is doing what we do best. We've found a shaky investment and we're going to ride in and rescue it from failure. The investors will be happy."

Michael nodded and walked toward his own office, pausing in the doorway to glance back at him.

"Sounds perfect, Gav. Really it does, but you and I both know that nothing is perfect."

"What's your point?"

"I don't think you're going to be as happy about this as you've always thought you would be."

"I'm not the only one who wanted it."

"I know. I'm not saying this is only about you, but I do think you've changed. And taking over Tempest's Closet has never been my goal."

"The hell it hasn't. You just toasted his downfall the same as I did."

"You're right. But when Tempest walked in, I

realized that no matter what we do we are never going to get Dad back. He's dead and maybe it's time we started thinking about living our own lives."

Michael walked away and Gavin just watched him leave. Those words lingered in his ears as he stepped into the outer office and saw Tempest smile up at him. He didn't want to sacrifice his chance to have a life with her.

Gavin was too quiet during the lunch. It had been two long weeks since that morning on his patio where they'd had that tentative talk. She'd been careful of everything she said to him. Trying to keep the peace and hoping that maybe they really were building toward a life together.

But something was off today. She didn't know what it was. Maybe it was the whole fashion week thing. It was kind of silly and kind of frivolous but she loved it. It was one of the few memories she had of her mother. Even though Tempest was supposed to be in school in October her mother would always pull her out and take her to New York for the week.

They'd stay at the Plaza hotel back when it used to be a hotel. She smiled to herself. Then glanced across the car to Gavin's harsh features. She put her hand on his thigh.

"Are you upset that I brought up fashion week?" she asked, as they drove back to Gavin's office.

"Why would I be? I know that it's something

you've been planning on. I'm sure Melinda will be thrilled to go with you if she can get the time off."

"I know but it can be kind of…I don't know… trivial."

"Considering you've been talking about trying to write for *Vogue* I think it would be foolish to skip going. Have you heard back from that editor?"

The relief she felt unnerved her. Maybe it was because he'd been so quiet during lunch and she had the impression that his silence had to do with her.

"Yes. She wants me to write an article on Tempest's Closet and its tradition of bringing haute couture to the masses."

He glanced over at her and she saw something in his gaze that she couldn't define. But it caused a chill to run down her spine.

"That sounds right up your alley."

She realized she'd touched a nerve from his past. The past that had shaped him and driven him to become the man he was today. She knew that he didn't think the masses benefited from Tempest's Closet coming into their small towns. Maybe her article would change his mind.

"I don't know how it'll turn out. I've never written anything other than press releases before."

He signaled to change lanes and then looked over at her. "It'll turn out good like everything else you try."

She flushed at the compliment and at the confidence and pride she saw in his eyes. He pleased her on so many levels that sometimes she woke up afraid that this was all a dream. The fragile bond they'd formed two weeks ago should have made her feel more sure of their relationship but it had only made her realize how vulnerable they were.

"I was thinking about staying in for dinner tonight. Kali's hosting a birthday party for one of her coworkers but I thought a quiet night would be better."

"I'm going to be later at work tonight than I thought. Why don't you go to the party and we'll catch up later?"

He hadn't mentioned that earlier. She didn't want to go to the party by herself. She was slowly coming to realize that socializing wasn't what she really took pleasure in. She'd come to really enjoy the evenings that she spent home with him. Just curled up on the sofa while he worked or watched TV.

"Oh. Okay. I'll go to her party."

"You don't have to go if you don't want to. I thought you might not want to stay home by yourself."

"You're right. What kind of socialite stays in when there's a party?" She tried for a flippancy she didn't feel and knew she'd failed miserably when he glanced over at her.

"What was that tone about?"

"Nothing."

"Tempest…"

What could she say that wasn't going to make her

sound like an idiot and make him tense up on her? She knew better than to confront him with anything to do with Tempest's Closet and her father. Yet it was so much a part of her life—she couldn't ignore her heritage any more than he could.

"I don't have to write the article. I know you don't really agree with everything that Tempest's Closet has done."

He didn't say anything but pulled the car into a parking lot and turned to face her. "I'm not bailing on dinner because of an article you're writing."

"Really?" she asked, doubting him. There was something going on here. Something more than he'd ever admit to. She wondered if it had to do with Michael and whatever the two of them had been discussing when she'd arrived in his office.

He nodded. "I'm proud that you're going to do an article for *Vogue*. I think it'll be a great career transition for you. A way for you to stand on your own and show everyone that there's so much more to Tempest Lambert than a high-society heiress."

The relief she felt was so intense she thought she might cry. What the hell was wrong with her? Her emotions were taking her on a roller coaster ride and she wanted off. She wanted to find a nice safe place in her relationship with Gavin and had the feeling that it would never happen.

"A high-society mistress," she said. That phrase always made her feel a little smarmy. Like she wasn't good enough for Gavin to consider her as anything other than a mistress. She knew it was just a scintillating title that the magazines used to entice readers. But it did tarnish a little of what they had together.

"I've talked to my lawyer about suing the tabloids but he said that would only add fuel to the fire."

"I wish there was some way to make them back off. Should we stop seeing each other?"

"No, baby. Move in with me permanently."

Throughout lunch all he'd been able to think about was what Michael had said. He was going to tear apart Tempest's heritage. *Her legacy*. But it was too late to swerve from that course of action. His entire life would be a lie if he broke the vow he'd made at sixteen.

The vow that someday August Lambert would fall to him. There was no way to stop everything he put in motion. By the end of October when Tempest's Closet held their annual shareholders meeting, Renard Investments would be the majority shareholder and he would demand that August step down as CEO.

And he didn't want to lose Tempest. The only way to keep her was to get her into his house now. To enmesh their lives so tightly together that when the changes happened at Tempest's Closet she would have something else. Something with him.

Oh, hell, she was staring at him like he'd lost his mind. Maybe he could have phrased it better. He should have waited until they were out of the car at least. He was acting like the animal he was beneath his Turnball & Asser designer clothes. The animal that he tried time and again to hide from her.

"Are you sure you want me to move in with you?" she asked. Her fingers were twisted together in her lap. She'd spent a lifetime by herself. Since her mother died she'd been on her own. Would she want to live with him? They were both loners, he thought. Of course with him it was obvious but only someone who'd really gotten to know Tempest like he had would recognize the solitary way she moved through her scores of friends.

"I wouldn't have asked if I wasn't," he said, but he sounded angry. And she was looking at him like he'd lost his mind.

"I'm making a mess of this."

He was known for his cool demeanor and had convinced more than one hesitant investor to go with an investment based solely on his word. He could convince Tempest to do this. He hadn't made himself into the man he was today by vacillating.

"You are. This isn't like you."

But he realized that it was like the man he wanted to be. This was the answer he thought he might have been searching for since that first night he'd made her his.

Reaching across the seat he cupped the back of her head and drew her forward until their lips met. He felt her surprise but her mouth opened under his. He thrust his tongue deep inside her, tasting her completely.

Hell, he really wanted to marry her. To legally make her his but he knew he couldn't do that until he had taken control of Tempest's Closet and that mess was behind them.

Her hands crept around his neck and her fingers slid beneath his collar getting closer to him, touching his skin. He wanted more. But this wasn't the place for seduction.

He pulled back, brushing his mouth over hers because he didn't want to stop kissing her. He never wanted to stop tasting her.

"Say yes," he said.

She stared up at him and in her clear blue eyes he saw all of her hopes and her dreams. And he hoped that he was man enough to live up to them. He was so afraid that he couldn't. Because he knew that he'd been doing the ultimate snow job on her. Convincing her that he was a whole man when inside he was empty. When inside he'd been eaten up by that long ago vow. And only now that she was in his heart did he feel like he was starting to be someone completely whole.

"I'm not an easy person to live with."

"Neither am I."

"My phone rings all the time."

"That's okay. I bring my work home with me every night."

"I can't cook."

"Mrs. Stanton takes care of that."

She was throwing up things that were inconsequential but he sensed there was more to her arguments. "What's this really about?"

"I've never lived with anyone. Not since my mother died."

He hadn't realized that. "You mean as an adult, right?"

"No, even as a child. When mother died, my father kept me at boarding school or summer camps. We'd meet at hotels for different holidays."

This was her legacy, he thought. This was what August Lambert had left her with. Suddenly he felt a hell of a lot better about his plans for Tempest's Closet. A man with priorities that screwed up deserved to have the rug jerked out from under him.

"Those things don't matter to me. We're practically living together every weekend. I think we do okay."

She looked into his eyes searchingly and he wondered what she wanted to see in his gaze. He really hoped she'd find it.

"Are you sure?" she asked. He recognized the hope underlying her words.

"I am very sure. I've never really had much of a home, either, but I want to try to make one with you."

She nibbled on her lower lip and then took a deep breath.

"Yes," she said at last. Her voice was so soft he

was afraid he'd misunderstood but he knew he hadn't.

"Great. I'll call the movers when I get back to my office."

"There's no hurry," she said. "I know you're busy."

"Not too busy for this, Tempest. I'm not too busy for you."

"I never thought you were."

He would do everything to make her feel like an integral part of his life. To make her see that even though he couldn't give up his revenge, he wouldn't give up on her, either.

# Eleven

Tempest had been to the Shedd Aquarium more times than she could remember for different functions and events. But tonight felt just a little magical as she entered on Gavin's arm. It could be that this was the first function they'd attended since she'd moved into his house. Or maybe it was just the fact that they'd been together for three months.

Earlier this evening, Gavin had made sweet love to her on his king-sized bed when she'd come out of the shower. Her entire body was still tingling. He glanced down at her and she blushed, thinking of the way she'd begged him to take her.

He raised one eyebrow. "What are you thinking about?"

"Nothing."

"Nothing, hmm, I'm thinking about the way you felt when I—"

She put her hand over his mouth. "Stop it, don't say that out loud."

He waggled his eyebrows, kissing the inside of her hand as he pulled it from his mouth. "Well, I am."

Someone cleared their throat behind them and Tempest glanced over Gavin's shoulder, meeting her father's disapproving gaze.

He wore his tuxedo with panache and ease. He'd always seemed so well put together that she felt she'd never measure up. But with Gavin's arm around her waist…she didn't feel like she was lacking.

She'd found her place in the world after a lifetime of searching. She wished she were alone with Gavin because she'd tell him right now. She'd confess the love that she'd been carrying as a secret in her heart. What good was love if it was kept inside?

She slid her own arm around Gavin's waist and leaned closer to him. He squeezed her hip.

"Good evening, Tempest."

"Hello, Father," she said. Gavin turned so they were both facing August. He looked tired and a little tense but then the retail business was a stressful one. She smiled at her father though she sensed an underlying tension between the two men.

Her mind was a total blank, which didn't surprise her. Her father unnerved her as no other person could. She always felt like she was thirteen years old and trapped between being a child and an adult. She felt awkward and gawky.

"Father, you know Gavin Renard, right?"

Her father nodded and held out his hand.

Gavin shook it. "Evening, August."

An awkward silence fell among the three of them. Tempest saw Kali over her father's shoulder trying to get away from the people she was with and come to the rescue.

"Doesn't the aquarium look nice tonight?" she said, desperate to overcome the awkwardness of this conversation.

Gavin glanced down at her. She hoped he realized that this wasn't the place for the conversation he wanted to have with her father.

"Yes, it does. But then it is always spectacular."

"Yes it is. Renard, will you excuse us? I'd like to speak to my daughter in private."

Gavin excused himself and her father led the way to one of the small quiet alcoves that had been set with cocktail tables.

Her apprehension about dealing with her father was stronger than ever tonight. There was something almost solemn about him and she just couldn't put her finger on what was wrong.

"What did you want to talk to me about?"

"About your being Gavin's mistress."

She wrapped an arm around her waist. Was he concerned for her? She cautioned herself not to read too much into his attention. The last time she had…well she'd been more than disappointed. But this was the first time since her mother died that he'd engaged her in a private conversation that had nothing to do with Tempest's Closet.

"I'm not really his mistress. The gossip columnists just keep saying that. But we are actually living together now. I think he might be the one." She hoped her father had gotten beyond believing what he read about her in magazines and newspapers.

"The one what?" August asked.

"The one I marry."

"I doubt that."

"Why?" she asked. Her father didn't know Gavin like she did.

"He's after Tempest's Closet."

"Dad, that's business. Gavin would never let that affect his relationship with me."

"What makes you so sure?"

She didn't know. She could say that it was her gut but she knew her father wouldn't accept that answer.

"I just am."

"Don't set yourself up for disappointment, Tempest. I'd like to think I raised you to be pragmatic if nothing else."

He turned to walk away and she almost let him go. "Father?"

"Yes?"

"You didn't raise me. Boarding schools and nannies did," she said, brushing past him. "And you don't know the man Gavin is away from the business world. He'd never hurt me the way you have."

He stopped her with a hand on her arm. "He already has. He's taking over Tempest's Closet and forcing all the family out. That includes you."

"What are you talking about?"

"Maybe you don't know your man as well as you think you do," he said.

"Just tell me what's going on," she said.

"Maybe we should let Renard do that. Tell her, Gavin."

Gavin stepped out of the shadows, coming to stand next to her and her father. She looked up into his eyes willing him to laugh and make light of her father's comments but he was too somber. There was more than a kernel of truth in her father's words. She shouldn't have been shocked by that. Her father never joked around when it came to business.

Gavin hated the way Tempest stood with her arm wrapped around her waist. His instincts had said letting her go off with her father had been a bad idea. But he wasn't about to shelter her from the truth.

"Tell me what exactly?"

"I'm not sure," Gavin said. He didn't know how much information August already knew.

"Something about your buying up shares in Tempest's Closet and forcing the family out."

August's information was complete. Gavin wondered if he had a leak in his own organization or if the boys at Tempest's Closet had finally gotten smart.

"I didn't buy up the shares; Renard Investments did on behalf of a consortium of investors. I've only just spoken with our investors this afternoon and we haven't made any decisions on what we will be doing with Tempest's Closet at this point."

Tempest was watching him with those wide blue eyes of hers and he had this sinking feeling that living with him wasn't going to be insulation enough from the shock brought in by his ruthless business maneuverings. That somehow she was going to slip through his fingers tonight.

"You are Renard Investments. Whatever you recommend to those investors they will do."

"That's true."

"Put my father's mind at ease, Gavin. Tell him you're not going to tear the company he built apart."

He stared at her and knew that this was going to be the moment when he lost her. Because he couldn't do what she was asking him. He wasn't going to put August Lambert's mind at ease.

He wanted the older man to spend as many sleepless nights as his father had. He wanted the older man to be forced to come begging to him for his job. And then he wanted—oh, hell, he craved—the opportunity to tell him no.

"This really isn't the place to discuss business. Call my secretary in the morning, August, and I'll try to squeeze you in."

"I'm not going to come to your office."

"That's your decision. But I think we both know that you are over-extended and I know I hold all the cards."

"And my daughter," August said.

Gavin nodded. He would have preferred to do this away from Tempest. To keep her out of the seedier side of what he did. The fact was hostile take-overs were never pretty. They were down and dirty fighting. The kind he was best at.

And she'd always seen him as something more than he was. Maybe this was for the best. Let her see the man he really was so that she'd know exactly what he had to offer her.

Except with Tempest he was a different man.

"I'm with him because I want to be. Our relationship has nothing to do with Tempest's Closet," she said.

"I'm not so sure about that. This is a man who has the money and power to control the media and yet he still allows them to refer to you as his mistress. He's not the one for you, Tempest."

She glanced at him and he saw the doubt in her eyes. But he wasn't about to defend himself against these ridiculous accusations. Tempest herself asked him not to bother with the stories the scandal rags had been running.

"I asked him to leave the media alone. These kind of stories blow over."

"You always were good at believing whatever lies you told yourself."

She visibly recoiled from her father and Gavin reached out, pulling her to his side and tucking her up against him. "You direct your anger toward me, Lambert. Tempest has nothing to do with this business between us."

"She has everything to do with it. You placed her squarely between us."

"Even I can't control who I fall for."

"Are you saying you care for her?"

Gavin wasn't sure he wanted to do this now. Do this here. But not confirming his feelings for her wasn't going to help anyone.

He glanced down at Tempest. Leaning close he whispered into her ear. "Yes."

She wrapped one arm around his waist, holding him tightly to her. "Me, too."

He wanted to pick her up and carry her away from this place. Away from the crowds filling the aquarium and away from the man who was watching them.

"If he really loves you, then he won't destroy the only legacy I have to give you."

"Of course, he isn't going to destroy it," she said. "That's not your intent is it, Gavin?"

Destroying Tempest's Closet had been his goal for far too long. There was no way he could give it up even for Tempest. Her legacy wasn't a chain of retail stores. Her legacy was the writing she'd be doing. Sharing her past with readers and talking about a unique point in fashion history that her father established.

"I'm not at liberty to discuss this right now. We can talk either in my office tomorrow, Lambert, or at the stockholders' meeting in two weeks."

August gave him a tight smug smile. "That's exactly what I thought. You'll never let my company stay as it is."

"It is a failing business," Gavin said.

"It's an institution like Macy's. You can't close us down."

"I'm not sure what course of action we will take. And I'm not discussing it further tonight."

"Why not? Afraid Tempest will see the real man she's involved with?"

"She already knows exactly who I am."

"Does she?"

"Yes."

"Then tell her the truth of what you plan to do with Tempest's Closet."

"Okay then, I will. I'm going to sell it off piece by piece. Are you satisfied, August?"

Tempest watched her father walk away and then she pushed out of Gavin's arms. Surely he wasn't really going to ruin a company that employed so many people. Surely his hatred of her father and Tempest's Closet didn't go that far.

"Did you mean that?"

"Yes."

The music started in the other room as the party got into full swing. But she felt less like partying than she ever had before. She didn't know how to reach Gavin. She knew that her father represented something dark and dangerous from his past. Something that had shaped him.

But the man she'd fallen in love with wasn't the kind of man who'd take away the livelihood of so many.

"You'll be little better than he is if you do this."

"It's not about him or you. Don't worry about it, Tempest."

"I'm not worrying. I just think that you haven't thought this through."

"I assure you I've thought it through. I've been running a successful company for more than a decade. I think I know what I'm doing."

"You're wrong."

"Wrong?"

"Yes, you're too emotional about my father—"

"Stop right there. I'm not emotional about this. Taking over Tempest's Closet is just another day at the office to me."

Except it wasn't and she knew it. Tempest's Closet represented something to him that no other company could. She took his hand in hers.

"Think of the families that will be put out of work if you do this. Families that have been making a good living—"

"Tempest I care for you, but I can't and won't change my mind on this."

She pulled back. "I'm not trying to manipulate you."

"Good because you can't."

She dropped his hand. "You're life will be empty, Gavin if you do this."

"Are you threatening me?" he asked.

She remembered the last time he'd said those words to her. And they'd come out of that moment stronger in their commitment to each other. She knew she just had to find the right words to say.

Find the thing that would relax him and once he got some distance from the confrontation with her father maybe he'd calm down and be able to talk to her rationally.

"I asked you a question, Tempest."

"Don't speak to me like that," she said. "You know I'm not threatening you."

"Really?"

"Really."

"The consortium has already agreed to tear the company apart and sell it off. It's the only way to make a profit. Are you still going to stay with me?"

"You're acting like a jerk."

"No, I'm acting like a man whose woman is trying to get him to make a business decision that makes no sense."

"I'm trying to get you to see that there's no prospect for a man who can only destroy things. For a man who doesn't see that only by building things and creating new opportunities can there be a real future."

"A real future with you?"

"With anyone, Gavin. You have to let go of the past."

"Would you be so concerned if my past involved any company other than Tempest's Closet?"

She stared at him for a long moment and realized that she had fooled herself into thinking that he really wasn't the man the media made him out to be. That he wasn't the man *Forbes* had called a 'cold-blooded profit maker.' Because the stories written about her were never true.

"The sad thing is that you have to ask me that."

"Sad because it's true. You know you like the money you make from Tempest's Closet. You haven't had a job for the entire time we've been together."

"I don't have to work because my mother left me a trust that pays me an annuity. I don't live off the profits I make from Tempest's Closet. They are re-invested in the company."

"Whatever you say."

"I don't have to explain myself to you."

"Neither do I."

There was a finality to his words that made her realize he'd anticipated this sort of ending for them. And it was an ending. She saw it in his eyes and in his stance.

"I wasn't asking for an explanation," she said, pushing a tendril of hair back behind her ear and re-alizing her hand was shaking.

"What were you asking for?"

She had no idea. This argument had gotten totally out of her control. To be honest she no longer was angry at him. Instead she was sad because she couldn't see a way around this situation. Couldn't find a way that she and Gavin could have something lasting. Ever. It wasn't about Tempest's Closet or the small town that he'd grown up in.

She had a moment of true clarity seeing Gavin as she'd never seen him before. He was an emotionally damaged man focused only on business, one who'd taught himself to hide away from the world.

She recognized that because she did it herself. She hid behind fashion and the paparazzi. But she'd always craved a man like him. A place like his arms where she could curl up and forget the outside world existed.

"I was asking for you to let go of the anger and bitterness that's controlled your life so long and take a chance on love."

"I'm not bitter," he said.

She just shook her head and walked away. Not knowing what else to say to him.

# Twelve

Tempest left the Shedd Aquarium and caught a cab out front. But she had no idea where to go. She couldn't go back to Gavin's place and she had no interest in going to her empty condo. She wanted to find a quiet place where she could just break down and cry.

She felt tears stinging her eyes but she forced them back. Actually she didn't want to cry. She wanted to find a nice numb place where she couldn't feel.

What was it about her that she couldn't see the men in the life for what they were?

The cabbie was looking at her, waiting for an address, and finally she sighed. She had no idea where to go. She thought Kali would take her in but that would be humiliating beyond measure.

How could she have been so wrong about Gavin? Her cell phone rang and she glanced at the caller ID display before answering the call. *Gavin*.

"Where are you going?" he asked.

"I don't know," she said. She hated the way her voice sounded thready and weak. She didn't want him to realize how deep his rejection had cut her. As if there were any way she could hide that. Gavin had always seen straight through the masks she wore to fool others.

"I'll crash at Michael's tonight. Go back to my place."

There was no way she was going back to his place. Not even to get her things. She didn't want to remember the illusions she'd bought into while she'd been there.

She didn't want to remember what it had been like to be happy for those few short months. It was almost the way she'd felt about her father's house on Lake Shore Drive. That big mansion that she'd lived in when her mother had been alive but had rarely set foot in after her death.

"Thanks but I don't think I'll do that. I can find a friend to stay with."

That weird sound of silence buzzed on the open line and she bit her lower lip hoping…what? That he'd somehow say he was an idiot and that he was going to give up making a huge profit just to make her happy.

She sighed, missing him more than she should, considering he'd just told her taking revenge on her father mattered more than she did. But her heart didn't care about Gavin's revenge. All her heart cared about was that she'd be sleeping alone in a big bed without him by her side. She'd be waking and reading the newspaper by herself. Her life would go back to its busy but empty schedule.

"Goodbye, Gavin."

"Tempest?" There was a note of pleading in his voice that made her hope. Was he going to alter his plans for Tempest's Closet?

"Yes."

"If I could change…"

"You can," she said, believing it with all her heart.

"But not on this. In the future I can be a different man, maybe start building things instead of buying them and then selling them off piece by piece."

She knew that it would be too late. Too late for them because, whether Gavin knew it or not, putting all those families who relied on Tempest's Closet for their livelihood out of work was going to affect him.

"I hope you do change," she said, softly.

"But it's too late for you. Is that what you are saying?"

She wished she had a different answer but she didn't. "Yes."

"I thought you cared for me."

"I do. More than you'll ever know but I can't keep shifting who I am to please you."

"I've never asked you to do that."

"You did tonight when you said that Tempest's Closet wasn't part of my legacy."

"This really is over?"

It broke her heart to say it but they both knew it was true. "Yes."

"Take care, then."

He disconnected the call and she hugged her phone to her chest. The cabbie was still looking at her and she figured she was making a fool of herself. "The Ritz-Carlton at Water Tower Place."

Her family had long kept a suite at the hotel. She'd crash there tonight and in the morning make some solid plans. One thing was—she needed to get a job, start working to get her mind off things. The article for *Vogue* was something, but not enough.

The sites of the city she'd always called home flashed by the window as the driver wove through traffic. She realized she was going to have to leave Chicago. Not just temporarily, but forever. She needed to get as far away from the men in her life and the humiliation she felt at having tried to make them love her. To make herself more important than their business machinations. More important than their workaholic schedules. More important than their game of one-upmanship. She'd lost but good and it was time to leave.

She wished the decision was an easy one, but inside she felt a tearing deep in her heart and she knew it was going to be a long time before she forgot Gavin Renard.

It started to rain as the cab pulled to a stop in front of the hotel. The doorman opened the cab for her and she stepped out, forcing a smile on her face. Time to start pretending she was Tempest Lambert, happy-go-lucky heiress.

The heiress who didn't care that the world knew her business. She made sure that she lingered in the lobby, chatting with a couple she knew from her childhood. She was careful to keep the smile and lighthearted banter foremost until the door to her 30th floor suite closed behind her and she sank to the floor leaning back against the wood door.

Gavin went to the table he'd reserved for the event and sat down. But he was scarcely aware of anything going on around him. He knew he should be making plans. Now that August knew he had enough shares to force him out there was a chance the other man would try to manipulate the stock somehow.

But he couldn't focus on that just now. Where was Tempest going? Why had he let her leave like that?

He just wasn't willing to give into any kind of ultimatum. It didn't matter that she hadn't really been telling him he had to choose between her or Tempest's Closet. He knew in his heart he couldn't have both.

And he'd only known Tempest for a few months. He'd been focused on Tempest's Closet since he was sixteen years old.

"Where's Tempest?" Michael asked as he seated Melinda and then took his seat.

Gavin hoped that he'd never have to answer that question again. But since it was Michael he knew he couldn't ignore it. In fact, considering that they'd become friends he was probably going to have to endure more than one question. "Gone."

"What? Is she okay? Melinda had a sinus headache earlier."

"Tempest's health is fine. August is here."

"Did he say something to her?" Michael asked. "You know he's the most arrogant men I've ever met. When I called him with your offer he said he'd rather rot in hell than do business with us."

Because of Tempest he had asked Michael to put together a package for August that would give the other man a figurehead position with no power but at least would let him hold on to his pride. And more importantly, to ease the shock and pain for Tempest. But that cold bastard had found another way to twist the knife in.

"He knows we have purchased all those shares that were available and somehow he knows that we're behind Hugh Stephen's loan, too. I think we need to go back to the office and look for a leak."

"Tonight?" Melinda asked.

"Yes," he said. Yes, definitely tonight. He needed to get to work. Work had been his salvation once and it would be again.

"Gav, are you sure about this? Shouldn't you go after Tempest instead?"

Michael was right—and it really pissed him off.

He wasn't going after her. Not now. He'd have to beg her to come back and he wasn't into begging.

"When have I ever asked you for advice?" Hell, he hated asking for anything.

"Never, but maybe you should start."

He admired Michael more than any other man he'd ever met but that didn't mean he was going to listen to him when it came to Tempest. Michael couldn't begin to understand that complex woman. Hell, half the time he didn't.

"You're not exactly a great example of success when it comes to relationships," Gavin said.

"I asked Melinda to marry me," Michael said, turning to her and drawing her into his arms.

A future. This is what Gavin should be planning instead of how to make August squirm. This is what he should be focused on instead of a quest for vengeance that would never bring him peace. "Wow, that's big. Why didn't you mention it to me?"

Michael ducked his head, rubbing one hand over his chest. "I wanted to make sure she said yes first."

"Congratulations, bro. I'm happy for you. Welcome to the family, Melinda."

Michael reached across the table, his hand falling on Gavin's shoulder. "You could be happy, too."

Not anymore. Not now that he'd seen the way Tempest had so easily believed the worst in him. Granted he hadn't tried that hard to convince her otherwise. Not that her opinion of him was what stopped him from going back to her. What really kept him in his seat was the pain he'd seen in those glittery blue eyes of hers.

Beyond the anger had been the kind of soul-deep pain that he wasn't sure he had the right to ask her to forgive him for causing. And the root cause remained, because he sure as hell wasn't backing down from August. The one tentative olive branch he'd offered had been rebuffed, and to be honest, he wasn't interested in trying that hard to win over her old man.

"You should get out of here and take Melinda some place nice to celebrate."

"I'm going to. We're just dropping in for a few minutes. I'm taking tomorrow off."

"Enjoy yourself."

His brother hesitated before walking away and Gavin forced a smile to reassure him. He was happier for Michael than he could express. The table filled up with business associates until there was only one empty spot left. The chair that should have been Tempest's.

He talked with those around him, functioned as close to normal as he could. He had the feeling that this was the life he'd made for himself. That there'd always be that vacant chair in his mind that should be filled with her.

Ah, hell, he was getting maudlin. Was he really letting her go? Was there really no way to keep her?

He left as soon as the dinner was served. Instead of driving home he cruised the city finding himself on Lake Shore Drive. He slowed at the gated mansion where August Lambert lived and glanced up there.

For Tempest's sake he knew he should at least make an effort to smooth things over with her father. He wasn't going to give in to her old man. But he was a shrewd negotiator willing to do whatever it took. And he wasn't going to leave the Lake Shore Lambert mansion until he and August had hammered out a deal that gave him what he wanted—a way back into Tempest's heart.

Revenge wasn't as sweet as he'd always hoped it would be. And seeing Michael get everything that Gavin had secretly dreamed of having with Tempest had twisted the sword of her leaving in his gut a little bit.

Sitting in his luxury car and watching August's house he realized that maybe it was time that he did become a better man.

He pulled up to the gate and rang the bell. He didn't know if August had left the Shedd yet or not. But Gavin could wait. He would wait as long as he had to and use the time to figure out a way to make the situation with Tempest's Closet right. August was going to agree to his terms because if he didn't the old man would really end up with nothing. And if he accepted Gavin's deal to remain part of the company then he'd still have not only a job to go to each day but also a chance at a relationship with the daughter he'd never had time for.

Then once Gavin was finished with August, he

was going after Tempest. Because even a few hours without her in his life was too long.

The bed was too big and the halls too quiet. After nearly a week at the Ritz she realized that her old habits were back. She was sleeping maybe two hours a night. No matter how she tried she couldn't get comfortable in her sleep, she kept rolling over and searching for Gavin.

She tossed and turned in the king-sized bed one more time before finally getting up. Wrapping herself in a robe she went to the windows and glanced down at the streets. Unlike Manhattan that was busy 24/7, Chicago did sleep in the wee hours of the night.

She pushed her hair to one side and wished that she could calm the voices in her head. The ones that warned her that maybe she'd overreacted and that she should go back and try one more time to make Gavin see reason.

She wandered around the room filled with a feeling of nothing, of that emptiness that made her want to do something crazy. Finally it was a six o'clock and she changed into her workout clothes and went down to the gym.

While she was running on the treadmill, everything coalesced. She didn't need to leave Chicago, she needed to find her place here.

She realized no matter how hard she ran or how far she moved away, the past would always be with her.

The past defined who she was today in a way that she'd never realized before. Asking Gavin to give up his revenge was like asking him to stop breathing. She'd heard his sparse tales of the past. Understood that her father and Tempest's Closet had changed the course of his life—and given him something to drive toward.

She left the gym, grabbed a bottle of water and headed for the elevator. She stepped into the car. After her shower she was going to make some real plans for the day.

"Hold the door."

She put her hand out between the doors to keep it from closing. She never could figure out which icon button meant door-open.

Gavin stepped into the car. He had on jeans and a rumpled Harvard T-shirt. His hair was mussed and he had stubble on his jaw. He looked tired but so good to her that she wanted to jump in his arms. She'd missed him more than she'd wanted to.

"What are you doing here?" she asked. Their last conversation had felt so final that she'd never expected to see or hear from him again. And clearly dressed the way he was, he wasn't here for a meeting.

"Looking for you."

"How did you find me?" she asked. The only people who knew she was here were the hotel staff and Kali. Kali had come over the first night she'd arrived.

"Kali."

"I can't believe she told you where I am." Kali had been as angry at Gavin as Tempest had been.

"Um…she didn't. I had to go to Michael and ask him for Melinda's help to call Kali."

"What?"

"Can we talk about this in your room?"

"Sure."

She couldn't believe he was here. Or that Kali had given up her location.

She led the way down the hall to her room with Gavin following closely behind her. He hadn't said another word on the ride.

She opened the door and stepped inside, seeing the mess she'd made of the room. The open box of chocolates on the table, the empty tea mug and the robe she'd left lying over the back of the couch.

She walked to the window and leaned against the wall next to it. The city was just coming awake.

"Okay, so explain to me what you're doing here."

"I wanted…I mean you were…ah, hell, Tempest. I don't know what to say."

She wrapped an arm around her waist and stared at him. He'd never really been too vocal about what he felt. But the fact that he was here meant something. But she was afraid to speculate on what it meant. Afraid to hope that he was here because he wanted a future with her.

"Start at the beginning. You went to Michael?"

"Kali wouldn't take any of my calls, well, except for one."

"And you asked her where I was?"

"I never got the chance. You should know that you have a really good friend in her."

"I do know it. I also know she has a bad temper."

"So I found out," he said.

She wanted to smile at the way he said it. "After that you went to Michael?"

"No. I called every hotel in the city but no one would give me any information about you. I checked the airlines and you weren't listed on any flights out. Same with trains so I had a pretty good hunch you were still in the city."

"Why did you do all that?" she asked, no longer caring how he found her.

"Because I need you."

"You need me?"

"You were right when you said that I couldn't keep living my life the way I always had. I treat everything like its temporary and try to insulate myself from disappointment. But when you left…there was no insulation."

"I never meant to hurt you."

"I know. I didn't mean to hurt you, either, but I did."

He crossed the room to her, pulling her away from the wall and into his arms. And though she wasn't sure she should, she wrapped her arms around his waist. He crushed her to his chest and she held him back just as fiercely.

Cupping her face in his hands, he tipped her head

backward. "I don't want a life without you. I like the man I am when you're around me."

Her heart sped up at his words and she saw real affection and caring in his eyes. "Oh, Gavin, what are you saying?"

"I'm saying I love you and I want you to marry me."

He kissed her then before she could say a word in response. His tongue thrusting past the barrier of her teeth and tongue. His hands sweeping down her back and holding her molded to the front of his body.

When he lifted his head, she started to speak but he rubbed his thumb over her lower lip. "I should have said this first. Your father and I are working out a plan for Tempest's Closet—it's not the role he's used to and he'll have to work for our new CEO but I think he's considering it. The consortium has agreed to allow Michael to step in as CEO for a year. Michael has a solid plan to get Tempest's Closet back on track."

"Dad agreed to that?"

"He didn't really have a choice. It was take the deal or walk away with nothing."

She stared up into his gray eyes finally believing that he really did love her.

"I love you, Gavin."

"And you'll marry me?"

"Yes."

He kissed her hard and carried her into the bedroom. Making love to her as if it had been years

since they'd been together instead of just an incredibly long week. Knowing they had both found
the home they'd been searching for.

# Epilogue

Her father's chauffeur-driven Mercedes arrived promptly at 7:35 p.m. Tempest nervously smoothed her hands down the simple lines of her white satin wedding dress. The last nine months had flown by and her new life was everything she'd always dreamed it would be.

Her father climbed out of the back of the car while Marcus, his driver, stood holding the door open.

Tempest stood at the top of the steps looking down at her father. Their relationship was still a little awkward but he'd been making an effort to get to know her and she was getting to know him, as well. He said that Gavin's take-over had forced him to realize there was more to life than Tempest's Closet.

So here she was trying not to smile too brightly but when her father glanced up at her, she couldn't help it.

"You're so beautiful, Tempest. You look just like your mother."

"Thank you, Father," she said around the lump in her throat, her nerves melting away at the compliment. This was her night. The night when she and Gavin were going to be married at her father's estate.

The tabloids had stopped referring to her as a high-society anything.

The drive to the Lake Shore mansion was quick. There was a silence between her and her father that wasn't exactly comfortable but it wasn't as strained as it would have been in the past. "Thanks for agreeing to let us have the wedding here."

"Your mother would have wanted you to be married in her gardens."

"She did love her garden," Tempest said.

"She also loved you, Tempest. Every night before she went to sleep she'd remind me how lucky we were to have you."

Tears burned the back of her eyes. She had so few memories of her mother, and her father had never spoken of her before. This small nugget about her mom was like a precious gift.

She blinked rapidly, stopping the tears that threatened.

"Are you sure about marrying Renard?"

"Yes," she said. She wasn't nervous about marrying Gavin.

Flashbulbs exploded as they passed a knot of paparazzi who were clustered around the gated drive of her father's mansion. She and Gavin had agreed to letting *Vogue* magazine—and only *Vogue*—do a profile on their wedding. After all, she had now made a full-time job of writing for them about the fashion industry from the inside.

Her father nodded once as they came to a stop in the drive. Marcus opened the door to the car, and her father came around and took her hand, escorting her through the house and into the back yard.

There were close to a hundred people assembled there. She glanced at the sea of faces not really seeing them. Her father walked down the aisle ahead of her and took a seat up front. She'd decided against asking him to give her away since he'd never really had her. Instead she glanced to the right and saw Gavin waiting for her.

"You are gorgeous," he said, coming to her side and kissing her passionately on the lips.

"So are you," she said, feeling the love he felt for her flow through her. Feeling surrounded by the love she felt for him.

"Even though I'm not model material?" he asked, making her smile.

"Even though."

He dropped another quick kiss on her lips.

"Can't you wait for the honeymoon to do that?" Michael asked coming up behind them.

"Mind your own business, bro."

"I guess I finally can now that Tempest is in your life."

Michael winked at her. "He needs a lot of advice, Tempest. Are you sure you want to take him on?"

"Very sure," she said.

"You messed up her lipstick," Kali said, stepping up beside Tempest. "Give me a minute to fix it then we can get this wedding started."

Kali fixed Tempest's lipstick and then hugged her. Leaning close to her to whisper, "I'm so happy for you."

The wedding fanfare started and Kali and Michael walked up the aisle in front of Tempest and Gavin. They had decided on a simple wedding with only Kali and Michael as their attendants.

As the Wedding March began to play, Tempest glanced up at Gavin and knew he'd given her the kind of happiness she'd always thought she could never find. She couldn't wait for the ceremony to be over so that they would be legally bound, though in her heart she knew nothing would ever take him from her side. They worked hard to build a future they'd both be proud of. And Gavin had been talking about children and building a dynasty together. She thought about what her father had said to her long ago about choices—and realized she'd made the right one when she'd approached Gavin.

\* \* \* \* \*

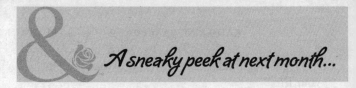

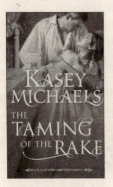
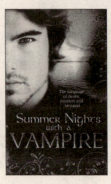
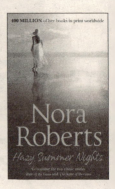